NEVER Leave NEVER Lie

THEA VERDONE

Cover by Get Covers

Edited by Alona Stark

To anyone depression has touched.

PLAYLIST

1950 | King Princess
Daylight | David Kushner
Haunted House | Holly Humberstone
Breezeblocks | alt-J
Palace | Sam Smith
Someone You Loved | Lewis Capaldi
Where is My Mind | Pixies
Say Something | A Great Big World
Summertime Sadness | Lana Del Ray
Don't Look Back In Anger | Oasis
Helena | My Chemical Romance
Hurt | Nine Inch Nails
You'll Never Walk Alone | Marcus Mumford
Cold Cold Cold | Cage The Elephant
Lithium | Nirvana
Wasteland, Baby! | Hozier
If The Book Doesn't Sell | Ritt Momney
You | Benny Blanco, Marshmello, and Vance Joy

Full list on Spotify

AUTHOR'S NOTE

Never Leave, Never Lie contains dark subject matter, including the discussion of depression and suicide.

A full list of content warnings may be found at https://theaverdone.com/nlnltw. (Please note: the list contains spoilers)

The mental health of my readers is extremely important to me. If you are struggling with depression, please reach out to a trusted friend or family member and a health care professional. https://nami.org/help is an excellent resource for mental health information and support.

Talking about suicide prevents suicide. If you're thinking about harming yourself, please visit https://988lifeline.org/ or dial 9-8-8 if you're in the United States.

Don't let the bad thoughts win.

CONTENTS

1. Alek   1
2. Ian   8
3. Alek   13
4. Ian   18
5. Aleksandar   28
6. Ian   33
7. Alek   38
8. Ian   46
9. Ian   49
10. Alek   55
11. Aleksandar   59
12. Ian   63
13. Alek   67
14. Ian   74
15. Ian   82
16. Aleksandar   88
17. Alek   95
18. Ian   105
19. Alek   117
20. Alek   126
21. Ian   132
22. Alek   142
23. Aleksandar   153
24. Ian   159
25. Alek   163
26. Alek   169
27. Ian   175
28. Alek   186
29. Alek   194
30. Ian   205
31. Aleksandar   218
32. Alek   220

33. Alek   234
34. Ian   245
35. Alek   251
36. Aleksandar   258
37. Alek   263
38. Ian   270
39. Alek   279
40. Alek   284
41. Ian   292
42. Alek   296
43. Alek   304
44. Ian   311
45. Alek   319
46. Alek   328
47. Ian   338
48. Alek   343

Afterword   349
Acknowledgments   351
About the Author   355

1

ALEK

Musical notes fluttered like fireflies in the dark parlor room. Alek sat at the piano, all ten fingers gliding over the keys, his gaze fixed on the window. Sound tangled with color and emotion. Fear was the color ochre, viridian love, chartreuse shame.

The sun disappeared behind the tree line and shadows clawed at the Gothic Victorian mansion. Ian would be home soon. Ian's favorite meal—eggplant parmesan—was in the oven. The casserole dish just fit on the rack beside the strawberry galette. The table was set, the wine poured.

Ordinarily, Alek would be waiting by the door. Ian joked that coming home to Alek was like being greeted by a 1950s housewife. Alek disagreed. He didn't need a medicine cabinet full of barbiturates and methamphetamines to marshal the courage to suck Ian's dick after handing him an aperitif. He was more than willing.

Besides, they weren't even married yet, though Alek had plans to remedy that. Tonight. Alek was going to propose, and when Ian said yes, Alek would feed him, and fuck him, all in time for the galette to come out of the oven.

Until then, he would play the piano, because if he was left alone with his thoughts—the thoughts that said *No one will ever love you* and *Ian will leave, like everyone else* and *You don't deserve him*—he'd never have the courage to ask.

He pushed the thoughts away, sending them through his fingers as he hammered the keys in a violent staccato, transforming his fear and doubt into music, like alchemy, until he felt nothing.

"Is that a new song?" Ian asked.

Alek's pulse stuttered, but his fingers didn't stumble as he finished the last few notes that remained. The scent of cedar and salt—Ian's signature scent—wrapped around Alek like a security blanket and behind closed eyes, his synesthesia built the image of a forest in summer when sunlight baked the trees and turned shadows sepia. It had been that way since the night they first met.

"It's beautiful," Ian murmured against Alek's neck, his dark stubble scratching Alek's skin like a match.

Alek turned and met Ian's lips, tangling their tongues, tasting the moments they'd been parted. The piano strings were still, not a single note reverberated, but Alek's music carried on seamlessly inside his head, playing an underscore to their kiss. Alek straddled the bench and pulled Ian down by the collar of his tee until he was on his knees.

"I missed you." Alek brushed the sawdust from Ian's umber hair.

"Likewise, love."

"How was your day?"

"The Queen Anne's almost finished. The Craftsman is down to the studs."

He and Ian restored historic homes. Alek oversaw interior design and sourced antique materials, while Ian threw sledgehammers against brick walls, carried loads of lumber over his shoulder, and did other hot construction things.

Ian's dark eyes narrowed. "You hate small talk. What are you plotting?"

Alek splayed his hand against his chest. "Me? Plotting? I have no idea what you mean."

He should ask Ian now. The more time that passed without music, the more his doubts crowded. He reached into his pocket, his fingertips grazing the soft velvet box... No. Not yet.

"Come on." Alek pulled Ian to his feet. "I'm sure you're hungry."

The kitchen was a 1970s nightmare with cheap cantaloupe-colored cabinets and laminate counters that peeled at the corners. They were renovating the Victorian one room at a time, and the kitchen would likely be last, given the expense and the fact that while ugly, it was functional.

Alek sat across from Ian at a narrow drop-leaf Georgian table. The tabletop was made of solid mahogany scuffed with the patina of two hundred years worth of history. Alek had told Ian he'd found it at a garage sale.

Ian's fork scraped against his plate. He took a swig of wine and twisted the bottle to read the label. "Single Berry Select?" His brows raised. "Sounds expensive. Are we celebrating something?"

"Celebrating? No. I just thought it would pair well with the red sauce."

"Hm," Ian grunted and nudged the bottle back to the center of the table.

An entire sentence of disapproval was wedged inside Ian's one-word response. They couldn't afford an expensive bottle of wine. They couldn't, but Alek could.

Their relationship was a house of cards built on lies. Reveal one truth and the whole thing would collapse.

"You're not eating," Ian said.

"I'm not hungry."

"You're always hungry."

Sweat tickled the back of Alek's neck. Ian knew him too well.

"The truth is… " Alek began.

Which truth to give him? That he was too nervous to eat? That he was terrified Ian would reject his proposal? *Fear is only proof you are alive*—one of his uncle's old adages. But Alek was a coward. He tore a piece of bread from the baguette, dipped it in the pool of sauce on his plate, and took a bite.

"Go on," Ian coaxed, voice low and quiet, as he leaned across the table.

"Oh, alright then. I despise eggplant." Alek exaggerated a shudder. "It's like eating a slug, or an eel. Too slippery."

"You should have said something. You don't have to cook something you don't like."

Of all the things Alek was guilty of, one of his worst sins was making Ian a fool. The real truth was that he *loved* eggplant parmesan because Ian loved it. Not to mention, he was far too skilled a cook to ever serve eggplant slimy.

"Besides, I'm leaving room for dessert," Alek added.

"Oh?"

Alek tutted. "I meant that literally. Though I might be persuaded if you ask nicely."

"Like I have to ask," Ian teased.

The velvet box was a telltale heart beating in his pocket. *Ask him. Ask him. Ask.*

He drained his glass, pulled the box out, and flipped it open with one hand to reveal the timeless titanium band he'd had custom-made to fit Ian's sizable ring finger. He set the box on the table between them.

Ian paled and his smile slipped from his face. "What?"

"Marry me." It was supposed to be a question, but came out more like a command. Alek had a whole speech prepared. Instead, he'd ripped his heart from his chest, still beating and bloody, and asked Ian to have it.

Ian's eyes widened on the ring, then bounced up at Alek. Somewhere unseen, a clock ticked.

"Alek, I love you..." Ian grimaced. "But I can't marry you until you trust me with the truth about your past."

Alek's ears began to ring. No. That wasn't right. They'd been together three years. They shared a business. A home. It was the next natural step. It was what Alek needed.

Ian reached for Alek's hand.

Alek jerked his hands to his lap and clenched his fists so tight he hoped his fingernails left crescent bruises on his palms. "You know all you need to know. You know me."

Gently, Ian asked, "Where were you born? What was your mother's name? Why do you sleep talk in other languages? What are you running from?"

Alek stiffened, stacking each vertebra one on top of the other as he lifted his chin. "None of that matters. What I've told you is enough. After three years, I should be enough."

"You are enough, Alek. I promise. But after three years, I should know something about your life before we met. That's all I'm asking for. You can trust me."

Trust—the only thing Ian wanted and the one thing Alek would never give him.

"I told you, there's nothing to tell."

A flash of hurt crossed Ian's stoic features. The faintest grimace. Downturned brows. Ian's disappointment hurt worse than if he'd hit him.

The oven timer dinged. Alek started.

"Leave it," Ian said.

Alek froze, the authority in Ian's voice hard to resist.

"Tell me just one thing," Ian said. "One thing that's true."

"I…"

"Whatever it is, I promise I will still love you."

"You can't promise that."

Alek bit into the soft flesh of his cheek until he tasted blood. Ian brushed his thumb over the spot, a silent reminder to stop. How could Ian say he didn't know him when he knew his bad habits? Alek buried his hands in his hair. He pulled until his scalp stung. He wanted to pull harder, rip his hair out in tufts, but he was rather fond of his hair.

When he lifted his head, an armor of apathy shielded his face. His voice was cold and empty as he said, "If you don't say yes, I'll have no other choice."

"No other choice?"

Alek was standing at the edge of a cliff and rocks slipped beneath his feet, but he would jump before he'd ever fall. He plucked the ring from the box.

"Marry me or it's over."

Ian's jaw turned sharp, the color returning to his cheeks. "You can't manipulate me into marriage."

It was just a game, right? Ian was calling his bluff. Well, Alek wasn't bluffing. Falling in love with Ian had made Alek weak, and Alek would never forgive him for that. Never.

Alek pushed back his chair and stalked to the sink. Wood scraped against floorboards. Ian's footfalls thundered. But Alek was faster. He turned the tap on full blast and held his hand out over the drain, the ring clutched in his hand.

"I'm serious, Ian," Alek said. "Say yes."

Ian worried his bottom lip between his teeth.

"Tick tock." Alek shook his hand. The ring bounced around like a bird flung against a cage.

"Alek, wait." Ian showed his palms. "Let's talk about this. We can figure this out. What if—"

"Wrong answer." Alek dropped the ring and flicked the switch for the garbage disposal.

The metallic racket of the ring ricocheting against the blades was so loud, all Alek saw was bright red.

Ian pushed Alek aside and turned off the garbage disposal. He cast Alek one warning glance, then shoved his arm down the drain.

Something was burning. The galette! Alek opened the oven. Smoke billowed out, carrying with it memories unbidden—a distant fire glowing like a rising sun trapped on the horizon, snow angels made in ash.

Without thinking, he reached for the pan, and snatched his singed fingertips back. Good. Now when he played, he would be able to feel it. The pain that he deserved. A reminder not to stray from the rules that kept him safe.

Deception is survival. People are meant to be manipulated. Hoping is foolish. And above all else, *Love is a weakness.*

2

IAN

F our rooms separated Ian from Alek, but nothing could mask the sound of the headboard banging against the wall. Ian didn't have to imagine what was going on. He was very familiar with the sequence of events.

The lover was sometimes male, sometimes female, but never, ever repeated. First was laughter and drinking, the smell of smoke curling in through the window. Then music—piano if Alek was in a conceited mood. Next came the quiet murmurs, the groans and squeals that grew into a crescendo.

A short time later, Alek would walk that night's lover out to their car and see them off, well-bedded and their brains just shy of being too sex-addled to drive. He would smoke some more out on the front stoop, the lit end of his hand-rolled cigarette like a beacon in a sea of mist and redwood trees. He'd look up at Ian's window from time to time, throw the cigarette on the ground, and squash it beneath his foot like it was a voodoo doll to channel all of his aggression into.

Then he'd come inside, not taking any care to prevent the front door from slamming, and stomp to his piano, completely unconcerned that it was two in the morning. Alek's expert hands would next twist notes into an oppressive fog of melancholy that climbed the stairs and slipped under doors until Ian could hardly breathe against the weight of it.

But tonight there would be no postcoital piano, because during the earlier cacophony, Ian installed a mute rail that could only be removed with hours of hand screwing and a smattering of curse words.

The front door slammed. Heavy footsteps crossed below. Ian imagined Alek's impatient confusion, then ire when he discovered what Ian had done.

The stairs creaked. Ian's door banged open.

Alek stalked towards him, his black hair ruffled, sage-green eyes promising revenge. He was tall like Ian, but the similarities stopped there. Alek's skin was a warm olive, except so pale it was almost sickly-looking—probably because he hardly ever saw the sun—and his body was chiseled in hard angles, sinewy like a big cat that hadn't had a good meal in a while, and with all the same threat of danger.

Ian backed away and before he realized the error of his actions, the scent of vodka and loose tobacco surrounded him as Alek pinned him against the wall. Ian could overpower Alek if he wanted to, but he wouldn't. Alek would like it too much. Instead, he allowed himself a fraction of a second to sneak a glance down Alek's shirtless chest to the 'V' of abs and trail of black hair disappearing into the gray pajama bottoms that hung low on his hips.

Alek smirked like he knew exactly what Ian was looking at, then leaned in until they were so close Ian could count the jade striations that made up his irises. All it would take was one deep breath for their lips to touch. Ian was desperate to close the gap, but he had enough self-respect left not to kiss Alek after everything he'd done.

"If you were lonely, all you had to do was ask." Alek's voice was saccharine laced with poison. "I would have been happy to let you watch."

"I hate you," Ian said.

Alek flinched, but recovered quickly. He fisted one hand in Ian's shirt, while the other reached down to palm Ian's traitorous dick where it tented his boxers obscenely. Alek tsked and squeezed. Ian sucked in a sharp breath, arched his back, and groaned from the shock of pain mixed with pleasure.

"That doesn't sound like hate to me," Alek said.

Alek inched downward, tortuously slow, until he was on his knees. Every muscle in Ian's body tensed with the effort not to drop his boxers and facefuck Alek into capitulation. It had been three weeks since he'd felt Alek's mouth around his cock. Three weeks left with only his hand while Alek stuffed his dick into anyone with a hole.

Alek grabbed the front of Ian's boxers. "What's this?" He showed Ian the spot of precome. Then, with only the thin fabric separating them, Alek pressed his mouth, warm and wet against the head of Ian's dick, swirling his tongue broadly. Alek's eyes were so dark, his pupils dilated so wide, they were two rings of green around a well of black.

Alek pulled back mere millimeters to say, "That doesn't taste like hate to me."

Mustering what was left of his bravado, Ian shrugged and said, "I can be turned on and hate you at the same time."

Alek's cheeks were as red as if Ian had slapped him, but not in shame; Alek had none.

"Fuck you," Alek said.

"I thought that's what we were doing."

"Careful. You're beginning to make me mad."

"I like you mad." The push and pull of power was what first brought them together and the only thing that held them together now. "Besides, what can you do to me that you haven't done already?"

Alek said nothing, but he didn't need to. Ian had won. He could see it in the way Alek's cheek hollowed out from where he'd bitten it to stop himself from saying something he'd regret, the way his fingers blanched where they gripped Ian's hips so tightly there'd be bruises the next day.

In a flash of motion, Alek brought his mouth back over Ian's cock and breathed out a slow gust of heat that forced a strangled and embarrassing whimper from Ian.

Alek rested his cheek against Ian's thigh and looked up at him with a sadistic half-smile. The once familiar sight of Alek kneeling before him, challenging him like that, made Ian homesick for the way things used to be.

"All you have to do is say yes and we can be happy again." Alek's tone strived for teasing, but desperation bled through. "Wouldn't you like that? Say yes." Alek dropped the facade, pleading, "Please. Just say yes."

It took every ounce of willpower Ian had left to shake his head. Their relationship was ruined beyond repair, like the Gothic Victorian mansion when they first bought it—foundation rotting, jagged cracks in the walls, one bad storm away from collapsing.

Ian never should have invested all his money into rehabbing the mansion with a business partner as mercurial and impulsive as Alek. "We could even cut costs and move in together," Alek had said. "This house will be our opus." Now the Victorian felt cursed, like the beginning of a horror movie where an unsuspecting couple buys their dream home, only for their lives to be ruined in the process.

Ian couldn't say yes, but he couldn't walk away either. All of his money was tied up in the house and Alek was self-destructing. He had no one. What would happen if Ian left him?

Alek took Ian's silence for the answer it was and said, "Fine. Have it your way." He removed his hands and stood.

Ian almost growled in frustration.

As Ian watched on, paralyzed against the wall, Alek walked over to the bed and sat down. He pulled his cock from his pants, spat into his hand, and jerked himself slowly, pausing only to rub his thumb over the head.

Ian's mouth watered. His balls ached. He hadn't come in weeks, because every time he tried to touch himself, all he could see was Alek. Before he could stop it, warm pressure foretold the inevitability. Ian came. It was short and unsatisfying and a spot of sticky come bloomed shamefully over his boxers as his dick deflated.

Alek's eyes widened, his tongue darted out to his lip, his hand stilled over his cock for a fraction of a second. That was the only indication Ian affected him at all. Then Alek put his cock back in his pants and walked to the door. He opened it and said, "Don't ever touch the piano again."

When the door closed behind him, Ian sank to the ground and leaned against the wall. Ian hated him and he loved him, but right now, he hated him more.

3

ALEK

The next morning, Alek got out of bed, sniffed the various discarded tumblers at the end table until he found the one that was vodka, emptied what was left, and wiped the back of his hand over his mouth. Then he went out into the long, dark hallway without bothering to dress.

The bottle green carpet runner beneath his feet was clean, the tall baseboards stripped down to the original hemlock wood. The peeling layers of wallpaper from every era, little snapshots of time like the rings of a tree, removed and replaced with blood-red flock wallpaper.

Ian had insisted on restoring the living quarters on the upper floor of the Victorian before they moved in. He was far too responsible to allow either of them to be exposed to an errant trace of lead or asbestos. Other more crumbling parts of the house were cordoned off with thick plastic sheeting and tape.

He pushed open Ian's door. Inside, his room was immaculate, the bed linen depressingly wrinkleless. No personal effects on the surfaces to indicate someone lived there.

The room smelled so intensely like Ian that Alek went to the bed, pulled the covers back, and climbed inside. He buried his face in Ian's pillow and breathed in, his cock immediately hardening, so Pavlovianly conditioned to Ian that the olfactory ghost of him was stimulus enough. He debated thrusting into his hand, but he hadn't been able to come since they broke up.

He dragged himself from the bed, leaving the linen askew, and crossed to the dresser. Inside the top drawer, Ian's boxers were folded into thirds and placed vertically in one neat row like the spines of books on a shelf. Alek took each boxer out, shook them free of their folds, and then shoved them all back inside the drawer in a tangled heap. Leaving the drawer open, he returned to the hallway.

He walked downstairs and out the front door, still naked, his feet bare. It's not like there was anyone around for miles, anyway. He shivered under the shade of the trees that had reclaimed every inch of land not built over.

Inside the detached garage, Alek snatched a screwdriver from his desk and marched back towards the house. Fog gray paint peeled from the siding. An ancient wisteria climbed and twisted gnarled trunk-like vines to the top of the three-story turret. All that remained of the attached greenhouse was a skeleton of rusted wrought iron.

By all appearances, the mansion was too broken to be fixed —and potentially haunted—but to Alek, it was home, and the only ghosts that haunted it were his own. They were supposed to renovate and resell the Victorian. That was their business model, what they'd been doing all along the northernmost coast of California for the last three years, but Alek would die before he left the Victorian. Or Ian.

He slammed the front door. A cloud of dust showered from the frame. Without Ian, the Victorian was too quiet. He could almost hear each speck of dust landing like a snowflake on his sleeve.

Back in the parlor, he lifted the piano lid, and spent the next hour removing the blasted mute rail. Each minute that passed left him more and more impressed with Ian for coming up with such an effective method of retaliation and simultaneously irate for vandalizing the piano in the process.

The piano had come with the house. Music was the only thing he brought from his childhood, and the abandoned piano had seemed more magic than coincidence when he'd discovered it, almost as if it had been waiting for a worthy suitor, like it had existed long before the mansion was built, a lone piano surrounded by trees until walls had caged it in.

Finally, he pulled the mute rail free and dropped it on the rug with a clatter. Ian could clean up the mess later.

He lowered the piano lid carefully, slid onto the bench, straightened his spine, and began to play. Each note rang with years of history suspended in time, and when he closed his eyes and inhaled, he could almost believe he and Ian were still together. That nothing had ever gone wrong between them.

Alek excelled at nearly everything he put even the smallest effort into, but his one weakness was understanding other people. He wasn't a sociopath. Empathy was a muscle that had atrophied under disuse. Ian was the only person Alek cared to understand at all, and he didn't understand why Ian came in his pants last night. Maybe the weeks of sleep deprivation via loud sex, piano, and edging were taking a toll. Were his tactics bordering on the wrong side of torture? That wouldn't do. Alek didn't get off on Ian's pain, psychological or otherwise.

The plan he'd forged before the dust of Ian's rejection settled was a complete failure. He'd expected Ian to surrender the first night he brought someone else home, and when Ian hadn't, he couldn't think beyond the pain. Why hadn't Ian fought for him?

Now Alek was three weeks into this wretched stalemate, and the only thing he'd accomplished was making Ian hate him.

Hate sex with Ian would be fun if the knowledge that Ian hated him didn't hurt so much.

Why wouldn't Ian just marry him? Alek knew better than most how meaningless a legal document could be, but a marriage license meant more to him than the foreign birth certificates and passports hidden in the safe in their garage. At least if they were married, it wouldn't be so easy for Ian to leave. Alek needed Ian to promise, to vow, to swear his fealty. He finished the sonata with a slam of his hands on the keys.

He spent the rest of the day hand-sanding the gouges that scuffed the exterior of a 19th-century trunk he bought off of eBay for five hundred dollars. It looked worthless to the untrained eye, but he knew from the detail on the handles it'd sell for at least six grand. He hadn't cracked the lock yet. He liked to draw out the anticipation because once he knew what was inside, he usually lost any interest in restoring it.

Night fell and Ian still hadn't returned, or called, or texted. Alek wasn't going to make the first move. Not because he needed to keep the upper hand, though he would prefer to, but because he didn't think he'd be able to survive it if he reached out and Ian didn't reach back.

He climbed to the third floor of the turret, cranked open the oversized casement window, and sat on the sill. A gust of wind tore through the trees. The sweet musk of flowering wisteria bloomed in the air, carrying with it flashes of memory—the sound of river rocks knocking against each other, the rough scrape of a piano bench over parquet floors, the warmth of his uncle's arm against his shoulder, initials carved into the side of a piano, ash over keys that cut like broken glass beneath his fingers.

Ian hated when Alek perched there, said he was going to break his neck, but that window sill on the front edge of the turret was the only place Alek could be free of the forest, the only place he could see the sky, be sure the horizon was still where it was supposed to be. Ian hated the wisteria too, the insatiable way it grew out of control and threatened to lift the roof up and pull the house down to rubble if he turned his back on it. Alek admired its perseverance.

Beneath the light of the nearly full moon, the coastal redwood trees stretched uninterrupted for miles. Alek's eyes caught on a flash of white, something that moved at the edge of the forest. He squinted and spotted the tip of a fox's tail. The fox looked at him and then turned and faded into the near-black understory.

The forest swayed as another gust of wind whistled through the trees. The hushed roar reminded him of the sound of Ian's steady breathing when he pressed his ear against his chest. If he could live inside that sound forever, he would.

An owl hooted. He pulled out his phone and opened the app that showed Ian's location. He was at his mother's home, which might work in Alek's favor. Ian's mother loved Alek. Sometimes when she hugged him, tears stung unshed.

Alek marked each hour that passed without Ian's return with more vodka while he gave the piano all of his anger and regret until he felt nothing. Then he staggered to Ian's room, stripped his clothes, and climbed under the duvet.

Tomorrow he would talk to Ian. He would apologize and rescind his demand, tell Ian he'd have him, marriage or no, and Ian would say yes. Wouldn't he?

A stab of panic threatened. He needed Ian, not like water—like oxygen. The way things were between them now, the fragile thread of financial obligation and attraction that frayed as it held them together, was slowly strangling him.

4

IAN

Ian kicked off his shoes under the dim light of the weathered brass lantern that hung beside the front door. He snuck inside, latching the door quietly behind him.

The parlor was empty. Upstairs, Alek's room was empty too. He climbed the front stairs to the third-story tower. Alek wasn't there either. Trepidation roiled in Ian's gut. Alek was prone to worrisome theatrics, especially when left alone for too long.

After checking each of the doors on the second floor, he was about to try downstairs again when he stopped in front of his own room. Alek was in bed, on his side, his body curled around Ian's pillow. Asleep.

Ian was going to end things with Alek. He'd spent the entire day tasting and testing the words on his tongue. He'd move in with his mom while he finished the Victorian and once the house sold, he and Alek could part ways forever. But the sight of Alek clutching his pillow, the proof that Alek missed him; he couldn't end things now. Maybe tomorrow. Maybe never.

Ian sat on the edge of the bed, but Alek didn't stir. He'd always been an easy sleeper, falling under as soon as he closed his eyes, like none of the things he did could ever keep him up at night.

The bags under Alek's eyes had become a pair of half-moon bruises since he'd last seen him. Alek breathed faster. His forehead wrinkled, luscious black lashes clenching tight. Alek muttered words in an indiscernible language. Romanian, maybe? But not quite right. Armenian? He had no idea. Alek's speech was accentless when he was awake. There wasn't even a hint of the New York from which he supposedly hailed.

Ian wasn't stupid. He had asked a hundred times already. *Why do you dream in other languages?* Alek had a different answer for every occasion. He aupaired in Czechia one summer so he could backpack through Europe without paying airfare. He taught English to students in Croatia. He went to an antique restoration convention in Macedonia.

How did a familyless loner even become a savant pianist and antique restorer? How did he subsist on a freelance income, yet never worry about money? Alek hadn't even paid taxes until Ian nagged him about it and then he paid it with little fanfare in one lump sum. None of it made sense because there were huge pieces left out.

He ran his hand over Alek's forehead, pushed away the hair from his face, and pressed a kiss in its place. Alek's face smoothed, and with the nightmare vanquished, Ian crossed to the dresser, pulling his shirt over his head. The sight of his underwear drawer left open, the mess Alek had intentionally left for him, brought an automatic smile to his face.

After undressing, Ian joined Alek in bed and spooned behind him, forcing himself to stay awake so he could bask in the warmth that Alek radiated, like his body temperature ran a half degree higher than his own.

———

WHEN IAN WOKE NEXT, the bed was cold and Alek was gone. Overhead, the floorboards creaked. On the third floor of the turret tower, Alek sat in his usual place on the window sill with his face turned towards the forest. He was wearing only a pair of drab olive sweatpants, a lit cigarette burning forgotten in his hand. Ian shivered, longing to wrap his arms around Alek for more than warmth.

"This isn't working," Alek said without turning.

Ian flinched.

"I thought that if I made you jealous enough, if I pushed, you'd fold, not break. I was wrong." Alek spoke slowly, likely unspooling the words for maximum suspense. "Can we just go back to whatever we were doing before?"

"I don't hear an apology anywhere in there."

"Is that what you need?" He gave the cigarette a flippant wave. "Fine. I'm sorry."

"If you're going to say sorry, turn around and do more than half-ass it."

Alek swiveled and leaned against the side of the window frame, his legs straddling the sill. He took a long drag from the cigarette, like he was only apologizing to humor him and only after he made him wait first. On an exhale, Alek rolled his eyes so slightly, anyone but Ian would have missed it.

"I'm sorry I brought home an assembly line of one-night stands. I'm sorry for torturing you with sleep deprivation tactics that violated the Geneva Convention. I'm sorry I teased you into a perpetual state of blue balls." Alek lifted a finger for each transgression, counting them off like they meant nothing to him, which was probably true. Then he looked at the three fingers held aloft, bit the corner of his lip, and lifted another. "I'm sorry I threw all your tools outside while it was raining and then put them back in your tool chest without drying them off."

"You're such a prick."

"I know, but you like that about me." Alek's jade eyes darkened. He was only a moment away from weaponizing sex to sweep this all under the rug.

"If I accepted your apology, just like that, would you still respect me?"

"Who cares about respect so long as you respect yourself?" Alek ran an aggravated hand through his hair. "I'm sorry. Of course, I would respect you. So much, in fact, that I'll drop to my knees and drain your dick down my throat right now to prove it to you."

Ian shook his head. "You can't fuck your way out of this, Alek."

"I don't understand. I told you I'm sorry. Why are you still looking at me like that?"

Ian's blood went hot with rising anger. He reminded himself that Alek was only so feral and ignorant of normal human customs because of whatever secret past he wouldn't share with him. Calmer now, Ian said, "An apology doesn't erase the fact that you slept with enough people to populate a small island under the comically misguided assumption that it would make me want to marry you."

"I'm sorry. I didn't..." Alek paused. He must be rattled. He never stumbled over his words. "I wanted—"

"What about what I wanted? All I wanted was the truth." Ian angrily brushed the tears from his cheeks. "I want to fix this. I don't want to walk away. But nothing will change, nothing will convince you that I'll stay, nothing will make you feel safe until you trust me. Please, love—" Ian faltered at the term of endearment that hadn't slipped past his lips since they broke up. He cleared his throat. "*Alek*. Trust me. Let me in. Please."

Alek stabbed out the cigarette and crossed his arms in front of his chest. "You think the truth will set me free, but it won't. If you knew the truth, you'd hate me."

"Let me decide. Don't I deserve that?"

"You want to know the truth? Here's one secret. One of hundreds." Alek's words came fast—manic—like he knew he was being self-destructive but he was going to go through with it anyway because he'd rather burn down his entire life than be vulnerable. "I can easily buy you out of the Victorian. I only let you assume we didn't have enough money because it kept you here with me. If you don't want me, then go. There's nothing keeping you here, least of all me."

"Wait... What?"

It was like Alek was speaking a different language. One Ian knew, but wasn't fluent in. When the words finally registered, it wasn't just a kick to the gut. Alek's betrayal was eviscerating. All of the extra jobs Ian had worked, the money he'd pulled from his retirement to pay his crew, the fears he'd lose his business if the Victorian didn't sell. He thought the only lies between them were the lies about Alek's past. But if Alek was lying to control him, what else was he lying about?

Alek rolled another cigarette on the window sill in the space between his legs. He lifted his eyes to Ian's as he licked the edge of the paper to seal it in place. After lighting the cigarette, Alek inhaled, and on the exhale said, "I told you you wouldn't like the truth."

"I wish I never met you," Ian said. "You ruined my life. You ruined me."

Alek shrugged, flicking the ash from the tip of his cigarette. "Likewise."

"Do you know what the worst part is? I could move across the country—the world, even—and it wouldn't be far enough. You're always here inside me," he thumped a fist over his heart, "like a tumor, and even if I could escape, I can't, because you have nobody in the world except for me. Do you have any idea what kind of burden that is?"

At first, Alek said nothing, his eyebrows raised imperiously, like Ian was a child too old to be throwing a tantrum. That was how Ian knew he'd really hurt him. When wounded, Alek leaned on apathy.

"There's no need to martyr yourself." Alek's voice was deadly cold, his face wiped clear of all emotion. "I'll buy you out of the Victorian and pay you for the work you've done."

"Would you really let me go?" Did Ian want him to?

"I don't know." Alek met Ian's eyes. His bottom lip trembled like he was trying not to cry, like he was scared. It was nearly undetectable. He almost thought he imagined it. Alek never cried. He was never scared.

Ian took a step backward. His thoughts were getting tangled. He had to think and he couldn't think with Alek looking at him like that. He took another step back.

Alek turned, throwing his other leg over the window sill and planting both feet on the floor. "Wait. Please. Don't go—" He lurched forward and grabbed Ian's wrist.

Ian couldn't bear to feel Alek's fingers on him, not after everything he'd done.

He wrenched his arm free and then time slowed down. Alek's eyes went wide as he lost his balance, fell backward out of the window, and disappeared.

Ian ran to the window and looked down.

Alek was hanging onto a branch of that godforsaken wisteria. The same monster wisteria Alek worried Ian would one day water with a gallon of Roundup, and although he might have considered it, he'd never destroy something that Alek loved.

Ian held onto the window frame with one hand and leaned out, any fear for himself overshadowed by the terror he felt at the sight of Alek hanging twenty-odd feet above the ground. Alek scrambled up the vine and Ian reached his other arm out, stretching his muscles farther than he thought they could go. Their fingers grazed. They were so close.

Alek didn't look afraid. More like he'd expected it. Of course, he would die in such a melodramatic way, falling out of a window after his lover told him he wished he'd never met him.

The trunk of the wisteria snapped ominously as it strained to hold him.

Alek said, "For what it's worth, I really am sorry."

The wisteria ripped away from the wall, inch by inch at first, and then all at once with a sickening crack like bones breaking. Alek was falling and Ian was running.

He pulled out his phone and nearly dropped it, then called 9-1-1 as he stumbled down the stairs and out the front door to where Alek was laying, flat on his back, lifeless, his face turned to the side, blood pooling around his head like a macabre halo.

"9-1-1. What's your emergency?" The female operator said.

"My—" What was Alek to him? After everything that was said, they were hardly friends and they weren't lovers anymore. "My partner. He... He's..." Ian's voice shook as badly as his hands did. "He fell. His head's bleeding. I think he's—he's not moving."

Alek's face was expressionless. Ian half expected him to jump up and say he was only joking; it was all an elaborate prank, another punishment for rejecting him, but he was so still.

"Help is on the way—"

"They'll need to send a helicopter. There's a two-lane paved road and a clearing half a mile east from there if the road is too narrow."

"Okay. I'll tell them." Ian heard typing in the background. She sounded so calm, it would have been contagious if life as he knew it wasn't ending. "Do you see his chest moving? Is he breathing?"

"No. I mean, I don't know. I'm not sure."

"That's okay. Take a deep breath and lay your hand on his chest."

But none of this was okay. How could he breathe, let alone deeply, when Alek might not be breathing at all? He felt Alek's chest as instructed but was trembling so violently he couldn't be sure.

"I can't tell."

"Why don't you try checking his pulse?" she asked like she was suggesting something as benign as turning Alek on and off again like a frozen computer. "Just put your middle and pointer fingers in the groove at the side of his neck."

Ian watched his shaking hand move like it was someone else's, his body only becoming his own again when he felt the frantic, thready ticking under the pads of his fingertips, the proof that Alek's heart was still beating.

"It's there. I feel it."

"Very good. Okay. Put your ear above his mouth. Do you hear anything?"

Ian did as he was told, his body working better now that he knew Alek wasn't dead. Even though he suspected the Alek he loved was probably lost forever, not being dead was a start. Ian felt as much as heard, the slow and shallow tidaling of Alek's breathing like the faint roar of the ocean in a shell held against a child's ear.

"He's breathing."

"That's good. Are you hurt?"

"No."

"Good. What's your name?"

"Ian Stewart."

"And your partner's?"

"Alek Katin."

"Okay, Ian. I'm Patricia. Can you get a blanket and a towel?"

"I can't leave him. What if..." He couldn't finish the sentence. The prospect of Alek dying alone was too painful to bear.

"I understand, but we need to keep Alek warm. Put the phone down next to him. I'll stay with him."

Ian thanked her, set the phone down, and pressed a kiss to Alek's forehead, tasting the metallic tang of blood on his lips. He wiped his mouth on his sleeve and ran on unsteady legs, time slowing down again as he ripped a blanket from the couch, grabbed a towel from beside the kitchen sink, and returned to Alek's side. Alek was even paler, the circle of blood larger around his head.

He covered Alek with the blanket and his mind projected the image of the blanket pulled over Alek's face if he died.

"I'm back. He's got the blanket."

"Very good, Ian. Can you check if he's breathing now?"

Ian repeated the action, ear over Alek. "Yes."

"And can you check his pulse?"

It was still there, tapping away. Ian was proud of Alek for holding on. "Yes."

"Does it feel about the same as before?"

"I think so."

"Good. Now I want you to leave me on speaker and look for any wound on Alek's head. Don't lift his head. Don't move him. Look for anything obvious. Can you do that?"

"Yes. Of course."

Ian tossed the phone aside, every nerve in his body going icy hot as he checked.

Alek's hair was matted with blood, but Ian could still spot the gash on the back of his head. "I see it."

"Sit down by Alek's head and very carefully use the towel to hold gentle pressure to stop the bleeding. Use your other hand to keep his head from moving."

Ian did so without hesitation, holding the towel against the wound like maybe he could keep all the blood from spilling out if he tried hard enough.

The operator asked, "Is the bleeding slowing?"

He'd forgotten she was still on the line. Ian quickly looked around. The towel was bright red where he pressed it to the wound, but it wasn't completely saturated, and the pool of blood didn't seem any larger. "I think so." Ian returned his gaze to Alek's chest and held his breath until he was sure Alek was still breathing.

"The helicopter is five minutes out. You should hear it soon."

While he waited, Ian told Alek everything; how sorry he was, how much he loved him, how stupid Alek was to hang out on a third-story window sill, how he would never cut down the wisteria after this, how he forgave him and nothing Alek did could ever be more than he could take. Ian would marry him, and he'd say *I do* as many times as it took for Alek to be satisfied that there would only ever be him, but Alek probably couldn't even hear him because it was too late.

Meanwhile, Alek remained so still he might as well be dead, except for the steady rise and fall of his chest that Ian now synched his own breathing to. Ian didn't stop talking to Alek, except to occasionally lay down verbal tithes and offerings and bargains and prayers to gods of all kinds until the distant sound of helicopter blades grew louder and he couldn't hear anything else at all.

5

ALEKSANDAR

BULGARIA

Aleksandar Velishikov was five in his first memory. His pudgy fingers hovered over black and white stripes. A gauze curtain blew lazily in the breeze, carrying with it the scent of sweet wisteria that bloomed in bunches of purple flowers like grapes where it climbed up and around the window. Beside him, Uncle Krasimir's fingers danced over the keys, turning sunshine into sound that floated around them like fireflies in the dark.

Uncle Krasimir was his father's brother and more his parent than anyone else. Aleksandar's father was very important and very busy. His mother had brown skin and pale green eyes the color of jade stones. When she hugged him, which was never very often, the scent of honeyed roses wrapped its arms around him and stayed long after she was gone.

One night, Aleksandar woke from a nightmare and left his room, following the amber light that glowed at the end of the hall until he found his father in his study, his enormous hands held over his face.

"Love is a weakness," his father had said. "Never let anyone see where they can hurt you."

Then he patted him on the head and sent him off into the dark hallway alone.

As Aleksandar grew older, his father continued to shape him into the heir he was intended to be. "Deception is survival," he told him and Aleksandar remembered that too, even after his father had forgotten.

Uncle Krasimir waited at the gates of Aleksandar's primary school every afternoon. They walked home together, their footsteps hollow on the dusty cobblestone, the sun warming their backs, as his uncle told him stories from history. Seemingly doomed adventures in which a bold hero conquered insurmountable odds, mysteries that had never been solved, love that didn't just start wars, but ended them too.

Afternoons were for music. Uncle said Aleksandar's hands were made for the piano, but that wasn't what made him gifted. It was how he used them, how they moved, almost sentiently, like music had stitched itself inside his fingers. It was the way that Aleksandar wielded his emotions like a sword that slashed into the listener until they couldn't be sure if their feelings were their own or if Aleksandar had put them there.

But mere talent wasn't enough for his uncle. "You have been given a gift you cannot squander. You must never let a single day pass without practice."

The first time that Aleksandar played for an audience, the lights were too bright, the eyes that watched him in the darkness burned holes in his skin, and he couldn't make his fingers work.

His uncle was not disappointed. He said, "Fear is only proof we are alive."

Uncle Krasimir's house was built into the side of a hill that overlooked a dense forest with a river running through it. Dark green ivy climbed up walls made from river rocks stacked one on top of the other like a vertical puzzle.

His uncle's ballroom-turned-workshop was a lonely child's

paradise. Enormous paintings in gilded frames leaned against walls, making tunnels for Aleksandar to drag books under and read. Wooden chests were filled with cabinet knobs and burlap grain sacks overflowed with tiny hinges and screws that made his fingers smell of copper the rest of the day. There were dark armoires to hide in and grandfather clocks that had forgotten how to tell time, an army of chairs standing in rows, yards of jewel-toned velvet hanging down from the ceiling.

On the less than rare occasion Aleksandar broke something whilst weaving down the narrow aisles of history, his uncle never yelled. Instead, he'd patiently teach him how to fix it.

"Nothing is ever too broken to be fixed," his uncle had said.

But he was wrong about that. People and hearts could break and never be fixed again.

———

ONE DAY, when Aleksandar was ten, school let out and Uncle Krasimir wasn't there. Instead, another one of his father's friends was waiting to escort him home. When Aleksandar asked his escort where his uncle was, he said he moved away.

That didn't make any sense. All of his uncle's things were here. His piano was here. Aleksandar was here. Surely his uncle wouldn't leave him, and never without saying goodbye.

His escort must be mistaken. Perhaps his uncle was sick or maybe he was delivering an antique. That had happened before. His uncle usually warned him, but maybe there hadn't been time.

When he arrived home, he looked for his mother. He would ask her where his uncle went, but only Ivet, the housekeeper, was home and Ivet didn't like him. So he ran to his uncle's house. It wasn't very far. Just across the river and along a path that wound east through the woods. He could make it there in twenty minutes—ten if, instead of using the narrow stone bridge, he crossed the river on foot.

Outside his uncle's house, he retrieved the spare key hidden behind a river rock that had come loose from the mortar. The courtyard was empty. His uncle's workshop too. He searched every room and did not find him.

Was his uncle really gone? No. He couldn't be. Aleksandar would wait for him.

He dragged the duvet from his uncle's bed into the closet. The scent of his uncle—clove and loose tobacco from his pipe— was strongest there, where all of his clothes were in one place.

If he closed his eyes and inhaled through his nose, he could imagine the sound of his uncle's voice when he said he loved him, the warmth of his hug, the sky blue color of his eyes.

Eventually, he fell asleep to a dream of the day his uncle carved *AV* into the side of the piano, right underneath *KV*, the initials he'd carved long before Aleksandar was born.

Aleksandar had felt guilty, like they were carving into an ancient tree, like they were defacing it.

His uncle had said, "Long after we're both gone, this piano will remember us, just like we will never forget it."

When Aleksandar woke the next morning, he was in his own bed and the lingering scent of honey and roses explained that his mother had carried him there.

Over the weeks that followed, Aleksandar went to his uncle's house to practice the piano every day. He didn't want his uncle to be disappointed when he returned. But his uncle was never there and he didn't come back.

Now that his uncle was gone, he was grateful for those initials carved into the side of the piano. When he traced his fingers over the *KV*, it helped him know his uncle was real, that he hadn't imagined him into existence.

Every time Aleksandar played, he gave the piano all of his

loneliness, all of his confusion, every stab of pain from his uncle's abandonment. The music that rose in the air and drifted out through the windows into the forest beyond, fluttered around like fireflies against the starless night sky inside his mind. Every note was the color blue. Lonely. Sad. Left.

6

IAN

The hospital surgery consultation room was slightly larger than a bathroom stall, the walls only thick enough to make the surgeon's droning words unintelligible in the room next door. The bone-chilling wail that soon followed explained exactly what these rooms were for. Would Alek's surgeon soon arrive and deliver equally wail-inducing news?

Ian sat at a flimsy white table that still rocked despite a scrap of cardboard shoved under one leg. Earlier, he'd rinsed the blood from his body the best he could in a shallow sink, his stomach rolling at the smell of iron and the red-tinged water that swirled down the drain. After, he'd changed into scrubs a nurse had given him, but he must not have washed his hands well enough because he spotted dried blood deep under his fingernails, a dark burgundy that reminded him of the paint on the walls in the parlor when the sun hit it.

The clock over the door said it had been five hours. It felt like five days, as far as Ian was concerned.

His cell had died an hour in, so he mapped the landmarks of the white acrylic tabletop to distract himself. There were black, oily scuffs on the edges, long scratches on the top right quadrant, and miniature potholes throughout. The artificial recirculated hospital air made him thirsty, but he couldn't bring himself to drink.

The door opened and Ian looked up. A short woman with brown skin, dark eyes, and a blue hair net smiled before sitting down across from him. She extended her hand across the table. Ian looked at it. Were those the hands that tried to save Alek? Had they been successful?

She dropped her hand and in a thick accent said, "I'm Dr. Modorovic, the neurosurgeon who operated on your partner."

When Ian originally said Alek was his partner, he'd meant in the business sense, but they'd assumed otherwise and he had let them.

She opened her mouth and Ian felt like his heart was pulled out through his stomach.

"Your partner has a subdural hematoma in his left frontal lobe. In some cases, surgery is not required, but in this case, it was. The skull is like a vault and if too much blood accumulates, it can compress the brain and damage it further. I performed a craniotomy, which means I cut a small window into his skull so that I could remove the hematoma and stop the bleeding. I then secured the skull back in place with screws. The brain damage appeared minimal, but we won't know how much the fall affected him until he wakes up, which will hopefully be soon."

"There was so much blood. I thought..."

"The blood you saw was from the superficial head wound. The hematoma was only about the size of a marble."

Ian burst into tears, loud wracking sobs that likely carried through the thin consult room walls and into the waiting room proper.

He really hadn't thought Alek was going to make it.

"Would you like to see him?"

He nodded. Dr. Modorovic filled him in on the rest of Alek's injuries as she led him down overbright hallways to the ICU. Alek's right arm had a nasty fracture at the wrist where it had hit the edge of the flagstone pathway, but the pine needle forest floor had cushioned him from any other major injuries. Just a lot of ugly bruises, she said. Ian hadn't even thought to check for other injuries. He should have.

They stopped in front of a glass sliding door. A curtain hid the room from view.

"Alek is going to look different. His body is swollen and both of his eyes are bruised. A strip of hair is shaved on the left side of his head and there's a bandage covering the incision. He's been breathing on his own rather well now that most of the anesthesia has worn off, so there is no breathing tube. But as I said before, last I heard, he was still unconscious."

"I understand," Ian said.

Dr. Modorovic slid the door open and pulled the curtain aside.

Alek's eyes were still closed. His skin color was remarkably better, the olive more brown than sickly gray. His right arm was in a cast. Alek would be devastated when he learned his wrist was broken. As long as Ian knew him, Alek never went a single day without playing the piano.

Now that Ian had laid eyes on Alek, the details of the hospital room filled in around the bed. There was a silver IV pole with pumps that blinked like lights on a Christmas tree, a standing-height computer on caster wheels, a whiteboard that said *Welcome Mr. Katin*, as if whoever wrote it thought he would actually be able to read it. A narrow, uncomfortable-looking couch was shoved against the far wall beneath a window that looked down on a parking lot.

A tall Asian man pulled a chair to Alek's bedside and

gestured Ian over. "I'm Michael. Your partner's nurse. He's stable, but hasn't woken yet."

Ian sat in the hard plastic chair and scooted closer. The metal legs screeched like nails on a chalkboard, but Alek didn't stir.

Dr. Modorovic frowned and crossed her arms over her chest. "Sometimes the anesthesia lingers. I'll stick around for a few minutes in case he decides to wake up."

Ian leaned forward and took Alek's hand. It was surprisingly warm, but his fingers weren't slender and graceful anymore.

"You can talk to him," the nurse encouraged.

"Alek... Alek, it's Ian." Ian cleared his throat. He wished he didn't have an audience, but on the other hand, if someone left them alone, he'd probably trip over the cord to some vital machine and accidentally kill Alek. He unfolded the fingers of Alek's good hand and kissed the center of his palm. "I love you. Please come back."

A series of shrill beeps sounded. Ian jumped. Was everything okay? Alek couldn't die. He had already almost lost him. He couldn't lose him again.

His heart raced as he scanned the room. Michael still typed at the computer. Nobody ran to their room. Alek looked the same—lifeless, unmoving, like a tall, dark, and brooding sleeping beauty. Ian forced himself to take a deep breath, even as his heart raced, and blood roared in his ears.

Dr. Modorovic pulled a pager from her waistband and squinted at the screen. "Sorry about that," she said, clipping the pager back on her pants.

He hadn't seen a pager since high school.

"*Zashto e tolkova tikho?*" Alek's voice was scratchy, like that time he had strep throat.

Ian swung his gaze back to the bed. Alek's eyes remained closed, his face expressionless. Had he imagined it?

But Dr. Modorovic must have heard Alek too, because she pulled off her surgical cap and asked, "He speaks Bulgarian?"

"Oh, is that what it is? He only ever speaks to me in English." Ian was disappointed Alek hadn't been the one to tell him first. "What did he say?"

"He asked why it's so quiet." Dr. Modorovic stepped closer to the bed. "Mr. Katin, can you hear us?"

7

ALEK

"Yes, I hear you," Alek said to the disembodied voice.

His head throbbed. His entire body hurt, actually. Everything felt heavy, like he was buried under an ocean of sand. He opened his eyes and blinked against the bright overhead lights. Maybe this was where *go towards the light* came from.

He looked for Ian—he'd heard him say "I love you"—and found him holding his hand. There were tears on his lashes like dewdrops on fern leaves after it rained. Alek wanted to taste them.

"Why are you crying?" Alek asked.

Ian looked at him blankly. Was Alek dead? Could Ian see him?

Alek asked the woman standing beside his bed, "Why can't he hear me?"

"He can hear you, but you're speaking Bulgarian. I'm Dr. Modorovic, your neurosurgeon."

Now that she said they were speaking Bulgarian, it was all he could hear. He hadn't heard it spoken aloud in more than ten years. He didn't even like to think in Bulgarian.

The doctor, whose name he'd immediately forgotten, looked to be in her late fifties. She was petite, tan with age spots under her eyes, and had long, black hair, peppered judiciously with strands of silver.

"You don't sound Bulgarian," Alek said.

"I'm not. I'm from Croatia, but have family in Macedonia."

That made sense. Most of the Balkan countries shared each other's languages as much as their borders and Macedonian and Bulgarian were nearly interchangeable.

"You fell from the window on the third story of your house and hit your head when you landed. I performed surgery to evacuate the blood in your brain."

"How did you reach?" Alek asked.

"I cut through your skull, but don't worry, I've put it back together again."

"No. Is there a step stool you use? I can't imagine it's easy for you to see." He'd be shocked if she was taller than five feet.

Her laugh was loud and unselfconscious.

Alek wasn't making a joke. He was genuinely curious.

The doctor asked, "Can you try to say something in English?"

"Is this English?"

"No."

He focused intently, trying to visualize the English words in his mind, but it was like they were obscured behind a haze of fog. "What about this?"

"Afraid not."

"Fuck."

"With time, it may come back." She paused, then asked, "Can you close your eyes?"

He closed them.

"That was English," she said.

He opened his eyes. "No shit."

She flashed a penlight into his eyes. "You're going to be fun to look after. Most of my patients are intimidated by the idea of speaking to a brain surgeon." The doctor turned to Ian, and in English, said, "Sorry about that. It's hard for me to switch between languages when interpreting. It appears that Mr. Katin can understand English, but cannot speak it."

Why wouldn't Ian look at him? Maybe he was only there out of obligation because Alek had listed him as his emergency contact.

"Do you mind if I sit?" The doctor dragged another chair over before either of them answered. "I've been on my feet for," she checked her watch, "seven hours now." She plunked down into the chair and slumped forward with appallingly poor posture for a medical professional.

"I don't understand," Ian said. "He can't speak English?"

"No, or at least, not right now, anyway. Without going too far into neurophysiology, most of our skills—speech, language, walking, and so on—arise from different areas in the brain. It's very common for someone with a brain injury to lose one ability while the others remain intact. Your partner's hematoma was near the communication center of the brain and it seems he's lost the ability to speak English while retaining the ability to understand it. I'm assuming you learned Bulgarian first?"

"Yes," Alek answered quickly, his mind very much distracted by her choice of words. *Your partner*?

"Then Bulgarian is likely more cemented in your brain, so not as easily lost."

Ian told them he was his partner. Alek tried to catch Ian's eye so he could raise his eyebrows in a silent question, but his attention was still focused on the doctor.

"Is this permanent?" Ian asked. "Can he relearn English?"

"Unfortunately, that's impossible to predict. It's rare to lose only one language and not the other—it's much more common to lose all ability to speak, or in rare cases gain fluency in an entirely new language. The intricacies of the brain are as vast and unexplored as the sea. Most patients regain their speech by three months, some later, and some never do. It would be foolish to pass a guess off as a guarantee."

Alek needed to find a better doctor. A neurosurgeon should be able to speak with certainty on all brain-related matters. Although, it was convenient to have her speak his language, and he did sort of like her.

"I can't promise everything will go back to the way it was," the doctor continued. Her eyes focused on Alek like he was an interesting laboratory specimen. "Do you remember falling?"

Alek remembered smoking on the window sill, but hadn't that been the night before last? How long had he been out? Had he fallen that night, and everything after was some sort of brain injury fever dream?

"I think I remember last night, but I'm not sure if last night was *last night,* if that makes sense?"

"You hit your head awfully hard. Give me your best guess. What's the last thing you remember?"

Alek's eyes flicked to Ian and away. The last thing Alek remembered was that Ian didn't come home. Everything between them was ruined.

"I remember going to sleep in Ian's room. Alone," he abbreviated.

The doctor checked with Ian, and having his ex-boyfriend confirm his story like he was a child not to be trusted was a new low, even for him.

"It's normal to have amnesia from the day of the event," the doctor said to both of them in English. "You'll likely never get it back."

Alek wanted her to go away so he could talk to Ian, but how would he even be able to communicate?

The doctor stood and moved to his feet. "Try to wiggle your toes."

His heart dropped. It hadn't even occurred to him that he might be paralyzed. His legs felt like they'd fallen asleep, but when he tested out each one, they did what they were supposed to. He blew out a relieved breath, his ribs aching with the motion.

"Good. Now squeeze my fingers." She held out two fingers in front of each hand.

That he could do too, though his right arm hurt and moved sluggishly, weighed down by... He caught sight of the cast. How was he going to play the piano with that?

She followed his gaze. "Your right wrist is broken. Are you right-handed?"

Luckily, he was ambidextrous.

He shook his head and then stopped, stunned by pain. His head throbbed like his brain was ricocheting against the inside of his skull. He'd have to remember not to do that again.

The doctor completed a series of other tedious neurological exams, including poking him with the sharp end of an unfolded paperclip to confirm he still had sensation to all of his limbs. When she finished, she said, "Tomorrow, we can test your ability to read and write in both languages, and see how you are on your feet. But for now, I'm pleased."

Ian opened his mouth, but Alek spoke first.

"Get me a pen and paper," he told the doctor, then added, "please."

The doctor repeated his request to a man in the room—the nurse, maybe?—who left and returned with a pen and paper pinned to a clipboard.

Alek picked up the pen with his left hand and wrote, *I'm sorry.* His handwriting was appalling, but it passed for legible. He could tell it was English. Or at least he thought it was.

"It's English," the doctor said, "and you don't need to apologize to me."

"I'm not."

She laughed again. Shouldn't a neurosurgeon be more serious?

"I'm going to write something for my *partner*," Alek said. He liked the taste of the word inside his mouth, though *husband* would have been better. "I don't want you to read it."

She steepled her fingertips. "Of course. I'll just wait here like a very expensive carrier pigeon."

Yes, he definitely liked her. Which was strange. He didn't like anyone except for Ian. It must have been some fall.

Alek wrote, *I could forget everything about myself and still know that I love you.*

He nodded to the doctor. She rolled her eyes, pulled the paper from the clipboard, and said to Ian in English, "I believe it's for you."

Ian took the note without reading it.

"We'll give you two some privacy," the doctor said in English. At least she had emotional intelligence, even if her neuroscience needed work. "I'll have Michael track down an iPad. We have a video interpreter—"

"No! No interpreters. Only you," Alek rushed to say.

In Bulgarian, she replied, "I assure you. It's secure. Your privacy will be maintained."

"No."

"Keep the writing implements then. I'll bill you later." A flash of a smile and then, "I'd tell you to stop writing when you get tired, but I doubt you'll listen."

To Ian, the doctor said, "*Da* is yes and *Ne* is no. *Ebasi* is fuck. I have a feeling you'll be hearing it a lot." Then she took Alek's pen and wrote her phone number on his clipboard. "I trust you not to abuse the privilege. Would you like me to translate anything else before I go?"

"Tell Ian to stop looking so sad. He can't kill me that easily."

She laughed again. "I'm not going to say that."

"Doesn't that go against your oath or ethics or whatever? Just tell him."

"He says stop looking so sad. I'm going to be fine," she told Ian, then in Bulgarian, asked, "Anything else?"

"Tell him to buy a keyboard and bring it back here."

"Like a computer keyboard?"

"No. Piano."

After relaying the message, the doctor and the nurse left, a cacophony of phones ringing and alarms dinging outside the room until they closed the door behind them.

"Read it," Alek said automatically and then growled. *Fuck this fucking Bulgarian.*

Ian must have understood because he looked down at the paper.

There were tiny flecks of dried blood like freckles on Ian's neck. He looked older, the wrinkles at the corners of his eyes deeper, but even wearing scrubs, the color a most atrocious spearmint gum green, Alek couldn't stop staring.

Ian folded the paper up into smaller and smaller squares and then held it in his hand. He looked less like he was about to be executed and more like he was about to be laid off, his eyes glued on the scratchy blanket covering Alek's lower half.

"I'm so sorry," Ian said.

Alek didn't know what *he* had to apologize for.

Ian raised his gaze. "Can I kiss you?"

"Yes." Alek cursed the fact he couldn't sit up and bring Ian's face to him.

Ian rose from his seat, but instead of kissing Alek's lips, he pressed a feather-light kiss to his forehead.

Alek wrote, *That's it?*

Ian lowered back into the chair and rubbed his hand over the back of his neck. "The last place I kissed you was there and... there was blood everywhere. I... I needed to erase it."

I'm sorry I scared you.

"I'm so glad you're not—you came back." Ian moved quickly and wrapped his arms around Alek's waist, pressing his face into his stomach. "Am I hurting you?"

"No." Alek reached for the clipboard and pen. *So what's this about us being partners?*

Ian lifted his head. "I panicked. I meant business partner, but they assumed otherwise, probably because of how upset I was."

Business partner was a woefully inadequate label for what they were to each other. *I like being called your partner*, Alek wrote.

"Me too."

I have to know. Is there still a chance?

Alek held his breath.

With dark eyes sincere and the line of his jaw sharp, Ian answered, "Yes."

Alek thanked him, but whether it was Bulgarian or not, he was too tired to care. He dropped the pen, pushed the clipboard to the side, and patted his lap. After Ian rested his head again, Alek ran his fingers through his velvety brown hair. It made everything hurt, but it was worth the pain.

8

IAN
THREE YEARS EARLIER

Ian had first met Alek over email when he'd reached out to inquire about some emerald and gold stained glass pendant lights he'd seen in an antique listing. Alek had suggested they exchange the priceless items at an Art Déco hotel at the old town waterfront.

Over email, Alek sounded like a stuffy, aristocratic professor clad from head to foot in tweed. Far too many five dollar words and a subtle level of condescension nestled between each letter.

But the man sitting on the third barstool from the left as they'd previously discussed was nothing like he'd imagined. He was dressed in all black with wide shoulders and a wiry build, the bones at the base of the back of his neck just visible as he bent over a paperback book. Glossy midnight hair flounced over his forehead, the perfect length for Ian to tangle his fingers in.

Ian dropped onto the barstool beside him, eyes trailing over the strong forearms revealed by a collared shirt pushed up at the sleeves, but by the time he opened his mouth to introduce himself, Alek turned and rendered Ian speechless. Alek had high cheekbones, an angular jaw, and striking pale green eyes that flashed in contrast with Mediterranean skin.

He looked close in age or a little younger. Late twenties, maybe?

"You must be Ian," Alek said in a voice low and lyrical.

"You're not what I expected."

His lips quirked into a half-grin. "I get that a lot."

Ah, there was the arrogance. "Where are the light fixtures?"

Alek mocked a pout. "I'm really rather attached to my antiques. How will I know if they're headed to a good home if I don't get to know you first?"

Alek spent the next hour seducing Ian between talking shop, finding any excuse to touch him, dropping a hand to his wrist under the ruse of getting his attention, leaning closer when the bar was loud to speak against his ear. His tactics were shamelessly obvious, but Alek was like a book Ian couldn't stop reading. There was something magnetic and dangerous about him. Ian nursed a single beer until it was lukewarm and still felt drunk, his words flowing freely, as if Alek wasn't just a book, but a drug.

"Why do you restore historical homes?" Alek asked, tracing long, delicate fingers around the rim of his glass. "Why not commercial buildings?"

"Still interrogating me, I see. Are you this thorough with every sale you make?"

"Certainly not. Most people are exceedingly dull, but you intrigue me. Now, answer my question." He wet his lower lip and leveled his jade gaze through thick black lashes. "Please."

"Commercial and new builds have no character. For me, every abandoned house is a person with its own secret history. Tarnished engraved doorplates. An old well in a basement. Built-in book cases layered with cheap paint. Hidden wounds, yes, but held together by the skeleton of a survivor. Scars that can be erased. For me, restoring a historical building is like traveling back in time. The closest thing to magic we'll get in this life."

Alek's lips had parted slightly. Ian wanted to dip his tongue inside and taste the single malt whiskey.

Ian flushed and looked at his hands. "I should go." He peeled a twenty from his wallet, tucked it beneath his beer and stood. The stool legs scraped, pulling the attention of the other bar patrons.

"I'll walk you out," Alek said, seemingly unruffled as he hailed the barman and closed out his tab.

Ian waited, stupefied for fleeting seconds, then shook himself and sped towards the exit. Footsteps followed him all the way outside into the briny night air, around the hotel, and to the alley that snaked behind.

"What about the light fixtures?" Alek called playfully, his voice echoing across the empty alley.

Ian stopped and turned, surprised to find Alek right behind him. Without thinking, he fisted his hands in Alek's shirt and pinned him against the wall. The faintest flicker of fear flared in Alek's eyes and disappeared so quickly, Ian wasn't sure if he'd imagined it. Ian brought his mouth so close to Alek's neck that he could have bitten him if he wanted to.

Alek lifted his chin, baring his neck, challenging him. Goosebumps lit up all over Ian's body like flash bulbs exploding. He could almost smell the ozone. His mouth watered. He wanted to kiss him.

But he wouldn't lose control. As fast as it had happened, almost as if it had never happened, Ian released Alek and left him in the dim glow of a rusted lantern. Ian could find some other light fixtures for his project. That man would be his end.

9

IAN

PRESENT DAY

In the fleeting moment between sleep and waking, the gentle rise and fall of Alek's breathing, the heavy weight of Alek's hand settled in his hair would have almost lulled Ian back to sleep.

Ian's eyes jolted open, his stomach lurching with the flood of memories. Alek fell, a halo of blood, a blanket pulled over his face. What if while he slept Alek had slipped back into unconsciousness, never to return again?

The room was dark, except for the blinking green glow of the lights on the IV pumps beside the hospital bed. Alek was already awake, watching him curiously. He pressed a button on his remote and a fluorescent light switched on overhead.

"How are you feeling?" Ian asked.

Alek already had the pen in his hand, his swollen fingers scrawling clumsily. *As bad as I look.*

Ian reached for the call light, but Alek grabbed his wrist with surprising strength and speed.

"*Ne,*" he said. *I don't need the nurse. I want to know what I forgot.*

"Before you fell?"

"*Da.*" Then he said something in Bulgarian, huffed impatiently and wrote, *Everything that happened since you left me.*

It seemed the fall had not made Alek any less demanding.

He told Alek about how he'd gone to visit his mom, how he hadn't told her anything about how bad things were between the two of them. As far as his mom knew, they were as blissfully content as ever. "Then after work, I came home..."

Should he tell Alek that he was going to leave?

Alek wrote, *No lies. Leave nothing out.*

"I was going to move out."

Alek stilled, watching him unblinkingly.

"I didn't know if I was really going to do it. I felt terrible for disappearing, for not calling. I looked for you everywhere and then found you in my bed." Ian took a deep, shaking breath. "I knew we could still fix this. I climbed into bed behind you and it was..." His voice cracked. "It was the only time I've been happy since we broke up."

Alek gripped the pen tightly, but wrote nothing.

"I'm sorry. I don't think I was going to go through with it."

"*Ne.*" Alek's pen scratched the paper. *Never apologize for telling the truth. Keep going.*

Ian told him everything else, pausing only to address Alek's interruptions when he wasn't satisfied with the level of detail. Ian told him everything, everything except that he'd called Alek a burden, a tumor, that he ruined his life. The truth was right there on the tip of his tongue, but Ian hadn't meant what he said. Besides, Alek had betrayed him with lies of far more importance, and omitted decades of backstory, and Dr. Modorovic said he wouldn't remember anything from today anyway. When Ian got to the part where Alek offered to buy him out of the house, Alek stopped him.

Why would I offer to let you go? I would never do that. He underlined the never with a jagged slash of his pen.

"Well... You offered, but you also said you didn't know if you'd go through with it." Ian hoped the kernel of truth would be enough to quell his suspicion.

Did you want to go?

"No! I was going to say no."

Alek studied his face and then must have trusted the veracity of the answer because he wrote, *Continue.*

"You were sitting on the window sill, facing me. I... I just wanted to give us some space. I wanted to calm down first. I didn't realize... You reached out for me. You asked me to stay, but I didn't—I pulled my arm away and you fell." Ian told him how the wisteria had saved him, how he thought Alek was dead, how he'd told him he would marry him and meant it.

When Ian finished, Alek grimaced.

"Are you in pain?"

"*Ne.*"

Ian read the words as Alek wrote them. *You only wanted to marry me because you thought I'd die?*

"No. I mean, the fall and seeing you like that... it was a contributing factor, but it made me realize how much I was willing to forgive if it meant I could have you forever. All of the fears I had, all of the things that happened between us were nothing compared to losing you. Does that make sense?"

"*Da.*" Alek tapped his pen against the page. He'd run out of space. Ian flipped it over to the unwritten side.

Alek wrote, *I'm so sorry I hurt you. I've made so many mistakes.*

Unsolicited apologies? Admitting he made a mistake? Maybe the brain damage was more severe than they'd thought.

"It's okay," Ian said.

Alek released a stream of unintelligible words. There was a no in there somewhere, if Ian heard correctly, but everything else was nonsense to him.

"You're not speaking English, love," Ian said as gently as he could.

Alek continued in Bulgarian anyway, a long diatribe with at least three *Ebasi* F-bombs. He put the back of his hand over his forehead, breathing fast, like he needed to catch his breath.

"Are you okay? Do you want the nurse?"

"*Ne.*" He sounded tired, defeated. *I was trying to say what I've done... It's not okay. I don't deserve you. Also, this stilted method of communication is annoying as fuck.*

"You're right. It *is* annoying. I thought we'd never talk again, though, so small victories, right?"

Ian reached forward and ran his fingers through Alek's hair. All the blood had been washed out. It felt dryer, rougher, like a very astringent soap was used to clean it, but it was still as shiny as raven feathers. Would the surgical incision leave a scar?

"Is this okay?" Ian asked.

"*Da.*" Alek closed his eyes and made a contented humming noise in his chest.

After a few moments, Ian said, "Everybody deserves love, Alek. Even you."

Alek started writing again and Ian prepared for another round, but all he wrote was, *Have you eaten?*

Ian shook his head. "Are you hungry?"

When was the last time you had something to drink?

"Don't worry about me."

Now that he thought about it, he *was* very thirsty. He looked at the clock. It was nearly four in the morning.

Call the nurse and ask for water, Alek wrote.

A few moments later, a young woman slid the glass door open and pushed a metal cart into the room, her long, swishy, blonde ponytail bouncing behind her. On the cart were two small gray plastic pitchers of water and a piano keyboard.

"Hello, Mr. Katin." Her lilting voice was a decibel shy of

being too loud for such a depressing place. To Ian, she said, "I'm Courtney, your partner's nurse tonight. Mr. Katin and I are already best friends. I've been in and out doing neuro checks all night, but he didn't want me to wake you."

She put the waters on the end table next to the head of Alek's bed.

"*Blagodarya*," Alek muttered.

Ian had no idea what that meant.

Courtney patted the top of the electric piano. "I scrounged this baby up from our Music Therapy department and I've never been so excited for a call bell to go off."

Alek nudged his arm. *Drink.* He tapped his pen as if to tell him 'now'.

Ian stood and picked up one of the pitchers. "Only if you drink first."

Alek's nod was nearly indiscernible.

Courtney pressed a button on the bed and a faint electric whirring raised the head of the bed until Alek was sitting completely upright.

Alek groaned.

"Any nausea or pain?" she asked.

"*Ne.*"

Liar.

Ian held the pitcher and guided the straw into Alek's mouth.

Alek looked up at him with those pale jade eyes, wrapped his lips around the straw and drank. Trust Alek to make drinking water on his near-deathbed erotic. Ian cleared his throat and once he was sure Alek wasn't going to throw up, said, "More?"

"*Ne.*" Alek pointed his pen to where he'd written *Drink,* as if to repeat the command.

Ian brought the same cup, the same straw that Alek drank from, to his lips. There was something very intimate about sharing a cup with Alek. Not in a sexual way. Just in an *I haven't kissed my boyfriend on the lips in three weeks and now we're sharing a straw* kind of way.

Ask for snacks, Alek wrote.

"I'll eat after you've tried the piano."

Alek huffed a sigh and wrote, *Deal*.

"Excuse me, Courtney," Ian called to where she appeared to be checking the fluid inside Alek's IV bags. "Could we try the piano now? As long as it won't be too loud?"

"Too loud? No way! These glass doors block more noise than you'd think. You should hear all the dinging alarms outside."

That was an unsettling thought.

Courtney wheeled a table to the opposite side of Alek's bed, positioned it over his lap, and Ian placed the keyboard on top.

From the side pocket of her cargo pants, Courtney pulled out a piece of paper. "Sheet music. Just in case. Okay, well, I'll leave you to it. Make sure you only use your left hand." She narrowed her eyes at Alek in a surprisingly stern way and then left, closing the door behind her.

Alek rolled his eyes and then winced.

"I know you're in pain. You don't need to suffer. Do you want me to ask her to bring something?"

After I play.

Alek lifted both hands to the keyboard and rested his fingertips against the keys.

10

ALEK

Ian was lying to him. Nothing explained why Alek would have been so acquiescent as to allow Ian's departure from the Victorian.

And Ian finally accepting his marriage proposal? Alek wished he'd lost all of his English so he wouldn't have learned that Ian only wanted to marry him because he thought he was about to die. Of course, the idea of marrying him was made more palatable if death would soon part them anyway.

Ian was watching the keyboard with as much intensity as if it were a bomb about to explode. He shuffled from one foot to the other, his arms hanging stiffly at his sides like he didn't know what to do with them.

Alek wasn't nervous. He already knew he couldn't play piano the way he had before the fall. Testing his theory on the keyboard was only a formality. He could tell as soon as he woke up that something was missing.

The endless soundtrack that played inside his mind was gone. The music that tangled with his senses until he couldn't smell without memories and see without sound and listen without feeling. All of it was gone. His entire life, he'd never existed with such silence.

Before the fall, when Ian talked, an entire forest grew inside Alek's head. The quiet roar of Ian's breathing was like wind through treetops. Even the nearly inaudible crackle of the strands of Alek's hair when Ian ran his fingers through it sounded like autumn leaves underfoot. Now when Ian talked only words came out. Every sound he made was just noise and nothing else.

Where Alek usually read the black and white piano keys as infinite potential combinations of sound, sense, and emotion, he only saw white letters A through G and black notes sharp and flat. Alek's hands weren't his hands anymore; they were ugly and didn't move the way they used to. It was like he had to manually pull the puppet string of each finger to get them to go where he wanted them to. But he would try, not because he hoped for a miracle, but to take inventory of exactly how much he'd lost.

The acrylic keys were a cold and hollow substitute beneath his fingertips, and when Alek pressed down, the keys grated against each other like teeth gnashing. He tried to select a song to play, but couldn't summon any of the songs he'd composed or the songs he hadn't composed but memorized.

Alek looked at the sheet music the nurse printed for him. The notes might as well have been characters from an entirely different language. They made no sense to him. His ears began to ring. He lifted his hands and laid them in his lap. He'd lost his music and would rather have died than face the world without it.

Ian knew without asking. He pushed the table aside and bent down, leaning his forehead against his.

"Alek, I'm so sorry."

What would Alek do with his emotions if he couldn't give them to the piano anymore? All of his sorrow, all of his regret—

it would consume him whole. The only time he'd ever skipped a day playing the piano...

River rocks knocking against each other, ash over keys that cut like broken glass beneath his fingers.

He couldn't breathe. His heart thumped like a train traveling fast over tracks, only one moment away from going off the rails.

He wanted to die. He should have died.

Ian pulled back, concern knitting his brows together, but Alek brought his good hand to the back of Ian's head, tangling his fingers in his hair and dragging him close enough to nip his lower lip. Ian gasped, and that should have taken the pain away some, but it only twisted the knife deeper because before the fall, Ian's gasps sounded like splotches of starlight and now it was all dark.

Their lips were so close that every fast, jagged breath Ian exhaled went right down into Alek's lungs. Maybe if he tried hard enough, he could pull Ian inside of him so he'd never leave. Without words, Alek dared Ian to steal the kiss, to stop treating him like he was fragile, to kiss him the way he always had, like death was on his heels and Alek was his salvation. Every atom in Alek's body strained to merge with Ian's, to fuse completely.

Ian lunged forward and when his lips crushed against Alek's with a bruising intensity, gravity imploded and Alek was flying.

It had been twenty-three days since they last kissed. Alek had kept track, marking the days he'd been trapped in a prison of his own design. Now it felt like he'd been counting the days down to freedom.

Ian mumbled a low, satisfied *mmm* that vibrated deep inside Alek's own chest.

"I love you. I love you. I love you," Ian chanted before their lips fully parted and Alek said the same and it didn't matter that it was in Bulgarian, because their language was their own.

But that was only an intermission, a comma joining the first kiss to the next, because Ian's lips were back on Alek's, and then Ian's mouth moved to Alek's temple and over to the space in front of his ear, before descending to his neck, kissing and licking and sucking as he reclaimed each and every inch of territory that had always belonged to him, had only ever belonged to him.

Ian moved to press his ear over the spot where Alek's heart cantered erratically inside his chest, like each beat was precious to him and maybe it was. Alek let his head fall back against the pillow. He was tired. His head ached terribly. He wanted to sleep, but he was afraid to miss even a single moment with Ian. They'd already wasted so much time.

Ian's face tilted upward, assessing Alek. "You're taking pain medicine. Now."

Before Alek could disagree, Ian pressed the call light and summoned the nurse. A handful of minutes later, the nurse came and went, leaving Alek with the obliviating buzz of opiates coursing through his veins. His eyelids were so heavy, it was impossible to keep them open.

"Go to sleep, Alek."

"Loving you is the only thing I don't regret," Alek tried very hard to say in English.

"I'll be here when you wake up. Go to sleep."

Bulgarian then. Maybe he'd be able to say it in English when he woke up.

11

ALEKSANDAR

BULGARIA. 11 YEARS OLD

Uncle Krasimir was dead. It was the only logical conclusion. When people died, they left and didn't come back. When his grandmother died, she didn't have time to say goodbye. Death was the only thing that would have made his uncle leave him. He was sure of it.

Enough time passed that one afternoon, when Aleksandar went into his uncle's closet, he couldn't smell him anymore. He ripped every item of clothing from their hangers and upended each of his uncle's dresser drawers, but there wasn't a trace of his uncle left. He sat on top of the pile of clothing and didn't stop crying until his mother brought him back to his bed.

After what felt to a lonely boy like an eternity later, but was really only several months, Aleksandar had his first taste of freedom. School let out early and Aleksandar's teacher was too preoccupied with scolding Grigor, who had punched Darian, to notice Aleksandar slip out through the doors without waiting for his escort.

His father would be furious with the teacher, and he felt a twinge of guilt, but he was never allowed to be alone anywhere except for his own house, or when he snuck to his uncle's.

On his way home, Aleksandar walked along the shady path that followed the river dividing his family's property from his uncle's. Birds chirped in the trees and shook the leaves where they landed. The river babbled merrily, unseen behind a copse of birch trees and curtains of overhanging willows bordering the shore.

Above the din of the gently rumbling water, Aleksander heard his uncle's voice.

He must have imagined it. His uncle was dead.

But the voice sounded so much like his uncle that he had to check. He ducked under a tree branch and pushed past smaller sharp branches that clutched at his clothes. A thick bramble of blackberry bushes blocked his view. He was about to turn back, but then he heard the voice again, raised this time.

"I'm not leaving without Aleksandar." That was definitely his uncle's voice.

"He's not yours to take," said his father.

Something splashed violently. There was a strange hollow thundering that reminded Aleksandar of the time his uncle took him to the sea. The beach had been covered in lemon-sized rocks all the way to the water line, and when Aleksandar tried to get close to the water, the smooth rocks were surprisingly painful under the arches of his feet. He had been disappointed that the beach wasn't sandy like the ones he'd seen on TV. But then the sea drew back, and the waves carried the rocks with them, and the roar of the rocks as they tumbled over each other was so beautiful, he didn't mind.

Aleksandar crashed through the thicket, desperate to see his uncle once more. Thorns pricked his cheeks as he squeezed through a narrow gap and the riverbank finally came into view. Rays of sunlight beamed down onto the water, sparkling so brightly, it momentarily blinded him.

Then he saw his father. Aleksandar darted behind the bush and peeked around to watch him.

His father was standing in the river, fully dressed as he bent over with his hands thrust into the water that went up to his knees. The muscles in his arms strained, like he was trying to pull something very heavy out of the water.

Behind his father, something thrashed and water splashed so violently it reached Aleksandar where he hid. Nothing made sense until he found the source of the splashing. Shoes. For a brief moment, Aleksandar wondered why his uncle would be swimming with his shoes on until it all snapped into place like a zap of electricity.

His uncle wasn't swimming and his father wasn't trying to lift something from the water and the sound of the river rocks knocking together was because his uncle was scrambling to stand. Hands reached from the water and scratched at his father's arms, but his father only forced his uncle under the water more violently.

Aleksandar lurched forward, his mouth opened to tell his father to stop. His uncle always said he should be brave, that he should do what was right even when it was scary, even when it was hard. *Fear is only proof you are alive.* But he was too afraid. His voice wouldn't work and he was paralyzed in place.

Then, the splashing stopped and the sound of rocks knocking against each other stopped and the silence was eerily still. Aleksandar's father spat into the water and sound came back all at once, like waves crashing forward onto the shore. Inside Aleksandar's mind, everything sounded red, like a river of blood leading to an ocean of rage that would one day rise up and swallow his father.

His father struggled to catch his breath, his hands on his knees, before he straightened and wiped the back of his hand over the sweat on his brow. He sloshed through the river to the opposite bank and disappeared into the forest on the other side.

Aleksandar ran to his uncle and tried to pull him from the shallow water, but his uncle was too heavy and he wasn't strong enough. He pinched his uncle's nose closed, put his mouth over his lips, and breathed air into him the way he'd seen it done on TV, but his uncle's chest did not rise.

He tried again and again and again while the current moved around them, the water babbling cheerfully against the rocks on the shore. The sun continued to shine. Offensively. It should have been mourning. It should have gone out like a snuffed candle, instead of stubbornly burning the skin on the back of his neck.

Aleksandar shivered so hard his teeth chattered, and his clothes were heavy with water, but he didn't stop trying to bring his uncle back. Not until he heard voices, and footsteps. His father's men.

Uncle Krasimir was dead. Aleksandar was too weak to save him. He looked at his uncle one last time—his eyes were made even bluer as he stared sightlessly up at the cloudless sky—then turned, and ran. He ran without seeing, without hearing, without thinking until he reached his uncle's house.

Aleksandar didn't deserve to ever step foot in his uncle's home again, but his uncle's was the only safe place he'd ever known, the only home he'd ever had. Aleksandar couldn't bear to return to his uncle's closet, so instead he slipped into the workshop and crawled under a large painting leaning against the wall. He cried until he had no more tears left and then he decided he would never cry again.

Aleksandar did not practice the piano that day. He hoped his uncle would understand.

12

IAN

Sweat made Alek's hair wet, his eyes moved rapidly under his lids, and his heart rate spiked on the monitor. Ian was about to call the nurse when Alek's eyes snapped open on a gasp. Alek rifled through the tangled sheets until he found the paper and pen.

No more pain meds, he wrote, his hand shaking so much Ian could hardly read the letters.

"Why?"

Alek circled his previous response. *No more pain meds.* His face was already smoothing into apathy, his hand no longer trembling as he wrote, *I want to play a game.*

"Okay, let's play." Alek needed the distraction, and the two of them played games more often than not, anyway. "What are the rules?"

You can ask me ten questions, and I promise my answer will be the truth.

"So like truth or dare, without the dares?"

"*Da,*" he said. *But no open-ended questions. Only yes, or no. I'll save the dares for when we're at home.* Alek offered a specter of his typical smirk and lifted a finger, then wrote, *You have nine left. Think before you speak.*

Ian didn't have to think. He asked the question he most wanted the answer to, the one he was least sure of.

"Do you love me?"

Alek rolled his eyes. "*Da.*" Another finger.

"Do you want me to go?"

Never.

Ian looked down at his lap. "But it's my fault that you fell. None of this would have happened... the fall. Your music. I'm so sorry."

Alek waited and when Ian said nothing else, wrote, *You made me sit at the window? You never warned me of its danger? You reached inside my brain and stole my music? Now ask me another question.*

"Do you hate me?"

"*Ne.*" *You might hate me, but I could never hate you. That's four.*

"I don't hate you."

You're lying.

"I'm not."

You are. I only lost yesterday's memories, remember.

"You'd think someone writing wouldn't talk so much."

If you want me to stop talking, just take my pen. It will be fun to see what happens if you try.

Ian didn't take the bait. "Do you think I pushed you?"

"*Ne.*" *Crimes of passion aren't your style.*

"Are you a spy?"

Alek laughed and then grabbed his stomach. "*Ne.*"

Ian followed Alek's hand to his stomach and frowned. He opened his mouth and Alek wrote the number seven.

"I didn't ask anything yet!"

You were going to. When I want pain medicine I will tell you.

Ian heaved a long-suffering sigh. "Why did you hide that you're from Bulgaria?"

Alek remained silent.

"You can write an entire sentence to taunt me but won't answer my questions with anything, but yes or no?"

Those are my rules. You have three questions left. I'm tired. You'd better hurry.

Quietly, as gently as he might carry a bird with a broken wing, Ian asked, "Do you really have no other family left?"

"*Da.*"

"I'm sorry."

Alek shrugged.

Ian watched the paper beneath Alek's hand until he was sure Alek would not elaborate.

"I don't want you to sleep with anyone else anymore," Ian said.

Alek said nothing. He was like one of those annoying Sphinxes in Greek mythology.

"Will you stop sleeping with other people?"

"*Da.*"

"I wish you never did."

Alek trapped his tongue between his teeth and wiggled a solitary finger.

"I know. I can count," Ian said. "Will you ever tell me about your life before you met me? About Bulgaria... and your family?"

That's more than one question, but yes. I will tell you. Alek stopped the pen, leaving its point against the page. *But, not today.*

Ian groaned again.

If you keep making noises like that, I'll have to force my cock in your mouth to silence you.

"Don't threaten me with a good time." Ian strived for irreverence but was betrayed by the gravelly rumble that snuck into his voice.

I find it very satisfying that with a single profane suggestion, I can get you to welcome the risk of being caught in such a shameful predicament when only a few moments ago you were afraid to kiss me.

"I wasn't afraid. I didn't want to hurt you."

Don't treat me like I'm weak. In the blank space underneath, he added, *I want things to be like they were before.*

"Things can never be the way they were before. I thought you died. You almost did." Ian paused to rein in his composure before it ran away from him.

Alek looked over at the hulking form of the electric piano.

If things can't be the way they were before, then I'd rather have died.

13

ALEK

Why hadn't Ian asked about the escorts? Didn't he want to know exactly what Alek did with them? Shouldn't he be jealous? Shouldn't he be obsessed with finding out what went on between Alek and his paramours? If the roles were reversed, Alek would have demanded Ian tell him every single detail and describe how inadequate each sexual interaction had been.

He wrote, *Why didn't you ask me about the escorts?*

Ian had fallen asleep in his chair with his arms crossed over his chest and his head tilted back. Alek poked him with the blunt tip of his pen.

"Hmm?" Ian mumbled, then dropped his eyes to the paper. "What escorts? You said... You said they were dating app matches. Wait, there were escorts too?"

Fuck. It was hard to keep all of the lies straight when he had a concussion to contend with. He really thought he told Ian about the escorts. He had the strangest sense of déjà vu.

Alek wrote, *The matches were escorts.*

Ian was even hotter when he was angry. His already chiseled jaw was carved into sharp relief, and the way his brows dipped to darken his eyes into the color of damp earth was exactly the same look he made before he held Alek down and fucked him the way they both liked.

"Why would you lie about that?" Ian asked. "It's all the same betrayal to me."

Alek wrote, *Escorts imply that I had to pay for your competition, whereas matches would be more likely to make you jealous since they wanted to come to me.*

Apparently, that was the wrong thing to say, because Ian glared at him with disgust, like he couldn't believe he'd ever seen anything in him. Alek thanked himself for the last resort he'd kept in his back pocket.

I didn't touch them. It was all an act.

Ian shot out of the chair. "Explain. Now."

"I didn't want to actually have sex with them. I needed it to look like I did. I wanted *you*."

Ian stared at him coldly. "That wasn't English."

Alek growled and wrote out the same on the paper.

"You didn't touch them? It sounded like they enjoyed themselves."

An angry pulse beat visibly in Ian's neck as he waited for an answer. His fists were clenched at his sides like he was resisting the urge to strangle him. Alek would quite like to feel Ian's hands, trembling with volatile rage, around his neck. He forced himself to focus and wrote, *I paid them to be convincing.*

"Why should I believe you?" Ian nearly whispered.

Alek didn't have an answer. Ian was right. Alek was the definition of dishonest. Lies coursed through his veins and slipped into his speech like second nature.

"Everything you do, everything you say... I can't trust any of it. There are too many lies. Why didn't you tell me that yesterday? Were you really going to get back together with me with a lie that big between us? How many other lies are there?"

"There are so many lies, I can hardly keep track of them all and if I tell you the truth, you'll hate me." Alek's voice grew louder and ended in a cough that made his head feel like it was going to explode.

"Write it down," Ian reminded him.

I'm sorry. I know I messed up. I knew it the first night I invited someone over and saw your face when I walked him out. But I didn't know what else to do.

Ian shook his head, like he was trying to shake Alek's words loose before they were committed to memory.

"You could have done practically anything else and it would have been better than what you've done."

But I didn't touch th— Ian snatched the pen out of Alek's hand and gripped it like a knife.

"You're done talking. You can have the pen back when I'm finished."

Ian reclaimed his seat, his back straight, his eyes flat as he stared through the window across the room. Outside, wisps of purple clouds drifted low over the early morning sky.

"I know empathy is hard for you," Ian said. "So let me put it in a way that you can understand. Imagine the roles reversed. You're not just in love with me. You're obsessed."

Really? Ian thought Alek had to imagine that.

"After three years, I still don't tell you much about myself, but you'll take what you can get. We move into the Victorian and when you see how much I love it, you plan for us to stay when it's finished. You can't wait to see my face when you tell me."

Alek's mouth fell open. No one ever caught him off guard, no one ever surprised him, except Ian. Alek tried to catch Ian's eye, but he appeared to have no interest in seeing his reaction now.

"The only time you leave is to go to work, but you miss me so much while you're gone that most nights you hardly get through dinner without bending me over the table and fucking me until the plates and cutlery slide off onto the floor."

Alek was relieved to know that his dick could still get hard.

"Then one day, I ask you to marry me." The side of Ian's face glowed golden as the sun rose higher in the sky. "Imagine saying no. Not because you don't love me. Not because you can't imagine marrying me one day. Obviously, you plan to be together for the foreseeable forever because you're rebuilding me a goddamn Victorian mansion.

"And then, I break up with you. Imagine the shock and disbelief. The denial that gives way to devastation. 'I don't understand,' you say. 'We're happy. We can fix this. I love you.' But I don't want to hear it. I won't compromise." Ian turned his face away, his Adam's apple bobbing as he swallowed. "Then, the very next night, I invite someone over and fuck them. Loudly. Imagine how painful that would be. Sitting there, listening to *that*. Totally discarded. The only conclusion you can make is that I moved on, just like," he snapped his fingers, "that. Like I never meant anything to you at all.

"Imagine being trapped. All of your money is tied up in the house, and even if money wasn't a problem, you can't help but stick around for the mere morsels of attention I give you when I feel like tormenting you. But worst of all, you can't leave because you're afraid of what will happen if you leave me to self-destruct. Because you still love me. You still care. You can't turn it off."

Ian said nothing for long enough that Alek wondered if he'd ever speak to him again.

"Imagine being so miserable," Ian began again. Slowly. Quietly. Almost whispering. "You long to sleep for even the briefest break from what is, essentially, a waking nightmare, but I make it so loud with sex and music that all you can hear are the thoughts inside your head. *He never loved you enough to tell you where he came from. You meant nothing to him. You don't even know him."*

Ian pulled a folded piece of paper from his pocket, unfolded it, and looked down at the page.

"Then, when it's finally quiet enough to fall asleep, you drop right into dreams about the way things used to be when we were still happy, when I still loved you, and that's even worse than nightmares because the next morning you have to remember that we broke up all over again."

With one hand, Ian crumpled the paper up into a ball and crushed it inside his fist.

"Repeat that. Every day. Every night. For three weeks. Then one day, you find out that none of it ever happened. That I didn't sleep with any of those people. That all the pain you suffered was a lie to manipulate you into doing what I want. Imagine if I did that to you."

But Alek couldn't imagine that. The only pain he let himself feel was the physical kind. It had to be that way. Besides, things wouldn't have gone down like that if the roles were reversed. Alek would have said yes. He would have never let Ian touch someone else.

That's not to say Alek couldn't admit that he was wrong. When he first started this monumental failure, he'd only thought of it as an equation. Ian plus jealousy equals marriage. He'd been so confident that it would work because it would have worked if it happened to him.

"Every time you hurt me, I think, this has to be the cruelest thing you've ever done. This has to be the lowest I'll ever have to degrade myself in order to forgive you. But every. Single. Fucking. Time. There's something worse than I can even imagine."

Without looking at Alek, Ian held out the pen. "Start talking."

Alek quickly scrawled, *Forgiveness doesn't make you weak. It's harder to let go than to hold on and I'm not just saying that so you'll forgive me. I didn't want to hurt you. I needed you to promise that you'd stay because since I fell in love with you, my heart has been outside of my body and with you, and I don't like how it feels.*

"You think you're the only one who gave their heart away?"

Alek ignored the question. Ian didn't get it. Hearts were fickle. They could be broken. Marriage was more permanent.

Ian rubbed his forehead with his palm and sighed. "Marriage is about two people, Alek. It's a choice you can't manipulate me into choosing. You cannot treat people this way."

Alek wrote, *I don't have to remember yesterday to know why I said I'd buy you out of the Victorian. Letting you go is the only apology that comes anywhere close to atonement. I was sorry then. I'm sorry now. The offer still stands. If you want to leave me, I'll let you go.* Each word Alek wrote cut him as sharply as if the pen were a knife, and the ink that bled into the paper was his blood.

Ian stood, walked to the window, and dropped the paper ball on the sill, before collecting his cell phone, wallet, and keys, holding them all in one hand.

Alek watched him, probably for the last time. He tried to catalog every detail, starting with Ian's hands, strong and unrelenting when Alek needed him to be and generous enough to surrender when Alek wanted him to. He wished he could ask Ian to touch him one last time so he could get it right.

His eyes followed the curves of the muscles in Ian's neck and the Adams's apple he loved to watch when he swallowed. The shadow of near-black hair along Ian's jaw that felt like sharp Velcro against his neck, lighting up like fizzing static electricity when Ian kissed him there. Those warm brown eyes that only ever brightened for Alek and would probably never brighten for him again.

With his back still to Alek, Ian said, "I'm so mad I can't even look at you."

Alek held his breath. Ian was going to leave him now. At least he wouldn't just disappear. At least he'd say goodbye.

Ian crossed the room and bent down so quickly that Alek flinched—which was stupid because Ian had never laid a finger on him in any way other than he wanted him to. Ian frowned and then pecked a chaste kiss to the side of his mouth.

As far as last kisses went, this one was all wrong. There was no passion. No angst. Up close, Ian didn't smell the way he usually did. He reeked of hospital hand sanitizer that claimed to be unscented but really smelled exactly like cheap vodka poured over an open wound to keep it from festering.

"But, I accept your apology," Ian said.

The noose around Alek's neck loosened.

"I'm going to go home and take a shower and change into something that belongs to me and while I'm gone, I'll deal with everything you've said because I don't have any other choice. Then, I will come back." Ian's eyes raked over Alek like he was committing him to memory too. "Don't you dare slip into a coma or die while I'm gone."

"Wait!" Alek begged. *Can you leave something with me? Something you'll have to come back for.*

Ian's brows darted together. "What? Like collateral?"

Please.

"You already have it."

Alek wrote a giant question mark and held the clipboard up.

"You're the collateral, Alek. I'll always come back for you."

14

IAN
THREE YEARS EARLIER

I an thought the bible was a work of fiction, something to make man less afraid of the fact that when death came, there was nothing after, that there was only that one existence between the first breath and the last, that toiling away their meaningless lives wasn't the best use of their time, that this purgatory was all they got.

But if he was wrong, if there really was a God, He wasn't the benign, indulgent benefactor in the New Testament. He was Old Testament through and through, and if the stories in the Bible were actually true, Alek was the snake and the apple, the devil and temptation. Alek would cast Ian out of Eden and they both would burn for it.

So that was why after nearly kissing Alek Katin in that back alley, Ian decided he would never see him again.

Over the last few months, Ian had thoroughly enjoyed ignoring each and every one of Alek's sexual innuendo-laden tangentially business-related emails. The first had been a seemingly innocent suggestion that the two of them should join forces and start a business. Alek could handle design, fixtures, and furniture, while Ian dealt with all the boring construction stuff and heavy lifting.

In the next email, Alek asked if Ian needed any *hung* windows. Were there any *hand-blown* light fixtures he should keep a lookout for? Wood trusses, tongue and groove, hardwood, load-bearing. And he shoehorned *caulk* into his one-sided conversations any chance he could. The emails kept coming as if Alek was completely undeterred by the lack of response, like he knew Ian was messing with him too, like it was all a game, which it was.

But whether it was fate or serendipity, kismet or destiny, or the fact that their county was as sparsely populated as it was vast, Ian had not seen the last of Alek Katin.

The Wells Building was a red brick and terracotta mixed-use property that took up an entire city block downtown. Built in 1898, the rectangular building's faded burnt-sienna exterior walls were covered by terracotta tile plates the size of sidewalk slabs that featured a spiral of stars orbiting around a crescent moon in the center.

Inside, the building was framed with a skeleton of redwood trees. A wide hallway—made Tolkienesque, thanks to a series of semi-circle mahogany arches—led to a theater converted into a warehouse for a furniture store. A mezzanine towered over pallets of surplus flat-packed furniture, and an enormous dark wood medallion hung in the center of the ceiling. Made in the image of a ship's helm, the medallion's wooden wheel was a less-than-subtle nod to the region's fishing industry.

With the aid of black and white photos, Ian had already pictured what the theater used to look like: the draping floral garlands hand-painted over pale pistachio walls, the autumn leaf-patterned carpet underfoot, the rows of red velvet chairs, the golden brass seashell light sconces that illuminated the stage.

Winning the bid to oversee the restoration of the Wells Building came as no surprise. Ian had made a name for himself in the restoration scene. Refugees from the more expensive parts of California read about him online and the locals knew him by name. The money he'd earn upon completion was motivation enough, but the real reason Ian took the job was because it had never sat well with him that the grand theater was turned into storage for surplus inventory.

A month into the project, there was an electrical issue. It took Ian a half day, but he finally traced the problem back to an apartment on the top floor. When he knocked on the door, it swung wide, revealing none other than Alek Katin.

He was naked, except for tight black boxer briefs. Apparently Alek was a grower *and* a shower. His raven hair was disheveled, tufts sticking up at the top and hanging over his face. His pale viridian eyes glowed against the backdrop of his olive skin and he wore a self-satisfied grin like a cat who hadn't just caught the canary, but tormented it for hours before eating it.

What was *he* doing here? Ian was as suspicious as he was surprised. But that was absurd, wasn't it? Alek wasn't stalking him. He was far more likely to be hiding a secret heroin habit than enough cash to move into a distressed historical building to get his dick wet. It had to be a coincidence that Alek lived in the Wells Building. Alek probably recognized Ian's work truck and sabotaged the electrical on purpose. It was the only thing that made sense.

When Alek's tongue darted out to wet his lower lip, Ian decided he would fuck him once. Right then. Get Alek out of his system and never see him again. Without words, Alek stood aside and Ian followed, closing the door behind them. Ian fisted his hand in Alek's hair, spun him around, and pushed him up against the door.

Alek looked over his shoulder, watching Ian with an almost

clinical detachment, like he wasn't the one who wanted this so bad he made it happen. Ian pulled Alek's head back and bent down to kiss and nip along his neck, not missing the pinprick goosebumps that lit up under his lips.

In the space behind Alek's ear, Ian said, "You messed with the electricity just to get me to talk to you?"

"It worked, didn't it?"

Shameless prick.

"Well, I'm here now. What do you want? I'm sure you didn't bring me here for more construction puns."

"I think what I want goes without saying." Alek pressed his ass back.

Even with jeans and boxers between them, the aching pleasure that radiated out from where they connected felt better than any sex Ian could remember. He hoped that if he scratched the itch, the chemistry between them would dissolve. Maybe the sex would be anticlimactic and disappointing. Nothing could live up to that kind of anticipation, right?

Ian readjusted his dick where it was stuffed against his zipper, then stepped back so they were no longer touching. "Get yourself ready for me while I watch."

Alek kept his cheek pressed to the door, still and silent long enough that Ian thought he was going to back out. Then Alek gave a petulant huff and rose on the tip of his toes, reaching around blindly on the sill of the rectangular transom window above the door.

Following his gaze, Ian spotted a travel-sized bottle of lube and moved closer, crowding Alek against the door. Ian's hips gave an involuntary thrust, like his body was on board with the idea of breaking Alek open on his cock without lube, without condoms, without delay. Ian reached up and grabbed the lube, then rested his chin on Alek's shoulder as he said, "You have sex in your doorway often enough that you stash lube there?"

Alek shrugged. "Help me out of my pants."

Ian hooked his fingers on the back edge of Alek's boxers and tugged, squatting to ease them down and off, enjoying the way Alek's balls tightened when he dragged his hand up the inside of his leg on the way back up.

"Go on then," Ian said, passing Alek the lube.

Alek squirted lube into his hand and tossed the bottle to Ian, then leaned into the door and brought one of his hands back to fuck himself with his fingers while he jerked off with the other.

At the sound of Ian's zipper, Alek snuck an obvious peek over his shoulder, his eyes widening at the sight of Ian's dick for only a fraction of a second before snapping back into apathy.

"Turn around and put this on me," Ian said. He'd reached into his back pocket, pulled a condom out of his wallet, and ripped open the foil.

With graceful, adept fingers, Alek pushed the condom down. The sight of Alek's long fingers encircling Ian's cock would preside in a place of prominence in his spank bank for years to come.

Instead of releasing Ian, Alek jerked him with more violence than was necessary. Each pump lifted Ian onto the balls of his feet, like Alek wanted to lead him to the edge of his restraint and push him over, like he wanted Ian to fuck him recklessly, using him with a single-minded focus to come.

Ian grabbed Alek by the scruff of his hair and swiveled him back against the door. Alek made the sexiest grunt, like Ian had surprised him, maybe even knocked the wind out of him. Good. Ian lubed his dick and dragged it slowly up and down Alek's ass, thrusting in the gap between Alek's legs, teasing them both. It would be irresponsible not to check if Alek had opened himself up enough, so Ian slipped one finger inside. They both gasped.

"Tick tock, Ian," Alek goaded, pushing back to work Ian's finger deeper into his ass. "I'm ready... unless you aren't."

The tenuous thread of Ian's control snapped. He swapped his finger for his dick and thrust forward faster than was polite. Alek met him inch for inch, silently asking, silently taking, until there was nothing else left.

God damn, Alek was tight.

Alek's eyes had closed, his thick black lashes pressed tightly together, his cheek as red as if Ian had slapped him.

"Is this okay? Am I hurting you?" Ian asked.

"Shut up and fuck me."

That answered that. Ian bit his lip as he pushed even deeper, lifting Alek up the door and off his feet, just the one time, to prove a point. Alek could try to tell him what to do, but Ian was stronger. He would only do what he wanted to.

Ian fucked Alek gently at first, but his strokes came faster and rougher as his mind was replaced by something primitive and scary. When Ian checked on Alek again, his eyes were still closed, but his face was lax, all tension eased out of him, his fingers splayed against the door.

Seeing Alek vulnerable like that was Ian's trophy. He had won—not the game, maybe, but definitely that round. With the hand still tangled in Alek's hair, Ian turned Alek's head back toward him and leaned forward, his tongue leading the way to an open-mouthed kiss he didn't even realize was their first until their lips joined and their tongues warred to claim each other. Alek tasted like cinnamon, so spicy it tingled and stung, like he'd chewed a fat wad of Big Red gum.

Ian gripped Alek's cock in his fist, relishing the way precome spilled into his hand with one touch. A few pumps later, Alek came against the door so hard Ian heard it splatter. Ian wedged his way deeper into the tight ecstasy gripping him. He tried to be patient. He tried to savor it. He knew he'd never feel this good again—he'd never let himself see Alek again—but he couldn't stop.

Ian shot his hand out, covering Alek's with his own, holding on tight, leaning all of his weight into him because he was seriously afraid his knees were going to give out. Every nerve in his body lit up as the orgasm exploded and white flashes rained like fireworks in his vision to the point that he distantly worried his retinas were in the process of detaching.

Alek pushed back hard and said, "If you don't mind, I don't have a suffocation kink, and you're as heavy as you look."

Ian's eyes opened slowly. "Sorry," he murmured and passed Alek his boxers before pulling out.

Alek slipped out from under Ian's arm, a single eyebrow raised and a condescending smirk on his face as he cleaned himself up with all the dignity of royalty, like Ian had been the only one who had the best sex of his life and only because Alek had deigned to let him.

Ian removed the condom and held it out to Alek, who rolled his eyes, but turned, walking slowly, gracefully, unfuckingaffectedly, across the room. Ian watched him the entire way. Alek's skin was blemishless, scarless, like he'd never climbed a tree or been fucked against one.

Dragging his eyes away, Ian looked around, taking in all the details of the apartment he'd been too distracted earlier to notice. Alek's apartment was one big studio with high ceilings and tall windows dressed with blue-green velvet curtains. A half-dozen squat glass tumblers sat forgotten under a cognac leather couch. On the couch, a blanket lay bunched on one end, like Alek had kicked it off while he slept.

What looked like a giant slab of polished sequoia tree trunk served as the coffee table and on it, Alek's laptop sat perilously close to a mug of coffee teetering on the edge of a coaster. There was a stack of paperback books—mostly supernatural horror and historical nonfiction, from what he could see, because half of the spines were upside down or facing the other way. An antique, black cast iron ashtray had a half-spent, still smoldering hand-rolled cigarette stashed in the tobacco well.

There wasn't a bed. The only door he spotted was ajar, leading to a bathroom with black and white tile floors and a clawfoot tub with an oval shower rod suspended from the ceiling. The kitchen consisted of a row of cabinets against one wall, a heavy black vintage range, and a milk-white retro fridge with a stainless steel lever that reminded Ian of a drawer pull at a morgue.

"Would you like to hear me play?" Alek asked.

Ian was about to say "Huh?" His brain was still pretty sex-fried, but then his eyes landed on a piano in front of a bay window in the far corner of the room.

"Sure." He was already in for a penny, so why not?

Without dressing, Alek sat down on the piano bench and began to play.

Ian should have left as soon as he zipped up his pants. Once he heard Alek play, it was over. Alek's music was like water or air. It spread out, filling up all of the space until there was no room left. It crept through Ian's bloodstream, sinisterly, like an infection, until it was too late and, with as much intensity as a sudden high fever, Ian's soul burned with the auditory embodiment of him.

Alek's music took Ian's thoughts and feelings and replaced them with his own. Simultaneously nostalgic and hopeless. It was lonely and selfish. Angry and sad. Tormented and haunting. Alek wasn't playing for Ian. He was playing for himself.

15

IAN

PRESENT DAY

On the long drive home from the hospital, Ian replayed every word, every betrayal. If he distanced himself from the situation, if he looked at things objectively, the way he usually did, all signs pointed to ending things with Alek, but loving Alek was confusing, addicting, mind-fucking.

The highs and the lows were extreme and often wound together so tightly that Ian couldn't have one without the other. When things were good, they weren't just good. It was so transcendent that Ian had a difficult time giving up, even when they were in the deepest of trenches.

The potential was there inside Alek. Ian really believed that. Alek loved Ian with unrestrained fervor, as if by withholding his love from everyone else, it overflowed when he finally had someone to give it to. It was just that the guy needed therapy—intensive therapy—but Alek didn't accept help, and he didn't ask for it either, and opening up to an outsider?

Impossible.

Pulling off the road and onto the Victorian's driveway

brought everything back in reverse. After Alek had been strapped to a narrow stretcher and loaded into a helicopter that then lifted skyward, Ian was left behind, empty, bereft, like a part of him was up on that helicopter with Alek.

Now fog wrapped around the Victorian, obscuring most of it from view, so that it appeared slowly and then all at once like a mirage. The Victorian looked different. Something was missing. It seemed colder, somehow. Maybe because of what happened? Or because Alek wasn't there?

When Ian parked his truck and got out, his eyes caught on a heap of branches with fronds of dagger-shaped leaves crumpled at the bottom of the house. In front of the ruined wisteria, a pool of dark red blood stained the forest floor, like the wisteria had bled out instead of Alek. The fallen pine needles were matted with coagulated blood, much like Alek's hair had been.

Ian's heart dropped just like it did on the more than infrequent occasion that his foot sank through rotting wood in a house he was restoring. He'd forgotten about the blood, that someone would have to clean it.

He went into the house and plugged his phone in. Then he cleaned the blood he'd smeared on the kitchen counter when he'd searched for a towel for Alek's head, packed a bag with clothes and toiletries for both of them, Alek's favorite snacks, and a book Alek hadn't yet finished.

As Ian went from room to room, his footsteps echoed jarringly against the tomblike silence. Now that he thought about it, this was the only time he'd ever been at the Victorian without Alek lurking around somewhere nearby. Alek was a total hermit. Even when they broke up, Alek didn't go anywhere. Ian's anger cooled rapidly inside the cold, lonely house. He shouldn't have left Alek alone after he'd lost so much. He picked up the landline and dialed his mom.

"How's Alek doing?" she said after the first ring.

"There's no privacy in EMS, huh?" Ian's mother was a paramedic and the first responders were as tight-knit as family.

"I figured your phone was off and I heard you were okay, but I've been climbing the walls worrying about Alek."

Sometimes Ian wondered if his mom liked Alek more than him. She always baked to his tastes. Alek favored desserts made with chocolate so dark, it was as bitter as espresso, cut with fillings made from tart, blood-red fruits like cherry, strawberry, and blackberry. She fussed over him constantly, hand-sewing and knitting heavy wool sweaters and coats in dark fabrics; blackest black, herringbone charcoal, and a mossy evergreen that cast his eyes the most beautiful seafoam.

Ian may have liked to tease them both—Alek for stealing his mom, and her for spoiling him—but he was grateful that his mother was so good to Alek, especially because of the way Alek practically preened like a well-tended house plant after he saw her.

"He's going to be okay." Ian ran his fingers over his eyebrows and tried to hide the threatened tears from his voice. "That's actually why I called. Could you head over there and stay with him? I ran home to shower and take care of some stuff and I don't want him to be alone."

"Of course."

He thanked her. "Before you go... He can't speak English, but he can—"

"He can't talk?"

"No. Um... the fall and whatever damage it caused... he can only speak in Bulgarian right now. That's where he's from." He paused, expecting her to interrogate him about the Bulgarian thing, but she didn't. "He can understand English and he can write it. So if you have to talk, there's that. Also, he can't play the piano, so don't bring that up."

"And you left him? Ian."

He could already imagine the look of disappointment, her eyes raised heavenward as if only divine intervention could knock some sense into him.

Solitude had always been Ian's coping method of choice. Even as a child, he never threw a tantrum. Instead, he'd disappear into a closet or his treehouse and return later in a much better mood.

"I want you to keep him company until I come back," he said. "There's some stuff I have to do here first."

"I haven't seen my favorite son in too long, anyway." She exhaled loudly on the other side of the line. "I'm so sorry, *E*. Are you okay?"

"No." His voice broke. He wouldn't be okay. Not until Alek was whole.

She clucked her tongue. "You guys will be okay. You'll get through this together."

She might not have said that had she known exactly what sort of 'this' they had to get through.

After ending the call, he went to the garage and returned to the front yard with a wheelbarrow filled with the items he needed to get the job done.

He scraped up all the bloody pine needles, using a shovel to dig up the top layer of soil that was stained red from Alek's blood, then carted the wheelbarrow around the garage, dumping its contents in the burn pit they kept in a small clearing.

After that, he set to work cutting the fallen wisteria into manageable pieces. He already knew about the care of a wisteria plant. First, because he'd researched how to get rid of it. Then, because Alek had voiced his affection for the monster plant, and Ian had wanted to make sure he didn't kill it inadvertently.

It would be perfectly fine to remove the bulk of the fallen

wisteria as long as he left a small stump for it to grow back from. Wisteria was meant to be pruned back twice a year anyway—maybe not pruned this heavily, but Ian had no doubt that by the end of summer, it would be taller than him.

A half-hour later, Ian was done. It took another hour and nearly a dozen trips back and forth to the clearing to add the wisteria to the burn pile, which was now so tall, it was only a hair shorter than him. On the last trip, he raked up each and every flower and when he added it all to the pile like kindling, not even a single stray leaf was left behind.

Ian doused the pyre of wisteria with lighter fluid, lit a match, and stepped back, watching it go up in flames. A cloud of nearly opaque smoke billowed, stinging his eyes and nose as it ascended. He stood there a while, the heat of the blaze warming him pleasantly under the misty forest canopy and the rapidly cooling sweat that saturated his clothes.

Destroying the physical manifestation of what happened to Alek was cleansing, like by burning the evidence of Alek's fall, Ian had erased some of the pain and panic from the day before. It wasn't the first time Alek drove Ian to aggressive demoing or home improvement. The fact that the Victorian was in such good shape after only one year was a testament to exactly how aggravating Alek could be.

Ian examined the revelations of the past few days as he watched the fire. Alek's confession that the one-night stands were all an act to weaponize jealousy really wasn't all that surprising. When Alek was threatened, he reacted very much like a cornered predator, lashing out without considering the damage he'd cause.

Alek's confession about how scared he was to be in love, and to have no guarantee that Ian would stay, also made sense for someone like him. Ian could only hope that one day Alek would feel safe enough to tell him the whole story. Who left him with such debilitating abandonment issues?

By the time the wisteria and blood-soaked pine needles were reduced to smoldering ash, Ian had a plan.

16

ALEKSANDAR

BULGARIA. ELEVEN YEARS OLD.

Aleksandar did not stay long at his uncle's workshop. The walk home through the forest was different now that it existed in a world in which Uncle Krasimir did not. The shadows were darker, the same gnarled knots and whorls on tree trunks that had always been there, now transformed into sinister faces.

When Aleksandar arrived home, he asked Ivet if his father was home. She looked down her nose at him like he was stupid, or maybe a bug crushed under her shoe.

"He's still out of the country on business."

Aleksandar did not argue. He lifted his chin. "And my mother?"

"With him."

Ivet removed her apron, opened the closet door and hung it on the hook inside, then turned and left, presumably to the room she stayed in when Aleksandar's parents were both out. Which was fine. Aleksandar preferred to be alone.

That night Aleksandar couldn't sleep for a very long time and, when he finally did, he dreamed of his uncle. The ocean roared and stones clattered and waves crashed over his head while his uncle called his name from far away. When Aleksandar tried to swim towards the surface, his feet were trapped inside a quicksand of river rocks that knocked painfully against his ankles and threatened to swallow him whole. The waves finally pulled back, the rocks released him and he stood in the river over his uncle's lifeless body, except it wasn't lifeless anymore and Aleksandar was the one forcing his uncle under the water, his own arms the ones his uncle scratched at. Aleksandar screamed but only water came out, and then he woke up.

Aleksandar smelled smoke. He got out of bed and looked through the open window. In the distance, a fire burned, glowing like a rising sun trapped on the horizon. Aleksandar knew what was burning.

Everyone around his father, the presiding Finance Minister of Bulgaria, seemed to have very bad luck. There were falls from great heights and so many suicides that a national mental health emergency should have been declared, but fire was his father's favorite, because it left nothing behind.

Uncle Krasimir's estate, the piano, his clothes, the artwork, the furniture, and clocks. All of it was burning and Aleksandar's heart burned like it was on fire too.

Aleksandar tiptoed out the front door, latching it quietly behind him, and ran for his uncle's, but it was too far. He was too late. By the time he reached the house, flames erupted from where the wood thatched roof used to be.

Up close, the fire was much louder than he expected. Glass shattered, flames spat and roared, and the wood beams glowed molten red, groaning like they were dying. Smoke stung his eyes and scratched the inside of his throat as he watched the fire consume his uncle and his things.

Aleksandar should have been sad—distraught even, but he felt nothing. Like he wasn't in his body. Like everything that had happened to him had really happened to someone else. A distant siren called. He backed away, then turned, and let the woods swallow him up. He would come back tomorrow night and see what was left behind.

Once home, Aleksandar stripped and stuffed his dirty clothes in a trash bag so he could get rid of them at school the next day. Then he stood under the shower, washing his skin and his hair over and over again until he didn't smell like smoke anymore, which was impossible, because everything smelled like smoke and he would never be clean again.

———

WHEN ALEKSANDAR WOKE the next morning, the fire was still burning. Smoke suffocated the town, shadowing the sun with a dirty haze that cast the world into a hue of melancholy. Ash fell from the sky and didn't stop, so that every breath Aleksandar took served as a grim reminder of his cowardice and everything he had lost.

The fire devoured the forest around his uncle's house and burned all the way to the edge of the river before the fire crews were able to stop it.

That night, Aleksandar sat in front of the piano at his own house. He hardly ever played his father's piano. It was more a status symbol than an instrument, and his father didn't like him to play it, but Aleksandar had already skipped one day of practice. He wouldn't skip another. He wouldn't let his uncle down again, and besides, he needed it.

His emotions were too big and uncomfortable. He had to put them somewhere.

Aleksandar sat straight, lifted his hands over the keys, and began to play, but stopped immediately, curling his fingers against his palms. The keys were covered with silky ash that cut like broken glass beneath his fingertips. He brushed the ash away with his sleeve, the piano protesting with loud jarring notes, but the keys still weren't clean enough, so then Aleksandar bent down and blew the soot away, over and over until he was lightheaded, not stopping until he could no longer feel grit under his fingers.

In the fraction of a second between his finger depressing the first piano key and the hammer striking the string, he worried that he wouldn't be able to play, that as penance for letting his uncle die, his music might have died with him. He didn't know whether he was disappointed or relieved when the first note reached his ears, stringing together with the next one and the next one into a melody that fluttered out the window and through the dark forest, some of them lost to the river and its current, the rest continuing onward over the burnt out woods on the other side, all the way to the ruins of his uncle's house.

He turned his mind off, losing himself to the music, disappearing inside of it, disintegrating into sound waves, so he wouldn't feel pain or love or loneliness ever again. He was music turned sentient. Senses without emotion. Sound, sight, scent, touch. He closed his eyes and let his music paint over all of his thoughts and feelings until the only thing left was a starless night sky.

———

AFTER IVET WENT TO BED, Aleksandar snuck out again. The cloud of stale smoke dimmed the light of the nearly full moon, making the journey more difficult. It didn't help that his uncle's side of the forest was burnt down to charred stumps and spindled trunks that ended in jagged burnt-off ends so that the once recognizable landmarks, and the path itself, were lost.

When Aleksandar finally found his uncle's house, he didn't

have to search for the key. The door had burned down and he could walk right in, the sounds of his footfalls muffled by the thick layer of ash covering the floor.

It was difficult to remember which rooms were which when almost everything inside was destroyed, but Aleksandar found the room he was looking for on his first try. In the corner, a large pile of embers still smoldered, a thin cloud of smoke drifting out a nearby window.

The piano was still standing. Barely. The piano lid had burned through completely to reveal metal strings curling away like they'd tried to escape. Aleksandar and his uncle's initials were no longer carved into the side of the piano. He touched the spot to be sure that not even a shallow etching remained, but the wood crumbled to ash beneath his fingertips.

The fallboard was blackened and cracked like bark on a tree. Piano keys warped by heat no longer lay flat, but like crooked teeth.

Middle C had survived. As the name implied, Middle C was the centermost 'C' key on the piano. It was the landmark from which all pianists oriented themselves to the piano, and sheet music. "This is the only note you need to learn," his uncle had said. "If you know where it is, you know where everything is."

Aleksandar pressed down on the key and the sound that didn't come hurt his ears. He lifted the key upward and pulled hard. The piano put up a fight, like it didn't want to let go, but in the end he was stronger. Wood cracked like branches snapping and then the front half of the key broke free, sending him falling backward with the jagged key held victorious in his fist.

He didn't care that the key broke in the process. What he had in his hand was enough; it was the part of the key that his uncle had touched, proof that his uncle had existed, no matter how his father had tried to erase him.

The piano would never make music again, but Aleksandar would take the key with him, and he would never forget.

He pocketed the key and turned to go. He still had to clean up and hide the key before Ivet woke. In his haste to leave, Aleksandar tripped on something hard, something so heavy that it didn't budge when his foot hit it. He bent down and brushed the ash away, revealing a rectangular metal box with a mechanical lock. A fire-proof safe! The spot for the safe was interesting. Had his uncle hidden the safe beneath the piano, revealing it only after it burned? He lifted the safe. Heavy, but he could manage.

On his way home, he stopped at the carcass of an ancient tree downed during a storm two years before. The tree lay on its side on the forest floor, its twisted roots, thick as branches, left exposed when the fall ripped them from the earth.

His uncle had told him that decades later, a row of trees would grow from the trunk, nourished and tended as the elder tree decayed. A nurse tree was what it was called. "The tree's sacrifice will lead to new life," his uncle had said.

There was a shallow hole hidden behind the dangling roots and Aleksandar stashed the safe there. He would come back later and try to crack it.

After locking his bedroom door, Aleksandar crawled under his bed, and lifted the loose floorboard his uncle showed him years before. Aleksandar's home had been his uncle's home first.

Inside, Aleksandar kept a velvet pouch filled with colorful shards of stained glass that glittered like gemstones and a tiger carved from amber wood. He put the piano key inside and replaced the floorboard with a small thunk as it slid into place.

He felt more settled now that he had the key in his possession. Less empty. Less alone. A mean, ugly voice in his head reminded him that if he'd been brave, his uncle wouldn't be dead, and his things wouldn't be ash, and the key would have been in the piano where it belonged.

Overnight, a strong wind blew through the town, sweeping away what remained of the smoke, so that when Aleksandar woke the air was clear, the sky a cloudless bright blue, and that was worse, because it meant all he had left of his uncle was the piano key under his bed and the lockbox in the woods.

Oh, and music. He had that too.

17

ALEK

A lek pushed up with his good hand and swung his legs over the side of the bed. He nearly fell forward onto the floor, but caught himself just in time by wedging his casted arm into the gap of the bed rail. A lightning bolt of pain shot up his arm, but he didn't care.

He had to follow Ian.

Before he could muster the strength to stand, the telltale dinging alarms and murmuring voices grew loud as the door slid open behind him. Had Ian returned?

"What on earth do you think you're doing?" The brain surgeon—whose name escaped him—rushed over and lifted his legs up, shoving them back onto the hospital bed, a disapproving scowl on her face as she continued to berate him in Bulgarian. "The last thing you need is to fall on your face. You can't get out of bed without help."

"Then help me."

She put both hands on her hips. "If you think I'll be able to hold you up when you fall, you have more brain damage than I originally suspected. You look terrible. Why aren't you taking the pain medicine?"

"I don't need it." Alek rested his head back on the pillow and shielded his eyes with his hand. The sun was too bright outside the window. It made his head throb.

Her eyebrows rose. "Really? You look like the type to enjoy a bit of legalized heroin."

"I'm more of a cocaine kind of guy."

"Too bad. We're fresh out of that."

Alek pressed his lips together to hide his smile.

In all seriousness, the idea of accepting hospital-grade narcotics wasn't as appealing as it normally would have been. Aside from the even-more-vivid-than-usual nightmare his last dose had conjured, concussion-induced vertigo made him seasick at baseline, and the narcotics only made the nausea worse. He'd thrown up once already, and the force with which he vomited made him feel like his head was going to explode.

Besides, the pain was a rather fitting penance.

The doctor sat down in the chair Ian had vacated and looked over at the piano keyboard. "A little bird told me there was no music overnight. Why didn't you play?"

"I can't."

"Why not?"

"The keys don't make sense when I look at them and I can't read music anymore. I've forgotten all the songs I know. I've lost the music I composed. When I hear sounds, I usually see colors and images, but now it's all dark."

She crossed one of her legs over the other and brought her hand to her chin. "Has anyone ever told you that you have synesthesia?"

"No," Alek lied.

Early on, Alek's uncle had explained that the way his senses tangled together until he couldn't isolate one without tugging on the other was different from how most others experienced the world. It was an uncommon gift shared by some of history's greatest artists—musical and otherwise—and often credited for some of the magic in their craft.

"Synesthesia is when you experience one of your five senses simultaneously with one or more of the others. For example, if you think of your partner, you might smell his cologne, or if you hear a sound, you might see a color in your mind. Does that sound familiar?"

Alek nodded and sneaked a glance at her badge. *Dr. Modorovic*. The picture on her badge was faded and she looked about ten years younger, her black hair smooth and with far less gray, the crow's feet and smile lines shallower than they were now.

"I want you to try to remember your earliest memory of the piano," she said.

Alek could already smell the wisteria, feel the wind blowing gently against his face, fireflies blinking in the dark. He stopped himself before he got to the part where his uncle turned to him and smiled, almost in slow motion when it played back as a memory.

"I was five and I was watching my uncle's hands move over the piano keys. I don't see how this is going to help. Where can I smoke?"

"I'll have my resident write an order for a nicotine patch."

"I take it alcohol is off the menu too?"

"Afraid so. How much did you drink before?"

"A glass or two of vodka."

"How big are these glasses?"

Alek picked at a piece of fuzz on his cast. "I don't use a measuring cup. Bigger than a shot glass but smaller than a carton of milk."

"You'll have to quit the alcohol. At least for a few months. Probably longer. You're going to have a hard enough time getting around; the last thing you need is to fall while drunk."

"I don't get drunk."

"Have you quit drinking cold turkey before?"

Last January Ian challenged both of them to go an entire month without drinking. It was a scout's honor sort of thing and Alek had considered cheating—how would Ian ever know?—but Alek was inherently competitive and it really wasn't all that hard to abstain.

He wasn't one of those textbook alcoholics-in-denial who insisted they didn't have a problem and could quit any time when, in reality, they could only quit after walking up and down twelve steps for the next decade. Addiction was something too sloppy for him to allow.

"I'm not going to go into withdrawal, if that's what you're getting at," Alek said.

"I'm sure you understand why I have to ask."

Alek waved a flippant hand. "It's fine. The only opinion of myself I care about is my own."

The doctor erupted in unrestrained laughter that certainly didn't belong in a place of death and dying and losing one's ability to play the piano. He watched her curiously. Was she unbalanced?

A knock sounded and Alek's eyes snapped to the doorway, but it was just another staff member—presumably a doctor, if the white coat that hung down to his knees was any indication. He held a pair of to-go coffee cups and a large brown paper bag.

"Thank you," Dr. Modorovic said, taking the items.

After the man left, she crossed to the abandoned piano keyboard. Alek tensed. He was in no mood to play.

Dr. Modorovic moved the keyboard from the table to the lid of a nearby laundry bin and pulled the privacy curtain to hide it from view. She rolled the table back to Alek's bedside until it was over his lap, then placed one of the coffee cups in front of him, and began removing food from the bag.

Inside were croissants—"Chocolate hazelnut filling," she

said—a small carton of smoked salmon, hard-boiled eggs, pre-sliced wedges of brie cheese, and fresh blackberries. There were two servings of everything.

"What is this? Some sort of adult Lunchable?" Alek scowled. "Why are you being so nice to me?"

The doctor smiled around a mouth filled with brie. She'd sat back down in Ian's chair and dug into the food with gusto.

"Who says I'm being nice? Maybe I'm just very hungry."

Suspicious, Alek said nothing.

"Go ahead. I'll put it on your tab."

"Tell me why you're being so nice and maybe I'll eat."

She wiped her mouth with a napkin. "You remind me of my cat."

"Your cat?" Alek was nonplussed.

"Wolfie. I adopted him from the pound, but he hated me for it, like he was insulted that anyone would dare help him. Whenever I tried to pick him up, he'd tense and hiss and scratch. He'd leave for days at a time, but he'd always come back."

Alek raised a single eyebrow, or at least he tried to. The muscles in his face felt like they were controlled by knotted marionette strings.

"You've inferred enough about me in the short time we've been together to determine I have the same temperament as your cat?"

"Your personality is," she looked at the ceiling like maybe she'd find a suitable word up there, "strong."

Alek tutted and plucked a blackberry from the table. It was bitingly tart. Exactly how he liked them. "Let me guess the ending... Wolfie is a fat, lazy, lap cat now?"

The doctor pushed up the sleeve on her right arm, revealing a series of angry, bright red, scabbed scratches. "These were a reward for trying to remove a burr from his paw."

He took a sip of the coffee. It wasn't as good as home-brewed espresso, but it wasn't bad either.

"I guessed you took your coffee dark like your disposition," Dr. Modorovic said. "Was I right?"

"You were."

"Cheers." She tapped her cup against his. "Now eat."

Ordinarily, Alek would resent being told what to do, but he really was hungry and the salmon looked delicious. It was sprinkled with fresh lemon zest and there were little crackers to sandwich it between.

"What's your name?" Alek asked between bites.

"You can call me Jane," she said with no hesitation.

"Is that really your name?"

"Is Alek Katin yours?"

He wasn't surprised she noticed. Katin was not a Bulgarian surname. That had been the point.

The doctor set down her croissant on a napkin and said, "I propose a trade. I'll tell you my Croatian first name if you'll tell me your Bulgarian one."

That was easy. "Aleksandar." His name was so common it was hardly identifying.

"Jana." She reached over and took the other half of his croissant. Alek's mouth opened in a scandalized 'O' but she ignored him. "Most of the staff and patients just call me Dr. M. Easier to pronounce."

"Are you married, Jana?"

The only impression Alek had of Jana thus far was that she was, essentially, a lonely woman who forced love onto a terminally feral cat. It was depressing. She wasn't wearing a ring, but were surgeons even allowed to wear rings?

She nodded. "I was. He died a few years ago."

Alek refused to entertain the thought of outliving Ian. Preferably, Ian would never die, but if he did, Alek had better already be dead and dust. He was not above pulling a Romeo and Juliet if Ian went first. Ian would be furious, but they'd both be dead so what could he do about it?

"I'm sorry about your husband," Alek said.

She shrugged. "There are things worse than death."

———

IT WAS a real dick move for Ian to leave Alek with no way to pass the time. Alek had nothing to read, no one to talk to, and the mere idea of watching TV gave him a headache. He'd already cataloged the items in his room, nearly all of them out of his reach except for a plastic jug urinal that hung on the side of his bed, displaying the contents to any passersby. He wished he had magic and could summon the phone to him so he could call Ian and beg him to come back in the only language he had.

Thinking was all Alek had left to entertain himself with, but his thoughts were stormy and sad and told him things like *Ian is never coming back* and *He would have been better off if you died.* Alek would have been better off too.

Without music, without Ian, he had nothing.

According to the clock on the wall across the room, Ian had been gone an hour and a half. Alek rolled onto his side, facing away from the door, because the last thing he would do was stare pathetically out the sliding glass door, pining away after his scorned lover. It was bad enough that the nurse forgot to close the curtain so that anyone walking by could inspect him like an exhibit at the Museum of Natural History.

When the door slid open, Alek didn't bother to see who it was. It was probably the nurse stopping by to ask him the same asinine questions she asked him every hour. *What's your name? What year is it? Where are you?* It was annoying. He didn't like to talk to people, especially strangers, and the nurse had a knack for arriving whenever he'd just fallen asleep. He was sure that she was fucking with him.

The mystery intruder stepped closer and Alek smelled spun sugar and orange blossoms. He snapped his eyes shut and slowed his breathing. Why was Ian's mother here?

Sarah's footsteps tiptoed closer and then, "I know you're faking it. Your eyes are too tense."

When Alek opened his eyes, her face was a few inches away from his. He'd never understood how a woman could be called handsome until he met Sarah. She had bold eyebrows, a patrician nose, and a jawline almost as strong as Ian's.

He wrote, *Ian sent you?*

"Yes. I would have come anyway, though. I was waiting to be invited."

Like a vampire.

She laughed. "Yeah, like that. Do you want to get out of bed?"

Alek nodded. Maybe he could convince her to spring him from the hospital.

Sarah hooked her arm around his elbow and helped him sit at the edge of the bed. All the blood rushed from his head. Shadows crowded the edges of his vision.

"Don't worry. I won't let you fall."

Alek didn't doubt it. Sarah was quite tall, but she was always so dwarfed by Ian, that whenever she was without him, Alek couldn't help but be taken aback.

"Just sit a while. There's no rush." She squatted down to his eye level. Ian had her golden brown eyes. "You know I love you, right? No matter what happens between you and my son."

He didn't know that, actually. There was only so much disbelief he could suspend. Sarah didn't know the whole story. How would she feel if she learned exactly what he'd done to her son?

In an unexpected show of emotion, Sarah pulled him into a hug that made his bruised ribs hurt and his eyes blur with tears he most certainly would not be shedding. He didn't hug her back. Instead, his arms dangled lamely at his sides.

"Do you have any idea how much you scared me? I didn't know if you'd ever wake up again. I wasn't just worried about what that would do to my son. I was so worried about *you*." She patted him on the back. "You ready?"

Alek blinked, then nodded, "*Yes.*"

Linking her arm again in his, she heaved him to his feet. He swayed and were it not for the scratchy non-skid socks, his feet would have slid out from under him.

"Nice and easy," Sarah coached.

She held his hands and took a single step backward, waiting for his unstable footsteps to follow. An eternity later, they reached a narrow recliner set in front of a small square table. Sarah held Alek's gown closed as he lowered on shaking legs into the chair. Breathing fast and only as deep as his battered ribs would allow, Alek looked back at the bed. It may have been four feet away, but it might as well have been four miles.

He pointed to the crumpled paper Ian had left on the window sill. "Could you hand me that?"

Her forehead wrinkled. "Sorry. I don't understand." She grabbed the clipboard from the bed and put it in front of him.

Thank you. Could you please pass me that? He pointed at the paper ball.

Following his gaze, she said, "Of course."

Trying to uncrumple it one-handed was an exercise in futility.

"Do you want me to help?"

"*Yes.*"

Looking away, as if to grant him privacy, Sarah opened the paper ball and set it down in front of him. Alek's own handwriting said, *I could forget everything and still know that I love you.* His stomach dropped. That wasn't exactly a good sign. He balled up the paper again and then wrote on the clipboard, *Did Ian say when he would be back?*

Sarah dipped her chin with an apologetic smile. "He didn't say, but he will be back—on his own, or because I dragged him here."

His pulse ticked faster. *Ian told you?*

She shook her head. "I don't know what's happened between you two, but I know my son." She pulled out her phone and held up a picture of a long-sleeved henley pattern she'd earmarked. "What about this one for Ian?"

Appreciating the abrupt, and obviously intentional, change of subject, Alek nodded and wrote, *What fabric are you thinking of?* He loved Ian in full sleeve shirts and pants. It emphasized how tall and long-limbed he was.

"I have some forest green jersey or gray waffle-knit wool."

One of each, please.

"You got it."

Ordinarily, Alek would have rather been alone, but having Sarah there was tangible proof that Ian planned to return. Surely Ian wouldn't dump Alek and leave his mother to pick up the pieces.

After lunch, and a harrowing walk back to bed, Alek was more exhausted than he'd ever been in his life, and though he hated sleeping in public places, his eyelids were too heavy to keep open. When he dreamed, he dreamed of his mother, something he never did.

18

IAN

The elevator stopped at the fifth floor, where the ICU and Alek were. Ian took a deep breath to steel his nerves, then slipped through the closing elevator doors. The nursing station was deserted. No alarms rang. His footsteps echoed against the waxed linoleum floors. At the turn in the hallway, he glanced up at the bubble mirror in the top corner. The hall leading to Alek's room was empty too.

It was eerie and unnatural.

The curtain behind Alek's sliding glass door was drawn. What if Alek had died and somehow Ian missed all of the calls? What if behind the curtain Alek's bed was empty and only his mother was waiting to deliver the news?

He pushed the intrusive thoughts away, opened the sliding door, and pulled the curtain back, exhaling when he saw Alek, turned on his side, facing away from him. His mom brought her finger to her lips, shushing him soundlessly, and gestured towards the door. Ian followed her into the hall.

She put both hands on his shoulders and looked him over, as if he was the one who fell out a window. "Are you good now?"

He wasn't. He wouldn't be whole until Alek was. "How is he?"

"He walked, ate lunch, and fell asleep. That's about all I know. You know how he is." She paused, probably to decide how much she ought to scold him. "I don't know what's going on between you two, but whatever it is, put it aside and be there for him. He needs you."

Ian nodded once.

She pulled him into a hug that hit him over the head with a wave of nostalgia like a flip-book flashback of all the times he'd cried in his mother's arms as a boy. Hard falls, skinned knees, the occasional broken bone. When his dad said he would take him to Disneyland and canceled at the last minute. Ian sniffed and pulled back.

"Keep me updated, okay?" she said.

"Of course." After she'd walked a few steps, his manners came back to him. "Mom?"

She turned.

"Thank you."

"You're welcome, *E.*"

Ian returned to Alek's room, shut the door, and pulled the curtain closed. He tiptoed around the bed and flinched. The bruises around Alek's eyes had darkened to an ugly purple and the swelling had smoothed away all of the hard angles of his face. The fingers peeking out from his cast were still pink and purple, but now the skin was shiny and taut.

A deep visceral pain burned inside Ian's gut. Alek may have hurt him—intentionally even, but the weeks of betrayal, every stab of devastation, the sum total of everything Alek had ever done was nothing in comparison to the pain Ian now felt. He would have given anything and everything to trade places with Alek, to travel back in time to the moment he pulled his arm away and made Alek fall.

Ian pulled a Sharpie from his pocket, removed the cap with his teeth, and bent over Alek's cast. Once finished, he recapped the pen and sat in the chair beside the bed. While he watched the shallow rise and fall of Alek's chest, the precious sound of Alek's breathing blended with the air filtration system into a white noise that had Ian's head bobbing.

"Mmm. You smell like you again," Alek murmured.

Ian's eyes jerked open to find Alek watching him with a drowsy, dreamy look to his heavy-lidded eyes.

"What?" Ian had been nearly asleep. It took a second for Alek's words to register. "Oh... Yeah. I told you I was going to take a shower—Wait!" Ian had understood him! Alek's accent was thick but it must have been English, right? Ian didn't know a lick of Bulgarian aside from Dr. Modorovic's crash course. "Alek, you're speaking English!"

"Really?"

It was definitely English, though Alek's accent shadowed every word with extra inflection.

"Yes, love, really."

Ian brought both hands to Alek's face, and kissed him. He meant for the kiss to be a celebratory *you got your English back* kiss, but the two of them could never just kiss, and soon Ian's dick was telling him to climb on top of Alek. A louder, more responsible voice reminded him that it was probably dangerous to have sex with someone so soon after a head injury.

Ian pulled away and Alek tried to keep him there by the bottom hem of his shirt, but Ian shook his head. "Say something else."

"I love you. Was that English?"

"I love you, too. Does that answer your question? Your accent is so hot. You can read me an instruction manual and I'll get hard."

Alek's face fell. "I didn't realize..."

"You don't like it?"

"Imagine how much work it required to switch my accent to an American one. Every word I've ever said took effort. I prefer not to even think in Bulgarian. Of course, I don't like it. I hate it. It reminds me of who I was when I moved here."

Ian's jaw fell open. Alek had revealed more in that one answer than he'd ever told him in their entire relationship.

"Why don't you try the American accent then, and see if it still works?"

In an accent that was accentless to Ian because it sounded like his own, Alek said, "I would rather have become a vegetable than contend with all of these tiresome post-concussion symptoms."

Ian grimaced. The thought of Alek suspended in a state between dead and alive, propped up by tubes and machines, stripped away of everything that made Alek Alek. Never hearing his voice again. Never seeing his eyes open. Kissing him without ever being kissed back. Wondering if Alek would be better off if they pulled the plug, but terrified to give up on him because what if he woke up tomorrow? Or maybe the next day. Or the day after that. But also, what if Alek never woke up and the less than half-life he was living was worse than death?

"Too soon?" Alek interrupted Ian's spiraling thoughts.

"Too soon," Ian agreed. "I think you should stick with the Bulgarian accent. Give your brain a rest. The cat's out of the bag anyway, isn't it?"

"You're only saying that because you think I sound sexy," Alek said, but he'd reverted to his Bulgarian accent.

Ian brought Alek's good hand to his lips and kissed. "Would you be jealous if I said it feels like I'm cheating on you a little bit?"

"Mmm. I like the idea of you cheating on me with me," Alek said. "Could you bring me the keyboard?"

"The piano! That's... Do you think it came back, too?"

"I don't think so, but I didn't know the English came back until you told me."

Ian retrieved the keyboard from behind the curtain while Alek pressed the button to elevate the head of his bed.

Alek lifted his hands over the keys.

Ian held his breath.

"What's this?" Alek's dark lashes shaded his eyes as he looked down at his cast.

Nerves made Ian hot all over. He'd forgotten all about his earlier plan when Alek started talking in a language he could understand.

Alek's face was expressionless as his perusal snagged on the crude heart Ian drew and what was written inside.

"I don't understand... *Is plus as*?"

An unconcussed Alek would have figured it out immediately.

Ian pushed the piano aside and sat on the edge of the bed. His heart beat fast as he pulled the small wooden box from his back pocket and flipped it open with one hand to reveal the two rings inside.

"Ian Stewart and Alek Stewart," Ian said. "I figured you could take my name since yours is probably fake anyway."

Alek frowned. "I already told you I don't want a deathbed pity marriage."

"It's not. This is different. I'm asking you."

"Shouldn't you be on one knee, then?"

"Do you have any idea how dirty hospital floors are?"

Alek rolled his eyes, then craned his head to look inside the box. "I see two rings there."

"One for me and one for you," Ian said in a voice that sounded far calmer than he felt. "Can I finish now?"

"You may."

"I'm asking *you* to marry *me*, but I've got conditions." Ian snapped the box shut and set it down out of Alek's reach. "And there's something I have to tell you first because I haven't been completely honest with you and you deserve to know everything before you answer."

Alek traced his fingers over the heart on his cast. "Maybe I love you enough to answer without knowing everything because what I know is enough. If you're trying to teach me a lesson, I don't want to be condescended to."

"No. That's not what I mean." Ian cleared his throat. "If we want this to work, we have to be honest. We have to choose to trust each other until we build up enough trust that we actually do."

Alek focused his sage green eyes on him. "Tell me."

In slow, even words, Ian said, "Right before you fell, I said you were a burden, and that I wished I never met you." Ian cringed. "I sort of equated you to a malignant tumor."

"Malignant tumor?" Alek raised his brows like Ian was a child trying to pass an impossible story off as fact.

The words had come out easily in the heat of the moment, but taking them back, repeating them, watching the subtle changes in Alek's body language as he closed himself off; the way his spine straightened to make the most of his height, how the muscles in his forearm flexed as his good hand clenched into a fist—it wasn't easy.

"I just meant that even if I tried to leave you, I couldn't, because you'll always be inside of me. I can't cut you out without destroying myself. See? It doesn't even make sense."

Alek said nothing. The silence was suffocating.

"I regretted it as soon as I said it. I was angry. I didn't mean it. I—"

"You meant it. You just wish you didn't."

"Alek—"

"What are the terms of our engagement? You said there were conditions."

Ian blinked. He should have known Alek would respond with apathy.

"That's it? You're okay with what I said?"

Alek shrugged. "You said I was inside you, which is something I will never take issue with, and I quite like the idea that you can't leave me completely, even if you wanted to."

"Alek," Ian leaned closer and cupped his cheek. "You can be mad at me. You can show me that I hurt you. You can be honest with me."

Alek waved his hand cavalierly. "You take yourself so seriously. It's fine."

It wasn't, but if Ian pushed any further he'd only push Alek away. "Okay, so my conditions..." He held up a finger. "You have to tell me everything. Not all at once, but as extra motivation not to drag your feet, I'll only marry you when I've heard it all."

Alek shook his head. "If you can't have me with my secrets, then you can't have me at all."

"Is that the brooding bad boy version of *if you can't handle me at my worst you don't deserve me at my best*?"

"Yesterday you said you would marry me even if I never told you about my past. Now you'll only marry me if I tell you everything?" Alek tried to cross his arms and sighed petulantly when his cast got in the way.

"It's not about your secrets; it's about trust. I don't trust you to tell the truth. I don't trust you not to hurt me. You don't trust me enough to tell me anything except what you absolutely have to. You don't trust that I'll stay. We need to start over and build this thing right because if we don't," Ian gestured back and forth between the two of them, "none of this is going to work, and I need us to work, Alek. I can't go through what I went through when I thought I lost you forever."

Alek looked away, his hand balling into a fist. Ian took Alek's hand, unclenched his fingers, and kissed his palm.

"How about we play another game?" Ian asked.

Alek looked back at him with wary, guarded eyes.

"I get to ask you two questions every day; one about your past and one about us, and no matter what the answer is, as long as it's the truth, I will forgive you." He paused, worrying his lip between his teeth. Alek was like a genie in a bottle. The rules needed to be specific. No loopholes. "You have to answer more than yes or no. I think you owe me that. With two questions a day, I might actually get to know you in a year or so. Would you like to play?"

Alek grumbled, "What choice do I have?"

Ian smiled. "That was hardly the acceptance of a marriage proposal I was hoping for."

"Now you know how it feels. What's the other rule? You said there were two."

"If you lie to me about the answers, about anything, the deal's off. We're over. Everything you say from now on has to be the truth. The same goes for me too."

"That's not very fair. You don't have any dark secrets."

"Are you in or not?"

Alek flicked his fingers impatiently. "Ask me your questions."

Ian held Alek's gaze. "Remember, whatever the answer, I promise to forgive you. Just be honest." He waited until Alek nodded his agreement, then asked, "Have you slept with anyone else since we bought the Victorian?"

Alek shook his head and Ian was about to open his mouth to tell him yes or no answers weren't good enough, when he said, "I haven't touched anyone, haven't even looked at anyone like that since I followed you into that alley. Three years. Three years and there's only been you. There will only ever be you."

Ian had not expected that. At all.

Alek looked away, his bottom lip pouted outward, like he'd already resigned to the fact that Ian wouldn't believe him. "I may have betrayed you in every other way, but my cock and my heart have always belonged to you."

Ian reached forward and palmed his hand around the side of Alek's neck, his fingertips spanning across Alek's jaw, all the way to his silky black hair. It was a gesture Alek would know well. It said 'good boy'. It said 'you've made me very happy'. It was a nonverbal, all uppercase 'MINE'.

In response, Alek pressed his neck into Ian's grasp. Alek's pulse drummed against Ian's hand, like Alek was steel and Ian a magnet. Ian released Alek's neck and gently turned Alek's chin back to face him.

"That pleases me more than I can say with words." Ian brought his other hand down to Alek's hardening dick. "When we get out of here, I'll show you exactly how happy you've made me."

"You believe me?" Alek's eyes widened slightly.

"Yes. You said you wouldn't lie to me and I'm choosing to trust you." Ian pumped Alek's dick a few times in a show of good faith and then removed both of his hands. Alek huffed a whine, but Ian ignored it, instead saying, "Let's get back to the game. Remember, you have to answer my next question, and if you don't answer truthfully, the game's over and I'm gone."

Alek gave a curt nod.

"Tell me the nightmare you have when you talk in your sleep. Tell me the truth and I won't think any less of you. I'll still love you. I'll forgive you, even if you can't forgive yourself."

"I won't answer that question yet. Wouldn't want to give everything away up front."

"You want to forfeit already?" Ian teased. "Let me say it

again. Nothing you've ever done is more than I can forgive, so long as you tell the truth."

Alek said nothing.

"What if I let you tell me in Bulgarian? Could you tell me then?"

"That depends. Does it have to be in great detail, or can I give you a sentence?"

"I give you an inch." Ian held his thumb and finger apart. "I'll take one sentence, in a language I don't understand, this one time."

"*Blagodarya.*"

Ian frowned. "That's it?"

"That's 'thank you'. I was checking if I lost Bulgarian when I regained English—not that I'd mind, but it's convenient in this case." Without preamble, Alek closed his eyes and said, "*Semeĭstvoto mi e martvo zaradi men.*"

Ian leaned forward and tapped a kiss to Alek's lips before he opened his eyes.

"Thank you for telling me. Whatever it is, I forgive you."

Alek's eyes opened. "How can you say that? There are things beyond forgiveness. People beyond redemption. For all you know, I could be a murderer."

"I may know nothing about your past, but I know you. You're not beyond redemption, not to me."

"I'm not a house, Ian, and if I was, I'd be condemned. A meth lab explosion. A nuclear wasteland where not even plants can grow."

"I hear plants grow in Chernobyl now." Ian plucked Alek's ring from the box and then went down on *both* knees. "If you want proof of my commitment, then you have it. You know I don't make promises lightly and I don't break them. Ever. As long as you keep giving me a little bit more of yourself each and every day, I will marry you and I'll never leave. I promise that there's nothing about you I won't accept. I love you and all of your dark corners and sharp edges. What do you say? Alek Katin. Whoever you are. It doesn't matter to me. Will you marry me?"

Ian rubbed his hand over the back of his neck. Now he understood where Alek was coming from. It was terrifying to lay his soul bare and ask the person he loved most to have him forever.

Alek brought his fingers to his chin and made a show of deliberating before saying, "I agree to your terms. Is the ring even going to fit around my finger now that I'm swollen all over?"

Ian exhaled and blinked back tears from his eyes. "Definitely not. I slipped a measuring tape around your finger when you were sleeping a while back—"

"A while back?" Alek's eyes narrowed nearly indiscernibly.

"Yeah. I mean, I might not have been ready then, but I'm always prepared. Now do you want the ring or not?"

"Want. So much want." Alek thrust out his hand. "Try it on my pinky."

With surprisingly still hands, Ian slid the ring onto Alek's finger. Nothing magical happened. No imaginary choir sang. No broken heart slammed back into place. But underneath the nerves that made Ian want to throw up, there was a delicate, fragile, yearning hope.

Alek looked down at his ring with a small smile. Ian had selected a thin gold band with a subtle Art Deco-style laurel leaf filigree etched into the inside like a secret. The ring had a patina of scuffs and scratches that Ian had considered polishing away, but it was almost as old as the Victorian so he'd decided to leave it the way history had.

Before Alek, Ian had never given much thought to the idea of an engagement ring. He worked with his hands. It would get lost or ruined or, worst-case scenario, deglove his finger. But now Ian understood. Alek needed to see Ian's love on his hand.

Alek's eyes met Ian's. "Give me your ring. It's my turn."

Ian dropped the ring into Alek's outstretched hand and then held his own hand out.

"How did you..." Alek's brow furrowed as he looked at the satin-finished titanium ring.

"It's the same one," Ian said. "Lucky for me, I found it unscathed in the U-bend after you went to sleep." After which, Ian had hidden both rings in an envelope inside an accordion file folder under the label 'Boring Tax Stuff' for safekeeping.

"Thank you," Alek said with genuine, unguarded-for-once, gratitude.

Alek trailed his fingertips lightly against the sensitive skin on the sides of Ian's ring finger as he pushed the ring down into place. They both looked at their joined hands and the rings adorning them. Ian smiled so wide his cheeks ached.

Alek grinned too. "So we're engaged?"

"Yes, we are, *fiancé*."

"Doesn't feel like anything's changed." Alek was still looking at his ring.

"That's what I've been trying to tell you." Ian tapped the tip of Alek's nose. "So close to self-awareness and yet so far away."

"Fuck off," Alek said with a smile as he reached out and dragged Ian up to his feet by his hair, not stopping until he'd pulled Ian close enough to kiss.

As far as Ian was concerned, this was their first kiss. Everything before was lies and games. This was the beginning of forever.

19

ALEK

I f Alek had known all he had to do was fall off a building to get Ian to finally commit, he would have fallen sooner, and from the second story, rather than the third. In all of Alek's marriage-related machinations, he'd never considered the possibility that Ian would be the one to propose, let alone with a ring. To have Ian choose him, to be the one to ask and not answer, to want him enough, to love him enough to claim him, was the happiest Alek could ever remember feeling.

There was that part where Ian basically called him a cancerous parasite that was slowly sucking out his soul, but Alek wasn't going to look at that too closely, or ever again. Ian had put words to exactly what Alek had always worried he was to him. Worthless. Unlovable. Unwanted. Too much and yet not enough.

"Did you still want to try the piano?" Ian asked.

"And ruin this? Not really, but it's probably best to get it over with."

"That's the spirit." Ian mussed Alek's hair.

Ian moved the keyboard to the rolling table and positioned it over Alek's lap.

Alek closed his eyes and scrolled through songs like a mile-long list of bootleg MP3s on an iPod. He needed something he could play upside down, one hand tied behind his back, while fucking someone in his lap. *Swan Lake* would do. He opened his eyes and began to play.

The acrylic keys grated against his fingertips and when the electric phantom of what a piano should sound like reached his ears, it wasn't *Swan Lake*. It wasn't even music. There was no fluency. No rhythm. Nothing.

Alek's ears began to ring. He took a deep breath and turned to Ian. "Let me try the sheet music." He had to be sure.

Ian held the piece of paper out for Alek. The nurse from the night before had selected *Hot Cross Buns*.

Alek looked at the nonsensical string of notes for a long time. He bit the tip of his tongue and tried to play but he didn't know where his fingers were supposed to go. He clenched his teeth together so tightly he hoped they would crumble and snap off.

Ian moved to take the piano, but Alek was faster. He slammed his hands down on the keys, cast and all, and the sound was so loud and ugly, it was like a car crash, a building collapse, a gunshot echoing in an empty room.

Ian's arms surrounded Alek, heavy and tight like he was pulling him back from the edge he'd leaped right off of. Alek breathed in cedar, but when he closed his eyes no forests grew. His mind was a black hole, darker than a moonless, starless, dead-of-winter, night sky. The steady vibration that resonated in Alek's chest meant Ian was talking, but all he could hear was the echo of the counterfeit piano and the roar of a fire burning in Bulgaria twenty years before.

He clung to Ian's shirt with his one good hand, while his other wrist throbbed hotly with each thundering beat of his heart and his skull felt like it had ripped apart at the seams.

When Ian pulled away, his jawline was devastatingly sharp and a thick line of worry was etched between his brows. "Is your wrist okay?" Ian's voice was more gravelly than usual, like he was talking through barbed wire.

"It feels as broken as it did before." Which was technically true. "Stop fussing over me." He'd been about to say that he felt much better now, that abusing the keyboard had been incredibly cathartic, but he really did want to give the whole not lying thing a try.

"I want the doctor to look at it." Ian gently lifted Alek's hand into his lap as if it was as priceless as a Fabergé egg.

Alek pressed the button on his call light to summon the nurse.

"Do you want me to get you something?" Ian asked.

Alek shook his head and told the voice that came through a speaker in the ceiling that he would like a doctor to come to assess his fractured wrist. Now that the dust of his tantrum had settled, Alek worried he might have ruined his hand irrevocably. He tried to wiggle his fingers. It felt like the broken edges of his bones were scraping against each other but he *was* able to move them.

A few moments later Dr. Modorovic strode in, wearing navy surgical scrubs, her thick salt and pepper hair escaping from underneath a disposable surgical cap.

"I believe I asked for an orthopedic surgeon, not you," Alek teased.

"When were you going to tell someone you got your English back?" she said.

Ian held a chair out for the doctor and gestured for her to sit.

She lowered into the chair, turning over her shoulder to thank Ian before saying, "A nurse called to tell me that my curmudgeonly Bulgarian patient was speaking heavily-accented

English, and seeing as you're the only curmudgeonly or Bulgarian patient on my service today, I put two and two together."

"I find that hard to believe," Alek drawled. "Surely there must be at least one octogenarian on your roster more curmudgeonly than me."

Dr. Modorovic opened her mouth, but was interrupted by the young doctor from before, who trailed into the room and flipped open a top-bound spiral notepad, his pen poised to take notes.

"Do you mind if my intern, Dr. Elias, is present?" she asked. "I'd like to loop him in on this so he can write up the progress note for me."

Alek nodded. He didn't plan to share anything important anyway.

"Sorry to interrupt," Ian said. "But, there will still be an orthopedic doctor coming to check on Alek's wrist, right?"

"Absolutely. The nurse called Dr. Fernandez before she called me." Dr. Modorovic looked closely at Alek's cast. If she noticed Ian's graffiti, she didn't say anything. "What's wrong with your wrist?"

Alek hoped the rule about lying didn't apply to everyone else. He avoided Ian's eyes as he said, "It's a little more sore than usual, but still in working order." Alek gave a small wave of his cast to show how in tip-top shape it was and a blast of pain wracked through his arm so intensely, he was in very real danger of vomiting all over the front of his gown.

"Hmm." She crossed one leg over the other and leaned forward on her elbows. "The spontaneous return of your English is a very promising sign. I'm curious if you've tried the piano."

Alek appreciated that she didn't pry about his arm, staying in her lane—or body system as it were.

"It's just the English, for now," Ian answered for him.

Alek traced his fingertip over the bumpy lines and ridges of the permanent marker heart on his cast.

"Well, it's early days yet. Alek?" She waited until he looked at her. "How exactly did your English come back?"

"I woke up and started talking." Alek wanted them to leave. He wanted to hold Ian's left hand for at least as long as it took to memorize the sensation of their freshly ring-cladded hands joined together.

"Try to think back to the moment you woke up," Dr. Modorovic said. "Which of your five senses do you remember experiencing first?" She put her hands up. "Don't tell me yet. Just think."

Alek closed his eyes. He didn't remember hearing anything, but he did remember the strong scent of Ian—nostalgic, freshly-showered, concentrated. Red cedar and pine. Ancient forests, still and silent.

"Now, I'd like you to recall your first memory of the piano again, focusing only on your five senses."

Wisteria wafting through the window, his uncle's hands moving fast over black and white stripes...

"Which sense is the strongest in that memory? And the other. You can answer now."

"Scent." Alek resented this game. Why couldn't she tell him everything all at once?

Dr. Modorovic beamed. "Exactly! Very good!"

"What does this have to do with anything?"

"Don't be a dick," Ian said from the end of the bed where he stood, arms crossed, with an attentive look on his face.

Dr. Modorovic waved her hand. "It's fine. I find his acerbic nature endearing." Alek stuck his tongue out at Ian as she continued, "If we were to rank our senses in order of intensity and importance, scent would likely be near the bottom, but that's not to say scent *isn't* important. Scent and memory are closely related. It's likely that everyone here has had the experience of smelling something and suddenly traveling back in time to the memory associated with it. Maybe it's the artificial strawberry scent of a child's toy. Returning to your house after vacation. A particular shampoo used on an important day. One sniff and it all comes back.

"Our sense of smell is connected to the hippocampus of the brain, where our memories are stored. There's a great deal of research that supports scent therapy for everything from dementia to head injuries like yours, Alek. I think it might be something worth trying once you're discharged. That is, if your musical ability hasn't returned by then."

"I want to start now," Alek said. "What do I have to do?"

"Alek," Ian said. "You need to rest. Your wrist needs to be checked. This can wait until you're feeling better."

"I *need* to be back to the way I was before." Ian could fuck right off.

Dr. Modorovic looked between Ian and Alek as if she was trying to decide whose side to pick. She sighed, her gaze settling on Alek. "You'll need to make a list of scents you associate most closely with the piano. Then Dr. Elias will round up some samples. Once procured, you will smell the samples while recalling a memory of your choosing. It should be a powerful piano-related one. You'll repeat the process twice each day. In the meantime, you can brainstorm that list while you rest."

"Piano polish. Loose tobacco. Cedar. Pine. Lemon," Alek said immediately. "I would like Dr. Elias to go to my home and remove a cutting of flowering wisteria from the front of our house."

"Fuck," Ian said.

"Fuck?" Alek asked.

"While I was at the Victorian earlier, I pruned the wisteria back to the ground, since it was damaged when you... by the... Anyway, it's gone."

"Gone where?"

"I burned it already." Ian grimaced. "I'm sorry. I wanted to get it done before you got home. I didn't kill it. I just pruned it."

"In four hours you cut down the wisteria and burned it?"

"Well, most of it was already on the ground. I'm so sorry. If I'd known..."

"There's no need to apologize," Alek said. "How could either of us have known?"

The entire thing would have been funny if it wasn't happening to him. It was an almost karmic retribution, cosmic symmetry, some sign that the gods had a sense of humor. Alek's antics had driven Ian to such rage that he aggressively pruned a house-sized climbing vine, and when that wasn't enough to erase what Alek had done, he'd burned it, consequently destroying the remote chance of bringing back Alek's music through some sort of magical sniffing test.

Ringing sounded in Alek's ears, bringing with it a wave of nausea. He snuck a glance to confirm his barf bag was on the bedside table where the nurse had left it.

"Are you okay?" Ian asked.

Dr. Modorovic looked at Alek closely. The young doctor too.

"I'm fine," he said sourly.

Ian opened his mouth, probably to tattle on him for not taking any of his pain or nausea medications, but Alek repeated again, "I'm. Fine."

"It's probably safe to assume the scent of wisteria is a one size fits all sort of thing," Dr. Modorovic said. "Dr. Elias, do you know what it looks like?"

"No, but I'm sure I can figure it out."

Alek had expected the young doctor's voice to squeak like a rusty hinge, but he sounded surprisingly poised.

"Perfect. Make a stop by their house, as well. See what you can find."

"On it." He flipped his notebook closed and tucked it in the pocket of his white coat.

In Bulgarian, Alek said, "When can I have sex?"

"Vigorous activity is prohibited for the first four weeks after head injury," she replied, also in Bulgarian. Grave-faced, like she was taking this all very seriously, she asked, "Would you say it's vigorous?"

"Do you want me to answer that?"

"I'm sure they aren't talking about you," Ian told the young doctor. "Right, Alek?"

Dr. Modorovic apologized in English. "Alek had a private question." She nodded at the other doctor. "You can head out and get started, though."

When the door closed behind him, Dr. Modorovic said in Bulgarian, "Can we speak freely in front of your partner or would you like me to continue like this?"

Before their engagement Alek wouldn't have hesitated to hide the doctor's order from Ian, but now when he thought about lying he felt an uncomfortable twinge in his stomach. Guilt, perhaps. Thirty-three years without a moral compass, and all it took was a single ring to shackle him with one.

"Anything you need to say can be said in front of Ian," Alek said in English.

She nodded, turning to Ian. "Alek asked about activity restrictions and I was telling him he'll have to wait one month before resuming any vigorous activity."

"Oh, sure. You don't have to worry about that. I'll do all the heavy lifting."

Laughter tumbled out of Alek's mouth before he could catch it. "I was asking about sex, Ian, not home improvement."

Ian grunted his understanding, the tops of his ears going crimson.

Dr. Modorovic rose from the chair. "For the sake of clarity, I consider everything leading up to intercourse within the realm of moderate activity, which can be resumed once you're discharged. The actual sex will have to wait the four weeks, I'm afraid."

"When can I go home?" Alek asked.

"Friday, if your CT remains reassuring."

"Fucking Friday?"

"Doctor's orders. It's much easier to crack your skull if the bleeding in your brain worsens when you're already here—"

"What a ghastly visual image," Alek interrupted.

All the flush from Ian's earlier embarrassment had drained from his face.

She followed Alek's gaze. "I apologize. I only meant that the risk of rebleed is much lower after days three to five."

"Tomorrow will be three days," Alek argued.

"I choose five." She crossed to the door. "I've grown very fond of your brain and don't want to see any harm come to it."

"I'm liable to remember my music sooner if I'm in familiar surroundings," Alek called after her.

"Five days," she repeated over her shoulder.

"But I hate it here," Alek said.

"Listen to the doctor," Ian said.

The stern, gruff tone of Ian's command only made Alek want to act out more, but his ribs still throbbed from his earlier laughter and his wrist felt like it had been crushed in a vise, so he did what Ian said and bid the doctor farewell.

20

ALEK

After another x-ray of Alek's arm and an agonizing physical exam, the orthopedic surgeon—a CrossFit enthusiast Alek disliked immediately—declared that although his fracture was unchanged, the swelling and soft tissue injuries were markedly worse.

Alek would have to keep his right arm completely immobilized with his hand above his heart. If the swelling didn't go down, the surgeon would remove the cast, and Ian's heart-shaped proposal along with it, so he could make a series of incisions that would allegedly relieve the swelling and spare his hand.

He'd asked if they ought to try leeches first if their approach was going to be so barbaric.

His newest accessory—a scratchy, black sling—restrained him in a decidedly unsexy way. The strap dug into his shoulder and the velcro snagged on his bed linen, picking up lint souvenirs each time he adjusted his blanket.

Ian had already barked at Alek twice when he tried to move his arm accidentally. Instead of snapping at Ian for being over-bearing, Alek was halfway through plotting how he was going to tie Ian up with the sling and pound the bossiness out of him once his arm healed.

Ian was sprawled out on his back on the pull-out couch with his hands under his head and his long legs spilling out over the armrest. Alek had made him drag the couch over to his bed and it felt like they were having a sleepover—or at least that's what he assumed it felt like, as he'd never had one as a boy.

"What room do you want to work on next?" Ian asked in a near-sleep rumble Alek knew well.

Alek rolled onto his side, hanging his good arm down to tangle his fingers in Ian's hair. "You know what room."

Since purchasing the Victorian, they'd taken turns choosing which room to tackle next. Alek always asked Ian to fix the attached greenhouse. Ian always said no. It was too expensive. It would take forever. The glass would have to be custom-made. And Alek would agree because he was supposed to have the finances of an antique furniture restorer.

Ian flipped over onto his side, resting his cheek on his bicep. "I was hoping the head injury would make you forget about the greenhouse."

Renovating the greenhouse *would* be a massive undertaking. All that remained of their greenhouse was a skeleton of rusted wrought iron wrapped around an octagonal red brick foundation. Oh, and a forest of blackberry brambles and volunteer trees.

"Come on, Ian. It'll be gorgeous. I can't wait to stand inside during a thunderstorm and watch the rain pour down overhead."

"That sounds like a highly effective way to be struck by lightning."

"Hardly," Alek scoffed. "Iron conducts electricity, which makes the greenhouse a gothic wet dream of a Faraday cage. It's perfectly safe. Now that that's settled, it brings me to my next point."

"Oh no."

Ignoring him, Alek continued. "I think you should take a sabbatical from work. Supervise the Queen Anne and the Craftsman as remotely as you can, and then we can finally finish the Victorian." Now that he had Ian back, he wanted to keep him close, lest distance break the fragile spell he still held over him.

"Wait. You have to slow down when you throw around vocabulary words. I'm not used to your accent."

Alek rattled off a series of his favorite curse words and then repeated back what he'd said before.

"I can project manage remotely until you recover, but I'm not closing up our business. I need to keep it solvent and present in people's minds." Ian pulled Alek's hand from his hair and kissed it. "Even if I have an independently wealthy fiancé."

Alek snatched his hand away. He could read between the lines. Ian wouldn't risk their business. It would be irresponsible to put his financial future in Alek's hands. Their relationship might not make it. Maybe he wanted to cache money for an escape plan.

"What makes you think I'm independently wealthy?" Alek said. "Maybe I was lying about being able to buy you out of the Victorian."

Ian smiled good-naturedly. "Were you lying?"

"No. I do have money."

"Okay."

Alek huffed. "That's it?"

"I don't care how much there is or what you do with it. It's your money, not mine."

Alek frowned. "But what's mine will be yours eventually..."

"Not in this case. You'll only convince yourself that the

money is why I stay with you."

Alek hated that he knew him so well.

"Can I ask a question though?" Ian said.

"I thought you already asked me two today, and a third now, but yes, I'll allow another."

"I didn't realize you were keeping count."

Alek pulled Ian's hair sharply. "Ask your question."

Ian uncurled Alek's hand from his hair and held it. He looked up at him, brown eyes serious. "Are you running from the law?"

Alek laughed. "No one's looking for me." He'd covered his tracks and there was no one left alive to come after him anyway. The perks of being a dead orphan. Besides, "The money came into my possession legally."

Ian let out a low whistle. "That's a relief."

"Would you have stayed if I'd answered otherwise?"

"I don't know... Let me enjoy that you're not a fugitive, okay?"

That was where they were different. It would have taken far more than the threat of prison or death for Alek to give Ian away.

Ian closed his eyes and moved Alek's hand back to his hair.

"I lied about our finances because it kept you from leaving me," Alek said as he massaged Ian's scalp with the tips of his fingers.

"I know."

"In retrospect, I realize that was manipulative."

"You think?" Ian's eyes remained closed.

"Are you mad?"

"Furious."

"Mmm. I like you furious." The make-up sex was going to be so good when they finally had it. "But you forgive me?"

"Yes."

"Because you have no other choice?"

"Yes," Ian said again. "But also because I don't think you thought you had a choice either."

"I'm sorry you worked all those extra hours." Alek gave an exaggerated pout. "I'd rather you'd spent that time with me—"

"You're such a prick," Ian murmured, nipping a biting kiss to Alek's forearm.

"Now that you know, though," Alek carried on as if he hadn't been interrupted. "We don't need to live in a partially condemned building anymore."

"Okay."

"Okay?" Alek's eyes narrowed.

"Yeah. Like I said, it's your money. I'm not going to tell you how to spend it."

"Fine. Then I want to finish the Victorian. I think my... Well, I just think it's what we should do."

"If that's what you want, then that's what we'll do, but you'll have to be patient. We're still talking years here."

Alek had already moved on. Maybe he could influence Ian into using his turn on the library after they finished the greenhouse. There was also the kitchen. Alek would use his turn for that next.

Ian's breathing began to slow and deepen. Alek worried Ian's cumulative sleep debt from the last two months had shaved a few years off his life, but he had another question.

"Knowing I have more money than you doesn't make you feel emasculated?"

Without opening his eyes, Ian said, "Do you want me to show you exactly how emasculated I don't feel right now?"

Alek wanted that, very much. "Another time. Go to sleep before I change my mind."

———

THE YOUNG DOCTOR—DR. Elias, Ian reminded him—returned before nightfall, carrying with him a large backpack.

Ian moved off the edge of the bed, where he'd sat facing Alek.

"No. Stay." Alek liked being able to reach out and touch Ian to prove that he was still there.

From his bag, Dr. Elias removed a series of individually labeled plastic bags, opening them one at a time, before passing them to Ian to hold under Alek's nose.

Fresh lemon zest, a cotton ball saturated with lemon essential oil, loose tobacco, tobacco-scented candles, pine needles, cedar bark, and so on and so forth. Dr. Elias was very thorough. There were four different cuttings of flowering wisteria he'd pilfered and a leaf from their own wisteria that Ian had missed. He'd also stopped by a music shop and bought a small bottle of piano polish, which Alek spritzed onto his side table.

There was no lightning bolt return of his musical genius. None of it worked and what little hope he'd foolishly allowed himself was extinguished. All the exercise had done was make him exceedingly nauseous.

"It would have been truly remarkable if this worked on the first round," Dr. Elias said.

Alek used to be remarkable. Things had always worked out for him effortlessly.

Ian thanked Dr. Elias and walked him to the door, closing it and the curtain behind him, before returning to Alek.

"I'm sorry." Ian held Alek's face in his hands and kissed his forehead.

Alek closed his eyes and breathed in cedar and pine, but no forest grew inside his head. Alek would be better off if he accepted that his music was gone forever. He'd have to find something else to fill that void.

Perhaps Ian would do.

21

IAN

Over a breakfast of scrambled eggs and low-sodium sausage rounds, Ian asked Alek who taught him to play the piano. He had expected a short answer or some sort of pushback, but whether it was because Alek wanted his music back, or he felt particularly motivated to work on their relationship, or maybe he was bored, Alek's answer was far more detailed than he'd anticipated.

Alek set his fork down beside his plate and wiped his mouth with a napkin before answering. "My uncle taught me to play. He was tall with hair as black as squid ink and eyes the color of a cloudless summer sky."

He told Ian about his uncle's house and his workshop, where Alek had learned how to fix ancient, broken things. Ian was afraid to say anything, in case it broke the spell. Alek described his piano in great detail, all the way down to the pair of initials—Alek's and his uncle's—carved into the side of it. He talked about the piano like it was a person. A person who died.

What had happened to the piano? It must have been a huge loss for Alek to leave it behind.

When Ian asked what happened to Alek's uncle, he said, "You'll have to ask that another day. Next question."

Ian respected that. What Alek had just told him was a precious gift.

"Why did you move into the Wells Building after I started working on it?" Ian asked.

Alek's eyes met his. "How did you know?"

"I was bluffing. You confirmed it for me now." Ian had assumed as much, but it still hurt. The apartment he had visited so many times had been curated to present the character Alek had created for him.

"That's cheating." Alek elbowed Ian in the stomach with his broken arm.

"If you move that arm again, you won't like what happens."

"Oh?" Alek's voice dripped with seduction. "What sort of punishment have you thought up that I wouldn't enjoy?"

Ian hadn't, actually. It was hard to punish someone with a propensity for kink and an insatiable sex drive.

With apparently no concern for how obvious it was that he was stalling, Alek cut his sausage into bite-sized pieces, one of which he ate, and then washed it all down with a gulp of instant coffee. Alek feigned a gag and thunked the mug down on the table.

"This coffee tastes like at least thirty-percent ground-up desiccated cockroaches. Are you sure you can't pop home and plug the espresso machine in here?"

"If you're buying time to select a suitable lie, I'd like to remind you again that lies aren't allowed. Why did you move into the Wells Building?"

"I don't need reminding. I have a concussion, not dementia." Alek ate another bite of sausage before continuing. "You wouldn't reply to any of my attempts at contact."

"Where did you live before then?"

"I have a place south of Big Sur."

That fit. The rugged stretch of coastline was sparsely populated. Sometimes mudslides made the roads impassable. It was right up Alek's alley.

"I want to see it," Ian said.

"Okay. We'll go. Whenever you want."

"Good. Now answer the question. Why did you move?"

"I already answered that."

"Only in the most literal way. Why me?"

Alek pushed his eggs around his plate. "What reward do you have for me today?"

"You naked. Me with a basin of soapy water and a hospital rag about as excoriating as sandpaper."

"A bed bath?"

"Yeah, but if you're not interested..."

Alek wet his bottom lip. "I'm interested."

"Then stop stalling."

Alek held out a plastic fruit cup. "Open this, please."

Ian snatched it from his hand and chucked it into the trash can.

Alek raised his eyebrows and smirked. Ian inhaled deeply. He wouldn't let Alek win so easily next time.

"At first it was because you surprised me," Alek began. "In that alley, you were stronger than me, more unpredictable than me. You scared me, and it made me feel alive, for the first time in a very long time. I wanted more."

"So it was a sex thing?"

"Of course, it was a sex thing. You said no lies, but that wasn't the only reason. You never lost control. I knew you wanted me, but you stopped yourself. You didn't give in." Alek met Ian's eyes. "Do you know how rare that is? Someone who makes you feel safe and scared at the same time?"

Ian wouldn't know. Loving Alek made him feel like he was walking a tightrope over a crocodile-infested canal.

Alek licked his lips again. Ian knew what he was doing. Taunting him. Tempting him. It was Alek's oldest trick, well-worn to the point that Ian would be more surprised if he didn't lean on sex for control, especially now that he'd lost so much of it.

Ian waited. He let the silence draw out between them. Alek's eyes darkened.

"The sounds you made," Alek said, somberly, like he knew it would never sound that way again. "Your voice, the scratch of your palm against the scruff of your five o'clock shadow. It made the prettiest pictures in my brain. And the way you smelled? It was like the forest in summer. I could see the entire thing if I closed my eyes and inhaled. I hadn't thought about anyone except myself since my uncle died."

If Alek noticed what he revealed, he didn't acknowledge it.

"I thought about you. Incessantly. What's Ian doing? Why hasn't he called me? Why won't he write back? What sound would he make when he buried his dick inside me? What would that feel like?"

Ian's stomach dropped. "Wait. That was your first time bottoming?"

Alek nodded.

After that first fuck, Alek and Ian had swapped topping each other, taking turns relinquishing control before stealing it back. They both liked it that way, or at least Ian thought they did.

Ian asked, "Why didn't you tell me you'd never bottomed before?"

"It was impromptu sex against a door. We barely knew each other. Why would I have told you?"

"That's fair, but what about since then? You never thought

I'd like to know? Do you even want me to top you? Have you just been tolerating it to keep me here with you?"

"I wouldn't have come if I didn't like it."

"Ejaculation is a physical response. I want to hear the truth."

"I never let anyone top me before because I never had the desire to. Maybe I didn't trust you enough to tell you, but I've always trusted you enough to top me. If you're worried I didn't want it. Don't. If you knew how many times I fantasized about it... I promise. I'm very satisfied with our current arrangement."

They were only words. Ian didn't want to believe them, but that was the deal, right? Alek was supposed to trust Ian with the answers to his questions, and Ian was supposed to trust his answers were the truth.

"Did I hurt you?" Ian asked.

Alek looked at Ian under his eyelashes in much the same way he did when he sucked his dick. "Only in the best way."

"I'm serious. Stop fucking me with your eyes."

Alek's face sobered. "No, Ian. You didn't hurt me. I still jack off to that memory. It was so good I'm surprised I don't get hard whenever I open a door. Can I have that bath now?"

Ian exhaled his relief, but as he went to fill the water basin, he started to worry that maybe Alek was right.

What if his lies were too much?

———

THE NEXT DAY, Ian took Alek to a park bench in the hospital's courtyard. The trip over had left Alek fatigued. A fine mist of sweat gathered on his forehead and the back of his neck.

Ian readjusted the ice pack he held to Alek's hand. "Are you sure you don't want to go back to your room?"

Alek shook his head. "Ask me your questions."

Ian took a deep breath and asked, "How did your uncle die?"

Alek narrowed his eyes. "I never told you my uncle died. I won't fall for your bluff again."

Gently, Ian replied, "I'm not bluffing. You mentioned it yesterday."

Alek's forehead wrinkled.

"You were really tired," Ian said.

Alek dropped his gaze and kicked the bottom of his shoes over the pebble rocks that lined the path. "He drowned."

Ian clicked his tongue. "I'm so sorry, Alek."

"It was a long time ago."

"He didn't know how to swim?"

Alek lifted his head, his face unreadable. "I've answered more than yes or no. Next question, please."

"When did you fall in love with me?"

Apparently, Alek had the answer on reserve.

"The night we closed escrow on our first restoration. The four square. I know you remember, but I'm going to tell you how I remember it." He smiled, his pale green eyes sparkling in a way Ian hadn't seen in months. "You said we should christen it. We sat on the front steps, getting drunk on champagne. A bottle for each of us, right? You were silly. You actually giggled."

Ian bent closer, straining to hear through Alek's accent.

"When we first got there, the sky was the most striking pink and we stayed until it turned purple, then black. I laid down and put my head in your lap and watched the stars blink awake overhead, but you weren't looking up. You were looking down at me. You kissed me and when I closed my eyes I could still see the stars behind my eyelids, like you gave them to me, so I'd never be alone, so it would never be dark inside my mind again. That's when I knew I loved you."

That was the night Ian had admitted to himself that he was

in love too.

———

ON FRIDAY, Alek's CT scan had improved and the logistical nightmare of a typical hospital discharge process made Alek even more petulant than he was at baseline.

"Let's play our game now," Ian suggested. "It'll pass the time."

Alek nodded his assent.

"Tell me about your mother." Ian almost took the question back. He felt like such an asshole, but Alek needed this too. Trying to erase everything from his past wasn't coping and it wasn't working.

"My mother..."

Ian held his breath and looked for any sign of emotion from Alek, but he wasn't pausing to stave off tears. He seemed entirely unaffected. Bored even. More likely, he was trying to choose his words carefully.

"My mother was beautiful. Her eyes were like mine, but greener. If she had to speak to me, she'd look just over my head. She thought I didn't notice, but I did." He picked at the Velcro on his sling. "Is the length of my answer satisfactory?"

"If that's all you have to say, then yes, it's enough." Not for the first time, Ian wondered if Alek was neglected as a child. Maybe his uncle, and the piano, were all that he had. "Are you up to answering the second one? I can give you the rest of the day off."

Alek scoffed. "Your expectations of me are insultingly low."

"Okay. This one's pretty serious. Remember, you have to be honest." Ian grinned. "Is January second your real birthday? I'd hate to think I'd been celebrating the wrong day." Ian suspected he had been. Alek had forgotten his own birthday more than once, and he refused any suggestion of fanfare on Ian's part.

"November second," Alek answered.

"Hmm. I would have guessed you were born on Halloween or Friday the Thirteenth."

"Haha," Alek deadpanned. "You're not going to ask me what year?"

Ian shrugged. "Would you tell me?" If Ian knew Alek's full birthday, he might be able to find his true identity. Not that he would try. He wanted to wait for Alek to tell him.

Alek smirked and raised a single eyebrow. "Of course not."

———

IAN FLICKED the switch for the blinker. Alek usually teased him for indicating the turn onto their driveway from the dark, tree-lined road. "I've literally never seen anyone else on our stretch of the road," Alek would say. "It's a habit," Ian would reply.

But today, Alek said nothing. In fact, he'd been silent the entire drive home. Dr. Modorovic warned about persisting nausea and vertigo after a head injury, and if Alek's ashen face was any indication, the empty pink emesis bag he clutched in his hand confirmed it. The winding mountain roads probably hadn't helped.

The truck rumbled over the gravel road and rocks flicked up and pinged against the metal undercarriage. Fog hung low and dewdrops misted against the windshield. After spending the last few days inside the four corners of Alek's hospital room, the trees seemed taller, and out of place, the familiar ones a few inches off from where he last remembered them, like they'd grown legs and moved around while he was gone.

Ian took Alek's hand and squeezed it, but he didn't seem to notice.

When the house came into view, Alek finally spoke. "It looks wrong without the wisteria."

"I think so too. I can't wait for it to grow back."

Alek gave a ghost of a smile. "I never thought I'd hear you say that."

"The wisteria earned its keep." Ian parked the truck and pulled the keys from the ignition. He turned to Alek. "Let me help you out."

Alek bristled. "I don't need your help."

"You're right. Don't deprive me of the chance to feel you up."

Alek rolled his eyes and unbuckled his seatbelt.

Ian fastened the seatbelt back over Alek's lap. There was no way he was letting Alek cross the uneven forest floor and climb the stairs by himself.

"I'm serious," Ian said. "Do this for me, okay? If anything happens to that pretty head of yours... I can't lose you again."

Alek's cheek hollowed.

Ian tapped his knuckle against the spot. "Stop pouting. You're going to have to tolerate some level of fussing from me. It doesn't make you weak. It means I care about you."

Alek said nothing, his eyes fixated on the Victorian until, at long last, he nodded once.

"Thank you." Ian hopped out of the truck and hustled to the passenger side before Alek could go rogue, but Alek hadn't moved an inch and he didn't turn to look at Ian when he opened the door. Ian reached over Alek's lap and unlatched his seatbelt.

"Come on." Ian swiveled Alek towards him and pulled him to the edge of the seat. "Let's get you inside."

"I think I need a kiss for courage," Alek said with an anemic half-smile.

Ian didn't hesitate. Emotions swelled, far too big and conflicted to contain. Alek was home and in his hands. He channeled all of his tangled emotions into a kiss he hoped telegraphed to Alek exactly how much he loved him, with or without his music, whether his body and mind were broken or not. Even if Alek never healed. If he never got anything back that he'd lost. Whatever Alek had done, whatever lies he had told, Ian would always love him.

Ian dropped his hands down to Alek's ass and pulled him closer. If he had any less control, he would have fucked Alek into oblivion right then and there, but even as the corners of his mind went fuzzy with want and need and Alek, Alek, Alek, he was still in control. He would keep Alek safe, no matter how much he wanted to feel him wrapped around his cock.

Ian helped him down from the truck and kicked the door closed with his foot, releasing Alek when he was sure he had his feet underneath him. He checked Alek over. He was breathing fast, but he looked well enough—his cheeks were flushed, eyes bright and alert—and besides, Ian was breathing fast too.

Ian began to ask, "Are you—"

"If you ruin that kiss by asking me if I'm okay, I will never forgive you."

Ian grinned. "I was going to ask if you were ready." He lifted two fingers. "Scout's honor."

Alek's nose wrinkled, his eyes narrowed into a suspicious scowl so distinctly Alek that Ian's heart twinged and he fought the urge to kiss him all over again.

"Come on, then." Ian linked their arms.

When they approached the patch of freshly disturbed earth where Alek had landed, Ian tried to steer Alek around it, but Alek trampled right through the spot, seemingly unaware.

Alek made it up the stairs, only tripping once and pretending, unconvincingly, that he hadn't. When they reached the front door, Ian thrust his key into the lock and twisted the knob. The door opened with a long, eerie creak. Alek disappeared inside the dark house, his footsteps echoing on the heart of pine floors.

Behind Ian, the forest was too quiet, like it was waiting, like it was holding its breath.

22

ALEK

"So, where are we sleeping tonight?" Ian asked, hanging his keys on the hook beside the door.

Alek closed his eyes and breathed in. Dust and old things, lumber, lemon, clove. Home.

He opened his eyes. "Our room."

Ian's brows darted together. "Our room?"

Before everything went to shit, Alek and Ian had shared a bedroom. They'd chosen the largest room on the second floor and cannibalized the room next door to make an ensuite bathroom. The windows were plentiful and the view of the forest stretched on endlessly. Their bed was a simple, solid walnut frame. The sheets were white, for obvious reasons.

As far as Alek was aware, Ian hadn't set foot in their room since the day they broke up. He'd nailed the door shut the very next night while Alek was entertaining an escort in his room.

Alek laid a hand on Ian's chest, feeling the steady thump of his heart under his fingertips. "Yes. You're too big to share a queen properly and I want a bath in our tub." Alek was starting to look and smell like he belonged in one of those plaid-wearing, chronically depressed, nineties grunge bands.

Ian grunted noncommittally.

"What's wrong?"

He cleared his throat. "It's stupid... It's just, the last time I was there, you were breaking my heart, you know?"

Alek leaned in until they were both touching everywhere that counted. "Let's do my room then. My mattress is much better than yours. You can give me another bed bath, instead."

"Nah." He dropped his hands to Alek's hips. "I'll open it up. Do you want to rest on the couch first?"

"Definitely not." Alek walked through the doorway, taking care not to look in the direction of the parlor room, where the piano was surely waiting for his return. He called over his shoulder, "If you want to help me up the stairs, you'd better hurry."

Upstairs, Alek sat on the floor and leaned against the wall, shamelessly studying the way the fabric of Ian's shirt tightened over the muscles in his back while he removed each nail and board that barred their entry. When he was finished, Ian stashed his hammer in his back pocket and held out his hand to pull Alek up. Alek would have protested, but his legs did feel rather weak between the stairs and their earlier kiss.

Ian held the door open and stood aside. "After you."

It was like walking into a time capsule. A pile of Alek's clothes lay crumpled on the floor beside the laundry basket, shed like a snake leaving the husk of its molted skin behind. A half-empty glass of water rested neatly on top of a coaster on Ian's side of the bed. Alek's vision snagged on the mirror over their dresser. He hardly recognized himself and it wasn't only because of the bruises and swelling that marred the landscape of his face. His reflection was a ghost, a phantom shell, a wretched beast that ought to be put down.

Alek walked to his side of the bed and ran his finger over the end table. A thin layer of dust, but perfectly habitable. He picked up the book he'd been reading and flipped to the page he'd last dog-eared. Ian had locked up the room just before the villain was revealed, but Alek already knew who it was, so it didn't really matter. He dropped the book down on the table and sat on the edge of the bed.

"Help me get undressed?" Alek asked.

Ian froze, his Adam's apple bobbing deliciously in his neck.

"I promise I won't bite."

"Liar."

The thick outline of Ian's dick strained against his jeans. Good. The only consent Alek would accept was enthusiastic, and despite all the heavy petting that had transpired since their reconciliation, Alek couldn't shake the fear that Ian might not want him now that he was broken.

Ian removed Alek's sling, then button by button, opened the front of Alek's shirt. Goosebumps rained over Alek's skin as Ian's fingers grazed up his chest and over his good shoulder to slip the shirt off. Ian slid the final sleeve around Alek's cast agonizingly slow, like he was playing Operation and Alek would emit a loud buzz if he hurt him.

With eyes downcast, Ian kneeled and removed Alek's socks. It was a strangely intimate thing, having his freshly minted fiancé take off his socks for him. Next, Ian tucked his fingers inside the waistband of the slippery black and white track pants Alek wore. The pants were Ian's. Alek wasn't fanatical about sports or athleisure, but Ian had been adamant that Alek size up to a looser fit. Given the Rorschach inkblots of bruises that had blossomed everywhere Alek landed, he'd been inclined to agree.

When Alek's dick bobbed free, full mast and ready to go—he may have lost music, but at least he could still get it up—Ian paused, swallowing hard. He sat back on his heels and chewed on his lip, his eyes focused on the tip of Alek's cock, where a drop of precome beaded.

Alek clenched and unclenched his left hand, his body coiling with unreleased sexual tension as he fought the urge to grab the back of Ian's head and show him where he belonged. But he'd have to tread lightly. He couldn't treat Ian the way he had before he dragged him through three weeks of simulated cuckoldry.

He stroked Ian's cheek with his thumb. Ian's eyes fell closed as he leaned into Alek's touch.

"If you're waiting for my permission, you have it," Alek encouraged.

Ian opened his eyes and lunged forward, his mouth enveloping Alek's dick in warm, wet ecstasy. A moan escaped Alek so fast he didn't know that the sound was coming from him until it hit his ears.

The once-familiar reality of Ian's mouth was so much better than Alek had fantasized about during the last three weeks of their separation. His imagination had failed to supply the details; how Ian's mouth vibrated as he hummed his appreciation, the squeeze of painful pleasure when Ian gagged on his cock, the hypersensitive zap when Ian twirled his tongue around his crown. Ian used his hand to milk what he couldn't fit in his mouth and sucked hard like he was starved for Alek's come.

If Ian kept that up, Alek would blow his load right down his throat, which was not necessarily something he was opposed to, but he'd rather come with Ian inside him. Maybe if he riled Ian up enough, he'd forget the doctor's orders. Alek grabbed Ian by his hair and pulled him off of him.

Ian wiped his mouth with his forearm. "Are you okay?"

"Mmm. Never better. I still want that bath though." He brought his fingers to Ian's chin and guided him to standing.

"Let's go." Ian held out his hand.

Alek took it, grateful for the boost because he was pretty sure all the blood from his legs was in his dick at the moment.

Historical houses had their drawbacks. Inside the walls, fraying wires were held together by chewing gum and a prayer —at least until Ian had wrangled them into order. The insulation was chock full of old corn cobs, newspapers, and forgotten toys. But in addition to the history and character and the money pit list of repairs the Victorian had to offer, there was at least one thing it had that modern houses did not: oversized clawfoot tubs. Tubs big enough for two. Alek and Ian could just fit inside, facing each other with their legs tangled together, dicks within easy reach.

Ian turned the tap on and plugged the drain, then spotted Alek as he lowered into the tub.

When Ian made no move to ditch his own clothes, Alek used his good hand to splash him. "Oops. Sorry about that."

"Dick," Ian muttered, though a smile teased at the corner of his mouth.

Ian brushed water droplets off the front of his pants and stood on one foot to remove his sock. It was like a bear trying to do ballet. When he switched sides and removed the other sock, he nearly fell over.

Alek's laugh was cut short by the stab of pain in his ribs.

Ian scowled. "You know you have one good arm, right? I don't actually have to help you."

"I think my good arm's not working so well, either." Alek lifted his middle finger in salute. "It seems to be stuck in this position."

A rumbling laugh exploded from Ian's chest. Making Ian laugh was almost as rewarding as earning his praise.

Ian shook his head, his eyes wrinkled at the corners with amusement. Then, he took his shirt off. Alek gulped. Ian was stacked with muscle, and not the kind manufactured by hours spent lifting weights. No, Ian's muscles were earned by hauling pallets of tile and demoing walls and turning a house destroyed by neglect into something beautiful.

Ian tossed his shirt by the door and brought his hands to the top button of his pants, undressing blindly, his eyes locked on Alek. When Ian's dick finally sprung free, Alek's heart leaped to his throat like he'd jumped off a cliff. There'd been plenty of involuntary angry boxer-clad boners, but Alek hadn't had the pleasure of seeing all of Ian since they broke up.

Alek braced his good arm on the lip of the tub and rose to his knees. Before Ian could protest the irresponsibility of allowing Alek to blow him in his "condition", Alek pulled Ian tight and wrapped his lips around his cock, plunging all the way down until he bottomed out at the back of his throat.

Ian sucked in a breath, rising up onto the balls of his feet. "Holy fucking fuck, Alek."

Alek smiled. He had Ian right where he wanted him.

Before Ian, Alek had almost always been on the receiving end of oral sex. It wasn't because hardly any man was worthy of a top-tier Alek Katin blow job, although that was true. It was that most of the people he'd been with had wanted to be dominated. What they didn't realize was how easy it was for Alek to control someone on his knees with a mouth full of cock. All it took was a flick of the tongue, a finger against the prostate, and Ian would beg and plead and promise anything and everything if Alek wanted him to.

But Alek wouldn't do that tonight. He wanted to make love to Ian's dick for as long as Ian would let him. There were so many things he wanted to say that he couldn't. So he used his mouth the only way he knew how.

"That's enough." Ian moved his hands to Alek's shoulders.

Alek whined, letting the tips of his teeth drag lightly as Ian pulled out of his mouth. Ian helped Alek turn around, then lifted a glass tumbler from the vanity, and climbed in opposite.

Water sloshed against the sides of the tub, threatening to spill out onto the floor as Ian's sizable body displaced it.

Enormous erection aside, Ian's intent appeared to be strictly business. He grabbed the shampoo and popped the cap, then climbed on top of Alek, straddling him.

Alek groaned in frustration. "If you didn't get in this bath to get me off, then you'd better drown me instead."

Ian's laugh splashed waves against Alek's chest. Alek frowned. There was nothing funny about torture via sexual frustration. Ian, of all people, should know.

Next, Ian flipped the shampoo bottle over and squirted a long thick dollop onto his hand. He was definitely messing with him. With light, careful fingers, Ian scrubbed Alek's scalp, avoiding the sutures knitting together the edges of the incision. A charged silence stretched between them like TV static turned on full blast.

"Tilt your head back and close your eyes," Ian commanded.

When Alek opened his eyes next, Ian was leaning over him, stretching to return the glass tumbler to the vanity. Ian's dick brushed against Alek's like velvet on velvet. Alek hissed. Ian froze. Their eyes met.

"You have to tell me if I hurt you," Ian said. "And remember, no lies."

Alek could practically feel his pupils dilate. He forgot all the words in all of his languages, dumbly nodding his assent. He didn't care what he was agreeing to. Whatever Ian was offering, he wanted it.

They collided. Lips and teeth clashed clumsily. Alek's thoughts came in shapes and sunbursts, flashes of color, flickers of mixed-together senses like a faulty ignition trying to start. He clenched his eyes tight and chased the images around a corner inside his mind, but his synesthesia slipped through his fingers.

Ian broke the kiss, breathing hard, his eyes scanning Alek's face.

Alek bit back the involuntary annoyance at the interruption. "I'm fine. I'll tell you if I'm not."

Ian nodded, his brow serious. "I trust you."

Not *I'm trusting you.* Not a warning to tell the truth, or else. No suspicion. Trust, given freely, that Alek hadn't earned and didn't deserve. The locked box around Alek's heart broke. He wrapped his arms around Ian's neck, pushed him back on his ass, and climbed into his lap. Alek's eyes slammed shut, his hips mindlessly undulating as he chased the pleasure that lit up his cock.

Ian's hands gripped Alek's ass, holding him in place. "Rest, love. Let me make you feel good."

Alek opened his eyes. "I'm not coming unless you are. Whatever you've got planned better include you too."

Ian grinned. "So demanding. Keep your eyes open and on me and I'll get off too."

Alek nodded. It would be hard to resist closing his eyes. Maybe the pictures in his brain would come back. What if he missed it? But he wanted Ian more than he wanted the stars and trees inside his head, more than music. He would trade all of it away if it meant he could have Ian forever.

"That's it. Eyes on me," Ian murmured against Alek's lips.

Alek wanted to look away. He felt like a door had opened and Ian could see every thought, every fear, every secret that he had tucked away, but he wanted to be good for Ian. He didn't want to let him down.

I love you, I love you, I love you, Alek said inside his brain, because it really felt in that moment like Ian had telepathy.

"I love you so much," Ian said, like he actually did.

Ian's hand forced its way in the tight space between them

and jerked them both, moving his hand up their combined lengths. A long moan wrenched free from Alek's mouth.

"Are you still okay?" Ian asked. His eyes were glossy, his mouth hanging open slightly.

"Yes. Don't stop." Alek tried and failed to thrust into Ian's hand.

Ian chuckled. "So impatient."

Alek wanted to kill him a little bit, but he wanted to come more. "Yes, I'm impatient. It's impossible to come without you."

Ian's hand stilled over their cocks. His eyebrows drew together. He said nothing, like he wanted Alek to fill in the gap with more details, which Alek was more than happy to do.

"I couldn't even get close without pretending we were still together. I need you."

Ian leaned in, touching his forehead to Alek's. "Kiss me and I'll let you come."

"Finally," Alek said breathlessly and then he did as he was told.

Alek poured every errant thought of adoration, every apology that went unsaid, every moment of gratitude, every debt that he owed into that kiss, and Ian's hand began to move. He jerked them both slowly, easing them to the edge of climaxing from the ground up all over again.

"Don't let your cast touch the water," Ian said, then moved both of his hands to their cocks, encircling them both.

All Alek could do was hold on and keep his eyes open as Ian thrusted upward, their dicks sliding together tight inside his hands. Warm pleasure tingled in Alek's stomach and the beginning sparks of ecstasy shot up the length of his cock. His balls tightened, his entire body trembled. When he came it was like an explosion. Scary and exhilarating. Ian came right along with him, dark eyes glazed with bliss, like twin windows into his soul, showing Alek every single corner of himself.

As Alek's orgasm receded, shadows edged into the borders of his vision. He was hot and cold at the same time. Sweat tickled the back of his neck. His mouth filled with saliva and his stomach clenched like a fist.

Ian's face went blurry, his expression turning grim. Alek shot up with a strength and speed he didn't know he had, and leaned over the edge of the tub, splattering vomit all over the floor. Blood roared in his ears and his head felt like it was going to explode, again.

Alek apologized between retches. What if Ian thought he'd lied about how he was feeling? The heat of the water had snuck up on him. By the time he realized he was nauseous, it was too late.

Ian rubbed circles over Alek's back as he emptied his stomach.

"It's okay, love. I'm so sorry. You're going to be okay. It's okay." Ian's voice shook so much his words were hardly reassuring.

When the retching finally stopped, it was replaced with violent, body-wracking shivers that made Alek's bones feel like they were grinding against each other. Distantly, Alek realized Ian had unplugged the tub and as the last of the water swirled down the drain, all of Alek's strength went with it.

Ian eased Alek onto his back. He looked stricken, a deep line of concern etched into his forehead.

"Are you okay?"

"Yes."

"You're telling the truth?" Ian pushed Alek's hair from his face.

"I haven't lied," Alek snapped. "The water was hot and I got light-headed. End of story."

Ian lifted his palms. "I believe you. I'm so sorry. I shouldn't have let this happen. "

"Please." Alek rolled his eyes. "Only you would apologize for giving me the best orgasm of my life. Can you help me out? I'm cold."

Ian hoisted Alek from the tub. At least Alek didn't swoon.

Alek shuffled back to their room with Ian trailing overbearingly close behind. By the time Alek got to the bed, another cold sweat wet his brow. With Ian's assistance, Alek lowered onto his back.

"Be right back." Ian disappeared into the bathroom, returning a few minutes later with mouthwash, a wet rag, and an empty glass.

Alek gargled and spat into the cup Ian held out, then cleaned his face with the rag, before turning on his side.

Ian climbed into bed and spooned Alek from behind.

"I shouldn't have let things get carried away." He pressed a kiss to the back of Alek's head.

Alek said nothing. He didn't trust his stomach enough to speak.

While Alek willed the world to stop spinning, Ian's chest vibrated against his back with deep, grumbling apologies and declarations of love that did little to soothe his fears. Ian could say what he wanted, but people were most honest when they were angry. In a moment of pure, uncontrolled rage, Ian said Alek was a burden. If Alek was a burden then, he was much heavier now.

23

ALEKSANDAR

BULGARIA. TWELVE YEARS OLD.

Aleksandar's parents remained abroad for the rest of the summer, leaving him alone with his grief and a locked box he still couldn't open.

First, he'd poured over his encyclopedia collection for any information even slightly related to locks and safe-cracking. And when they didn't work, he tried bludgeoning the safe with a hammer, but all that did was make a clanging so loud, he was shocked no one came to investigate.

One afternoon, Aleksandar's parents returned. He wasn't expecting them, but that was how they were. It was not an uncommon occurrence for him to go to sleep with two parents and wake with one or neither. The reverse was also true.

Aleksandar was sitting at the piano when his father entered the room. His father's black hair, slim build, and blue eyes were so much like his uncle's that for one fleeting second Aleksandar convinced himself that his uncle was still alive. There was no fire. It was all a nightmare that he hadn't realized he'd woken up from.

All too soon, his brain cruelly reminded him that his uncle had died. Aleksandar would never see him again. None of what happened was a nightmare. It was like witnessing his uncle's death all over again.

His mother dropped her bag by the door and went up to her room without sparing Aleksandar a glance or word. His father ruffled the hair on top of his head. Aleksandar did not flinch. Deception was survival. Now more than ever.

He looked at his father closely. His smile seemed as genuine and friendly as it usually did, but charisma was always his strong suit.

"How was your trip?" Aleksandar asked him.

"Exhausting." He gripped Aleksandar's shoulder. "Come eat with me. I brought cake."

Aleksandar nodded and subtly shifted out of his father's grasp. Those were the hands that murdered his uncle. He'd rather die than feel them on him again.

Honey cake was Aleksandar's favorite, but the shock of his father's return had spoiled his appetite. He could hardly think because the knocking of river rocks against each other was louder than thunder. He wanted to scream, if only to hear something else. But it would draw attention if he didn't eat, so he forced himself to take one bite. And then another. Even though the taste was so sickly sweet, he wasn't sure he'd ever be able to eat sugar again.

Between bites, Aleksandar answered his father's questions. How was his summer? Hot. What had he been up to? The piano mostly. Aleksandar asked none of his own questions, though he had many. Had he grieved his brother's death or was getting rid of him a tick in a box on his list? A line struck through his name? Was he relieved? Victorious? Conflicted? Did his father feel anything at all?

His mother did not join them. Aleksandar knew why. If he was honest with himself, he'd known for a very long time. He didn't care to learn whether his real father was his uncle or the brother who killed him. It wouldn't change anything. Whether his uncle was his father by blood or in spirit, Aleksandar's betrayal remained the same.

It was all very tacky and uninspired, though. A secret affair between brothers? Falling for his mother was a weakness he wished he'd never learned about his uncle. How foolish his uncle had been to trade his life for a woman as fickle and faithless as her.

Aleksandar finished his cake and pushed the plate to the side. His father set his fork down.

"I heard about the fire," his father said.

Aleksandar was surprised he acknowledged it, but a destroyed house *was* a lot more difficult to ignore than an uncle on an extended 'business trip'.

"And my uncle?" Aleksandar asked.

"What about him?" He wrinkled his brow, playing every bit the part of benign confusion.

Aleksandar didn't answer. He was curious to see if his father might fill the silence with his own interpretation of the question, but his father had been the one to teach him that trick and he appeared quite serene in the quiet tension that grew between them.

Aleksandar broke first. "Does my uncle know about his house?"

"I think you're too old to play pretend." His father ducked his head and smiled knowingly.

Underneath an impassive facade, Aleksandar's thoughts raced ahead of him. Did his father know what he saw? What would that mean? Was he in danger?

"I know you know your uncle is dead." He tilted his glass back and swallowed.

Aleksandar widened his eyes in faux surprise. "May I ask how he died?"

"I said stop pretending," his father growled.

The only other time he'd seen his father show anger was that day at the river.

Aleksandar said nothing. They weren't going to talk about this. Ideally, they'd never talk again.

Calmer now, his father poured a fresh glass and leaned against the fireplace mantle. He bowed his head, his gaze focused on the soft pile of ashes left behind in the hearth.

"Good night, Aleksandar," he finally said.

"Good night, *father*."

Aleksandar pressed his lips together to hide his pleasure. In a game of apathy, his father had lost, and Aleksandar had won.

———

ALEKSANDAR WOKE LATER that night to the sound of a door latching. He ran to the window and spotted his mother passing through the garden gate. Still in pajamas, he sneaked out of the house and followed the distant glow of her flashlight into the forest.

The ash-laden forest floor felt like hallowed ground as the charred husk of his uncle's house came into view. Judging by the stuttering light that illuminated the windows, his mother was already inside. Aleksandar crept around the outside of the house, tracking his mother's movement from room to room until she stopped at the room he knew best.

Aleksandar crouched beneath the window where the wisteria used to grow. It was the same window he'd looked out of when he learned to play the piano. He could almost hear the phantom notes.

Holding his breath, he peeked over the sill. His mother was like a ghost. Not a single hair was out of place, like she hadn't even put her head to the pillow. It was late summer, but she was shaking like snow was on the ground. She walked to the piano, looked under it, and circled the area several times. Her feet kicked up clouds of ash that Aleksandar could taste where he hid.

The flashlight flickered and dimmed. She banged it against her hand, but fumbled. It hit the ground with a heavy metal crash that echoed around the room and out the windows, shooting between the narrow spikes of burned tree skeletons that surrounded the house.

"Fuck," she whispered, looking to the window.

Aleksandar ducked. Had she seen him?

He carefully looked back over the window sill, half expecting her to be staring right at him. The fall must have fixed the flashlight. It now cast a beam across the floor from where it landed. He found his mother on the floor, raking her hands through the ash.

It was absurd. His mother was graceful. She bowed to no one. Yet here she was crawling through debris on her hands and knees.

Ash settled onto her hair, painting it gray like she'd aged before his eyes. She ran a shaking hand over her face, leaving a trail of smudged soot in its wake. Her clothes were ruined. How would she hide this from his father?

"No, no, no," she chanted in a near-silent hush as she sifted through the ash over and over again.

Aleksandar could have told her where the safe had gone, but she'd never told him anything. He couldn't trust her. He shifted his feet. A twig snapped.

His mother gasped and scrambled to the flashlight, turning it off. At first, Aleksandar thought she disappeared, but when his eyes adjusted to the darkness she was standing in the center of the room holding a pistol in her hand.

She looked at the gun like it was a friend, even as she shook so violently the metal rattled. In a motion so fast he could have blinked and missed it, she brought the gun to her temple and pulled the trigger.

A flash of light. Aleksandar leaped to his feet. Time slowed. His mother fell back. It was a pity no one was there to catch her. A fall like that could hurt her head.

When she landed, time sped back up and Aleksandar's ears exploded with ringing so loud it overrode all the music in his head.

His mother settled in the ash like it was dirty snow and she wanted to make an angel, but she wasn't the kind of mother who would ever make snow angels. Her chest was unmoving, which was a relief. Aleksandar had no idea what he would have done if that first shot hadn't stopped her heart and left her somewhere in between.

The air smelled of fire and spent gunpowder, but underneath it all there was an electric scent, like the second before lightning struck—metallic almost, like the ringing in his ears spun into molten sound. His mother was supposed to smell of honey and roses, not blood and broken hearts.

Aleksandar didn't know why she did it, though he knew enough to guess. What he did know for sure, was that now, more than ever, he needed to open that safe. Whatever was inside had been important enough that his mother would rather die than live without it.

24

IAN

Ian checked his watch again. Two thirty-five. Another hour of staring at the wall had passed while Alek snored lightly behind him. Earlier they'd swapped spoons and Alek fell asleep with his arms wrapped around Ian's waist.

Ian carefully slipped from Alek's clutches and sat at the edge of the bed. A glance over his shoulder confirmed that Alek was still asleep. It would be risky to leave him. What if he needed to use the restroom, or was sick again? What if he fell down the stairs trying to find him? What if he had another nightmare and Ian wasn't there to wake him?

But Ian was one more sleepless hour away from walking into the middle of the forest and screaming at the top of his lungs. He wrote a quick note for Alek, then unlocked both their phones. After checking the phones were on silent, Ian called Alek's phone, answered, then put his own phone on mute. He left them both on speaker as a makeshift baby monitor and slipped out of the room.

The Victorian was so quiet that Ian could hear the fibers of the rug squish beneath his feet. He stopped by his room and threw on jeans, a long-sleeved shirt, and a pair of socks, then descended the staircase, careful to avoid the squeakier steps.

A full moon illuminated his footsteps on his way to the garage. Wind rustled the ferns and icy dew drops dripped from branches overhead. Ian grabbed a machete and a pair of over-sized garden shears, double-checked the contents of his old canvas tool bag, then set off around the exterior of the house to the northern wing where the greenhouse was located.

Their room was in the southern wing, so there was little risk that Ian's work would disturb Alek. Still, Ian pulled out his phone and confirmed that the call hadn't ended. He turned the volume up and heard Alek's faint snoring.

The door to the greenhouse was made of wrought iron vines that tangled and wound their way around the edges before branching inward to frame a keyhole-shaped window. Ian pulled the door open with a rattling screech that made his hair stand on end.

The greenhouse was as overgrown as he'd last seen it. Thorny blackberry bushes strangled the trunks of cedar and redwood saplings. Big leaf maple elbowed in between. There wasn't so much a glass ceiling than a young forest canopy as most of the glass panels had been punched out by some of the more overzealous trees.

Maybe they'd be better off going scorched earth with it, but he didn't like using herbicides, especially when he lived in the middle of a forest, surrounded by native plants and animals. As with all things—home improvement and otherwise—the best way out was through.

Ian propped the door open with his tool bag. The glow of the moon and clear conditions made for enough light to work by, but he donned a headlamp just in case. Wearing a pair of rose-pruning gloves that went to the elbow, Ian attacked the blackberry first, ripping vines from the earth by the fistful.

Once he cleared what he could reach, he picked up the machete. He lifted it high overhead and sliced downward, felling the first sapling in his path with a satisfying thwack. After throwing the sapling behind him, Ian moved on to the next tree. Metal slashed through the air. Another satisfying crack. He cut down branch after branch and ripped whole plants out of the ground. In no time, the pile of brush outside the garden door had grown as tall and wide as he was, but he kept going.

Snapshots flashed in front of his eyes with each swing of the blade. Alek sick and shaking in the bathtub. Alek hitting the keyboard with his cast. Alek sliding a ring onto Ian's finger. Alek's face when Ian told him the worst thing he'd ever said for the second time. Alek playing the piano before the fall. Alek breaking Ian's heart night after night and then taking all of it back. Alek reaching out. Ian pulling away. Falling. Falling. Falling. A bloody halo around his head.

Fooling around with Alek earlier had left Ian raw and untethered. It wasn't that it wasn't good or that he didn't want it. Ian had come so hard he felt like he'd been wrenched inside out. What they did in that bathtub was the most honest form of sex they'd ever had. Alek had let himself be vulnerable. He was really trying. Ian hadn't realized how guarded his heart still was until Alek bared his own heart to him.

Ian had not prepared for, or even expected, the wave of post-nut clarity that knocked him over the head in the fleeting seconds between their shared climax and Alek throwing up. What was he thinking? Alek had a giant scab inside his brain and a cast on his arm. Ian's heart was still broken.

Ian meant what he said when he promised he would forgive Alek as long as he told the truth. Ian *did* forgive Alek. He understood Alek's motivations. Everything Alek did stemmed from love warped by abandonment issues into something toxic and painful.

But forgiveness wasn't the same as forgetting. Alek had humiliated him. Bullied him. Broken him. Forgetting that would take time.

Ian hacked at a tree trunk that really should have been chopped into firewood with a chainsaw. He swung the machete over and over again, his mind forgoing all thought and emotion. He lost track of time as he lifted the machete on each inhale and sliced it down through the air with each breath out. Finally, the teenaged maple tree broke in two and Ian dragged it out through the path he'd already made and heaved it onto the pile. He paused, breathing hard as he wiped the sweat from his forehead with the back of his hand.

A frog croaked, but it was otherwise silent. Ian checked his phone. Either the call had dropped or Alek had hung up. Ian didn't stop to collect his tools. He turned and hurried back to the house.

25

ALEK

lek woke in the dark feeling decidedly less morose. He reached out for Ian, but instead of Ian's warm, solid frame, a piece of paper crinkled beneath his hand. He switched on the bedside lamp.

Alek,

Couldn't sleep. Decided to start demoing the greenhouse. DON'T COME DOWNSTAIRS WITHOUT ME! Say my name and I'll come. I have you on speaker. Your phone's on the end table.

Love, Ian.

Middle of the night demoing? That wasn't a good sign. Alek unplugged his phone from the charger and disconnected the call. There was a text from Ian.

I mean it. Call me. I'll come right up.

Alek scooted to the edge of the bed and stood. When the fuzz cleared from his vision, he walked to the staircase, and with his good hand gripping the rail tightly, made his way to the first floor. At the bottom of the stairs, he paused only long enough to catch his breath, then marched into the parlor room before he could change his mind.

The piano was waiting.

He considered leaving without playing, but the only reason he came into the parlor was to get it over with. Prove to himself that even the magic of the Victorian's piano couldn't find the music he'd lost.

His footsteps echoed beneath his feet and when he sat on the bench and scooted in, the scrape of the legs against the wood floor struck him with deja-vu like a zap of static electricity. He was so close. It was right there. If he could just get the memory right, it would all come back.

After a cursory search on his phone, he found a how-to video series for the novice adult. It was insulting to start at the beginning all over again, but if he could learn, he could practice.

Alek knew he'd likely never be what he was before. He'd never be able to stitch together his emotions into musical notes he could write on a page and remember forever inside his head. He'd never be able to bottle up the moment when Ian proposed to him and pour it into the piano to spit out a song with a joy so contagious it was intoxicating.

But if he could learn the basics, maybe he could parrot back songs written out for him by someone that wasn't him, and it would be unsatisfying and boring and there'd be no color, no pictures, no connection between him and the piano and the memory of his uncle on the other end, but it would still be practice. He could keep his promise.

The production value of the Youtube video he selected was on par with 1970s amateur porn, and Walter, the how-to host, had a mustache Stalin would be proud of. About every thirty seconds, in between an exceedingly tedious abridged life story, Walter reminded his viewers to hit the subscribe button.

While Walter blathered on, Alek decided to try to play on his own. Maybe he wouldn't need Walter. He moved both hands to the piano. Pain shot up his broken arm while the sling kept it firmly in place. How many brain cells had the fall cost him?

He shook his head, rolled his shoulders, and readied his one good hand over the keys. He knew these keys. Before the fall he could have recognized them by touch. It was quiet and distorted and far away, but he thought he could remember what the keys would say when he touched them. He reached out and pressed one, but the sound it made wasn't the sound he was expecting. He tried another and another. None of them matched. It was like someone had shuffled them around while he was gone.

Alek's ears began to ring. He stared at the keys until his vision became unfocused and the black and white stripes blurred together.

"I'm sorry," he told the piano.

While Alek apologized to an inanimate object, Walter had reached the end of his introduction. First, he explained the visual landmarks to determine which notes corresponded to which keys.

"The black keys repeat in a pattern of two and three. Think chopsticks and forks," Walter said in a tinny, echoing voice. "Start with middle 'C'. It's the white key in front of the center-most chopsticks on the keyboard. 'C' for chopsticks. Is it starting to make sense?"

Alek wondered if Walter had a secret sex dungeon in a shack that he pretended was storage for his instruments. Meanwhile, Walter demonstrated the exercise. Starting with his pinky, then ring finger, and so on and so forth, he depressed the next five keys, one after the other.

Next, it was the viewer's turn to follow along with him. Alek's eyes shifted back and forth between the keys and the video while he tripped and stumbled over his fingers, until he finally caught up near the tail end of it. It was literally the simplest of exercises at the slowest speed, led by a video instructor, but he did it.

On the screen, Walter smiled wide. "Now give yourself a pat on the back." Walter paused, waiting for his viewers to do as he said.

Alek scowled. It was almost as sociopathic as when public speakers made crowds repeat back "good morning" until the response was suitably enthusiastic. He paused the video and tried again by himself. He was able to play. Agonizingly slow and imperfect, but he could remember and he could learn. So there was that.

He tried again, faster this time, but the rhythm slipped through his fingers and he lost his place and his head started to ache and the nausea came back. He clenched his eyes closed and considered slamming the fallboard shut just for the satisfaction, but it would be sacrilegious to treat his piano that way. Abusing the keyboard the hospital loaned him was one thing, but hurting his piano in a fit of rage? No. He'd find another outlet.

"You played."

Alek turned. Ian stood in the doorway. Sweat stained the neck of his shirt and a line of dirt smudged his forehead. When he stepped closer, Alek spied a stray leaf in his hair.

"How's the jungle?" Alek asked.

"Overwhelming." Ian sat down, straddling the bench, a stern look on his face. "I told you not to come down without me."

Alek turned to face him. "I don't like to be told what to do."

"That's debatable." Ian kissed Alek's forehead and pressed a single key on the piano. "Is it starting to come back?"

"No, but I think I'll be able to learn."

"Have you thought about lessons?"

"Absolutely not. I can learn much faster by myself than with a pedantic instructor fussing over my fingering technique."

"Fingering technique, huh?" Ian's lips pressed into a smile. "I bet you're a master at that."

"I think you know exactly how masterful my fingerwork is." Alek smiled back.

"If you're going to teach yourself, do you mind taking on another pupil?" Ian asked. "You only ever taught me when you wanted to sit on my lap, and we never got very far without getting distracted."

"That depends. Do I get to sit on your lap during our lessons?" Alek scooted closer to Ian and looked at him.

Ian answered by pulling Alek into his lap, then reached his arms around to rest his hands lightly on the keys. Alek would stay that way forever if he could; sandwiched between Ian and the piano with the warm rise and fall of Ian's chest against his back and the scent of sunbaked pine and cedar curling around him.

"Am I hurting you?" Ian asked.

"I'll let you know if you hurt me in a way that I don't want you to."

"Alek, I'm serious."

"So am I." Alek cued up the video and while Walter repeated his introduction, Alek turned to Ian. "You can be my right hand."

Alek had picked up many paramours in much the same way. "Sit on my lap and follow my fingers," he'd tell them. If it was a piano he didn't particularly care about he'd have the lover perch on top of the piano, legs spread so he could sneak his hand between their legs. But, this was better. It was like their minds and bodies had united and even though they were only playing the most banally pedestrian piano exercises, the fact that they were doing it together had turned it into music.

26

ALEK
ONE MONTH LATER

"What do you want for breakfast?" Wearing only boxers, Ian stood in the dim glow of the open refrigerator. His silhouette cast a long, angular shadow across the kitchen. "There's bacon, eggs, yogurt..." Glass containers rattled against each other as he rummaged around inside.

Alek had never been a morning person. The way that Ian could launch out of bed at five in the morning and start his day without lingering over several cups of coffee had never sat well with him, but now it was nearly insufferable.

"I'm really not hungry. If I could just have some espresso. I could make it myself..." If Ian would let him. Alek had been home for a month and Ian still wouldn't let him lift a finger. Suffocating, was what it was.

"You can't have coffee on an empty stomach." Ian closed the fridge door and crossed to the full-length double-door cabinet they used as a pantry. "There's still chocolate brioche here. You can have that and some strawberries first."

"You can fuck off and die if you get between me and caffeine" is what Alek would have said if he wasn't trying so hard to earn back Ian's affections.

Despite Alek's best attempts to corrupt Ian otherwise, Ian hadn't touched him below the belt since the bathtub incident. Ian said he shouldn't have lost control, that it was a mistake, that they should wait until Alek was feeling better, but Alek *was* feeling better. The fog of hangover-esque nausea and vertigo was improving. He'd even gotten rid of the sling, though the cast wouldn't come off for another month and he still wasn't allowed to play with both hands.

Ian's excuse wasn't enough to explain why he was keeping his hands to himself. Before the fall, Alek would have stopped at nothing to get the truth out of Ian, but now he was afraid of what Ian's answer might be.

Was Ian even still attracted to him? How could Ian be in the same room as him and not touch him? Alek still wasn't sure if Ian wanted to be with him or was staying out of guilt. Tracing his fingers over the heart on his cast helped. Swirling the vintage band around his ring finger did too. But not completely.

Alek needed to feel Ian's warmth, his heartbeat under his fingertips, the silky strands of his dark hair, the scratch of his beard. Alek didn't have music. There was no place to turn the feelings he couldn't face into something external and separate from himself. Sex was the only distraction he had and Ian was suddenly celibate.

Ian sliced the strawberries—totally unnecessary—while the bread toasted. After the toast ejected from the machine with an unsettling beep, Ian added it to the plate and placed it before Alek, along with a glass of milk.

Alek turned up his nose. "I don't understand this sudden emphasis on feeding me. Is this a new kink? Couldn't you feed me your cock instead?"

Ian dropped into the chair across from him and slathered

peanut butter onto his slice. "It's not a kink, though if that motivates you, I'll have to do some research." Ian took a large bite, before washing it down with a swig of milk he stole from Alek's glass. "I want you to start the day off with food in your stomach. It'll make me feel better when you spend the next eight hours at the piano."

Anger simmered in Alek's veins. Ian was smothering him. He pushed his plate away. "I'm not hungry."

Ian dropped his crust on the plate. "You're acting like a child."

"You're treating me like one!" Alek erupted from his seat.

In an infuriatingly even tone Ian said, "I didn't say anything when you cut back on sleep to spend more time at the piano, but I won't sit idly by if you start skipping meals too. What would Dr. Modorovic think?"

"Oh no!" Alek mocked as he backed toward the doorway. "Don't tell mom!"

"I'm worried about you."

"There's nothing to be worried about. If I wanted to kill myself there are much faster and more effective ways. Swallowing a lethal dose of opioids and washing it down with the barrel of a gun comes to mind."

Ian burst from the chair and corralled Alek against the wall. His dark eyes scanned him intensely. "Have you been thinking about hurting yourself?"

"It was a joke."

"Forgive me if I don't find casual jokes about your suicide very funny."

"Fuck this." Alek slipped under Ian's arm and marched back to the table, ripped the slice of bread off his plate, and shoved the entire thing in his mouth. He chewed and chewed and chewed, his stomach gurgling ominously until he could finally swallow, then grabbed the glass of milk and drank without pausing, even as milk dripped down his chin and onto his shirt. He pushed aside the impulse to vomit out of pure spite and slammed the empty glass on the table so hard he was disappointed it didn't break. The sting of broken glass against his palm would have taken the edge off.

Alek turned on his heel. "I'll be in the parlor. You can bring me my coffee there."

By the time Alek sat down at the piano his anger had ebbed. Ian was only trying to help. He was a fixer.

Alek flared his hand over the shiny lacquered wood of the piano. His reflection stared back at him with darkened hollows beneath his eyes. Maybe Ian had a point.

With the help of a half-dozen apps and even more books, Alek had relearned sight reading sheet music and mastered most beginner-level songs with his left hand, but it wasn't enough. He couldn't stop until everything came back.

Orange flashed in his peripheral vision. He looked out the window to the forest line and spotted the source of the color. A fox paced back and forth along the sword ferns, its tail floating behind like a wind sock. She, he decided, was a touch too thin and stepped lightly on her front paw, not quite limping, but favoring it. Maybe she was injured? It wasn't common to see a fox during the day, or at all. What if she was rabid? He squinted, straining to see more details, but she was too far away.

"Alek?" Ian dropped his hand on Alek's shoulder.

Alek started. "You snuck up on me." He pulled Ian's hand from his shoulder and held it against his cheek. "I'm sorry for what I said before I had coffee. After thinking it over, I'm willing to take snack breaks more often and get to bed earlier as long as you make an effort to stop annoying the ever-living fuck out of me with your incessant nagging."

Instead of laughing, Ian flashed a tense smile that didn't reach his eyes and moved his hand to Alek's forehead. "Are you

feeling okay? I said your name twice. I have your coffee here."
He pointed to the mug, nested atop a coaster on the bench.

Alek thanked him and lifted the cup to his lips. He closed his
eyes and inhaled through his nose. He could almost see the rich
scent in the steam rising from the cup, imagine how it would hit
the back of his nose and slingshot through his nervous system
until it hit the olfactory center in his brain. He was trying to lean
into what was left of his synesthesia, embracing the way scent
and taste still seemed to tangle with color and images. He had
no evidence, just an instinct that maybe if he worked out that
muscle the only way he could, the other parts might get stronger
too.

"What were you looking at?" Ian asked, settling onto the
bench beside him.

Alek scooted over. "Have you seen a fox?"

Ian frowned. "No."

They both looked out the window, but the fox had
disappeared.

"I saw her the night before the fall, and again now. I think
she's hurt. Maybe we can get her cat food."

"Her?"

"It's just a feeling."

Ian's eyes turned tender. "Don't go naming her. She could be
sick."

"I know, but maybe she's not. Maybe she's injured."

"I'll call animal control today. They'll help her if they can
find her." Ian squeezed Alek's thigh, sending sparks of desire up
his spine. "What are we learning today?"

"Let's practice major scales and then we can try that blasted
Yankee Doodle again."

Teaching Ian was the only thing Alek looked forward to. It
was like he was putting a part of himself inside of Ian that would
stay there forever.

All the history between them faded into the background, the echoing arguments, the look on Ian's face each time Alek betrayed him, the sharp words that shouldn't have been said. The electric charge of tension—sexual and otherwise—was replaced with light flirtation and Ian's honest effort to learn what Alek taught him. The pleased look in Ian's eyes when Alek praised him for a job well done almost made up for how frustrating it was to teach someone with enormous hands and no musical talent.

By the end of the lesson, Alek's vision blurred from staring at the sheet music and his good hand throbbed. The idea of making it upstairs to take a nap was out of the question.

"Do you feel like getting some fresh air?" Ian asked.

"Not particularly."

Ian kept pestering Alek about spending time in sunlight each day like he was a plant. Ian had read that the vitamin D in sunlight could help ward off depression, which was apparently more common after a head injury. Alek wasn't depressed. He was simply reacting to the situation he found himself in. Anyone would be melancholy in similar circumstances.

"Come on." Ian pulled him to standing. "I want to work on the greenhouse."

Ian working on the greenhouse meant Ian sans shirt, sweat glistening, muscles rippling, sounds that bore a striking resemblance to Ian during sex. "You should have led with that."

27

IAN

Sunshine filtered through the treetops, scattering shadows and beams of light. Ian carried a rolled up blanket under his arm and held Alek's hand as they walked around the perimeter of the house. It usually took about five minutes at Alek's pace, maybe longer today, if the drawn look on his face was any indication.

When Alek was discharged from the hospital, Ian had kept Alek in bed or bubble wrap, until he learned that exercise could improve memory loss and recovery after brain injury.

Ian kicked aside a small branch that blocked their path. "Can I ask you today's questions?"

"You may."

"How did you end up here?" Ian gestured around them.

"Because of you, remember?"

"You know that's not what I'm asking."

"I came for school and decided to stay," Alek said crossly. "Next question."

Ian stopped in his tracks, inadvertently yanking Alek to a halt. "Sorry." He patted a nearby tree stump.

Alek raised a single eyebrow, but sat on the stump as directed. Sunlight reflected off of his inky black hair, some stray strands lifting up with the gentle wind that shook the branches above them to expose the nearly healed surgical incision where the hair hadn't yet filled in.

"I'm sitting because I'm tired, not because you summoned me like a pet."

Ian squatted until he was just below Alek's eye level. "You have to start giving me more."

"I said more than yes or no." Alek lifted his head and looked away.

Ian gripped Alek's chin and forced him to return his gaze. "You're not playing by the rules."

"Those literally are the rules." Alek turned his head, pulling his chin from Ian's hand.

Ian scrubbed a hand over his face. "I'm trying to build trust here, Alek. That's the whole point of this. Haven't I held true to my word? I've listened to weeks of answers and I'm still here. Give me more. Please."

Alek traced his fingertips over the heart on his cast, then clenched his hand in a fist. "It was customary in my family's social circle to send their children to college overseas. I chose America, but not because I was interested in the finance program I was accepted into. America was big. I could easily disappear."

Ian frowned. "Why would you—"

"The life I would have had back home wasn't what I wanted," Alek explained with a flick of his hand. "While I attended classes, I invested the money my uncle left for me and established my furniture restoration business. Multiplying my inheritance wasn't difficult. I'd learned enough by being my father's son. And obtaining a new identity was child's play. Back then you could throw a dart on a map and land on a former USSR territory with dubious government documentation. I flew to a country that no longer exists and Alek Katin was born." Alek lifted his eyes to Ian's. "It was too easy. I think my father knew. I think he let me go. It settled his debts."

"Did you ever see your dad again?"

Alek shook his head, hopped down from the stump, and started off down the path.

"In my family, we did not apologize," Alek continued when Ian joined him. "I was raised to be above remorse, that every decision I made was calculated. An admission of regret was an admission of guilt. Guilt wasn't allowed either."

They rounded the side of the Victorian and the greenhouse appeared before them.

"One afternoon there was a knock at my door. A courier held out a cardboard box. It had no postage. I wasn't expecting any local deliveries. My father was the only person I knew who would pay someone to chaperone a parcel across ocean and land. He had no way of knowing my address, but he always knew everything."

Alek stopped in front of the door to the greenhouse and turned to face him.

"Inside the box was a hammered gold olive branch crown from the fifth century. The gold leaves were as thin and delicate as if they'd been plucked from a tree. In handwriting I could never forget, my father wrote '*Sazhalyavam*'. *I'm sorry*. It took me two days to work up the courage to call him. When I did, I learned he'd died the night before." Alek shook his head and looked over Ian's shoulder to the forest surrounding them.

They were standing so close Ian could count each band of jade that made up Alek's irises.

"I don't know that I ever thought of my dad as mortal until

that moment. He was an invincible foe. Too powerful to die, let alone from something as boring as cancer."

"And the crown... did you keep it?"

"Of course. It's a priceless artifact from ancient Macedonia. History I could hold in my hands. I'm not that petty." Alek pushed his hair away from his face and flashed a smile before snatching it back. "It was tangible proof that my father was monster *and* man, and if he, of all people, could be both, then maybe I could be both too."

"You're not a monster, Alek."

Alek turned to face the greenhouse and looked through the keyhole window. "I know you've been toiling away in there, but I have a sneaking suspicion that the blackberry grows back while we sleep."

Ian drew nearer until he could look over Alek's shoulder. He had a point. The blackberry looked no less daunting than the day before despite the small mountain of torn-up vines outside the door.

Ian pressed a single kiss to the pulse on Alek's neck, leaving his lips there as he said, "All this time I thought the wisteria would tear the house down when it's the blackberry that will devour us whole."

"Death by a thousand thorns." Alek's voice was a nearly inaudible rasp. "I've always wanted a poetic death."

Careful to hold the bulk of his weight back, Ian leaned closer until he'd pinned Alek against the door. He nuzzled his face into the hair at the nape of Alek's neck. In the span of a single breath, Ian imagined ripping Alek's pants down and prepping his ass only long enough to be sure he wouldn't hurt him before pounding him hard enough that the iron door left a mirror imprint of bruises on his skin, but he wouldn't do that. Not until Alek was medically cleared, not until he was acting more like himself, and not until Ian was ready. He stepped back and readjusted his dick in his pants before he started thinking with it.

Alek growled in frustration. "You are such a tease." He tore the blanket out from under Ian's arm and stalked to a shady spot beneath an alder tree. He snapped the blanket violently, lowered it to the ground, and threw himself down on top of it. "I really thought I had you with the door."

Ian paused in the middle of taking off his shirt. "What?"

"The door," Alek was on his back with his hand behind his head. "You have a thing for door sex."

"I don't have a thing for door se—"

"My apartment, the Victorian, your truck—"

"I don't think a car door counts."

"The theater, the building permit office staff restroom... Shall I go on?"

"That last one was your idea." Ian finished pulling off his shirt and threw it at him.

Alek snatched it from the air and covered the top half of his face with it. "Don't wake me unless you find a door you actually want to have sex against."

Ian picked up his machete. He normally used the chainsaw during daytime hours, but Alek really did need his sleep. "Sweet dreams, Alek."

"Wet dreams, if I'm lucky," Alek grumbled.

Ian put the machete back down. He still hadn't come clean to Alek about the real reason behind his hesitancy to move things past kissing and heavy petting. Given the conditions of their proposal, Ian felt more than a little guilty, but Alek's mental state was so fragile and only getting worse. If Ian confessed that he didn't want to have sex because he still wasn't over what Alek had done, Alek would catastrophize.

But Alek was smart. He suspected something. They were locked in a stalemate where neither one of them wanted to talk about it. Maybe Ian's avoidance was making things worse. He should rip the bandaid off and see where things went from there. It's not like he didn't want to have sex on a physical level. It was his head that was the problem.

Alek had given Ian his honesty. Ian knew how difficult that must have been for him. Ian could at least try to be vulnerable too.

Careful to step lightly, Ian padded over to Alek's side and sank to his knees. He laid his head on Alek's stomach.

Alek pulled the shirt from his face and looked down. "Can I help you?"

Ian lifted his head and shook it, then pushed the hem of Alek's shirt up and tugged his sweatpants down low enough to kiss below his belly button.

Alek's eyes darkened. "I won't tolerate any more teasing."

"I'm not teasing. Promise."

With fingers that trembled, not with fear, but anticipation, Ian pulled Alek's sweatpants off and tossed them aside. Alek's dick pointed in an arrow over his abs where his shirt had shifted up. He was perfect.

"Turn over to your stomach," Ian said and helped Alek into position, making sure his casted arm didn't get trapped underneath him.

Ian straddled Alek and planted kisses down his spine, then sucked a hickey over each of the twin dimples on his lower back. He rubbed his thumb over one of the marks.

Before they broke up, Alek would demand Ian leave bite marks, hickeys, and bruises on his skin. "I want something to remember you by," Alek would say, like he needed visual proof that Ian had been there.

Alek looked over his shoulder with eyes glazed by lust. Moving lower, Ian gripped Alek's hips, dropped his mouth to Alek's tailbone, and kissed.

"Please," Alek said. "I need more."

Ian's mind went blank as he melted into ardent compliance. He kneeled behind Alek and parted his cheeks with his thumbs, then licked a long path from the base of his balls to his entrance. Ordinarily, Ian would take his time teasing, but that was the last thing Alek needed, so he traced just one circle around Alek's rim, then hardened his tongue and pushed it inside.

"Oh, fuck," Alek said, his body sagging into Ian's hands.

Ian hummed lowly and fucked his tongue into Alek with debauched enthusiasm. Without even meaning to, Ian found himself thrusting against thin air as he devoured him.

It was only when Alek started begging in an accent so thick, Ian wasn't even sure it was English, that he realized he was probably tormenting Alek with only a tongue in his ass and no way to reach his dick. Ian lifted his head, drawing out a mewl of protest from Alek that turned into a gasp of anticipation when Ian spat into his hand.

Ian hooked his arm under Alek's stomach and jerked him onto his knees just enough to take his dick in hand. Now Ian was certain Alek wasn't speaking English. A steady litany of unintelligible words mixed with *Ebasi* F-bombs spilled from his lips.

"Alek, you're not speaking English," Ian gently reminded.

"Take it as a compliment," Alek gasped in English.

"Or a challenge. Let's see if I can do it again." Ian slicked up his fingers with spit and rubbed the outside of Alek's hole.

Alek stilled.

"No words?" Ian teased. "I'll take that as a compliment too."

He pushed a single finger inside. Alek's prostate was swollen in arousal and Ian massaged it softly.

Alek groaned, his entire body tightening around Ian's finger.

Ian groaned too as a fresh gush of precome wet the inside of his pants where his dick already strained painfully against the zipper.

"Fuck, fuck, fuck," Alek gasped in cadence with Ian's hand up and down his cock.

Ian spat onto the spot where his finger disappeared inside and added a second finger. He was watching Alek so closely for any sign of pain that he saw Alek's orgasm coming before it hit him.

"Come now, love," Ian said. "Make my dick jealous of my fingers."

Ian tightened his grip on Alek's cock and focused his fingers on his prostate. Alek exploded with a guttural moan and a spurt of come over Ian's fist.

That one sound of ecstasy was like a record scratching. Night after night of listening to Alek fuck through the walls came roaring back with a stab of betrayal. *It wasn't real*, he reminded himself, but it was no use. His dick instantly deflated. It was like a switch had turned off and Ian wanted to get as far away from Alek as he could, but he couldn't do that either.

Alek collapsed onto the ground. The bones in his back rose and fell beneath his sweat-slicked skin like the flapping wings of a fledgling bird. His dark eyelashes smashed together against the apples of his cheeks. It had been a long time since Ian had left Alek in a sex-sated heap.

Ian cleaned them both up and dressed, then joined Alek, who hadn't moved from his position, flat on his stomach with his limbs sprawled wide like a ragdoll thrown on the ground.

"You okay?" Ian cleared his throat. He hoped Alek hadn't noticed the way his voice shook.

With his eyes still closed, Alek answered, "I think I'm still coming."

Even as shaken as he was, Ian grinned. "You're not still coming."

"Shh." Alek rolled to his side and pulled Ian into his arms.

Shade shielded their bodies and the wind whispered softly

through the treetops. Finches called as they flitted between trees. Alek's breathing was deep and even, already asleep behind him. The moment should have been peaceful, but all Ian felt was trapped. He wouldn't risk waking Alek, though. Alek had only slept ten hours in the last three days.

Ian was a firm believer that as long as he worked hard, he could have whatever he wanted. That was the American Dream. It was what was fair. If he put in the time and effort, things should work out. But life wasn't fair and maybe he was banging his head against a brick wall that he'd never be able to climb over or break through.

———

IAN WOKE to Alek straddling him. The sky had turned light gray and the wind that gusted around them was spiked with an icy chill. Ian hadn't meant to fall asleep. He must have succumbed out of pure exhaustion.

Alek leaned forward. A lock of hair hung down over his brow and his eyes smoldered with mischief.

"What's up?" Ian yawned as he tried to clear the haze of sleep from his thoughts.

"You've been taking such good care of me." Alek rained kisses down Ian's neck and nipped over his collarbone. "I think it's time I return the favor."

Ian tensed. "There's no favor for you to return."

Alek sat up and narrowed his eyes. "Why does it feel like I'm trying to convince you to let me blow you?"

"I'm sorry. It's not you, it's—"

"If you're about to say what I think you are, you'd better choose a more original statement."

"Sorry. I'm just..." Ian cringed. "I thought I was ready for this."

"I don't understand. You were happy to tongue-fuck my ass but you draw the line at reciprocal blow jobs?"

"I thought I was over the things you put me through—I forgive you, but I can still remember my heart breaking."

Alek's brows darted together. "But none of it was real."

"It was real to me," Ian said with more anger than he'd intended. He took a deep breath and in a controlled voice continued, "You spent weeks torturing me. It's messing with my head."

"You let me think my head injury was the problem. I knew something was going on with you." Alek shook his head in disgust. "You should have told me. Here I am telling you things I don't even let myself think about, and you can't tell me this? I would have backed off. I don't want you to do anything you don't want to do." Alek pressed his fingertips to his temple. "I cannot believe I have to say this, but keep your hands off of me until you're touching me because you want to. Don't do me any favors. Don't pay me back for my honesty with sex you're not even into. If the only reason you touched me was to reward me for answering your question or to put me out of my misery, then I'd rather you not touch me at all."

"That's not what—" But that was exactly what Ian had been doing, wasn't it? "I'm so sorry." He tried to wrap Alek back up against him but Alek pinned him down with a hand to his shoulder.

"You expect me to tell the truth, but you're lying to yourself," Alek said. "You think you want me, but you don't. You think I'm worth loving, but I'm not. You say you'll never leave, but you will."

"I won't," Ian insisted.

"And that's the biggest lie of them all." He climbed off of Ian and rose to his feet.

"Alek, wait." Ian moved to follow.

"No. It's my turn to leave in the middle of an argument." Alek pulled on his pants. "I'm going to practice. Do not follow."

"Please stay. Let me explain. I don't want you to go."

"Now you know how it feels." Alek turned and disappeared down the path.

28

ALEK

Leaving Ian behind in a fit of rage wasn't exactly as satisfying as Alek thought it would be. He was already tired from their earlier escapades and couldn't exactly tromp back around the house.

When he did finally reach the front porch, he heaved himself up the steps and slammed the front door with all the force he could muster. Dust rained down from the top edge of the door frame and a crystal soap dish they used to store loose change fell from a shelf and shattered.

Heading for the piano had been an automatic reaction, but practicing wasn't playing. There would be no magical transference of emotions into sound. Coping with music was a lifelong habit that he would have to break.

He set off towards his old room. He rifled through his top drawer past lube and lighters, rolling papers, crumpled receipts, bags of weed, and unused prescription pills before finally finding the silver cigarette case and satchel of loose tobacco he was looking for. He hadn't smoked a single cigarette, hand-rolled or otherwise, since the fall. At first because he wasn't allowed and then because he couldn't be bothered, but he needed something to do with his hands or he was going to pull his hair out.

Contrary to what the niche habit implied, Alek was not a monocle-wearing, unicycle-riding hipster. He'd only started smoking hand-rolled cigarettes because it was what his uncle smoked. The rich wafting scent helped him remember the sound of his uncle's voice, that he'd ever even existed. He pocketed the case and left the room without closing the drawer.

Alek hadn't been to the third-story turret since he fell from it. Maybe if he had a chance to see the horizon, the sky without trees obscuring his view, he would feel better. Or better yet, maybe he could go back to when he felt nothing at all.

The iron spiral staircase creaked under his weight as he gripped the cool rail and climbed upward. Each step swayed and Alek wasn't certain if it was the stairs that had him so unmoored or his vertigo. At the top, he twisted the doorknob and leaned into the door—it was locked. He should have seen that coming.

No matter. Reenacting the ax scene from *The Shining* would be cathartic. Anger gave him a second wind. He stomped back down to the first floor without pausing, slammed the front door as hard as he could, again, and went into the garage. He ripped the ax off the wall—and nearly dropped it. It was much heavier than he remembered.

Fuck the fall and fuck Ian too. Oh wait, no he couldn't fuck Ian because Ian didn't fucking want to. The weeks of rejected advances stung sharper now that Alek understood exactly how unwanted said advances were. All those occasions he had joked and teased and attempted to coax Ian towards any kind of physical intimacy made him cringe with shame in retrospect.

Alek might have been a very bad person who'd done very bad things, but he'd always been wanted, at least in that one way. Nearly always only in that one way.

Ian should have told the truth. The tenuous strand of trust that had started to grow between them was already broken. Being vulnerable had been a mistake.

Alek lugged the ax out of the garage and up the front steps. Black spots crowded the edges of his vision. He dropped the ax on the floor with a clatter and sat down on the top step, putting his head between his legs.

"Alek?"

His eyes snapped open. Ian kneeled in front of him. One hand hovered above Alek's knee, like his first impulse had been to touch him but he decided against it at the last minute.

"Were you asleep?" Ian asked.

Alek bristled. "Of course not. I was merely taking a break on my way to go hack a hole in the turret door because some prick locked me out of it."

Ian's eyes narrowed on the ax. His jaw sharpened. He took a deep breath. "I locked the door to keep you safe. I'd prefer if we pretended that part of the house doesn't exist, but I assume that's out of the question?"

Alek answered with a glare.

"I figured. I thought we could convert the tower rooftop into a balcony. Weatherproofing a trapdoor is going to be tricky, and you'll have to be careful on the stepladder, but I think we can make it work."

Alek wanted to tell Ian how much it turned him on when he made thoughtful construction gestures, but the sexual banter that came as natural as breathing was no longer appropriate. He gnashed his teeth together.

"What if I took you to the clearing?" Ian suggested. "You could see the sky there. Would that make you feel better?"

Alek shook his head. The clearing smelled like cinders and sorrow now that there was so much brush from the greenhouse to burn.

"Can I sit down?" Ian asked.

"If you must."

After sitting, Ian leaned his head on Alek's shoulder.

Alek shrugged out from under Ian's head and scooted over until he was crammed against the stair rail and they were no longer touching. It was petulant and childish, but he didn't care.

"Alek..."

"Don't *Alek* me. You said you didn't want me. I'm only doing as you asked."

"I never said I didn't want you. I said I wasn't ready." Ian pinched the bridge of his nose like Alek was giving him a migraine, which was patently unfair. Surely only Alek had earned the right to be exasperated in this situation. "This is why I didn't want to tell you. I was worried you'd take it the wrong way."

"What way am I supposed to take it?"

Ian stood and dropped in front of Alek a few steps below. He opened Alek's knees like a book and rested his cheek on Alek's thigh.

"Let me be very clear," Ian said in a gravelly murmur. "I want to touch you." He spread his left hand wide and dragged it up the inside of Alek's thigh. "I want to have sex with you." He squeezed the growing erection Alek had been trying to ignore. "I am still attracted to you." He removed his hand and lifted his head. "What's going on with me has nothing to do with my desire for you, or my love for you. I haven't done anything I haven't wanted to. That's always been the case and that will never change. Understand?"

"Understand? Yes. Convinced? No."

Ian rose up on his knees and forced Alek's good hand to palm the enthusiastic hard-on that tented his pants.

"Earlier today, I wanted it. I knew I wasn't ready, but—" Ian released Alek's hand. "I don't trust myself anymore. I second-guess everything."

As long as Alek knew Ian, he'd been decisive, self-assured, confident. Alek had made Ian question himself. He changed a core part of Ian's personality for the worse.

"I second-guess everything except choosing you," Ian amended as if he'd mistaken the reason behind Alek's sudden despondency. "The two times we've been together since we broke up have been perfect, but then I get these flashes of the nights I thought you were sleeping with somebody else." Ian's Adam's apple bobbed. "In those moments when I'm spiraling, I can't help but think what is wrong with me? I want to have sex with you after everything you've done to hurt me. What does that make me?"

Alek bit the inside of his cheek to avoid answering, "Horny?" Instead he said, "The only respect that matters is the respect you have for yourself. It doesn't make you weak to take me back. I can tell you exactly what kind of man that makes you. Someone who forgives. Someone who is so much more than I deserve."

"Alek..."

"I won't make any excuses. What's done is done," Alek spoke over him. "But I never, ever thought you would let me bring another person into our home. When you did, I couldn't think beyond how badly that hurt. That you could let me go without a fight. I didn't know what to do. I didn't have a plan B. I should have known you'd be stubborn.

"It was a stupid ultimatum. I could have ended it before it began but I was stubborn too. I hate myself for what I did. For causing you a moment of pain. I hope you know how much I suffered alongside you. How much I didn't want to do what I did. I'm so sorry. The things I've done to you are unforgivable."

"Not unforgivable to me." Ian kissed the back of Alek's hand. "I know you only did what you did because you love me. It's not your fault that no one taught you what love is supposed to feel like."

"I stand by what I said. You are more than I deserve."

"Agree to disagree." Ian's face sobered. "I still have one more question to ask you."

"Let's hear it, then." Alek braced for yet another vexing question.

Ian looked up with earnest eyes. "How can I make this right?"

Alek scoffed. "How should I know? Sex was the only thing that always came easy for us."

"I wasn't talking about sex. I lied to you..."

Alek picked at the cotton fluff on the inside of his cast. "If I recall correctly, your rules said that if one of us lies, our relationship is over."

"No. Alek, I don't want that. Wait. Is that what you want?"

"Hardly, but what I want isn't always what's best." Alek looked over Ian's head. He felt like someone was watching them. Maybe the fox was lurking unseen. He forced his eyes back to Ian. "I don't think I make you very happy." He twirled the vintage band wrapped around his finger. "If I was out of the picture, you could find someone who doesn't break things."

Alek's heart thrashed in his chest like a bird beating its wings against a too-tight cage. He meant what he said, but he was terrified of what would come next. What if Ian agreed? Would he want him to leave straight away? What if Alek wasn't ready to say goodbye yet?

"Look at me." Ian tilted Alek's chin up. His voice was gentle, but his face was furious. "We're not doing that. I don't want you to ever suggest something like that again."

Alek let out the breath he'd been holding, but instead of relief, he felt like a coward. Instead of hope, he was filled with self-loathing.

"I get to decide what's good for me, not you," Ian said. "You think you don't make me happy, Alek, but you do. You're the only person who makes me laugh. You're my best friend. I want to know every thought inside your head just so I can have more of you. Yeah, there've been some dark times, but that was three weeks. Three weeks out of three of the happiest years of my life. So don't misunderstand me. You may have hurt me, but when it comes to you, I'd take nothing back. Now tell me you won't leave."

"Fine." Alek crossed his arms. "I won't leave." *Yet*, he added silently.

Ian moved to hug Alek so fast he flinched.

"I know we can still fix this." The timbre of Ian's deep voice rumbled against Alek's chest. "I know it seems like it's too much, like we'll never be able to move past this, but we can. We will. I'll be patient with you. Please be patient with me."

Alek wanted to believe Ian, but he wouldn't allow hope to make a fool of him again.

"I feel like I'm hugging a rock." Ian pulled back but kept his hands on Alek's knees.

"What's allowed and what's not?" Alek eyed Ian's hands. "You're touching me now, but is it because you want to or because you feel obligated to?"

"Nothing's not allowed. If I do something, it's because I want to do it. But if I tell you to stop, do what you did today. Listen to me and stop."

That was a lot to ask. There was only so much threat of rejection Alek could tolerate.

"I think we should take sex and other such spelunking off the table. Consider us queer fiancés that are saving themselves for marriage." He cackled mirthlessly and grabbed a hold of the rail to pull himself up.

Ian followed. "You still didn't answer my question. How can I fix this?"

Alek opened the front door, and nudged aside the shards of broken glass and scattered coins with the tip of his shoe, ignoring Ian's questioning look.

"Some things are too broken to be fixed," Alek said. "We'll have to wait and see if this is one of them."

29

ALEK

ONE WEEK LATER

D r. Modorovic's office was in a red brick building that faced the harbor. The waiting room was empty. Ian pulled a paperback out of his back pocket and plopped down into a loveseat. Alek leaned against the wall.

"Come sit with me." Ian patted the space beside him.

"I'd rather not. We don't know what that couch has seen. Countless brain-addled patients in various states of incontinence, I assume. No. I'll stand right here."

"It's perfectly clean."

Alek ignored him.

The tension between them—sexual, and otherwise—was tangible. Each night, Alek respected the new imaginary line between Ian's side of the bed and his. Ian started the night off with similar intentions, but always migrated closer and closer to Alek while he was sleeping. Meanwhile, Alek ended up scrunched at the very edge of the bed, wide awake until he conceded defeat to insomnia and went to play the piano. Sometimes he fell asleep on the couch after. Most of the time he kept playing until Ian came down in the morning.

Despite Ian's reservations about sex, he was unceasing in his efforts to rekindle their physical intimacy. Ian reached out for Alek's hand when they were walking side by side. He sidled up next to him at the piano bench.

Alek had to watch his back when they were in the kitchen. Ian had *accidentally* pinned him against the counter in an effort to reach an object on a high shelf on more than one occasion. Alek hadn't rebuffed Ian's affections, but he hadn't initiated either, and he wouldn't.

Not until Ian was sure that he was ready.

Dr. Modorovic strode through the door in a white coat that drowned her petite frame. "Alek Katin!" Her dark eyes sparkled with fondness as she took his hand in both of hers.

Alek was surprised by the shadow of delight that bloomed in his chest upon seeing her. Maybe they could go for brunch after he recovered completely. Was that allowed?

She nodded at Ian. "Will you be joining us?"

"Yes, ma'am." Ian pocketed his book and followed.

She ushered them through the door, down a hallway of empty exam rooms, and into her office.

"Is business slow?" Alek asked as he lowered into a leather armchair across from an oversized live edge desk. Ian joined him in the other chair armchair.

"Today's one of my paperwork days," she explained, sitting behind the desk. "I thought it best if we didn't have to rush."

She flipped open a chart.

"Your CT scan results were excellent. Most of the blood in your brain has been reabsorbed and the contusion is healing. How have your symptoms been?"

"Abating. Some nausea, rare vertigo. Occasional headaches, but nothing I can't handle."

"That's to be expected, but definitely call if your symptoms worsen or increase in frequency." Her shrewd eyes focused on him. "How about your synesthesia and musical abilities?"

"I haven't noticed any improvement."

He leaned forward and lifted a framed photo of a sour-looking dark gray cat from the desk. Wolfie, he presumed. He exchanged the frame for another; this one of a much younger Jana in a floral dress, perched sideways on the lap of a handsome man in a wheelchair. She'd smiled at the camera, but the man had not—his eyes were reverent and on her. She didn't comment as he put the frame back.

"And you've been doing the scent therapy?"

"Twice a day. Exactly as instructed." More than twice a day, in all honesty.

"Any other symptoms? Mood changes?"

"No." Alek scanned the floor-to-ceiling bookshelf. There were rows of thick medical tomes, anatomical encyclopedias, leaning stacks of glossy scientific journals, scattered plastic brains in varying levels of dissection.

"I'm not going to waste any more of our time," she said.

Alek jerked his attention back to her.

"I've been in contact with Ian. He's worried about you. *I'm* worried about you."

What the fuck?

Everything was lies. As far as Alek was concerned, the deal was off. Ian couldn't expect him to be honest when all he ever did was lie.

Alek clenched his good hand around the arm of his chair and kept his eyes on the doctor even as he felt Ian's burning gaze like flames.

"I'm sorry. Is this some sort of medical coup?" Alek strived for amused, but sounded cold and sneering instead.

"Think of it as an intervention," the doctor said, steepling her fingertips. "Ian, would you like to speak first?"

Alek held up his palm. "If Ian wanted to talk, he wouldn't have recruited you to do his dirty work."

"The suggestion to approach you together was mine," she said.

Ian said, "Alek, I'm sorry—"

"Dr. Modorovic, what exactly is your medical concern?"

She unfolded her hands and raised a finger to tick off each of Alek's supposed maladies. "Irritability. Insomnia. You've been withdrawn. Difficult to arouse—"

Alek scoffed. "I don't see what that has to do with anything."

"I apologize. It means that it's been difficult to get your attention. Bouts of mania—"

"Mania? I wish."

"Ian mentioned you've purchased fifteen different wisteria cuttings over the internet—spent hundreds of dollars on them..."

Alek's stomach tightened with betrayal. Ian might have sighed as he lifted each cutting from atop the piano lid when he dusted, but he hadn't given any indication that he disapproved.

"I'm trying to get my music back," he told the doctor. "Our wisteria is a stump, but it's blooming in other climates." He brought his hand to his chin and pushed his lips into a thoughtful pout. "Sidebar: you know what's manic? Chopping down a house-sized vine and burning it in the same day."

"This isn't a personal attack, Alek," Ian said.

"How many hours do you spend playing the piano each day?" Dr. Modorovic interjected before Alek could sling a retort back.

"I don't know. Maybe four? Six?"

Ian's mouth turned down. "Alek, I've been keeping track. You practice twelve to sixteen hours every day, and that's what I've witnessed." He looked at Dr. Modorovic. "Sometimes I wake up and he's already at the piano."

Alek wasn't sure if he was more turned on or annoyed that Ian was stalking him in his own home.

"Alek!" she scolded. "Even four hours is excessive in your condition. Doesn't it make your fingers sore? Your arm? The muscles in your back?"

Alek didn't mind the pain. It was a delicious distraction from the guilt and self-loathing that took up all the space in his head now that he didn't have music.

Dr. Modorovic reached across the table, grabbed his unbroken hand, and pulled it towards her. Alek flinched and gasped at the pain that lit through his hand and up the tendons in his wrist.

Ian sucked in a sharp breath.

For obvious reasons, Alek hadn't mentioned the pain he'd been dealing with.

"There's swelling here." She clucked her tongue, her eyes narrowed hawkishly as she prodded the palm of his hand and flipped it over to inspect the other side. "It's very likely you're developing a repetitive stress injury." She released his hand and shook her head. "You could end up with two hands that don't work as well as they should."

Alek doubted that. He could play through the pain.

Ian's face was grim, his voice gritty as he asked, "How many hours can he safely play?"

"At this point, complete rest would be ideal—not forever—just until the injury heals." Her eyes softened. "I know how important the piano is to you, Alek, but we're talking about more than just pain here. You could lose grip strength, finger agility, precision. You'll start dropping things without meaning to. Your joints will slowly stiffen from chronic inflammation until you can hardly move them. How will you play then?"

Her diagnosis seemed rather dramatic. His hands weren't going to ossify like petrified wood. Underneath the ringing of his ears, Dr. Modorovic explained where they could purchase a wrist brace and how to use it.

"I'll make a referral to a hand and wrist surgeon to have a closer look. They'll be able to determine if permanent damage has been done."

Ian looked crestfallen. "I didn't realize the piano could hurt him..."

"You can't be expected to know everything. The only reason I know is because my job requires my hands to be in perfect working order."

"There will be no more piano," Ian declared. "Right, Alek?"

Alek feigned surprise, his eyes wide and the tips of his fingers splayed on his chest. "Oh? I didn't realize you wanted my opinion. I thought this was a conversation reserved for those with all their mental faculties intact."

"I apologize. Would you like to speak privately?" In Bulgarian, she said, "You and I can talk like this if you wish or I could ask Ian to step out."

"No," Alek said in English. "Are we just about finished here or are there more lifelong passions that you'd like to ruin for me?"

Ian leaned over and growled in Alek's ear, "Stop being an asshole. She's trying to do her job."

That was true. He should direct his anger at the source: Ian. He couldn't wait until they were alone.

"I have a few more questions, if you'll bear with me," Dr. Modorovic said. "Have you ever seen things no one else could see? Heard things that no one else could hear? Before the accident, or after?"

Alek turned to Ian. "You told her about the fox?"

Ian winced. "I'm not saying the fox isn't real. It's just... I haven't seen it. Animal control didn't find it. I thought she should know."

"It's a fox, not a dog. It doesn't come when it's called."

The doctor cleared her throat. "Foxes aside, there are very real issues here. Ian said you've mentioned suicide."

"It. Was. A. Joke."

"So if I ask if you've had thoughts of hurting yourself, even fleetingly, the answer would be no?"

"Resoundingly," Alek said.

Not that he would admit it if he was. Confessing suicidal ideation was a one-way ticket to a psych ward, and that was a place he would never find himself in.

"Good. If that should change, you must tell someone. Mental illness is exactly that. An illness. When the brain is sick, it lies. It tells us to give up when we should do anything but."

"Is that your diagnosis, surgeon? I have a mental illness? That isn't your specialty—unless you're planning to lobotomize me, or is scrambling brains like eggs no longer a thing?"

"Alek!" Ian barked.

"It's fine," she told Ian. "I'd be more concerned if he wasn't so sharp-tongued. That would be out of character. I'd rather not talk in circles, though. You're absolutely correct, Alek. Psychiatry isn't my specialty." She pushed a business card across the table. "Dr. Dhawan specializes in mental health issues following traumatic brain injury. I'd like you to make an appointment with her."

Alek looked at the dark purple business card. Making an appointment might placate Ian enough to lay off, but on the other hand, Alek didn't see what good it would do. He'd suffered a loss, for which he was grieving. His brain chemistry didn't need balancing. Before Alek could decide, Ian peeled the card from the table and tucked it into his wallet.

Dr. Modorovic donned her glasses and jotted something down on a prescription pad. "Here's a prescription for trazodone." She passed it to Ian, as if Alek wasn't to be trusted with such matters. "Take it at bedtime daily until you can see Dr.

Dhawan. It's a sleeping pill that is non-habit-forming. Extreme sleep deficits have been known to cause psychological symptoms. I'll order an MRI too. It can show us more subtle signs of brain damage."

"Is there a surgical treatment if you find anything?" Alek asked.

"Not likely, but it's still worth knowing. As I mentioned before, damage to different areas of the brain can result in different symptoms. It can help us determine if the mood changes are structural in nature, or something else."

"I'll consider what you've said." Alek stood. "It was nice to meet you, Dr. Modorovic. I appreciate the care you've taken—"

"Are you firing me?" Her eyes widened.

Alek shrugged. "I have no use for a doctor I cannot trust."

"You are not firing Dr. Modorovic," Ian grumbled. "Sit back down."

As far as Alek was concerned, he'd stand for the rest of his life.

In Bulgarian Dr. Modorovic said, "You can trust me, Alek. I want to help you. You simply cannot carry on like this."

"Last I checked, I'm an adult of sound mind. You can't force me to do anything."

"Perhaps. For now." Her countenance turned conniving. "All it takes is one phone call from me and I can have you committed for seventy-two hours on a psych hold."

She was as wicked as he was.

"Resorting to empty threats is beneath you."

"Call my bluff. See what happens." She smoothed her face back into professional interest. "See the psychiatrist, rest both of your hands, and take the trazodone."

"Or else?"

"Or else," she answered in English. "I'll see you next week to follow up."

Ian stood. "Thank you so much, Dr. Modorovic." He ducked his chin and extended his hand, shaking hers.

Alek paused at the doorway, pointing his thumb down the hall. "I can wait outside if you want to have another private chat."

Before Alek could make it to the elevator, Ian's heavy footfalls sounded behind him.

"I'm sorry." Ian grabbed Alek's arm, pulling him to a stop.

Alek looked down at Ian's hand until he let go. A bell chimed and the elevator doors parted for them. An elderly couple stepped aside to make room.

"Thank you," Ian murmured, holding the door as Alek crossed over the threshold.

Alek seethed in silence while they descended to the first floor, weaved through the crowded lobby, and out onto the street where Ian's truck was parked at the curb.

Ian put his keys in the ignition, then stopped. "Aren't you going to let me have it?"

Alek crossed his arms and looked out the window. A pair of gulls were squabbling over an abandoned, or perhaps pilfered, bag of chips.

Despair had already replaced his earlier anger. What if Dr. Modorovic was right? If he lost the use of both of his hands, if he lost his mental agency, he was going to find a bridge and jump off of it. Figuratively speaking, he added as he shot Ian a withering glare.

Ian turned on the truck and pulled into traffic, but his silence only lasted until the first red light. "If you won't talk, I'm more than happy to. I'm so sorry, Alek—about the piano, for going behind your back, but I'm not sorry for getting you the help you need. Something is wrong. I'm afraid to leave you alone. I'm afraid to sleep."

If Alek was talking to Ian he would have suggested that maybe Ian was the one who needed a psychiatrist.

"Tell me what you're thinking. Please. Say something. Even if it's that you hate me. Say something."

But what could Alek say? Ian had lied to him, again. There was no one he could trust, except for himself, although even that wasn't necessarily true because according to the doctor, his brain was completely unreliable. He had to choose between two shit choices: quitting the piano and thus breaking his uncle's promise, losing all of the progress he'd made, or risk losing the use of *both* of his hands.

How was he going to jerk off? He couldn't rely on Ian to lend him a hand.

By the time Ian parked the truck in front of the Victorian he was practically begging.

"Please, Alek. Please. I love you. Please."

Alek was unmoved.

Ian reeled back and hit the steering wheel. The horn bleated. Alek jumped. A murder of crows started from the trees. The silent treatment was turning out to be anything but.

Alek unbuckled his seatbelt and gripped the door handle. "If it means you'll shut the fuck up, fine. I'll talk. You lied. Again. I don't know what I want to do about that yet, but I do know one thing: the game is off. You don't get to ask me questions anymore. You don't get my trust."

"Alek, please. I'm sor—"

Alek opened his door and slammed it shut on Ian's apology, then had to wait at the front door for Ian to unlock it, which ruined the smooth getaway he had been trying to make. While Ian trailed behind him like a ghost, Alek went to his old room.

He closed the door, snicking the lock shut before Ian could follow. Perhaps slamming the door in Ian's face could be his new hobby. He searched the top drawer of his dresser until he found the bottle of oxycodone that Ian had insisted he pick up from the pharmacy just in case. He tipped the bottle, tapped a single pill into his palm, and tossed it into his mouth, washing it all down with a glug of vodka from the bottle pre-fall Alek had left on his dresser. Maybe if he got some sleep, as Dr. Modorovic suggested, he'd wake up as the same Alek'd been before the fall.

"Alek," came Ian's muffled voice through the door. "Are you okay?"

"Things are going just swimmingly here. I'll be sure to tell you if that changes and I feel like ending it all."

Alek crawled underneath his bed frame and lifted the loose floorboard hiding place he'd made for himself. He retrieved the velvet sack that contained his uncle's piano key and then crawled back out from under the bed. Clutching the key to his chest, he got into bed, and stared at the ceiling until the beginning tingles of narcotic-induced bliss sparked up and down his nerve endings, and he finally fell asleep.

His dreams were the same as they always were, but when he looked down at his arms as he forced his uncle under the water, the lifeless body that floated to the surface wasn't his uncle's. It was Ian that he drowned.

30

IAN

There was a nailhead poking out of the baseboard across the hall from Alek's room. Ian would have to fix that. He was sitting with his back against Alek's locked door, had been for an hour now. Alek was asleep. Hopefully. If Ian pressed his ear against the door, he thought he heard snoring.

He'd talked himself out of taking the door off the hinges twice already. What if Alek had slashed his wrists and his blood was coagulating in a puddle on the floor?

Would Alek really leave him? By suicide or less fatal means?

If Alek broke up with him, if he disappeared, the way he was right now... Ian couldn't let that happen. He rubbed his hands over his face. The stress was getting to him. Since Alek fell, nearly every minute felt like the moment before a jump scare in a horror movie.

Sitting outside Alek's door wasn't going to fix anything. He rose to his feet and crept quietly down the hall. In the kitchen, he ripped the calendar off the fridge and sat at the dining table. He called the psychiatrist first.

"I was about to call you," the receptionist said. "Dr. Dhawan has been updated by Dr. *Mordor*—Sorry. *Modorovitch*. We were able to save a virtual appointment for him at 8 AM tomorrow morning."

"He'll be there."

The hand surgeon was not as accommodating. The earliest appointment was six weeks out. He shot a text to Dr. Modorovic. Maybe she could pull some strings.

If he dropped off the prescription now, Alek could try the sleeping pill tonight. He had left Alek before for groceries or work, but the more Alek's mental state deteriorated, the more he worried what he'd come back to.

Shoving his anxiety aside, Ian wrote a note and left it in front of Alek's door.

On his way out, he swiped the truck keys and Alek's own car keys off the hook by the door. Alek could escape on foot. He could hurt himself in any number of ways. But Ian did what he could.

The pharmacist was able to fill the prescription while Ian waited. The bright fluorescent lighting of the drugstore reminded him of the hospital. His chair was too small and the square linoleum tile under his foot lifted up at the corner. He toed it with his boot and pulled out his phone, passing the time by responding to work emails. He'd mostly been able to manage the business remotely, but he felt like he was treading water.

He couldn't stop or he'd be in over his head.

————

IAN HEARD the piano before the Victorian came into view. Alek was laying on the keys hard. That obstinate prick. Ian grabbed the prescription bag with a crunch and hopped out of the truck.

The music was even louder outside. Haunting and gorgeous. A heavy black thundercloud that rained down anger and sadness and regret. It was music and it was Alek's. It was the song he played every night after he broke Ian's heart. Ian would know it anywhere.

Ian raced up the steps, through the door, and into the parlor. Alek sat at the bench, spine straight, silky black hair flung down over his forehead. All ten fingers flew over the keys while his foot pumped the pedals in seamless synchrony. Ian stepped closer. If Alek had caught sight of him, he didn't show it. Alek's face was blank, peaceful, his eyes not on his hands, or on the sheet music, but out the window and on the trees.

Ian brushed the tears from his cheeks. Later, he'd be mad that Alek had risked his hands, but even though the music was baleful and mourning, each note burning with ire and shame, the sound of Alek's music returned filled Ian with a magic sort of joy and hope.

The song came to an end and the peaceful expression faded from Alek's face.

"It's only the one song," Alek said, resting his hands in his lap. "I woke up and it was there. Like a single book in a library was returned to me, but I'm not allowed to see the others yet."

Ian sat on the bench and pushed a stray tuft of hair back from Alek's brow. He braced for Alek's rejection, but it didn't come.

"It was beautiful, Alek."

"It was *sorry*. Every night when I played this song, I was playing it for you." Alek turned to Ian and hugged him.

Whether it was the music, or the moment, the apology, or that Alek was touching him, talking to him, renewed tears fell down Ian's face. He dropped salty kisses everywhere he could reach while his hands roved over Alek's back, clutching him closer, though it still wasn't close enough.

Ian pulled back and stroked the side of Alek's face. "I'm sorry too. I should have warned you or tried talking to you again." He sniffed. "I have no idea what I'm doing."

Alek looked out the window and back again. "You were right to get me help."

"What are we going to do about your hands, Alek?"

Alek's face hardened. "I won't quit the piano."

"I know, love, but I don't think your uncle would want you to destroy your hands to keep your word." Ian chewed on his lip. "What if you taught me every day? Wouldn't that count?"

"Perhaps..." It sounded like an answer meant only to appease, like Alek was hardly listening, which might have been true, considering Alek had turned to stone, his eyes fixed on the window.

"Alek?"

Without looking, Alek shushed him, his eyes locked on the forest, or was it the forest?

Ian's hair stood on end.

Alek rose from the bench and walked around the piano like he was in a trance, drawn to the window by something sinister.

"Alek," Ian called, following him.

This wasn't the first time Alek's attention had been difficult to catch, but it was the first time it happened while Alek was in motion. It was almost like he was sleepwalking, except his eyes were open and alert.

Ian crept up behind Alek and laid a hand to his shoulder. Alek tensed, but didn't turn.

"Do you hear that?" Alek asked.

Ian's blood ran cold. The only sound in the room was his pulse pounding in his ears and the tick of the clock on the mantle. "What do you hear?"

In the reflection of Alek's face in the window, his brows darted together.

"What do you hear?" Ian repeated.

"She's screaming."

Ian peered over Alek's shoulder. The forest was dark, seemingly empty. Not even birds flew between the trees. The branches were still. The ferns did not sway. There was no one there.

"Who is?" Ian asked.

With his eyes still on the window, Alek pointed. "You don't see her there?"

"Who?" Ian crowded behind Alek until he was so close that fog flared on the glass with each breath. He looked for a long time. He strained to listen. But there was nothing.

"Alek, who?" Ian prodded.

If Alek didn't snap out of it soon, Ian was going to take him to the hospital. Ian grabbed Alek by the shoulders and turned him away from the window. Alek went willingly. His jade eyes weren't absent, but distracted. The lights were on and Alek was home but someone else was there with him.

"Alek, you're scaring me," Ian said with a squeeze of his shoulder. "Alek!" Ian repeated louder, shaking him.

Alek blinked and his gaze focused on Ian.

"The fox," Alek said. "I think she's dying."

Ian's heart broke. He didn't know what to say. He guided Alek to the couch, forcing him to sit.

"It's a strange feeling..." Alek said.

"What is?" Ian sat down beside him and took both of his hands.

"Loving someone so much that you wish they never met you."

It took Ian a moment to interpret what Alek said through his accent, but when he did, he climbed on top of Alek and straddled him.

"I would meet you over and over again no matter how hard this gets. You're never more than I can take." He framed Alek's face with his hands and held his gaze. "I want to be here for you, Alek. None of this is your fault. None of this is too much. Whatever's going on inside that precious head of yours can be fixed."

He willed the words to be true. It could be fixed, right? It had to be.

Ian kissed Alek and it wasn't just a kiss—Alek was dangling from a cliff and his hand was slipping, but Ian wasn't going to let him fall. At first, Alek froze, but then his tongue flickered along the seam of Ian's lips, asking for permission, instead of taking possession the way he usually did. When Ian opened his mouth to let Alek inside, Alek moaned, but this time it didn't hurt.

Fuck the past. Their love was bigger than that. Their love could fix anything. Anything.

Alek broke the kiss. "What are you doing?" His pale green eyes roved over Ian in equal parts suspicion and lascivious perusal.

"I want this," Ian said. "I want you to fuck me."

The reasons were abstract and a little bit irrational, but that didn't make them any less true. He was losing Alek more and more each day, to lies and secrets, to whatever was happening inside of his head.

"How do I know you're telling the truth?" Alek's brow furrowed. "How can I trust you to tell me to stop if you want me to?"

"I know I haven't given you any reason to trust me lately. If you don't want to... it's okay."

"Oh, I want to." Alek's eyes darkened. "Tell me why. I want to be sure you aren't doing this because I'm going crazy—"

"I'm not and you aren't."

Alek shushed him. "I don't want you to do it if you think it will make me stay. Whatever I said before, I didn't mean it. I'm not going anywhere."

"It's for none of those reasons. I want you to write over everything—what you did and the things you let me imagine. The lies we told. The fights we had. Everything we can't take back. I'm ready."

Alek paused for one tense second. "I'll do it, but I have conditions."

"Anything."

Alek lifted one finger, which Ian promptly sucked into his mouth. Alek pulled his finger back and grabbed Ian's chin. "Patience. Listen."

"Sorry," Ian said, even though he wasn't. What was the harm in leading him by the dick? It's what Alek would have done.

"I'll only fuck you if you fuck yourself on my cock. You on top. You have to stop if your feelings change. You have to be honest."

"I promise."

Alek patted Ian's cheek lightly. "Are you sure? You know I don't forgive the way you do. If you thought a week without my touch was bad, you won't like what will happen if you lie to me again. Do you understand?"

"I need this, Alek. Please."

And he really did. Alek probably felt like he'd lost all control, that he no longer deserved to take Ian in hand, that Ian wouldn't trust him to, but Ian wanted to show Alek that the phantom specter of his dominance *could* become corporeal again, that Ian needed to see it as much as Alek did.

Alek lifted his chin with leonine grace. "Undress me."

Ian pulled off Alek's shirt and greedily mapped every inch of his olive skin. Obsidian hair traced a fairy ring around Alek's belly button before disappearing inside his pants. He was too thin, his ribs poking ridges beneath his skin. Ian would fix that. He would feed him. He would make him well. He would love Alek enough for the both of them until Alek learned to love himself.

Ian swallowed thickly, then said, "You are the most beautiful creature I have ever seen."

Alek only pressed his lips together, one corner lifting up slightly to betray the pleasure Ian's compliment had given him.

Ian kneeled on the floor and removed Alek's pants. Stark naked and completely shameless, Alek reclined back on the couch and spread his legs wide, palming the cock Ian knew so well he could already sense the ghost of how it would feel inside.

"Go get lube," Alek said.

Ian didn't trust his voice to work so he nodded instead. Where had he last seen the lube? Alek stashed bottles around the house like Easter eggs. Ian dropped to the floor and looked under the armchair.

"Cold," Alek said.

"Huh?" Ian paused on his hands and knees.

"I thought it was obvious. I'm doing that thing Americans do on TV. Cold means you're far away. Warmer means you're closer. Is that not a thing?"

Ian bit back a grin. "No, you've got it right." He crossed to the built-in bookshelf. "How about now?"

"Warmer."

Ian headed for the cabinet.

"Colder!" Alek smiled unguardedly and it was as rare as it was adorable.

Ian tried the fireplace next.

"You're getting warmer," Alek coached.

Hanging over the mantle was an antique giltwood mirror featuring a formidable lion with a mane of scales. When they first moved in, Ian had complained that the parlor was too dark. Alek countered that he preferred it that way, the more clouds of tobacco smoke the better, just as the Victorians had intended. That was another thing. "No smoking in the Victorian," Ian had declared. "I won't be stifled," Alek retorted, going on to smoke enough cigarettes in the following twenty-four hours to give himself a ten-year head start on emphysema. The mirror was his apology. "The lion reminds me of you and mirrors reflect light," Alek had said with a shrug. He'd only smoked outside from then on.

Ian tilted the bottom of the mirror up from the wall and a travel-size bottle of lube fell out.

"Hot." Alek smirked, then patted his lap. "Come here."

Ian rushed to comply, moving to the space between Alek's thighs.

Alek tucked his fingers inside the top edge of Ian's pants. "Get yourself out of these clothes," he said in a low, velvet purr. "Leave the boxers on."

In his haste, Ian pulled his shirt off with a rip of a stitch and nearly fell over when he shimmied out of his pants.

Alek looked up at him with wide, dick-sucking eyes. "Are you sure you want me to write over everything I made wrong?" Alek leaned towards Ian's boxers until his mouth hovered a whisper away from the head of Ian's cock. "Even this?"

"I know what you're trying to do."

Deja vu mixed with pleasure, but Alek's test didn't hurt.

Ian gave a small thrust, nudging his dick against Alek's teeth before tugging a handful of Alek's hair. "I'm ready. Unless you want to reenact the part where I busted in my boxers, you'd better stop fucking around and get your dick inside me."

Alek pouted. "I thought it was my turn to be bossy."

"Sorry," Ian said.

With cold efficiency, Alek jerked Ian's boxers down. "Turn around so I can get you ready for me." Once Ian turned, Alek outstretched his hand and ordered, "Lube."

Ian's stomach felt like it was where his heart should be. He was surprised his fingers didn't shake when he dropped the vial into Alek's hand. Unseen behind him came the sound of the cap popping, the squirt of liquid, and then Alek's fingers were rubbing lube around the outside of his hole.

"Fuck, Alek," Ian groaned, trying not to push back, and failing.

"Patience." Alek slapped Ian's ass sharply with his casted hand.

"I don't care how turned on I am. If you misuse your broken arm again, we're going to stop."

It was bad enough that Alek was using his hands at all, but Ian had already decided to let go of what he could to give Alek back some of the control he'd lost.

"My mistake," Alek drawled.

Another squirt of lube and then Alek's finger slid inside him. Ian lifted up on the tips of his toes and moaned. When Alek added another finger, Ian dropped his head, the pattern of the Persian rug blurring as he gave himself over to Alek's expert ministrations. He was so far gone that he didn't even care if he came without Alek inside him. They could always go again. Ian was on the doorstep of no return when Alek's fingers left him. Ian growled.

"Be a good boy," Alek crooned. "Turn around and climb on my cock."

Ian straddled him. They hovered just over the edge of sex, their lips only a kiss away.

Alek's eyes moved to Ian's mouth and back to meet his gaze. "No second guessing?"

Ian shook his head. "You?"

In answer, Alek launched upward, closing the gap between them in a kiss that was so intense, Ian only distantly recognized that Alek was pulling him down, reeling him in, until the tip of his dick had nearly pushed inside.

Breathless against Ian's lips, Alek said, "No more power games. Just us."

Ian nodded. "Just us."

Every nerve fired at once as Ian slowly, so slowly, lowered down onto Alek's cock.

"You're shaking," Alek said, stroking Ian's cheek.

Ian hadn't noticed. He was more focused on trying not to come the fuck apart. He swore he could feel Alek's heartbeat deep inside of him.

"Do you want to stop?" Alek asked.

"No." Ian gripped the back of the couch, lifted himself up, and plunged back down again.

"I didn't think I'd ever... I... Oh fuck." Alek's words came out stilted and heavily accented as he met Ian thrust for thrust.

They made love like they were fighting, but not against each other. The past had tried to destroy them and the future loomed with uncertainty, but maybe if they pulled each other closer, they could fuse together completely, so nothing could ever separate them again.

"I'm not going to last long," Ian said, pulling them sideways.

They landed with a collective grunt.

"What the hell, Ian?"

"I want you on top."

Alek scowled. "That's not what we discussed."

"I trust you to stop if I tell you to stop." Ian scooted and twisted until he was on his back.

Alek chewed on his tongue. His eyes shifted to the window and back again. Did he see the fox?

"Please," Ian begged.

In a burst of motion, like he couldn't stand another second of Ian's anguish, Alek hooked his arms under Ian's legs and pushed all the way in.

"Mine," Alek said on a groan, emphasizing the declaration with another thrust.

"Yours," Ian somehow managed to say, even as his back bowed and all cogent thought escaped him.

Alek pulled back and fisted Ian's cock in his hand.

"No," Ian grunted.

Alek froze.

"No hands," Ian explained. "Rest your hands."

"You prick." Alek pushed Ian playfully into the sofa. "I thought..." He raked his hair back from his face. "Okay. I'll try to be good."

Alek curled back over Ian and fucked him with unbridled fervor. His emerald eyes made promises without words. Declarations of love and devotion. Vows to cherish and keep.

Ian was going to come, but he wouldn't go without Alek. He lifted up and said against Alek's ear the only word he knew would push Alek over the edge too, *"Mine."*

Alek's eyes burned with unabashed reverence, his mouth falling open as his body chased its last frantic, desperate thrusts. In the end, they came together, like they'd held hands and jumped off a cliff, but there wasn't any gravity and instead of falling they were flying.

"Yours," Alek said as he collapsed and buried his face in Ian's neck.

Alek didn't pull out until long after his dick softened, like he didn't want to let go, like he wanted to stay inside of Ian forever. When they did finally part, it was only to clean up and then Alek was back on top with his head resting over Ian's heart.

Ian absentmindedly toyed with Alek's hair. "Thank you for that."

"I take it you enjoyed yourself then?"

"You think?" Ian kissed the top of Alek's head.

"No spiraling?"

"No." Ian hugged Alek tighter against him. "I hope you won't be mad, but the psychiatrist has an opening to see you on video chat tomorrow morning and I told her you'd be there."

Alek sighed. "No. That's good."

Ian looked to the window. "Is the fox still there?"

Alek followed his gaze. "No, but I can hear her. Not as loud. Like she's far away."

Ian looked at the clock. "Why don't you try the sleeping pill and see if you feel better when you wake up?"

Alek nodded and let Ian lead him up the stairs to their bed where he held Alek tightly in his arms. Instead of counting sheep, Ian counted each strand of midnight hair on Alek's head with a prayer to a god he didn't believe in. *Please let Alek be okay. Please let him be happy. Please let him be whole again. Please.*

31

ALEKSANDAR

BULGARIA. TWELVE YEARS OLD.

leksandar was sent to boarding school the morning after his mother died. Boarding school had always been the plan, but not this soon.

Aleksandar's father wasn't home to see him off, but he'd left a guard to ensure Aleksandar arrived at his destination. There was no time to bring the safe and where would he have put it? He'd waffled over whether to bring the piano key. What if someone found it? But what if his father found it? In the end he decided to bring the key, and by extension, the memory of his uncle with him.

The school was in an old monastery with dreadfully boring stone masonry architecture plopped in the middle of a field of tall grass dotted with oak trees. Terms didn't start for two more weeks, but the headmaster made an exception for Aleksandar's father.

Only the caretaker and a few teachers were there for an early start, but they stayed mostly in the staff dorms on the back edge of the property. The first thing Aleksandar did when he arrived was track down the school's music room. The door was locked, but he picked it easily. The piano was decent. It was a school for Europe's elite offspring, after all.

Over the two weeks that followed, Aleksandar filled the cold, empty building with music that wrapped itself around him like a heavy blanket, protecting him from the loneliness and despair that chilled him.

When the term began, the students arrived, and Aleksandar was no longer alone. In order to play the piano, he had to book time in the music room, and tolerate the fanfare of admirers while he played. Intimidated teachers tried to correct his technique as if they weren't completely mediocre by comparison.

Aleksandar understood. This was his punishment. Before he had loneliness and freedom and now he had neither.

When no invitation to his mother's funeral arrived, Aleksandar assumed he wasn't invited. Imagine his surprise when his father appeared one Friday afternoon to tell him his mother had died after a long and private battle with breast cancer at a top hospital in France.

"I take it death by suicide is too cowardly for a Velishikov?" Aleksandar asked.

His father didn't ask how he knew. He only nodded. "Now come along, and don't forget to look sad."

32

ALEK

Propped against the headboard with his laptop flipped open in his lap, Alek felt far more like he was about to have cyber sex than have his head examined. He hadn't gotten around to putting on pants yet because Ian let him sleep in.

It was too soon to forgive Dr. Modorovic for having the audacity to do her job, but he could begrudgingly admit that the sleeping pill worked nearly without fault. His dreams had been more vivid and nightmarish than usual—he'd drowned his uncle in an endless loop that left Dream Alek's arms slashed to shreds because the trazodone-fueled Uncle Krasimir had grown knife-like claws, but other than that, he felt well-rested and alert.

Ian appeared well-rested too, though Alek wasn't certain if he was simply relieved that Alek had slept, or if his serene expression was the result of finally getting properly fucked.

"I'm going to go downstairs," Ian said as he returned from the bathroom, freshly showered and ruggedly handsome in a gray tee and dark navy sweatpants that accentuated the outline of his dick. "There's a few bids that needed itemizing."

"As sexy as that idea sounds, I want you with me."

Ian crossed the room and kissed Alek's forehead. "Don't you want privacy to speak freely?"

"I don't intend to share anything that matters. Surely this doctor can treat my budding psychosis without knowing the details of my life story."

Ian frowned, chewing on his lip. Alek could already hear the lecture that he should take this seriously, be as honest as possible, but all Ian said was, "If you insist."

"I absolutely do."

"Okay." Ian moved toward the armchair beside the fireplace.

Alek tapped the space beside him. "Here."

Ian dipped his head in a nod and changed course, dropping down onto his side of the bed and pulling a paperback out from beneath his pillow.

Dr. Dhawan's video flared to life at precisely 8 AM. The psychiatrist was around his age, or perhaps a little bit older. Her thick black hair was cut into a posh jaw-length bob and generous lashes framed large brown eyes.

In the space above her shoulder, a rainbow flag was pinned on a bulletin board next to a sign that proclaimed, *All are welcome here.* Above the sign was an anthropomorphic uterus raising an ovarian fist into the air. Alek suspected she curated the bulletin board for each of her patients. Perhaps her more conservative clients found a crucifix pinned to the board, along with the reminder that a make-believe god would never give them more than they could take, and a print of that abhorrent *Footprints in the Sand* poem.

"Mr. Katin, I presume?" she said.

"You can call me Alek." He turned the laptop to Ian. "My partner, Ian, will be joining us."

Ian waved. "I can leave if you want."

"No, that's alright. Although I will require you to step out for a moment so I can ask Alek some questions."

"I'll go down the hall?" Ian said.

"Perfect!" She flashed an asymmetrical smile that revealed a single dimple.

Once Ian left, closing the door behind him, Alek said, "If you're worried I'm battered, don't be. It's him you should ask."

The psychiatrist was stony-faced.

"That was a joke. Ask your questions."

She clicked her pen. "Do you feel safe?"

"Yes."

"Are you being forced to do anything you don't want to do?"

Alek discarded the sexual innuendo his brain immediately supplied. "No."

"One last question. Why do you want him to stay?"

"My reasons are my own. Shall I go get him now?"

Dr. Dhawan would have to do whatever the psychiatry version of buying him a drink first was before he would admit that he needed Ian with him because he was terrified.

What if the fall had knocked loose an unseen insanity that had always been lurking inside him? What if he was really from Indiana or some other such cornfield-laden place? What if he'd imagined his entire life story?

After last night's revelation that the fox was a hallucination, Alek had snuck into the bathroom and googled *Aleksandar Velishikov*, rushing through the search results. His heart rate hadn't slowed until he double-checked the photograph that went along with his obituary against the reflection in the mirror and even then, he still wasn't certain.

Once Ian had returned to his rightful place in bed beside Alek, the psychiatrist said, "Let's get right into things." She tucked her hair behind her ears in much the same way one would roll up their sleeves. "I'd like for our work to be a partnership. I promise to always be honest, but I'll need you to be honest in return. Dr. Modorovic may have consulted me, but what you say will stay with me. The only time I will betray that trust is in the event a serious crime has occurred or I believe you are a threat to yourself or others. Does that make sense?"

Alek nodded.

"I'm told you are a gifted musician?"

Alek blinked. He'd expected prying questions of childhood trauma. Maybe she was trying to lull him into complacency.

"I used to be," he answered.

"Can you tell me more about that?"

"There's little to say. I hit my head and lost my music."

Alek clenched his hand into a fist, but Ian was there already, loosening his fingers and joining them with his own.

"That must have been a huge loss for you."

Alek shrugged.

"What are you able to do now?"

Alek listed off the beginner skills he'd remastered. Scales and chords. Arpeggios. An entire childhood's worth of rudimentary nursery rhymes and lullabies. Some very simplified arrangements of Bach and Chopin. The one song out of the hundreds he'd composed.

"So you didn't lose everything, then?" Her pen moved fast over the yellow notepad he could just make out the top edge of.

"No. You misunderstand. I lost everything when I fell. I had to start over. *That* is what I've relearned."

Her eyes widened. "In six weeks? You learned all of that? With only one hand?"

Alek didn't answer.

"Dr. Modorovic mentioned you've had trouble sleeping?"

"If I could sleep, I would."

"Are you familiar with the concept that neural pathways form while we sleep, that when learning a new skill, like the piano for example, it's recommended to practice every day, so that every night your brain can connect the dots?"

Alek nodded. During the countless hours he had spent scouring the internet for a way to find the music he lost, he'd stumbled upon the science behind the promise he'd made to his uncle.

"I wonder what might happen with your music if you get a few weeks of solid sleep under your belt…" she mused.

Probably nothing more than make him look a little less haggard.

Ian cleared his throat. "He started trazodone yesterday and slept through the night. Right, Alek?"

Alek resented his sleeping schedule being monitored like a colicky infant, but nodded once in agreement.

As if sensing Alek's irritation with the line of questioning, Dr. Dhawan said, "Why don't you tell me what you'd like to get out of our partnership?" She gave a lazy flick of her wrist. "If I could wave a wand and give you exactly what you want, what would it be?"

Music was the obvious answer, but it wasn't what he wanted most of all. In a rare moment of honesty born from desperation, he admitted, "I don't want to hurt people anymore."

She frowned, lifting her hand to her chin. "How do you hurt people?"

"How long do you have?"

Dr. Dhawan smiled and inclined her head.

Alek cast a glance at Ian. His eyes were glued to the page of his book, but Alek would eat his piano if he wasn't eaves-dropping.

"I say things even though they hurt, even though they might not be true. I've done unforgivable things—"

"Let me stop you there," she said.

How unexpected. Weren't psychiatrists supposed to listen in

benevolent silence while their patients espoused a lifetime of trauma?

"What is the worst thing you've ever done?" she asked.

River rocks knocking against each other, the rough scrape of a piano bench over parquet floors, the warmth of his uncle's arm against his shoulder, initials carved into the side of a piano, ash over keys that cut like broken glass beneath his fingers.

Breaking Ian's heart was a very close second.

"Let me pose a question," Dr. Dhawan prodded. "What if Ian did the things you've done? Would you say he was a bad person?"

"Ian wouldn't."

"But if he did," she pressed. "Would you still love him? Think highly of him?"

Alek pulled his hand free from Ian and crossed his arms. "No. It would change who he is. It would make him a coward."

With a wry smile, the psychiatrist said, "Ian, I apologize in advance."

"Do what you have to do," Ian said, flipping to the next page of his book—rather exaggeratedly, in Alek's opinion.

"So Alek, you're saying Ian has never made a mistake? He's never done something that hurt someone, even inadvertently? He's perfect, all of the time? No flaws?"

"This exercise might work on your other patients, but I'm afraid it won't work on me. The things I'm guilty of aren't on the same level as Ian's inability to cook anything remotely edible and his neurotic fanaticism for house cleaning."

Undeterred, Dr. Dhawan asked, "Have you ever heard of cognitive distortions?"

Cognitive distortions sounded like a fitting name for a band, or perhaps a strain of weed.

"*Things will never get better. I am unlovable. Everyone would be better off without me,*" Dr. Dhawan said. "Sometimes the thoughts we have about ourselves, or the world, can be incorrect. Those erroneous thoughts are called cognitive distortions.

"Just as with the piano, there are neural pathways that form when we think these thoughts, and the longer we believe them, the more they become cemented in our mind. But if we can identify and change those thoughts; talk back to them, if you will, we can reshape those pathways into something more healthy, something more honest."

Alek stifled a yawn. He roved his eyes over Ian, snagging on the prominent veins drawn across his forearms. Now that Alek had been rendered nearly handless, he'd become very familiar with the way those muscles flexed and tensed whilst Ian jerked him off.

"If we go back to the cognitive distortions I mentioned earlier, we might change them into something else. Things could get worse, but they could also get better. I *am* worthy of love. The world would not be better off without me. There are people here who would miss me if I died."

"I thought most psychiatrists pushed pills, not talk therapy," Alek said.

"I consider medication and therapy equally important. Research supports it, especially for long-term outcomes."

Alek was doubtful; talk therapy might work for the masses, but his demons weren't so easily exorcized.

"Most psychiatrists share the same opinion, though they usually don't have enough time to conduct the therapy themselves." She shielded one side of her mouth with her hand like she was sharing a secret. "I'm a little controlling, and prefer to dig into therapy myself, especially in the beginning." She dropped her hand. "Having said that, if you're not comfortable speaking to me, I'm happy to refer you to one of the therapists I employ, or help you find one elsewhere."

He shook his head. The fewer people he had to talk to, the better. "Please continue."

"Very well. Let's move on. Does Ian know the worst thing you've ever done?"

"No."

"Do you think Ian loves you?"

"I think he thinks he does."

"That makes perfect sense." Dr. Dhawan surprised him by agreeing. "I imagine you don't actually feel like Ian loves you because he doesn't know the whole truth about you. If it's really so terrible, doesn't Ian deserve to know?"

Alek scowled at Ian, half-expecting him to mouth "I told you so", but far from haughty, Ian was chewing thoughtfully on his bottom lip, his book abandoned on the duvet.

"Shouldn't Ian get to decide if he loves the real you?" she continued. "How would you describe the current state of your relationship?"

Alek stiffened. "Why are you so fixated on my love life?"

"It can speak to the state of your mental health. If you'd rather not answer—"

"Our relationship is in its death throes and we're both in denial," Alek said.

"Ian, what would you say?" Dr. Dhawan asked.

Ian reached a heavy hand out to muss Alek's hair.

"Other than that being the most dramatic thing he's ever said?" Ian framed Alek's face with his hands so Alek had no choice but to make eye contact. "It isn't denial to fight for someone that's worth fighting for."

The fervency of Ian's vow left Alek so flustered, he felt like he'd stuck his finger in a light socket. Charged and giddy, his heart racing and body hot.

When Ian released him, Alek said, "There you have it. Denial."

"I can see why you'd think that, Alek." Dr. Dhawan nodded enthusiastically. "How could you be worth fighting for? Ian doesn't even know what he's fighting for, right? He doesn't know the parts that make you unlovable. That's what you think, right?" She smiled and dropped the intensity in her voice. "You won't be able to feel his love, or love yourself until you're honest with him, and yourself."

"Are you this pushy with all of your patients?" Alek said. "It seems rather irresponsible."

The psychiatrist laughed heartily. "You're very honest." She sobered. "I push because sometimes that's the only way to challenge those cognitive distortions. Why don't you tell me about the symptoms you've been experiencing,"

It was a welcome change in topic.

"Hasn't Dr. Modorovic already given you her laundry list of concerns?"

"She has, but I'd like to know what concerns *you*. Which of your symptoms do you find most troubling?"

"There's a fox—" Alek stopped because he couldn't think over the ringing in his ears.

At first, he had thought his brain injury had triggered the tinnitus, but now he knew the truth; that the ringing had always been there and his music was covering it up. His ears had been ringing since the day his uncle died. It had only grown louder when his uncle's house burned to the ground, and his mother shot off a gun a few feet away from him in an empty room that echoed like ricochets, and louder still when he fell from the top floor of the Victorian after he'd decided that the only way he could love Ian was to let him go.

He should have died in that fall. Then the ringing would have stopped. Then they'd both be free.

Ian squeezed Alek's thigh and Alek returned to the present, the ringing quieter now like it was locked back inside a box that didn't open, hidden in a secret place beneath the roots of a dead tree in Bulgaria.

"You saw a fox?" Dr. Dhawan prompted.

"I thought she was real, but only I can see her. Only I can hear her. I first saw her a few days before the fall."

Dr. Dhawan's brow wrinkled. "You worry that you've been hallucinating even before your head injury?"

"What if I can't trust my thoughts?" Alek's voice cracked. "How will I know what's real?"

"Ian, if I can borrow you for a minute?" Dr. Dhawan asked. "Was there ever any concern for Alek's mental health before the fall? Did you ever notice anything abnormal?"

Alek held his breath.

"No," Ian answered immediately. He took Alek's hand and held it against his heart like he wanted Alek's own heart to follow his slow, steady pulse like a metronome. "He's always been a little brooding. I've occasionally worried about depression, but the other signs weren't there. He's always been energetic and passionate, slept well, no appetite changes, no substance abuse."

The revelation that Ian had worried Alek had depression wasn't a surprise. Ian was a fixer, and a researcher, and he'd brought his concerns to Alek before.

"Melancholy aside," Ian continued. "I've never seen anything suspicious. I never saw any sign that he was seeing or hearing things I couldn't—not until after the fall."

"Do foxes bear any sort of importance to you, Alek?" Dr. Dhawan asked. "Perhaps your mother read you a story when you were a child that featured one?"

Alek shook his head. His mother never read to him. Sometimes his uncle had, but mostly he told stories from the time when old gods ruled the world, when civilizations were born in blood, when heroes died because it was what had to be done.

"Why can't the fox be real *and* a hallucination?" Dr. Dhawan proposed. "Maybe you really saw a fox before the fall. Maybe that fresh experience made an impression on you."

"I thought we weren't supposed to entertain my psychosis."

"No, we should not, but we also shouldn't entertain the idea that everything can be explained by psychosis. Has this fox ever told you things?"

"No."

"Does the fox make you feel persecuted or paranoid? Or maybe like you're a god? More powerful, all-knowing?"

"Of course not."

"Does it ever tell you to hurt someone or to hurt yourself?"

"I told you, no. It doesn't talk. This isn't *The Lion, the Witch, and the Fantastic Fucking Fox.*"

She smiled again. "I think you have major depression with a psychotic component. Psychosis, like the fox hallucination you've experienced, can occur in the setting of severe, untreated depression. We'll still do an MRI to rule out structural changes from the fall, but the treatment remains the same regardless—"

"Why depression?" Depression felt like a personal failure, though Alek couldn't pinpoint exactly why.

"Depression occurs in over half of patients who suffer a traumatic brain injury. You've lost your music, the use of your hands, your independence. Depression isn't just being sad. It can manifest as anger, insomnia, a negative perception of yourself—"

"You're sure it's not schizophrenia?"

"Based on the presentation and duration of your symptoms, it's very unlikely. I know you worry about seeing the fox before the fall, and I understand your concern, but if you had schizophrenia, I think Ian would have noticed something amiss."

Alek looked to Ian, who nodded his agreement with Dr. Dhawan's assessment.

"You can continue the trazodone and I'll add an antidepressant and antipsychotic, but medication alone won't be enough. You'll need to change the way you think about yourself, and your past. Talk to someone. Whether it's me or a therapist. Someone. But you don't need to get bogged down with that now. Let's start some meds, get you some sleep, and when you're feeling better, we can look at the harder stuff."

"Couldn't I try the trazodone first?"

"You could, but I'd rather come on strong so your symptoms improve rapidly. The antidepressant will take six weeks to reach full effect. Remember, untreated severe depression is terminal."

The silence that followed was oppressive.

"It's important to think about your depression as a medical condition. If you had an infection, you'd take your antibiotics, right? If you had diabetes, you'd take your insulin."

While Alek understood the metaphor, it didn't make the pill any easier to swallow. He'd already lost so much of who he was. Would the medications make him even more of a stranger to himself? What if they kept his music from coming back?

"I'd like to see you twice a week until your symptoms stabilize. Do Tuesdays and Thursdays work?"

"My social calendar is surprisingly empty."

"Wonderful. Start the meds as soon as you can get the prescriptions filled, ideally today. I must warn you that there is a small risk of suicide when starting an antidepressant. It's postulated that the initial increase in energy that comes from feeling better might spur those with suicidal intent to act on their previous plans.

"But that doesn't mean that the medications are bad. Antidepressants save lives all over the world every day. It's just something to look out for. If you find yourself having suicidal thoughts, you must tell me. Both of you can reach out to me. If I'm not available, head straight to the emergency room, okay?"

Ian's face was pale. Alek squeezed his hand.

"I understand how upsetting the topic might be, but I'm not worried," she said. "I've seen this before. I know how to treat it."

Ian nodded, some of the color returning to his cheeks.

"Remember, you can always call or email me. Unless you have any other questions, I'll see you on Thursday."

Alek ended the call and passed the laptop to Ian.

"That was very brave of you," Ian said. "Being as honest as you were, admitting that you need help, and accepting it."

Alek dipped his head to hide his face. "I'm not brave. I was so afraid of losing you, I tried to break you just to keep you with me." Alek bit into the side of his cheek until he tasted blood.

Ian grazed his thumb across Alek's cheek. "*Fear is only proof you are alive.* Isn't that one of your Alekisms?"

"Excuse me? *Alekisms?*"

"Yes. Sage advice and proverbs. Let me think of another one..." He chewed on his bottom lip and then snapped his fingers. "*Hoping is foolish. Lying is survival.* I don't agree with all of them, but the one about fear is on point. You can be afraid and still be brave. Do you think an outnumbered army slaughtered on the battlefield wasn't brave? Wasn't afraid?"

"So now that I've fucked you at your own behest, what does that mean for us?" Alek changed the subject. "Any regrets?"

Ian rumbled a laugh. "No. You?"

"I got to put my dick inside a place I never thought I'd be allowed back in. What do you think?"

"I think you owe me an apology for that death throes comment," Ian said in an erection-inducing baritone. He grabbed Alek by the scruff of his hair and pulled him down to his lap.

"I am sorry about that—" Alek's voice was cut off by a mouthful of cock.

As was typically the case, Ian turned Alek's punishment into a reward, lavishing heaps of filthy praise as he held an approving hand around the side of Alek's throat and jerked him skillfully until they both came, breathless and messy and together.

33

ALEK

TWO MONTHS LATER

"No. Not C-D-E." Alek massaged his temple. "C-E-G."

"Like this?" Ian asked, his fingers bashing three clashing keys that were definitely not C, E, and G.

"Yes. That's it," Alek lied. "Let's stop there. End on a high note, and all that."

Alek tried to rise from Ian's lap, but he pulled him back down before he could escape.

"I know you're lying," Ian said with a light nip to the side of Alek's neck. "I'm terrible."

"You really are."

But teaching Ian was the closest Alek got to practicing. The hand surgeon's prognosis was even more pessimistic than Dr. Modorovic's. If Alek didn't rest his hands, he risked permanent disability that surgery could only attempt to palliate. The surgeon had sentenced him to thrice-weekly physical therapy appointments, during which time his wrists and hands were iced and fussed over and occasionally injected with cortisol.

At first, being banned from the piano had been unbearable, but now it was inconsequential. He didn't enjoy music anymore.

Nothing else had come back since that earlier miraculous development, and it hadn't been for lack of trying.

He'd sniffed over a hundred fresh wisteria cuttings like an insane person, which for all intents and purposes, he was. He'd tried the oxycodone again while Ian was at work, but there was no divine revelation that time and he liked the high so much he emptied the pill bottle in the toilet and flushed before he could sink to a new low and scoop them back out. He'd surreptitiously fondled the piano key any chance he had and when that didn't work, quit his endeavors entirely.

"Let's go for a walk," Ian said.

"Let's not."

Alek didn't like to go outside anymore. It was much harder to ignore the fox when she was circling between his legs and nipping at his heels.

The first few weeks after Alek started his mental health treatment had been filled with such hope—stupid, willfully ignorant hope, in retrospect.

At first, he'd been honest with Dr. Dhawan about the problems with his medication regimen. When his nightmares became so bad that he dreaded taking the sleeping pill for fear of what sleep would bring, he'd reached out to her.

That misstep earned him fifty-five minutes worth of needling questions—*What do you dream about? Why are the dreams so distressing? What do you think it means?*

Inventing an answer for each of her questions had been exhausting. After that first appointment, Alek had ditched the training wheels and banished Ian from future sessions, but Ian's absence hadn't loosened his tongue.

After the nightmare nonsense, Dr. Dhawan had swapped out one pill for another with fewer reports of vivid dreams, but the new drug dampened what little remained of his synesthesia until not even his sense of smell tangled with his memories. Dr.

Dhawan took his concern seriously; thus suggesting a newer medication from an entirely different class. The new drug was the worst of the bunch because it amplified the ringing in his ears until it was as loud as the moment after his mother pulled the trigger. It was like she was haunting him, which was the absolute last thing he needed when the ghosts from his past already consumed nearly every waking thought.

It wasn't Dr. Dhawan's fault that the medications weren't working. Each adjustment to his prescriptions eliminated the side effect that he complained of, which was actually pretty remarkable, but the medications themselves only scratched at the surface of his depression. The whole process was futile.

Alek didn't want to hurt the psychiatrist's feelings—a sign that he really had gone around the bend—so he commended her for a job well done. He was finally feeling more like himself. She was a genius! In reality, he had quit the meds altogether.

It had been a few weeks since then.

Hiding his crumbling mental health from Ian was easy. All it took was pocketing his pills under his tongue and spitting them back out into the toilet while he was peeing. When Alek couldn't sleep, he pretended to, laying still in bed, slowing his breathing until Ian fell asleep, not daring to get up in case Ian noticed his absence. Some nights, he didn't sleep at all, kept awake instead by the dark thoughts chasing each other inside his head.

Hiding the fox from Ian proved more difficult. When the fox called for Alek, he tried to ignore her. When he saw her at the edge of the forest, he turned away. But he could only resist the call for so long. He couldn't leave her alone. She was dying. What if he could save her?

Dr. Dhawan suspected he'd fallen off the wagon. Her questions focused more on his symptoms and how he was tolerating his medications. She'd asked him point-blank if he'd quit his medications on several occasions. But for all her vexing questions and restrained concern, she was true to her word. As far as Alek could tell, what they talked about, which wasn't much, was kept in confidence, and she kept her suspicions to herself.

"Come on." Ian stood quickly, lurching Alek from his lap and back into the present. "I found a statue in the greenhouse. I think it's original to the Victorian."

Alek groaned. "Couldn't you take a picture?"

October was usually a mild time with pleasant breezes and clear skies, but that autumn was plagued by a drought that turned the meadows to tinder and the rich, dark forest floor dusty. Last week, smoke from a nearby forest fire settled ash over everything and turned the sky into a burnt orange hellscape.

Today was uncharacteristically humid. Angry clouds kept threatening thunderstorms and failing to deliver. "Earthquake weather," Ian had said cheerfully. Alek despised hot weather and became increasingly histrionic the higher the dew point climbed.

The Victorian didn't have centralized air conditioning, and the walls were practically sweating. He'd bought portable AC units for their room and the parlor—he didn't want the piano to wilt and warp under the humidity—and he didn't stray from the rooms that offered Alek-approved climates. The constant, droning hum of the AC unit was slowly driving him insane, or more insane, and the hulking appliance really killed the whole Dark Academia aesthetic he was going for, but at least he wasn't hot.

Weather was only one of the reasons Alek hadn't been to the greenhouse in two weeks. It had all been very exciting when Ian first started renovating the greenhouse. There was the promise of Ian eye candy and sex alfresco, but the greenhouse was like a vortex. Ian had spent hours there, building enormous piles of hacked-up trees and ripped-out vines and yet hardly put a dent into the vegetation. Last week Ian had one of their crews out to help—so they would still get paid while he took a break from accepting new jobs—and despite days of headache-inducing cacophony, the greenhouse looked as packed with brush as before.

Yellow grass crunched beneath Alek's feet as they wound their way to the greenhouse. Ian tried to hold Alek's hand, but he batted it away. Alek's palms were already sweating. Why couldn't his mental breakdown have had the decency to arrive before the heatwave?

"It's hotter than Satan's nether regions," Alek complained.

The forest was uncharacteristically silent, probably because the heat had made the birds and squirrels lazy, so when Ian exploded with laughter, it was as startling as it was bittersweet, because like all of the other times Ian laughed lately, Alek wondered if he was hearing it for the last time.

Alek had already decided he was going to kill himself two weeks ago. Since then, every beat of his heart was another reminder of his cowardice.

Suicide suited Alek. A coward's death for a coward. A selfless act from a selfish person. If Ian was too loyal to leave him, then Alek would do it for him. Ian would be mad at first, but he'd be better off. One day he'd see that.

Alek would have killed himself already, but planning a suicide was dreadfully time-consuming. It was a lot to ask of someone with depression. First, there was the business of leaving. He couldn't very well kill himself at the Victorian, leaving Ian to clean up whatever mess was left behind.

There were also financial affairs to settle. The last thing Alek wanted was his money and treasures tied up in probate and auctioned off. Everything would go to Ian, or mostly everything. He'd set aside a chunk of cash to settle Ian's mother's mortgage, just in case Ian refused to spend Alek's money out of some misguided sense of honor. He'd already anonymously paid off the remainder of the Victorian's mortgage via money order for the same reason. Alek would have to be gone before the deed came in the mail, lest the letter foiled his plans.

They were nearly at the greenhouse before Alek realized he had been walking without his bewhiskered invisible-to-every-one-but-him companion. Instead of feeling relieved by a brief break of sanity, Alek was unsettled. Had he upset his fox? She didn't understand when he pretended she wasn't there. The other day when he'd gently nudged her back with his ankle, she'd tucked her tail and ran away like he'd kicked her. That must be it. She was off sulking. Probably watching him from a shady knoll in the woods.

But his fox was getting sicker every day, and it was so hot, and he couldn't leave water out for her this morning because Ian had very nearly caught him filling the bowl at the kitchen sink. Alek had said he was doing the dishes, something he never did, and had to actually see the task through to completion in order to keep his cover.

Before they rounded the corner, Ian covered Alek's eyes with his palms. The sudden blindness heightened the rest of his senses. He could feel each beam of sunlight, the heat that slowly seeped into his skin, the rise and fall of Ian's breathing like the tide of ocean waves.

Alek tried and failed to duck out of Ian's grip.

"I said I wanted to surprise you," Ian said. "Keep walking."

"This is ridiculous. I could close my own eyes, or you could have used a blindfold."

"You would peek in an instant."

"Is the surprise that you finally greased the hinges?" The door to the greenhouse usually opened with a distinctly unpleasant screech.

"Patience," Ian chided. "We're almost there."

Alek minded his footing as Ian led him down the brick path.

The walk took longer than usual. Maybe Ian had carved the remainder of the path out from the blackberry brambles.

Water flowed somewhere up ahead. Was the statue a fountain? That was hardly a surprise. A fountain in a greenhouse? Who'd ever heard of such a thing?

Ian dropped his hand without warning and it took a few seconds for Alek to blink back the glaring daylight. When his vision adjusted, his eyes first caught on the fact that they were in a large clearing. Ian-sized saplings and leafy shrubs surrounded them, blocking the rest of the greenhouse from view. At his feet was a crystal-clear man-made pool, wrapping like a moat around an enormous oxidized-copper statue of Neptune perched atop an open shell. Neptune's trident was cast downward, water arcing gracefully from the prongs.

"Surprise," Ian said. He settled his hands on Alek's hips and kissed the side of his neck.

Why did the Victorian have to be so magical? Why couldn't they be living in a characterless 1960s ranch rambler with central AC? It was going to be difficult enough for him to say goodbye to the Victorian. Not as difficult as saying goodbye to Ian, but he wasn't planning on saying goodbye anyway.

"The water's clean." Ian took Alek's hand and unfastened his wrist brace.

"How did you..."

"It was a mosquito-infested swamp when I stumbled upon it two weeks ago. There was a huge crack in the soapstone. I don't even want to think about what the steady leak would have done to the foundation if we neglected the greenhouse any longer."

Alek faux shuddered. "The horror!"

"I had the guys drain the water and repair the crack. We only finished yesterday. It was very convenient that the heat wave had you squirreled away in the house."

"How serendipitous."

Ian pulled off Alek's shirt and dropped to his knees, untying Alek's shoes next.

"Repairing the fountain was tricky." Ian removed Alek's shoes and set them aside. "Especially since I couldn't ask my antique restorer fiancé for his advice, but I muddled my way through in the end."

Ian unbuckled Alek's belt, his hands making quick work of the button and zipper, and then Alek was naked. It was far too hot for underwear and he'd finally been freed from his cast the week before. Despite the heat, goosebumps pebbled across his body.

Leaning forward, Ian grabbed Alek's ass and wrapped his mouth around his cock. Alek pressed his lips together to stave back the involuntary moan that threatened. Sex just wasn't something he was into anymore. He dropped a hand to Ian's shoulder and pushed.

Ian sat back on his heels and ducked his head to wipe his mouth.

"It's the meds," Alek lied.

"I know." Ian stepped away and began undressing. "You'll swim with me, though, won't you?"

Alek nodded, forcing a smile.

The water was delightfully freezing, like an alpine lake that made his ears hurt and his heart pump with exhilaration. It was deep too. When Alek's feet touched the bottom, he was completely submerged. His fingers didn't even break the surface when he lifted his arms.

Ian swam a few laps around Neptune, then threw a towel down beside a pallet of neatly stacked bricks. He rested on his stomach, head turned, cheek pressed against the earth, dark eyes pensive. Sunlight made the water on his skin glisten and scattered shadows over the muscles in his back. Alek allowed himself a long look. For all he knew, this could be the last time he'd lay eyes on Ian in all his naked glory.

He swam over and propped his elbows on the pool's edge. "Thank you for this, for everything you've done for the Victorian, and for me."

Ian made a grunt that could be construed any number of ways.

"What room are we going to work on next?" Alek asked, emphasizing the *we* because he didn't like the way that Ian was looking at him right now like he knew everything inside of his head.

"I haven't given it much thought yet." Ian gestured his hand in a lazy circle. "There's still too much to do here."

"Have you considered the library?"

"I have considered it each of the times you've tried to direct me into choosing it next," Ian said dryly. His gaze still lingered unnervingly on Alek.

Silence stretched between them, charged and heavy.

"I'm ready to marry you," Ian said, and it was like a rock dropped into a pond. Alek could see the ripples. "We could go to the courthouse. They accept walk-ins. I already checked."

Of course he had.

"We could go today." A hint of hope slipped into Ian's voice.

Alek hated Ian a little bit then, for having such terrible timing, for finally giving him what he wanted most when it was too late. It wasn't that Alek didn't want to marry Ian anymore. There just wasn't any point.

Now he would have to say no, and Ian would look sad for a fleeting second before he pretended that it hadn't hurt because they were both fucking lying.

Gently, Alek said, "What about your mom? She's working today, isn't she?"

Alek heard from Ian's mother every day at lunchtime. Not by choice. She'd started the routine when he was discharged. If he didn't answer the phone, which was more and more often lately, she left a one-sided conversation of a voicemail that rambled about her day, what she was eating for lunch, what she was sewing for him, almost as if she knew he was on his way out and she wasn't going to let him go without warning him that she'd be left with a bunch of unworn shirts that wouldn't fit anyone but him.

"I haven't told you everything yet," Alek tried next. They'd never resumed their game of question and answers since their last big fight.

"I know enough."

"But I want to get married here."

There it was. A flash of hurt. A quick blink of Ian's eyes.

"Before the fall, you would have said yes," Ian said.

"Nothing is what it was before the fall, least of all me."

Alek exhaled all of his air and sank down until he was sitting at the bottom of the pool. There used to be a pool in his uncle's courtyard. On hot days, Alek would sit on the bottom and pretend to pour tea until he ran out of air. His uncle had taught him the game, said he and his father played it when they were young.

Alek's uncle and his father had always been close. There was one Christmas when Alek—No. Aleksandar—had been very young. He was sitting on his uncle's lap at the kitchen table. Both brothers had been drinking. His father slung his arm around his uncle as they sang slurred versions of old songs uproariously. Aleksandar felt very special to be included. The song crescendoed. Both brothers leaned back and extended their arms wide. The world tilted and slipped out from under Aleksandar as all three of them fell backward. His uncle had scooped him up, so when they landed he was completely unscathed. It was silent for a breath and then both brothers erupted in laughter.

He'd better get back up there, unless he wanted Ian to dive in after him. He kicked up from the bottom and broke the surface, breathing fast to catch his breath.

Ian was nowhere to be found.

34

IAN

I an hadn't expected Alek to say yes, but the answer still stung. Not because he had really wanted to marry Alek that day, but because of what his refusal meant.

After leaving Alek in the greenhouse, Ian picked up his demo kit and headed for the library. Maybe the promise of a fully-restored Victorian library would keep Alek around a little bit longer. Because Alek was leaving. Ian just didn't know when and he didn't know how.

Ian donned his respirator, unzipped the plastic dust barrier, and stepped inside. Thick white canvas covered towering rows of plastic bins filled to the brim with books. On their first walk-through of the Victorian, Ian and Alek had discovered that many of the library's books had been spared from the ravages of water and time, safely ensconced in the glass-fronted bookcases that bordered the walls.

The farthest wall was composed entirely of stained glass windows depicting scenes ripped from the pages of classic stories. Alice falling through the looking glass. Dracula. Dragons. Romeo and Juliet, in death. A bleeding, tell-tale heart. All trapped forever as colored glass between lead. When the sun started to set, like it was now, the wall of windows turned the library into a kaleidoscope of rainbows.

Some of the stained glass had cracked and shattered into shards. Between that and the greenhouse, Ian's glazier bill was going to be astronomical.

The crumbling ceiling was painted a purple so dark it was nearly black. White flecks of stars and barely recognizable planets orbited a boarded-up skylight. The floor beneath had significant water damage, though the rest of the checkerboard-patterned parquet was in good shape.

The bookcases would need to be refinished, the skylight replaced with sun-colored stained glass, the damaged floor-boards exchanged, everything put back together like pieces of a puzzle.

Ian needed the satisfaction of a job well done on a spiritual fucking level, so he started with the only task he could finish in one sitting. Going from one bookcase to the next, he removed the framed glass doors and leaned them against a wall.

He'd known for a while that Alek wasn't as well as he let on. Alek took his medications exactly the same way every night before bed. There was a swish of the sink as he filled the cup, the rattling of pill bottles, the hard sound of the glass against the counter, then he peed, every single time, flushed, and washed his hands—all of it loud enough for Ian to hear through the door.

Alek was nimble, quiet, calculating. The only time he ever made noise was when it was on purpose.

If Ian was in the bathroom at the same time as this nightly ritual, Alek would make a sarcastic show of swallowing the pills and lifting his tongue while opening his hands to prove he'd actually swallowed them. Then he'd hold his wrists together and say, "Take me to bed, warden."

Ian had voiced his concerns to Dr. Dhawan, but though empathetic and equally worried, there was nothing she could do. The law didn't allow doctors to force-feed medications or lock away someone in an institution on word alone. They needed probable cause that Alek was a danger to himself or others, or that he couldn't take care of himself. Even then, that would only buy them seventy-two hours. Alek was a skilled liar, he could easily pass for sane, and then he'd be right back to where he was before.

But Alek was wasting away, slowly strangled by the demons inside his head. In a way, it already felt like Alek had died. His eyes were dull. He seldom spoke. He never wanted to do anything anymore. He rarely laughed, or smiled. Anhedonia was what it was called. Alek had been hedonistic, if anything, when they first met.

Ian felt like he was dying too. He had no one to turn to. No one to lean on. Loving Alek had made him isolated; first, because he only ever wanted to spend time with Alek, and then because his relationship with Alek left little time for anyone else. He couldn't talk to his mom. He didn't want to burden her with his worries and Alek's troubles were too big for a mother to fix anyway.

No amount of demoing would make what Ian and Alek were going through any easier. No solution could fix what went wrong between them. It wasn't that Ian didn't want to fight for them anymore, it was that he didn't know how.

By the time he finished with the bookcases, the sun had set, extinguishing the colors that spilled over the floor so that everything was cast in dark grayscale.

He wiped the sweat from his brow with the edge of his shirt and left the library.

Alek wasn't at the greenhouse. He wasn't in the parlor. Or the kitchen. Upstairs, Ian followed the sound of running water to their bathroom. Breath held, bracing himself for whatever he might find, he pushed open the door.

Steam billowed out from behind the shower curtain. Alek only ever took scalding hot showers, even on hot days.

Ian peeled the curtain back and swallowed hard. Alek was turned away from him, leaned over with one hand pressed flat against the tile, water sluicing down his back. His head hung low and his raven hair blocked his eyes like a blindfold.

Quietly, carefully, Ian let go of the shower curtain and left the room. He paused, waiting to see if Alek had heard him, for the tap to turn off. When Alek didn't emerge, Ian swiped Alek's laptop off the bed and left the room. He went a few doors down to his office and closed the door.

He sat down at the desk, pushed his own computer aside, and opened Alek's laptop. The password to Alek's computer hadn't changed in the two years since Ian had bought it for him. He typed *loveian* and pressed enter. The password box shook in place and the asterisks erased. No luck.

He tried several variations, alternating the capitalization and adding in Alek's favorite number, which was three. When that didn't work, he got creative. Finally, in a fit of fury, he typed *fuckian* and the loading screen cycled.

Alek's desktop was as messy and disorganized as he was. Neurology research articles were interspersed with photographs of antique items he'd been working on, application shortcuts clumped together at random.

Ian opened the internet browser and clicked through each of the tabs Alek had left open. The first was a Google search results page with a list of vodka sauce recipes. Next, a website called *The Piano Bay*, which turned out to be a message board where users swapped sheet music. The last tab was the most recent video upload from Walter Graves, the rounded, bald-headed, mustachioed piano instructor Alek followed. His browser history included more of the same.

It all felt curated, but what had Ian expected? It's not like Alek would have left open windows to gun shop websites, highest bridges within fifty miles, or other such clues to his nefarious plans.

Ian opened a new tab and checked Alek's inbox, which was riddled with spam and the occasional professional correspondence. He scrolled quickly, past furniture ads, hot singles in his area, and the rare author mailing list. Distantly, Ian heard the shower stop. He scanned the emails faster.

His eyes caught on an email from a man called Mercer Llewyn. The subject was *Re: Re: Re: Living Will*. It was a chain of seven emails exchanged between them, the last of which was from a week ago.

ML,

> *I forgot about the Big Sur house. That goes to Ian too. Call me to discuss.*
> *Alek*

Quickly, Ian expanded the rest of the email. Alek had contacted Mercer Llewyn first, shortly after he fell.

ML,

> *I'm finally ready to put together that will you've pestered me endlessly about.*
> *Alek*

That seemed reasonable. A near-death experience might have inspired Alek to get his affairs in order. Ian read on.

Can I call you?

-ML

Alek replied:

You may.

The following day, Mercer Llewyn sent back a response with a file attached.

E-sign this and you're good to go.

Alek's next response came a few weeks later.

ML,

*   I'd like for you to add an additional benefactor. Sara Stewart. $250,000 to be used to pay the remaining balance of her mortgage. Another 500K for her, as well. Say it's for bespoke clothing... because it will amuse me.*

*   Alek*

That fucking prick.
ML had written back a single word:

Done.

It wasn't concrete proof, but it was enough to quell his guilt.

Forget Alek's plans. Ian had a plan of his own. He'd almost gone through with it that afternoon, but had been too afraid, because his plan was another lie. Another betrayal. One too big for Alek to forgive. It would make Alek hate him. It would ruin things between them, but he had no other choice.

35

ALEK

Showers used to be a very productive time for Alek. His mind would weave webs of music, turn thoughts into sound, spin memory into melody. But now showers were just showers—no stroke of genius, only circling sad thoughts.

Alek would leave that night. It was time. The decision made him feel a hundred pounds lighter. His suffering was nearly over.

Soon they'd both be free.

After Ian fell asleep, Alek would take his uncle's piano key, and something to remember Ian by—a sweater or a shirt he'd worn so he could smell cedar and summer-baked pine and love and the only thing that ever mattered one last time.

He wouldn't need anything else where he was going.

Ian still hadn't returned from wherever he'd sulked off to. Ordinarily, Alek would have worried. Had Ian left? Had Ian left him? Left him for good? But Ian had become as codependent and afraid of abandonment as Alek was, which was another reason why he had to leave.

He toweled himself off and pulled on a pair of sweatpants

and a tee. He usually slept in the nude, but it'd be easier to slip away if he was already dressed. Hopefully, Ian would attribute the change to some other antidepressant-induced peculiarity or the air conditioner that chilled their room.

"How was your swim?"

"Christ!" Alek jumped and turned.

Ian leaned against the doorframe. A twitch of a smile tugged the corner of his mouth.

"Sorry." Ian shrugged off the frame and stalked over. "You didn't shave." He palmed the side of Alek's face.

Shaving was hardly a concern when he would be dead soon.

Ian crowded Alek backward until his ass bumped against the vanity.

"I can shave you," Ian said.

"No, thank you."

Ian had shaved him before, usually when his hands were particularly incapacitated. It almost always devolved into fucking, but not until Ian had deemed Alek's face clean-shaven.

"Come on," Ian said. "I know you hate having stubble."

Alek bit the tip of his tongue. The idea of having Ian so close with a sharp object pressed against his neck, of putting his life in Ian's hands one last time, might prove to be a rather climactic send-off.

"Oh, all right," Alek finally said.

"That's the spirit."

Ian gripped Alek's hips.

"That's hardly necessary—" Alek protested, but Ian had already hoisted him onto the countertop.

Ian plucked a fresh towel from the neat stack he kept in the space between the dual sinks and looped it around Alek's neck. When Ian reached across the vanity to bring the razor and their shaving cream closer, their dicks grazed.

Alek gasped—he was only human—but if the sudden contact affected Ian, there was no sign of it.

Ian only turned the tap on and set to work.

Aside from the running water, the room was silent. The only words Alek had left to say couldn't be said aloud. Words like *Goodbye*, and *I don't want to go* and *Loving you used to be the only thing I didn't regret, but now it's the thing I regret most because I never wanted to hurt you.*

Alek's vision hazed as tears pooled unshed. He blinked, shifting his focus to the details of Ian's face so he could summon the image to keep him company later while he waited for his life to end. There were faint, feathered crow feet around his eyes— eyes that weren't just brown, but the color of the forest floor after it rained—and his beard had more gray than when they first met. Each fresh strand of silver stabbed Alek in the heart with grief that they wouldn't grow old together.

Alek wanted to call it all off then, but that was exactly why he wouldn't. He was greedy. If given the chance, he would steal the rest of Ian's remaining years, poisoning them with misery, and even that wouldn't be enough. They could both live until they were one hundred and it wouldn't be enough. Alek would take no less than forever no matter the cost.

The scrape of the razor against Alek's skin sounded like the striking of a match as he lifted his chin to grant Ian easier access. He could almost smell the sulfur and brimstone. All it would take was one slip of the blade and Alek could go now. He wished Ian could be the one to take the light from his eyes, to steal the breath from his lungs, to have Ian usher him from living to dead.

But Ian finished with nary a nick, gently cleaning and toweling Alek's face dry with tender, focused attention. When he was done, Ian leaned his forehead against Alek's.

"Stay," Ian begged, his voice rough and desperate. "I want you to stay."

So, Ian knew?

Alek wanted to ask what gave it away, but he'd stay the course. Deception was all he had left.

"I'm not going anywhere."

"Liar."

Alek hopped down from the vanity. "If you're trying to turn *Liar* into a pet name, I'd really rather you not."

Pale-faced and jaw sharp, Ian stepped back to let him pass.

Over his shoulder, Alek said, "Come along and fuck me now before I'm neutered by psych meds again."

For the first time in far too long, Alek wanted it. Maybe they couldn't say goodbye with words, but they could have sex that said goodbye. They could be together one last time.

He shed his clothes on the way, climbed into bed, closed his eyes, and waited.

Ian's heavy footfalls resonated on the floorboards like music. There was the metallic clinking of his belt buckle undone, the ragged swish of his pants shed, the creak of the bed, the weight Ian displaced as he climbed on top of him. The scent of ancient forests and sun shining through leaves.

"Open your eyes," Ian said.

"I don't want to."

"Come on, love. Let me see those gorgeous eyes."

Alek opened his eyes with a pout and Ian rewarded him with a hand to the side of his neck that made Alek shatter into a thousand shards like broken glass that cut and pricked fingers and spilled blood because he didn't deserve Ian's approval, he didn't deserve Ian's claiming of him, he didn't deserve anything and Ian deserved so much more than him and soon he would have it.

Ian took Alek's mouth in a kiss that pointed fingers, flung accusations, said *I know what you're doing and I hate you for it.*

Then he snatched a bottle of lube off the end table, popped the top one-handed, and poured it over his cock.

Just as impatient, Alek spread his legs and pulled his knees up. With the hand still at Alek's neck, Ian pinned him to the mattress and pushed inside with one quick roll of his hips.

Alek's back bowed at the shock of pain cut with pleasure, at being filled to the brim with no preparation. Digging his nails into Ian's biceps, Alek bit the inside of his cheek to stifle the cry that almost tore from his mouth.

Ian fucked him rough and angry and sad and resigned as tears fell from his eyes for Alek to catch with his tongue, but it wasn't enough so Alek arched up to taste them from his cheeks, and it still wasn't enough, so Alek opened his mouth and tangled their tongues in a kiss that tasted like salt and the end of everything and it still wasn't enough. Ian could paint Alek's insides with come and drown him in an ocean of tears and slit their palms in a blood bond, and none of it would ever be enough.

Ian's tears dried. His eyes turned predatory. He slammed into Alek like he was a hole to rut in until he got off, like he hated him, like he didn't care at all and as much as Alek deserved that, this couldn't be how they said goodbye.

"Stop," Alek said.

Ian stopped and pulled out, but the emptiness was worse.

Wordlessly, Ian climbed off of him and left for the bathroom. The lock clicked shut, the tap ran. Alek could imagine him there, hands braced on the vanity, head bent over the sink, castigating the fuck out of himself for losing control, for taking instead of giving, when it was Alek who was guilty.

Ian came back and sat at the edge of the bed. "Did I hurt you?"

Alek shook his head. "Can we try again, but make it a little less hate-fucky?"

"No."

"But you always give me what I want."

"And you never do." Ian's tone was flat, his emotions clamped down so tightly, that Alek could hear the bomb ticking. Pleading now, Ian said, "Why can't you give me what I want? Stay. Take the medications. Don't do this."

"I am taking my meds."

"Lies. Lies. Fucking lies!" Ian roared. He jumped to his feet, fisting his hands in his hair while he paced beside the bed.

Even though he was completely broken inside, Alek forced himself to become cold and sneering. He shot Ian an incredulous look, like he was a child throwing the most ridiculous of tantrums. That's what the old Alek would have done.

Ian halted his pacing, the stillness so sudden and eerie that a shiver pricked and poked its way across Alek's body.

Calmer now. Stoic even, Ian loomed over him and said, "This is your last chance. If you don't come clean. If you don't let me help you, you won't like what happens."

"Oh?" Alek taunted. "What are you going to do? Leave me? I thought you said you'd never do that. *Liar*."

"Alek, please." Ian leaned down to press his forehead to Alek's again. "*Please*."

Alek breathed in deeply and hoped that he'd inhaled some of the air from Ian's lungs and if he had that he could take it with him, so his last breath wouldn't be alone.

Then Alek pulled away and turned onto his side. "I'd like to go to sleep. Would you turn out the light?"

Things skidded and clattered onto the floor. Alek turned back in time to catch Ian yanking the lamp off the side table. The electric cord ripped from the wall. The light went out and the sudden darkness blinded him, but he didn't need his eyesight to know that the sound of shattering china and broken glass was Ian throwing the lamp onto the floor.

"Good night," Ian said in a sad, gritty refrain.

The door slammed.

"Goodbye," Alek said quietly.

He wished he hadn't ruined their goodbye, just like he wished he hadn't ruined everything else.

36

ALEKSANDAR

BULGARIA. SEVENTEEN YEARS OLD.

T he years Aleksandar spent banished at boarding school proved most informative.

Aleksandar had always known he was superior to others—in wit, in talent, in appearance, but it had never occurred to him to use that superiority to his advantage. People were meant to be manipulated. Everyone was for sale. Wasn't that what his father taught him?

Blackmail and bribes were particularly useful. Sex was as good a currency as any. If Aleksandar wanted something, all he had to do was determine whom to fuck or fuck over. Ten minutes on his knees was the only effort he'd had to put into securing two hours of daily solo practice at the piano.

Boarding school was much more tolerable after that.

Aleksandar was invited home for the summer and every summer thereafter, but he seldom saw his father, and when he did he wished he hadn't. After a respectful period of time, his father remarried.

Aleksandar's new stepmother was seven years older than him. She was fair-skinned with golden hair and hazel eyes on a face rounded with youth—nothing like his mother's olive skin, green eyes, and sharp beauty.

Their marriage was a loveless one. A match made in politics and power. There were no half-siblings, the fact of which was not lost on Aleksandar.

After stealing a classmate's login information—in case his own browsing history was monitored—Aleksandar used the school computer to learn everything he could about lock picking and safe cracking. Apparently, a fireproof safe was more for protection against damage than protection against theft. A combination lock could be cracked if a would-be thief knew what to listen for. Drilling a hole through the lock was another more fool-proof option, but Aleksandar wouldn't cheat unless he had to.

His mother might have known of the safe's location—perhaps she even knew the code, or planned to pick the lock—but the safe wasn't for her. His mother was prone to migraines, brought on or worsened whenever Aleksandar played. His uncle would never leave something for her there. Then again, for all he knew, his mother loved music, but couldn't bear to listen to what only reminded her of what she couldn't have.

All the same, Aleksandar knew with complete conviction that as much as the piano belonged to him and he belonged to it, that locked box only belonged to those whose initials were carved into the side of the piano. His uncle, and him.

At first, hiding the safe with the piano had seemed reckless. Whatever was inside must not be very important, or valuable, especially because it was locked away in a safe that could easily be cracked, but his uncle was never reckless. Exactly like Alek-sandar's father, and like Aleksandar himself, everything his uncle did was for a reason.

The Velishikovs played chess, not checkers.

The only likely conclusion was that the safe, and its

contents, were a backup plan. His uncle had left what Aleksandar would need most in a place he was most likely to find it.
That meant the combination to the lock wasn't random. His
uncle would have selected a series of numbers Aleksandar
would be able to guess. It was the most frustrating of failures
that he hadn't solved it yet.

That was why he wouldn't crack the safe with tools or tricks,
not unless he had no other choice. He wanted to earn the
contents contained within. He wanted to know that he was right,
that even though there were secrets that his uncle had kept from
him, that he'd likely never learn the truth, at the very least, he
knew his uncle.

––––––

IT WAS a hot night in midsummer when Aleksandar finally
cracked the safe. He was eighteen. Boarding school was done
and over and after reminding his father that all the other *heir-
lings* went to nepotism-ridden business schools in the United
States, he would leave for Wharton in the fall.

It was all a farce, one that they both were in on. It had been
years since his father had seriously expected that Aleksandar
would one day replace him. Aleksandar could not be controlled.
He wouldn't fall in line. The corrupt family business would end
with his father.

Aleksandar wasn't sure why his father let him live when he'd
killed his own brother with impunity. He suspected his father
didn't care what happened to him, as long as he didn't have to
look at him, because when he looked at him all he saw was
everything that he'd lost. A brother. A wife. The idea of a son
that Aleksandar had failed to become, and never would.

That night, the forest behind his house was alive with the
calls of crickets and frogs, providing a perfect cover for his foot-

steps. His father and stepmother were away, and aside from the guards at the gate, the grounds were empty.

Like every time Aleksandar approached the fallen log that nursed four new trees, he expected the safe to have disappeared, to never have existed at all, erased from existence the way that his uncle had been. But just like all the other times, when he reached his hand into the dark hole, pushing past roots that tangled like spider webs, the box was still where he'd left it.

Aleksandar propped his flashlight on the ground. Over the years, he'd tried dozens of alphanumeric cipher versions of his name, hundreds of historical dates, some so obscure they were only tangentially related to the stories his uncle had told him.

That night he would try only one code. The date of birth of something that never breathed, that had died, but would live as long as Aleksandar didn't forget it. He'd spent months researching the history of his uncle's piano, a task made difficult by the need for secrecy and the fact that all identifying features of the piano had been destroyed in the fire.

With the tip of his finger, he scrolled through each number disk until the combination read 1-8-9-3. There was a click, and the lid popped open. It was an anticlimax, really. Opening a box that had been locked for years. Discovering what his uncle had left for him, what his mother had so desperately wanted.

When Aleksandar lifted the lid, he found a single envelope addressed to himself in his uncle's meticulous script. He pocketed the letter without reading it.

Beneath the letter were stacks of bearer bonds, thousands of dollars that required no identification to redeem. There was a small jar of loose precious stones—emeralds, rubies, sapphires, and diamonds. Under the surname Vasquez, were fake birth certificates and passports for Aleksandar and his mother. His uncle had left them with a new identity and enough untraceable cash to finance their escape. He could only assume that he and his mother were meant to leave together, to join his uncle.

Was that why his uncle had left? Was he setting things in motion, laying the framework of their escape? Was that why he came back? Was he coming for Aleksandar? His mother was abroad during that time. Was Aleksandar supposed to have joined her? Had she left him behind?

Knowing that his uncle had planned for exactly what Aleksandar wanted to do was as good as getting his blessing. He felt less like a coward eschewing his familial duties and more like a son living the life his *father* wanted him to have.

He emptied the safe and returned it to the hole under the nurse tree. He did not read his uncle's letter. He didn't know if he'd ever be brave enough to read it, but along with the jewels and bonds and forged identities, he took the letter with him to America just in case.

37

ALEK

Escaping would have been easier if Ian had slept on the couch instead of plastering himself to Alek's backside with their legs tangled together like he thought maybe Alek wouldn't leave if he didn't let go. Waiting for Ian's breathing to slow was torture. The solid warmth of Ian's body surrounding him, Ian's breath against the back of his head where he must have nuzzled his face into his hair. It was all a grim reminder of what Alek would forfeit in death.

After an hour, when Alek was very sure that Ian was asleep, he disentangled himself from Ian's limbs and he didn't look back, because if he did he wouldn't be able to leave, and he had to leave. So without a kiss goodbye, he left, and he already felt like his heart had ripped in half, like he'd left it back in bed with Ian, like he was halfway dead, and it hurt so bad that Alek could hardly breathe, but he had to keep going.

This would all be over soon.

In his own room, he packed a single bag with his wallet and cell, and the black shirt of Ian's he'd pilfered from the laundry. He crawled under his bed and removed the piano key, and though the single key was hollow in his hands, guilt made it weigh as much as if he was carrying an entire grand piano.

Sweat tickled the back of his neck as he tiptoed through the oppressive heat of the upstairs hallway. He sneaked his way down the stairs, out of the house, and into the garage, then crossed to the fire-proof, humidity-controlled, double-doored safe.

Early on in their relationship, Alek had explained the safe was used to store his client's priceless artifacts while he was restoring them. He'd been secretive about its contents and Ian had respected that. If the roles were reversed, Alek would have cracked the safe the first chance he had. Which was why Alek had selected a safe with biometric and two-factor authentication to ensure that no one laid eyes on what was inside without him to chaperone.

He pressed his thumbprint to the scanner, approved the request on his cell, and used a key to open the door. He shoved aside the piles of historical love letters and photos that Ian had guilt-tripped him into preserving. Bending down, he used another key to unlock a drawer that contained the olive branch crown and the letter his uncle had written—the letter that he was still too afraid to read. He put his uncle's letter into his backpack then pulled an overstuffed envelope of his own from his pocket.

Inside the envelope was a letter that told Ian every last secret that he didn't know, Alek's entire life story as he remembered it. One hundred apologies that would never be enough. Words of adulation and love and undying devotion that Alek would hold until his last breath and even after that. And Alek's wedding ring. The one Ian had given him. Alek had been torn on the decision. He didn't want to part with the ring; he wanted his body to be marked as Ian's even in death, but what if it was lost to the ocean? It was Ian's as much as Alek's heart was.

He placed the letter front and center in the space he'd cleared and perched the olive wreath crown on top, because it said sorry and that's what he was.

Sorry.

Beside the crown, he dropped a handful of glittering stones, all that remained of his inheritance.

After leaving the door to the safe open for Ian to find, Alek left the garage and headed for his car. When he put the key in the ignition, the lights didn't turn on and the car wouldn't start. Alek popped the hood, the sound echoing unnervingly through the too-quiet woods. The battery wasn't dead. It was missing. That prick.

Ian's keys were in the pocket of the jeans he'd pulled off before climbing into bed earlier. Alek remembered the distinct metallic jingle. There wasn't a spare set, because Alek had misplaced them—well, misplaced them by melting them with a blowtorch he used to flambé crème brûlée when Ian had threatened to leave during one of their pre-fall spats.

Returning to their bedroom to fish the keys from Ian's pants wasn't the kind of calculated risk Alek got off on taking, and surely Ian would have removed the truck's battery anyway. There were dozens of rooms he could have hidden the batteries in, and dozens more wardrobes and built-ins and drop cloths over furniture to conceal them further.

Even if Ian had left the battery intact, the truck had a loud diesel rumble sure to wake Ian, who would no doubt alert the authorities if only to get Alek back. Alek didn't much care to delay his suicide whilst locked inside a cell that reeked of urine on the charge of grand theft auto.

No matter. Alek would walk down the double yellow line of the deserted mountain road while he waited for an Uber to meet him. He set off on foot, and he didn't look back at the Victorian either, because if he did, he'd see that first day he found it, when the wisteria climbed to the sky, when Alek and Ian's happily ever after had just unfurled before them, back when he could play the piano, and he didn't feel anything except that he loved Ian.

He didn't make it very far down the driveway before he saw her at the base of the tree on the edge of the woods. Bright orange and white, nearly fluorescent in the darkness. There was the fox, curled up on her side, her nose tucked under her tail.

He rushed over to her with unbridled relief. He'd all but accepted that he was going the rest of the way alone, the fact of which made him feel more lonely than he'd ever felt in his entire life—even more lonely than when his uncle had died and he had cried under the painting that leaned against the wall of his uncle's workshop.

Alek wasn't entirely sure how the physics of an imaginary fox were supposed to work, but he hoped now that he'd found her, she could stay by his side to see him through to the end, and maybe once he was gone, she would be free, unburdened and healthy once more.

But hoping was foolish. Something was wrong. She didn't hear him coming. Her eyes didn't open. He dropped to his knees and touched a light hand to her silky fur, but she did not stir. She was cold amidst the stuffy summer air. Stiff. Unbreathing.

That couldn't be right. He shook her, gently and then roughly. Her bones were sharp. She'd grown so thin, the haunches of her hips protruding through her velvet coat. When she didn't wake, he lifted her into his arms.

How could she die? How could she leave? She was his fox. She was his hallucination. And now she was dead and why couldn't she have waited a little bit longer so he could go first? Why did she have to leave him alone?

He had to bury her. He knew that. The dead were meant to be buried. Not burned to ash or made to disappear or, worse yet, left to be found.

She didn't deserve the salty, watery grave he was headed for, the craggy bluff that jutted out over the Pacific. He couldn't wait for the freedom of a fall that felt like he was flying as gravity yanked him down to icy water made harder than rock by the distance of his descent. He couldn't wait for the instant black nothingness of death that would wash away all of his pain, all of the things he'd done, everything that he was. The waves that would rush to swallow him whole.

But the fox hated getting her paws wet. He couldn't leave until he put her in the ground.

Alek would need a shovel. Carrying the fox with him, he ran back to the garage, but the shovel wasn't there. The greenhouse! He'd seen the shovel propped against the back door. Shooting a glance at the still-dark windows of the Victorian, he set off around the side of the house.

By the time he made it to the greenhouse, the wind had shifted. A sharp breeze sliced through the air. Clouds moved fast to cover the light of the moon and snuff out all the stars in the sky. Distant thunder boomed. Just his luck.

He cradled the fox in the crook of his arm and pulled his cell from his back pocket to light the way. The woods were like a labyrinth as he weaved between trees, crushing ferns beneath his feet, sharp branches snagging at his clothes like claws. At the base of an ancient redwood, he placed the fox atop a clump of gnarled roots—so that her fur wouldn't get dirty—then dropped his backpack beside her.

The first raindrop landed on the back of his neck at exactly the same moment his shovel pierced the earth. The storm started as a smattering sprinkle of fat raindrops, like someone had grabbed a fistful of water and hurled it down from the heavens, but only a few shovelfuls later the rain had gathered into a downpour that not even the interconnected treetops could shield him from.

A flash of lightning reflected off the water that already filled the hole he was digging. Another burst of thunder cracked. He pushed his hair from his brow and stepped down on the shovel. His hands slipped on the handle. Gritting his teeth and willing his hands to work, he readjusted his grip and lifted another shovelful of dirt from the earth.

Each strike of the shovel stabbed a jolt of pain up the nerves in his forearms, but he kept going. He had to hurry. The greenhouse was far enough from their living quarters that Ian had no chance of hearing him, but the storm was so loud. Ian would surely be up. Then he'd know Alek was gone.

Alek looked over his shoulder, but he couldn't see the windows of the Victorian through the veil of rain and tangled trees. He returned his attention to the grave with renewed urgency.

Finally, the grave was big enough and he threw the shovel aside. He wiped his hands on his pants and scooped the fox into his arms. Her coat was matted from the rain, but even in death she was beautiful; she looked like she was sleeping, like she was alive.

How could she be dead? How could she not be real?

It had been decades since he had cried and the rain washed away the proof, but he thought he might be crying. Over a fox. That wasn't real.

His teeth chattered violently; he trembled with such force that rigors wracked his body, and he couldn't be certain if it was because he was terrified, or a result of the rain that drenched his clothes, or perhaps even the burning pain that licked from his wrists to his fingertips—likely all three.

Marshaling the last dregs of his courage, he placed the fox in the hole in the ground. He checked one last time that her chest did not move, that her eyes remained unseeing, and then he stood back and picked up the shovel, piling the dirt over her before he could change his mind, because he wanted nothing more than to pick her up and hold her to his chest and will his fucked up head to bring her back to life like magic because how could she leave him?

He sank to his knees and pressed his palms against the freshly tilled earth.

"Goodbye."

And he wasn't just saying goodbye to her. He was saying goodbye to the only time he'd ever been happy in his entire life. The only time he'd ever felt love after his uncle died. He was saying goodbye to the Victorian. To quiet moments in bed with Ian's hands in his hair. The rumble of Ian's voice when he said "I love you", the squeeze of his hand wrapped around the side of his neck. To be taken care of. To be loved.

His fingers fisted in the dirt like his body didn't want to let go, like his muscles and tendons, the blood that coursed through his veins, still had the will to live and knew what was coming, because his job was done. The fox was buried.

It was time to go.

38

IAN

Lightning lit up the forest. *One one thousand.*

At the base of a redwood tree, Alek was on his hands and knees.

Two one thousand.

Mud covered Alek's arms up to his elbows. His body shook.

Three one thousand.

Ian wasn't sure if Alek was sobbing or shivering.

Thunder boomed. Alek flinched.

It had been precisely four seconds since the lightning struck.

Ian stepped closer to Alek's hunched-over form.

"Alek?"

Alek scrambled to his feet, a feral gleam in his eyes. His face was so pale he looked dead. A slash of mud was smeared across his brow.

"Love..." Ian lifted his hands. "What are you doing?"

"Just some impromptu gardening," Alek said, brushing his hands on pants that were just as filthy.

Ian eyed the freshly disturbed earth. It was about the size of a small animal.

"Oh, Alek." He pulled him into a hug.

"The fox," Alek sobbed, burying his face in Ian's jacket. "I know she's not supposed to be real, but she died and I wasn't there and I've been ignoring her because I didn't want you to know that I still see her, and I think that's why she died. She thought I abandoned her. She thought I left her. And then she died. Alone. Like that."

"It's okay, love. I've got you. I'll take care of you."

Ian pulled Alek's sopping shirt off and shrugged out of his own jacket, before throwing it around Alek's shoulders. He helped Alek's hands through the armholes and zipped it up to his chin, then pressed Alek back against his chest and shushed him consolingly.

Then Ian reached into his pocket.

Another flash of lightning. *One one thousand, two one thousand—*

Thunder.

Ian had bet on the storm moving closer and he'd timed it just right. Using the thunder as a diversion, Ian kicked his leg out and swept Alek off his feet. He tried to ease Alek's fall, but the ground was so wet, the mud thick and slippery, and rain obfuscated everything.

Alek landed on his stomach, hard. Hard enough to knock the wind out of him, because that could be the only explanation for why he wasn't yelling at him yet. Alek's fingers were stark white against the dirt as he tried to crawl away, but before he could make much progress, Ian grabbed his ankles and pulled him back, then climbed on top of him.

With as much care as he could manage, he trapped Alek's hands behind his back and looped the length of rope he'd pulled from his pocket onto one wrist, and then the other, before knotting it tight and snipping the excess with the scissors he'd stashed in his back pocket.

"What the fuck, Ian?" Alek roared over the storm, wrenching his wrists back and forth as he tried, and failed, to free himself.

Ian had worried about the restraint part of his plan, but he couldn't risk failure. He'd only have that one chance. Without answering, he lifted Alek to his feet and heaved him over his shoulder. Ian would feel it tomorrow, but he'd carry an entire house to save Alek if he had to. Careful not to trip, or slip, he held onto the back of Alek's thighs and lugged him towards the glowing light of the Victorian.

"What are you doing?" Alek growled from where his face bounced against Ian's lower back.

"I'm saving you," Ian grunted as he kicked open the greenhouse door and set off down the brick path.

Alek struggled to get down. "Let me go!"

"I didn't want to do it this way, but you left me no choice."

A few feet from the edge of the pool, Ian lowered to one knee and dropped Alek on his back in an empty flower bed. As soon as his body touched the earth, Alek twisted onto his stomach, bowed his head in the mud, and pushed onto his knees in a valiant attempt to get to his feet.

Ian pushed him back down before he could escape.

Roaring in rage, Alek yanked his wrists against the rope.

"If you don't stop that, I'll choke you out," Ian threatened. "I won't have you ruining your hands."

Alek stilled. "You say you'll choke me like it's a bad thing." He lengthened his neck, dragging the side of his face through the mud. "Go ahead." Then he struck out again, kicking his legs and thrashing his body side to side.

"I'm bigger than you. I'm stronger than you," Ian ground out as he straddled Alek's ass and sat all of his weight on top of him before taking his ankles in his hands. "Stop fighting."

Alek only screamed in frustration and fought harder.

Ignoring him, Ian knotted Alek's ankles together, then

hogtied his hands to his feet. He climbed off and surveyed his work. Alek wasn't going anywhere.

"I don't do bondage," Alek grunted between futile attempts to free himself.

"I know. I'm sorry. I feel bad about that, I do."

"What are you going to do?" Alek asked again.

"I know you aren't taking your meds," Ian yelled over the squall.

"What gave it away? The fact that I was having a funeral for an invisible fox?"

"You were going to leave? Without saying goodbye? Without a note?"

"I thought we already had goodbye sex. We could go again if you'd like," Alek said, like cutting him out of his life was as painless as snipping an errant thread.

"You were going to kill yourself," Ian said, and the enormity of it all, how close Alek had come to death, how close Ian had come to losing him, how precarious this all still was. All of the fear, running on adrenaline, feigning sleep, hardly able to sleep, to even blink for fear of what might happen. It all rose up like a rogue wave. Through the tears that threatened and the panic that loomed and the sudden bone-weary exhaustion that made his knees weak, Ian went on,

"Did you really think I would let you do that? That I'd let you go? When will you get it through that thick skull of yours that you matter, that you're worth the fight, that I love you?"

When Alek said nothing, Ian checked that his bindings were secure and crossed to a pile of leftover building materials—stacks of bricks, heavy bags of mortar, scattered tools, thick garden shears with blades so sharp they could sever a limb.

"This is no time for construction, Ian." Alek's bravado was thinning. His tone might have been teasing, but his voice cracked with a streak of fear.

Nine bricks over from the left, Ian started lifting bricks and tossing them aside. Five rows of bricks down was a pair of cinder blocks Ian had hidden there for when the time was right. He'd already prepped and tied the rope around each block. His years in construction had given him a pretty accurate sense of measurement.

Carrying one cinder block in each hand, Ian walked to the edge of the pool, and tossed both blocks in. The storm was so loud he couldn't even hear the splash.

"No. Ian, no!" Alek thrashed violently.

"You're so smart," Ian said as he returned to his side. "I love that about you."

Ian had a few other scenarios stashed around the house like a game of Clue. A blue tarp and an unloaded gun behind the cleaning supplies under their kitchen sink. A razor blade tucked beneath the crown molding in their bathroom. A noose to hang from the third-story window.

"It's very convenient, this thunderstorm," Ian remarked. "I'm glad I didn't have to throw you in the pool first, or dive in after you."

He'd stolen the idea from Dr. Modorovic, or maybe, the beginning of an idea. It's not like she called him up one night and suggested he frame Alek for suicide. Thanks to Ian's surreptitious study of Bulgarian—so he was prepared in the event Alek somehow lost his English again—he'd overheard Dr. Modorovic's long-ago threat to call in a fake complaint for suicidal ideation. Ian had just taken it one step further.

"Please. I'll stay. I won't leave. I'll take the meds. I'll tell you everything," Alek begged as he fought his restraints like he was fighting for his life.

Ian wanted to believe him. He didn't want this. But Alek was lying and if Ian had to make Alek hate him to save him, then he'd do what he had to do.

"My name used to be Aleksandar Vel—"

Ian rushed to cover Alek's mouth. "Don't say another word. You'll tell me when it's because you want to. When you've forgiven yourself. Besides, telling me won't save you."

Alek unleashed a muffled litany of curse words in a mix of English and Bulgarian.

Ian lifted his hand and snipped the rope that had Alek hogtied, leaving him with only his wrists and ankles restrained. While Alek struggled in vain to free himself from his remaining bindings, Ian removed his phone from his pocket.

"9-1-1. What's your emergency," said the male operator.

Good. He'd worried he'd get the same operator from before. What if she remembered him? What if he didn't sound convincing by comparison?

Channeling the very real fear he had for Alek's life and adding a dash of anguish over losing him, Ian said, "My fiancé. I just pulled him out of the pool! He's mentally ill. Cinder blocks tied to his ankles. Please. You have to come help him." Ian listed off the Victorian's address.

"Is he breathing?"

Ian looked at Alek. He'd turned onto his side, eyes cold, eerily watching in silence.

"He's okay. I got him right after he jumped in, but he's not acting right. He's off his meds. I'm afraid I won't be able to keep him safe," Ian said with faux desperation.

"I'll dispatch a sheriff to your location. It'll be about twenty minutes. I'll send an ambulance too, but they're farther out."

"Thank you," Ian said before ending the call.

Next, Ian fastened a new set of rope to each of Alek's ankles, leaving a small tail to match the ropes tied to the cinder blocks at the bottom of the pool. Now that the scene was set, Ian didn't want Alek any more restrained than he had to be. He severed the original rope that tied Alek's ankles together, and repeated the process to free his wrists. Ian chucked the scrap rope far into the uncut vegetation, and threw the scissors into the pool, roughly where the cinder blocks were.

Alek tried to get to his feet, but Ian was there already. He flipped Alek onto his back and sat on his chest, trapping his hands. With the sleeve of his shirt, he wiped some of the mud from Alek's face.

It was a mistake. Alek freed one of his arms and lashed out with a punch to Ian's gut.

Ian and Alek had wrestled before, for fun, usually as a pretense to sex. Alek didn't have the brawn Ian had, but he was scrappy and he fought dirty. Before the fall, Alek could have won. If he hadn't obsessively practiced the piano until his hands were as weak and battered as the gnarled, arthritic hands of a ninety-year-old, he would have had a chance. But even as Alek tried to scratch and bite, and buck Ian off of him, Alek was only a cardboard version of his former self and with little effort, Ian had him pinned to the ground like a moth to a board.

"I'll tell them you did this," Alek said. "They'll find the rope you cut with my DNA on it."

The fact that Alek thought that would work was proof of how much he wasn't himself.

"Do you have any idea how crazy that sounds?" Ian said with kindness. "If they believed you, which they won't, they'll assume it was a trial run. That you misjudged the length of the rope."

"I'll be out in seventy-two hours. Then I can do whatever I want."

"No. I don't think you will. I caught you mid-attempt, drowning yourself in a Gothic Victorian greenhouse. You said you wanted a poetic death. The best I could do was a poetic failed suicide attempt."

Sirens wailed over the storm.

"You'll have to go to the hospital first, but I found a private behavioral treatment center. The patients are all high functioning. They can make special accommodations." Ian didn't add that he'd be supervised around the clock, or that Ian's retirement would foot the bill. "When you're feeling better we can video chat. You can keep teaching me the piano. I can visit."

"If I never see you again, it will be too soon."

Ian knew that. He knew this was likely the end for them, but he pressed on. "They'll be able to keep you safe until the medications work. You can get help. Talk about what you can't tell me. You don't have to tell them the truth. Tell them a shadow of it. Get better. Stop hating yourself."

"I hate you!" Alek roared.

Through the sleeting rain, Ian could just make out the Victorian glowing red and blue. Whatever last words he had for Alek, the only time he had was now.

"I know you hate me and I know what that's like. But you know what you taught me? You can hate someone and love them too. You can hate someone so much you think you'll never be able to look at them without your heart breaking, only to fall in love with them all over again. Whether it's a month, or a year, or the rest of my life, I'm not giving up on you. I won't ever leave you. I won't let you go without a fight. I'll wait for you. Leave me if you want. Never come back if that's what you decide. But there will never be anyone else for me. Only you. Only fucking you."

Alek turned his head to the side, his cheek hollow. Ian rubbed his thumb over the spot and it killed him to think that he wouldn't be there to remind Alek not to bite the inside of his cheek. Ian's watch had ended. He'd done all he could and it wasn't enough. It was someone else's turn.

Car doors slammed. Distant voices called.

Ian kissed Alek one last time. Alek bit Ian's lip so hard he tasted blood, but it was okay, because it would be proof that Alek had been there for as long as it took to heal, even after Alek was gone.

"I love you," Ian said, pulling away. "He's here," he yelled over his shoulder.

Then he helped Alek to his feet and handed him over to the deputies, but only after Alek had been handcuffed—Ian didn't trust Alek not to attempt suicide by cop. In the end Alek did go quietly. He was smart enough to know he had no alternative, that he'd be better off biding his time. Acting as sane as possible. He'd wait and plot and strike when the timing was right. Ian wouldn't expect anything less.

Ian followed them to the patrol car, watching as Alek ducked his head gracefully and slid into the back seat. The car door slammed shut with heavy finality.

Through the darkness and the storm that still raged, Alek's jade eyes remained locked onto Ian with such intense loathing that his skin prickled like he was being cursed, like if Alek only possessed the ability, he'd summon a bolt of lightning from the heavens to smite Ian for his sins. Then the car pulled away and even after the flaring red and blue lights were swallowed up by the trees, Ian could still feel Alek's eyes on him. Accusing him. Hating him.

39

ALEK
DAY SEVEN OF PURGATORY

I t was day four of Alek's tenure at *Alder Grove, Elm Bridge* or whatever bourgeois bullshit the mental hospital was called—sorry—private behavioral treatment center, because that was supposed to make it sound like the patients were the tortured, artistic, well-connected kind of crazy, and not the government-insured peasants over at the state hospital.

At a small round table in the most secluded corner of the cafeteria, Alek marked another day of purgatory in a paper-bound notebook he'd been given to journal in, should he feel so inclined, which he absolutely did not. Pens and pencils were not allowed, so his tallies were written with an infantilizing black crayon.

Four days, plus the three at the hospital. One week without Ian. Seven days forced to live on borrowed time he'd never asked for or wanted. Countless heartbeats that chanted: *You should be dead. You should be dead. You should be dead.* He could hardly breathe. He didn't want to. He wanted to die.

He wanted Ian.

Meal time in the cafeteria was compulsory. The intent was obvious. Even the most reclusive patients had to eat. Alek was on day two of a hunger strike. Not for suicidal reasons; that would take far too long. He was trying to negotiate a room service arrangement.

"Fuck me, you're pretty," said a wisp of a young woman dressed in all dark like a shadow.

Alek started. He hadn't heard her approach over the cafeteria's ever present soundtrack of grumbling conversation, plates clashing against tabletops, blunted sporks scraping like nails on a chalkboard.

He'd seen the girl before, but she'd never made contact. Usually, Alek's resting fuck-off-and-die face was enough to keep the other patients away.

She dropped into the seat across from him.

Alek scowled at her over his egg scramble.

The girl had black hair with blonde roots and anemic, nearly-translucent skin. It was difficult to guess her age as there was neither a wrinkle nor sunspot on her face, but she had to be at least eighteen. Minors were not allowed.

"What did you do to get put inside here?" she asked.

Wasn't there an unspoken rule that fellow patients weren't supposed to ask each other that? It was like prison, but with better accommodations.

"Oh, I see," the girl continued. "You can't control anything so you'll eat your words and starve yourself while you push your food around your plate and do what you can to feel like you're not completely powerless. Right?"

She was. That was precisely what he was doing.

The girl piled her hair into a messy bun on the top of her head, securing it with a telephone wire hair tie she'd slid off her wrist. There were a series of pinprick holes along the delicate shell of her ear and rows of shiny scars carved into her forearms.

Absently, he wondered if it would be possible to fashion a garotte out of one of her hair ties.

"I'm Briar," she said. "What's your name?"

If he responded in Bulgarian, would she go away?

"I've been here for eight months, but don't worry. That's not typical. I mean, there's definitely some lifers here."

She flicked her gaze to a catatonic woman at the neighboring table who was frozen with her spork a few inches in front of her mouth.

"But most people don't stay long—not because they get better—they're hidden away somewhere with a private nurse to keep them out of sight. I'm hiding too, but not like that. Every time I'm about to go home, there's a sudden setback." She shielded her mouth with her hand and leaned across the table, stage whispering, "It's all an act. I don't want to go home."

If she thought he'd believe that, she was as insane as he was.

She sat back in her chair.

"If you don't tell me your name, I'll have to make one up for you and I must warn you that I'm very bad at naming things. I once had a goldfish named Cat. I named my dog Doug and it was very confusing for everybody involved. 'Your dog is named Dog?' the person would ask. 'No. Doug. Like the human name,' I'd say. Then they would say that was a funny name and I would ask how so and then there would be a long awkward pause, which was fine. I thrive in silence."

He should have left, but this girl—Briar, was it?—was strangely magnetic, and inpatient psychiatric hospitalization was exceedingly boring, especially when his schedule was stacked with group and individual therapy he refused to participate in, and forced attendance to holistic classes called *Yoga Your Way*, *Art of the Heart*, and *Reap What You Sow*. That last one was gardening without tools because some study alleged that humans needed to feel their hands touch the earth to connect with their prehistoric ancestors, when really it was because most garden tools could double as a weapon.

He didn't like the garden. It reminded him of the fox, and if he thought about the fox, in addition to experiencing the loss of her death all over again, he thought about the last time he saw Ian, and he couldn't think about Ian. He'd tried to get out of gardening on the grounds that his hands were still mangled, but an aspiring Nurse Ratched said he didn't have to garden, but he still had to be there. At least he was excused from *Music Moods*.

"Are you going to tell me your name or not?" Briar nudged.

He stared at her.

"Very well, then." She chewed on her bottom lip and it reminded Alek so much of Ian that he wanted to cry. Everything could remind him of Ian if he wasn't careful.

"Broody? No. That's something chickens do. What's that guy's name? The one Dracula was named after... *Something the Impaler*—don't get the wrong idea. I'm not implying I'd like you to impale me..." She looked at his lap as if he needed help grasping the innuendo. "Although I wouldn't say no if you asked nicely. It's just that you have a goth, I live in a haunted mansion and get turned on by the sight of blood sort of look about you."

Pot, meet kettle.

"God! What was his name?" She looked at him.

If Alek was talking, he would have said, "How could you not remember that it's Vlad the Impaler?" but he wasn't talking and he wasn't sure if he would ever talk again.

He'd already said his last words. He shouldn't be here.

"Scratch that then. Poe, maybe? You give me telltale heart vibes. Or... you could just tell me your name. I'll figure it out eventually. Someone is bound to address you while I'm around. We're locked inside the same cage, aren't we?"

Alek said nothing.

"No? Give me some time to think about it, then."

After looking furtively from side to side, Briar leaned close. Her bottom lip had bloomed a rosy red from where she'd chewed on it. Before Ian, Alek might have entertained the idea of passing his time in purgatory buried inside Briar's various holes, but bisexual as he once was, the only way he swung anymore was Ian's way.

Briar moved fast, snatching the spork from his hand and shoveling several heaping spoonfuls—sporkfuls?—of eggs into her mouth before dropping the spork on his plate.

"There. Now it looks like you've eaten some. You don't want to call their bluff when it comes to eating. There's this feeding tube they'll threaten you with and the threat isn't empty." She tapped the side of her nose. "Ask me how I know."

When he didn't, Briar rose from her chair.

"Wait," he said, surprising even himself.

She stopped and wrapped her hands around the back of the chair. Her nails were trimmed short and scuffed with peeling black polish.

"My name is Alek."

She flashed a grin. "Alek, huh? Are you sure you don't want me to call you Vlad? Especially with that accent..."

His responding smile snuck up on him before he could catch it.

"It was nice to meet you, Alek." Then, as if Briar knew a return exchange of social niceties would be too much for him, she left.

He watched as she navigated around the scattered tables, squeezed through a gap between a group of people in her path, and disappeared down the hallway that led to the living quarters. She didn't stop to talk to anyone else along the way. No one tried to talk to her either. Was she real? Or was Briar another fox?

40

ALEK

DAY TEN OF PURGATORY

D r. Dhawan wore a black silk top that knotted at her neck, a rather insensitive choice. Alek would give anything to feel the tight embrace of a knot tied around his neck and here she was flaunting a business casual noose in front of his face.

It was the first time he'd seen the doctor without a computer screen separating them. He preferred the digital experience. It was easier to hide.

"How are you liking it here?" She crossed one linen-clad leg over the other.

Her pants were the color of the crust of crème brûlée. Alek could hear the hollow scrape his spoon would make. Crème brûlée reminded him of the blowtorch to truck keys incident, which led his thoughts back to Ian and he was not thinking about Ian.

"It certainly appears nice enough," she said.

He followed her gaze to the modern windows that made up nearly every westward-facing wall. Miles of ocean stretched to the horizon, the water sparkling beneath a cloudless sky. The view might have been picturesque if it wasn't marred by the chain link fence with barbed wire curled around the top.

The irony of building a mental hospital on top of a cliff of rugged coastline to taunt its patients with a perfectly lethal method of dying was not lost on him.

"You've missed three appointments in a row," she said.

"Apologies for the no-show."

She smiled, and up close, in all the high definition that reality had to offer, he realized that her asymmetrical smile was not a quirk. She couldn't move the left half of her face.

"It's nice to hear the sound of your voice again. I was told you've become willfully mute."

"I talk when it suits me."

She tapped the tip of her pen on the yellow notepad in her lap. "I'm glad you're still with us."

"That makes one of us."

"What happened?"

He crossed his arms. "I'm sure you've been told precisely what happened."

"I want to hear it from you."

"Ask a different question." He looked down and plucked a piece of lint from the black shirt he was wearing.

The shirt was Ian's, the one Alek had tried to take with him. Ian had dropped it off when Alek transferred to *Elmsdale*, along with the piano key and his uncle's letter. At first, Alek wanted to rip the shirt to shreds with his bare hands, but his plans were thwarted by a beastly security guard and a stab of sedation, and now he was grateful he hadn't. Later, when he could move again, and later still when they'd released him from his restraints, he had put the shirt on and held the key to his chest.

"How are your meds treating you?"

"I remain as depressed as ever."

Whilst in purgatory, Alek had been forced to take his medications exactly as prescribed. None of the methods he'd used to fool Ian worked on the staff at *Alder Home*. They'd seen it all.

"Give the medications time. Remember, it can take up to six weeks for them to work. What about the nightmares? The ringing in your ears?"

Now that he thought about it, the ringing *had* quieted some. The nightmares were worse than before, though that could be due in part to the fact that he was actually sleeping more than a few hours each night.

After he relayed as much, Dr. Dhawan said, "And the hallucinations?"

"The fox is gone." In more ways than one.

"How do you feel about that?"

"Alone."

"Dr. Hills told me you've been declining visits, refusing all phone calls, and correspondence."

Dr. Hills was the psychiatrist Alek had been assigned at *Cedar Refuge*. He was toxic positivity personified. Alek suspected that it was an act, that each night the doctor came home to an empty house and drank a liter's worth of box wine before staring longingly at the barrel of a gun until his self-prescribed sleeping pills carried him off to sleep.

"What happened between you and Ian?" she tried.

"I don't want to talk about Ian," he said.

"Why?"

He fisted his hand until his fingers dug into his palm, but there was no bite from his nails. They'd been trimmed short, and filed down even shorter after he'd failed to sever his carotid with brute force three nights before.

"Ian's called my office to ask after you," she said. "There's nothing I can say without your consent. As far as I know, no one has updated him and you won't speak to him. Why won't you speak to him?"

"Hmm?" Alek was trying to decide if he felt satisfied or guilty that Ian had been forced on an information diet. Maybe both.

"I was asking about Ian. Why won't you speak to him?"

Alek wasn't thinking about Ian, which meant he wasn't talking about not talking to Ian.

When Alek didn't break the silence, she asked, "You said your relationship was in its death throes when I first met you. Did your relationship die? Is that why you tried to kill yourself?"

Alek scoffed. "Don't be ridiculous. I'm not a teenager with a Tumblr account."

"Why did you try to commit suicide then?" she pressed.

"I didn't."

Her eyes narrowed. "You didn't try to kill yourself?"

"I don't try things. I do them, or I don't."

She frowned. "Do you still want to kill yourself?"

"Does anyone ever answer that question honestly?"

"Yes. Talking about suicide saves lives. If you're honest about how you feel and what you might do, we can make a plan to prevent it. What would you do if Alder House discharged you today?"

He would summon a drug dealer to deliver him fentanyl-laced heroin. He'd enjoy the prick of the needle in his vein. The flash of blood. The way his pupils would dilate so wide, so fast, he could feel the stretch when it happened. He wasn't picky though. He could always jump from a high rise, buy a gun of dubious origin, take a nap on train tracks. Still, an overdose was preferable. Aside from the better user experience, he didn't want to ruin a train engineer's day or leave a splattered body for someone to scrape off the asphalt. But he wasn't going to tell her that.

She leaned forward, elbows perched on one knee, a fresh

flush of pink on her cheeks. "If you don't talk, I can't help you. If you don't try, I won't recommend your release."

When he said nothing, she got to her feet, took a few steps, and then stopped.

"Here you are in a glorified psychiatric spa resort, with a fiancé desperate to see you and a personal psychiatrist who specializes in exactly the type of condition you have..." She shook her head. "Most people wait months to see a psychiatrist, and when they do, the doctor doesn't have the time to do talk therapy. They refer you to a therapist, but they don't help you find one, and you're depressed so you don't have the energy to look, or call, but if you do call, that therapist might not be accepting new patients, or doesn't take your insurance, or the next appointment is five weeks from now and maybe that therapist you waited for isn't even the right fit for you, or the next therapist either.

"I squeezed you in for that first appointment because Dr. Modorovic is a friend. I keep doing therapy with you because I know how difficult it is for you to open up to new people. So many people would still be here if they had the resources you have. Money. People who care. Privilege.

"Not everyone has someone to talk them off the ledge, to stop them before suicide wins, and if they do make it, they get shipped to whichever hospital takes their insurance, or MediCal if they don't have any, and at those sorts of places the staff tries, but the best they can do is provide you with a place to be safe until you're not actively suicidal and then they bounce you right out so that someone else can have your spot.

"You have everything you need to get better, and you won't even try?"

She walked the remaining length to the door. "I keep showing up, even though at least half of what you tell me every session is a lie, but I wait because maybe one day you'll trust me enough to let me help." Her hand paused on the doorknob. "If you don't start trying, I'm afraid I won't be able to see you anymore. It's nothing personal. I'd like to free up my schedule for someone I *can* help. You can work with Dr. Hills from here on out."

She had a point, just not the point she thought she made. Alek already knew he was pissing away world-class psychiatric care that literally anyone else deserved more than him, but he didn't feel bad for wasting something he never asked for. The point was that she could leave and for some reason, that thought had never occurred to him. He'd always assumed that psychiatrists weren't allowed to give up on their patients, but she was giving up on him, and he didn't have another goodbye in him.

Besides, revealing the bare minimum required to please Dr. Dhawan might kill two birds with one stone. Regrettably, the handful of thwarted suicides he'd attempted during his first few days of hospitalization hadn't done him any favors. According to his attorney, Mercer Llewyn, it would be easier to bust Alek from *Sitka Village* if he'd actually succeeded in killing himself. The only path to Alek's release—so that he could kill himself without anyone's interference, obviously— was through Dr. Dhawan, or Dr. Hills, and Alek would rather chew his own leg off to escape than confess his secrets to Dr. Hills.

"Does guilt-tripping your suicidal patients ever actually work?" Alek called after her.

She turned, her smile more of a grimace. "It got you to start talking again, didn't it?"

"Come sit back down. I'll tell you a story, one that's true." What did it matter what he told her when—ideally—he'd soon be dead?

"I'm listening," she whispered lowly like she was afraid to spook him.

After she'd reclaimed her seat, Alek kept his eyes on the window and said,

"Once there was a lonely boy. He lived with his parents, but his uncle raised him, at least until his uncle disappeared. No one told the boy anything. Months passed and then his uncle returned. The boy was so happy, but it didn't last. There was fighting and the boy was scared, so he hid like a coward while his uncle was killed.

"When his uncle died the boy felt everything all at once. All of his fear. All of the shame. All of his sadness. All of the rage. Until there was nothing left. He was alone then, except for his music.

"His mother died not long after. The boy was there. She did it to herself, but he didn't stop her. He wasn't sad. He felt nothing. Then the boy was sent away because his father couldn't look at him without seeing all that he'd lost, and the boy wasn't sad. He felt nothing. When the boy was old enough, he ran away, and he still felt nothing.

"Many years went by with only the boy, and his music, and nothing. Until he met a man who was special because he made him feel more than nothing. He made him scared. So the boy took the man and ruined him, so he could never leave.

"When I lost my music—" He met her eyes. "Sorry, the whole boy-man thing was becoming rather tedious."

She nodded for him to continue.

"Without music, there's nothing to keep the fear and the shame and the sadness away and all I feel is everything and I don't want to feel anything anymore." He sniffed. "That's the truth."

"Can I tell you the story the way I see it?"

"You may."

She smiled that crooked smile, took a deep breath, and said,

"Once there was a boy—maybe he was lonely, but he was

resilient too. He watched his uncle die, and he blamed himself. The boy thought he should have done more, that it was his fault, but he was a child, and the only person guilty was the one who killed his uncle.

"Once there was a boy who lost so much and was hurt so badly that he had to turn off his emotions to survive. He saw his mother kill herself—" her eyes lifted. "Did I interpret that part correctly?"

He nodded once. "You did."

"He saw his mother commit suicide, and he blamed himself, but he was a child, and it wasn't his job to save her. The boy didn't do anything wrong." She paused as if to emphasize the point. "Once there was a boy who finally made it, who escaped, but he couldn't escape his past, and everywhere he went, he brought with him that trauma of being left behind, of not being loved, of the violence he'd seen. And maybe the boy hurt people, but he was hurting too, and he would have done better if he could. Maybe he made mistakes, but everyone does. Maybe the boy could forgive himself. Maybe he could be loved and feel like he deserved it. Maybe he could learn how to cope without music. Maybe he could live."

41

IAN

Perched high atop the library on a scaffold, Ian sanded the shelf of yet another built-in bookcase. The double-decker bookcases and rolling library ladder that seemed charming when they first bought the Victorian had lost all allure about three bookcases into the renovation. There were still a few days of sanding left, then Ian would stain the book-cases and return the books to their refinished homes, and then he'd be done.

He hadn't seen or heard from Alek in two weeks. The silent treatment wasn't surprising, but it still stung. Ian was climbing the walls with worry. He suspected Alek still remained at Alder House because they'd continued to charge his account their weekly rate, but that was the extent of his knowledge. There'd been no fictional marital partnership this time and as such, Alder House wouldn't even confirm if Alek was there, let alone share any other information.

Ian's phone vibrated in his back pocket and like every time, his heart leaped at the hope that it would be Alek, and like every time, it wasn't, or at least he didn't think it was. The number wasn't one he recognized, and it wasn't the area code from Alder

House that he'd memorized. Probably spam, but Ian answered all the calls he caught just in case, so he'd answer this one.

It wasn't Alek. After answering and confirming to the male baritone that he was indeed Ian Stewart, the man said, "Mercer Llewyn, here. I'm Mr. Katin's attorney."

So this was the asshole from the emails?

"Is this a good time? I wanted to go over some legal matters with you."

Ian tossed the sandpaper on the shelf and sat at the edge of the scaffold, dangling his legs at the knee. He should have seen this coming. He and Alek's lives were so entangled, they couldn't part ways without the drafting of legal documents and hours of billed attorney fees. Wasn't that why Ian had said no to the marriage in the first place? What difference did it make now? Ian should have said yes. Then none of this would have happened.

"I'm listening," Ian said.

"Per Mr. Katin's request, I've compiled the separation agreement to dissolve your business partnership. I will email you the E-Doc for your signature, but there are other matters to settle. Mr. Katin has already paid the remaining balance of the mortgage on your shared property, and I've filed the quitclaim to remove his name from the deed. I mailed a check to reimburse you for what you've spent on Mr. Katin's treatment thus far. Moving forward, Mr. Katin will pay for his medical—"

"How can *Mr. Katin* make decisions about his finances from within a psychiatric hospital?"

"The separation claim will be filed upon his release. You don't have to cash the reimbursement check if you don't want to. The mortgage and deed were completed before the date of his hospitalization and didn't require your signature. The house is yours. Feel free to run a check on the title."

Instead of telling Llewyn to feel free to go fuck himself, Ian said, "Tell *Mr. Katin* I won't sign anything without speaking to him first."

"I'm sorry, but Mr. Katin was very clear that all contact will go through me."

"Then do your job and tell Alek I won't sign the separation agreement, and if the Victorian's only mine, he better come get his stuff, or will you be packing his boxes for him?"

Llewyn gave an exasperated sigh. "I'll be in touch."

That paperwork, Ian's signature, what it meant... This wasn't Alek lashing out in anger with a predictably cold and calculating insult. This was real. If Alek wanted, he could end things without even speaking to him, instead only communicating through Mercer Llewyn until the last ties between them were severed.

Ian picked up the sandpaper and returned to his work. He'd been working, with his crew or on the Victorian, nearly every waking hour of every day since Alek had left. He'd work until he was too tired to stand because he couldn't sleep unless he was exhausted. He still couldn't bring himself to sleep in their bed, or worse yet, move back into his old room so, in an act so melodramatic Alek would have done it, Ian slept in the library on a chaise he'd dragged in from another room.

He only returned to their room to shower and dress; the parlor was avoided entirely. He had no appetite, but he forced himself to eat the casseroles his mom kept bringing over, alone at the dining table, across from Alek's empty chair, because while Ian was melodramatic, he wasn't so melodramatic as to take his meals in the library, another thing Alek surely would have done.

As the library neared completion, far ahead of schedule for obvious reasons, Ian needed to plan the next room for restoration. He could do the snuggery, which was like a Victorian man cave, or one of the several unused guest rooms, but it was Alek's turn to choose, and Ian knew what he wanted, but what would Ian do with a kitchen if Alek never came home?

How could he ever do anything again if it wasn't Alek he was doing it for?

42

ALEK
WEEK SIX OF PURGATORY

"Are you having any thoughts of suicide today?"

Closing his laptop on Dr. Dhawan was one way to avoid answering. He could always tell her the connection dropped. She asked the same question at the beginning of every session they'd had over the last six weeks, and every session Alek struggled with his answer.

"It's not a trick question," the live video version of Dr. Dhawan insisted. "I won't lock you up forever if you give the wrong answer."

"So there is a wrong answer?" he teased.

She clicked and unclicked her pen. That was one of her tells when her patience was wearing thin.

"Any answer is the right answer as long as you're telling the truth.".

"I don't want to kill myself," Alek finally said.

Dr. Dhawan's dark eyes narrowed. "That's your answer? After all the suspense?"

"Don't sound so disappointed." Alek feigned offense, bringing a hand to his chest. He dropped the sarcasm and added, "In all seriousness, admitting that I don't want to kill myself is nearly as difficult as admitting when I did."

Her mouth pushed to the side in a thoughtful pout. "Why?"

The urge to lie was strong, but Alek was stronger. "If I don't commit suicide, my future is uncertain. Where will I live? What will I do? What will life be like after this?"

"After what?"

"Depression. Losing music." Losing Ian.

"I can see how that might seem daunting, but you have so many new coping tools in your arsenal. You'll continue to see me outpatient. I will help you feel prepared."

She wrote something with a flourish on her notepad.

Suspicious, he squinted at the screen. "What are you writing there?"

She held the page up. It was blurry and pixelated but read, *denies suicidal ideation.*

"Denies?" He crossed his arms. "That sounds accusatory."

"It's not. It's medical jargon. Before today, your answer was always a nonanswer or abrupt change in subject or the frequent," she lifted her fingers in air quotes, *"If I wasn't already suicidal this place would make me want to kill myself.* Today is the first day you've said no, so today is the first day I can write that."

"Do I get a reward of some kind? Perhaps a party?"

"Unfortunately not, but it is major progress that should be acknowledged. Well done!" Smiling, she pushed the stray strands of black hair back behind her ears and met his gaze, and even though he was sitting on his bed and she was in her office, her eye contact almost felt like the real thing. "Why don't you want to kill yourself today?"

"I'm not entirely sure."

Alek couldn't pinpoint exactly when or why it happened, but his thoughts seemed to have shifted. When he'd first arrived at

Poplar Porch, he'd been plagued with guilt and loss and over-whelming hopelessness intermixed with frequent and prolonged bouts of suicidal ideation. He'd operated without the future in mind because suicide was on pause, not permanent hiatus.

But now? Without even meaning to, he'd started to plan. Small things at first, like schemes to unearth the truth about Briar, who he'd been happy to learn was not another fox. He'd check the weather forecast, order something online, or plan a weekly movie night with Briar that they'd titled *Netflix and Mentally Ill*. Then the plans became broader; how to get better enough to get out, what he would do when that happened.

His depressive thoughts hadn't completely disappeared, but they'd been pushed to the shadows, and when they tried to creep back in, they were far more easily vanquished. It was like a fragile wisp of hope had sparked to life in the ashes of his depression.

"It's okay if you don't know. Maybe it has something to do with weeks of therapy, good sleep, and medications under your belt..."

She was teasing him, but it was certainly possible. Over the last six weeks, he felt like he'd climbed up a mountain through a thick fog, and now that he was at the peak, the fog had cleared, and he could look back on everything that had happened and see how unwell he had been.

"With suicide off the table," she said. "I'm curious to know if your thoughts about Ian have changed."

Alek shook his head. "My lawyer is tying up loose ends with our joint ventures and then Ian will be free to do as he pleases."

There was that snag where Ian refused to sign any paper-work without seeing him, but no matter. Alek could remain a silent and completely unreachable business partner if Ian was going to act so childish. Worst-case scenario, Alek could explore other avenues of litigation.

There was also the issue of what to do with all his things back at the Victorian but he was ignoring that for now because he couldn't stand the thought of a pair of movers traipsing through the Victorian, packing and carting away his things to a storage warehouse, leaving Ian with less than half of what he had before.

"The relationship has run its course," he supplied when Dr. Dhawan still hadn't replied. "Really. I'm fine."

Still nothing but silent skepticism from her.

After a harrumph, he said, "I want to try to be healthy without him."

"Why?"

"What if I get bad again?" In more ways than one.

"Recovery isn't linear. Maybe you do well for a while and you have a setback. That's okay. But as long as you take your medications and continue your therapy—as long as you're honest about how you're feeling, you'll continue to get better, and stay better, too."

"Ian could find someone else, someone stable, someone he doesn't have to worry about dying in one body of water or another. If I let him go, he can have that."

Alek hadn't told her, or anyone, that Ian framed him, and not just because no one would believe him. At the end of the day, framed or not, Alek *had* been suicidal and he would have killed himself that night. He couldn't fault Ian when he would have done the same if the roles were reversed, though he'd have tied Ian to the bed and force-fed him medication, which was a far better idea that required no separation. That wasn't to say, however, that he hadn't spent the first two weeks of purgatory plotting Ian's untimely demise.

"What's the worst that can happen if you get back together with Ian?"

That was one of her therapy tricks, asking what the worst-case scenario was, so she could try to convince him that the worst wasn't really so bad, but it didn't work when it came to Ian. The stakes were too high.

"I could hurt him again. I could ruin the rest of his life."

"An altruistic answer, but I'm asking about you, Alek. What you want. What you think. What is the worst thing that can happen to *you*?"

Alek looked at his hands. "If I go back... If I love, then I can lose. He could leave and if he leaves..." he trailed off, his thoughts derailed by the fox in a grave and a specter of himself standing in the rain at the edge of the cliff he'd planned to jump off.

"You worry you won't be able to survive it?" she suggested.

Tears gathered, clouding his vision. "Saying goodbye once was hard enough. It's over. We're over. I won't go through it again."

There was a heavy pause wherein Alek worried she wouldn't accept his answer, that she'd argue until he couldn't talk through the tears, but she flashed a half-smile.

"If things with Ian are over, then we need to pivot our focus."

Silently thanking her, Alek cleared his throat and leaned back against the headboard. "Pivot away."

"Very well." She looked at her notes. "Have you read your uncle's letter yet?"

"Not yet." Alek groaned, burying his fingers in his hair. "I'm sorry. I... I'm still afraid."

"It's very brave to admit when you're scared."

Alek's cheeks warmed, and like every time she compli-mented him, he wanted to argue with her, that he hadn't even tried to be vulnerable, that being a coward was the opposite of being brave, but he'd earned enough lectures from her about accepting compliments that he kept his mouth shut.

"What are you afraid the letter will say?"

He could have lied. He could have said he was worried that after all this time his uncle had left him nothing but a list of instructions on how to plan his escape, but he wanted to tell her the truth. Talking about his past was still about as uncomfortable as he imagined urethral sounding to be, but there was something to be said for therapy because it took his thoughts and feelings out of his head in a way that music used to, but unlike music, with Dr. Dhawan's help, he'd then take those thoughts and feelings and put them back together into something that didn't hurt as much.

Dr. Dhawan's version of his abridged life story was a perfect example. Alek made her retell the story during several of their subsequent sessions, filling in more details so that he could argue against her contrasting points, but she'd argued too, until he finally started to admit that maybe he hadn't been the villain in his story. He was no hero, either, but perhaps he'd merely been a bystander, a passive observer, as it were.

"I don't want my uncle to be my father because that would mean he didn't love me at all."

Dr. Dhawan's pen stopped mid-stride. She gestured with her pen that he should continue. A silent why.

"If he loved me, how could he have loved *her*? My mother was cold. She didn't hug. She didn't touch me. I don't know if she ever loved anyone, let alone me. When my uncle died, she knew. She knew he was dead and she didn't spare a passing thought for me before she killed herself. I was a child. I was alone. If I hadn't found that box, I still would have escaped, but she couldn't have known that." He shook his head. "She didn't love me and if my uncle could love someone like that, he couldn't have loved me either."

"You've made an important insight," Dr. Dhawan said. "It wasn't only your uncle who left, was it? Your mother had already abandoned you without going anywhere."

Alek shrugged. "It could be argued that someone who was never there to begin with couldn't actually leave."

"But that's not how psychology works. Children are born loving their parents, no matter their faults. It takes time for that innocent, unconditional love to wither. You've said your mother's death meant nothing, but I'm not so sure. A child who grows up without his mother's love might think that he doesn't deserve love, and what does that sound like?"

"One of those detestable core beliefs you keep going on about," he answered, crossing his arms. "Yes. Yes. I know. I deserve love. Everyone deserves love, except Hitler, and so on and so forth. I know that."

"Your value as a person has nothing to do with how your mother felt about you. And your uncle? Maybe he wanted to bring her along so that you wouldn't be parted from her. Or maybe he did love her. People are imperfect, Alek. They have flaws and love people with flaws and they can love more than one person at a time, even if it doesn't make sense because sometimes love doesn't make sense, it just happens. Let us use another one of our tools."

Alek sighed loud enough for her to hear because, though he was no longer suicidal, he was still an asshole.

Ignoring him, she continued, "When you have a thought, look at the evidence. You say your uncle didn't love you? Where's the evidence of that?"

"My mother neglected me. He left me with someone who neglected me," Alek reported in a monotone.

"It sounded as if your uncle didn't have much choice when he left. Remember, more often than not, people act without intending to hurt."

"Not in my family."

"Let's look at the facts in favor of your uncle loving you..." She lifted a single finger. "He made plans for your escape at great financial and personal expense." Another finger. "He took care of you every day before he disappeared." Another finger. "He taught you to do the things that he loved to do." And she went on and on until there weren't any more fingers left and Alek had started to believe her.

"You have been loved. You are loved. You are worthy of love. Whatever it says in that letter, that is the truth."

43

ALEK

ONE WEEK LATER

A yellow-padded envelope arrived for Alek in the mail most days, already opened and searched for knives and drugs and other such contraband. Inside the envelope was always a letter from Ian, one that Alek didn't read, and a handful of individually wrapped chocolates, but not the waxy, overly sweet American kind; they were from Alek's favorite chocolatier, dark chocolate mostly and some espresso-flavored.

Every Saturday Ian hand-delivered a small care package, irrespective of the fact that he was never granted admittance. Inside would be tea, a new release book from one of Alek's favorite authors, or a pair of lounge pants his mother had made. There was the occasional cutting of wisteria carefully packed from one local nursery or another.

Each time the package arrived, Alek went straight for the previously-worn shirt of Ian's that he never failed to include. To the outside observer, it was creepy in a serial killer sort of way, but to Alek it was everything. He'd close his eyes and inhale and forests would grow inside his head, and an image of Ian too, and he could almost hear Ian's voice, and even feel Ian's skin beneath his fingertips, and in addition to the abject yearning that inspired, Alek felt a flicker of hope.

His synesthesia was coming back, but he didn't let his thoughts linger on it, and even though his hand surgeon had given him permission to start practicing the piano in short bouts again, he wouldn't try the mistuned travesty of a piano at Alder House—he'd finally committed the name of the hospital to memory.

"It's not fair," Briar whined. She plucked another chocolate from Alek's desk and dropped down onto his bed, lifting the back of her hand to her forehead like she was a debutante aswoon. "I wish I had a man who loved me enough to send me a steady supply of chocolates and love letters."

"It's not love. It's guilt," Alek said from where he was sifting through a backlog of Ian's envelopes at his desk.

He tipped the next envelope and tapped more chocolates out onto the tabletop. Then he pulled out the letter to add to the growing collection of letters he wouldn't read but couldn't throw away.

A thick card stock advertisement came out with the letter. In glossy colored print was a picture of the Victorian, the sight of which sucker-punched Alek with a near-terminal case of home-sickness. In obnoxious red letters, it said:

Just Listed!!! Now's your chance to own a piece of history.

He gasped and flipped it over to the other side. A grid of pictures featured the completed greenhouse, the remodeled bedrooms and bathrooms, *his* piano in the parlor, a fully-restored library. At the bottom, beside an air-brushed decade-old picture of their realtor, a faux handwritten scrawl font read:

Calling all investors and aspiring fixer-uppers. This well-loved mansion has been partially restored by a celebrated contractor. Perfect for a bed and breakfast. Seller is extremely motivated. Give us your best offer!

"What?" Briar asked for the second time.

Wordlessly, Alek handed the ad to her.

"He wouldn't!" she said.

He would. Alek should have anticipated such fuckery. That was the trouble with surviving suicide. He'd made plans without considering the consequences because he wasn't supposed to be around for said consequences.

Briar held the paper up to her face and squinted. "Your place is exactly as I imagined. Is it haunted? Please tell me it's haunted." When he said nothing, she returned the ad to him. "You think he'd really go through with it?"

"I don't know…"

It could be a ruse, another one of the games they'd played with each other, a ploy to get him back, but what if it wasn't? What if selling the Victorian was an ultimatum? Alek didn't like the odds. Ian's threats were never idle. The fact that Alek was alive and at Alder House was proof of that.

He tore the letter that accompanied the ad back off the desk.

Alek,

The listing is real. Check the MLS. If the Victorian is mine, then I don't want it.

Ian

PS I won't sell it to you or any shady overseas LLC, so don't get any ideas.

Alek stood, pushing the chair back from the desk. "Briar, out. I need to think."

Briar eyed the chocolates. Alek nodded once. With a dimpled smile, she snatched a handful and left the room.

In the hall, she said, "I'm here when you want to talk. It's not an empty platitude." She popped another chocolate in her mouth. "I find your love life riveting."

"Haha," Alek deadpanned, closing the door.

He returned to his desk, and the letters. He would simply work backward, skimming only the most recent letters for clues, reading clinically, from a purely investigative standpoint. He wouldn't let Ian's words weaken his resolve. That's why he hadn't read the letters in the first place.

A half dozen letters down, Alek spotted 'the Victorian' and read:

Alek,

I don't know if you're getting these, or if you're even still at Alder House, but I moved out of the Victorian and I want you to know it's not because I've stopped waiting. It's because I can't be in the Victorian without you there with me. I'm still waiting... just in a fifteen-year-old twin bed in my childhood bedroom.

Ian

Alek gathered the rest of Ian's letters and climbed onto his bed. He started at the beginning, with the oldest letter first. As he read, his mind filled with Ian's voice rumbling apologies and vows of love, insistence that he'd wait, desperate pleas that Alek talk to him, and the occasional update on how he was getting on.

He kept reading letter after letter, long after the excuse of investigating Ian's real estate motives could apply. In one letter Ian had detailed the night they first met, the moment he fell in love, how he felt when Alek fell and he thought he lost him forever.

A series of several letters outlined the progress of the library, complete with pictures, and complaining of how he'd agonized over this decision or that without Alek there to weigh in.

There were assurances that the wisteria was still alive and well, whole essays on what he loved about Alek, what he planned for their future, why he knew they could make it work, the research he'd done to prepare for any future depressive episodes should they arise.

One letter was written entirely in Bulgarian—not very good Bulgarian, but Bulgarian nonetheless. In the letter Ian confessed, the tone rather guilty, to learning Bulgarian in secret.

Bless him. Ian might have hidden the staged suicide from him, but that was only because he was literally psychotic at the time. Alek knew all about the Bulgarian. He'd stumbled upon Ian's flash cards during the first month they'd been home. He'd even made the effort to hide them for him better.

By the time Alek finished the last unread letter, Ian's voice echoed endlessly against the inside of his head, and if he closed his eyes he could see Ian's squared, neat handwriting and smell the ink that bled into the page.

Alek walked to the front desk and requested to use the phone, then dragged it down the counter as far as the cord would allow. Turning away and resting his back against the counter, he dialed Ian's number and waited.

The phone rang once...

Twice...

When Ian answered, he sounded the same as he always did, a little bit gruff, his voice clear, confident.

"This is Ian," he said and each of those three uttered words unleashed a torrent of butterflies that coalesced until Alek felt like he was flying.

He closed his eyes and let his mind fill in the details, the ghost of Ian's scent—cedar and pine—the way his dark brown hair stuck up at the back when he woke up in the morning, the scrape of his beard against Alek's neck, the warmth of his body wrapped around him...

"Alek?" Ian asked with a dash of hope bleeding through.

"Did you read my note?" Alek asked without preamble.

"I figured since you didn't die, I shouldn't read it."

Good. Now he could tell Ian the way he'd wanted to be told, when Alek wanted to, when he had forgiven himself, because as with everything else, Alek wasn't sure when or how it had happened, but he had started to forgive himself. That version of his story was the one he wanted Ian to know. No matter how hard it would be to tell him.

"I presume you checked the grave?" Alek asked.

A pause. "I'm so sorry, love. She wasn't there."

The term of endearment stabbed nearly as sharp as the empty grave.

"You're sure?"

"Yes. I kept digging until I hit clay. I filled it all back in after. It felt wrong to leave it like that... I'm sorry."

"No need to apologize," Alek answered briskly. There wasn't. He'd probably want to see the grave for himself, to have that closure, but it would only affirm what he already knew. "You aren't actually selling the Victorian, are you? The Victorian turned into a bed and breakfast? Really?"

"So you *have* been getting my letters?"

Smiling, Alek teased, "I eat those decadent chocolates you send and throw the letters away without reading them. It makes the chocolate taste better."

"Asshole." On the other end of the line, Ian cleared his throat. "I meant what I said. I won't stay at the Victorian without you. I can't."

Alek said nothing. Fear had already snuffed the courage he'd caught from Ian's letters.

Ian said, "Listen, I need to know you're okay. It's been so hard not knowing. Not talking to you." His voice broke. "Are you feeling better?"

"I am."

"Good. That's... I'm happy."

Before all bravery left him, Alek said, "I've decided that you may call on me this Saturday. I assume you've planned another visit?"

"I'll be there," Ian said before Alek finished his sentence.

"Good. I'll speak to you then."

"Wait. Alek?"

"Hmm?"

"When you woke up in the hospital, you asked me if there was a chance. You asked me after all that happened, and I said yes. I'm asking, Alek—*love*—please, tell me there's a chance."

"Do you want the truth or a lie?"

"You know what I want," Ian answered breathlessly.

"Yes."

A release of air, Ian's held breath perhaps, snuffled against the line.

"Okay. That's... Thank you. Thank you for talking to me. I love you, Alek."

"I've got to go. There's a line for the phone."

Alek hung up before he did something dangerous like admit that he loved Ian too.

44

IAN

Nerves wriggled like snakes in Ian's stomach as he forced himself out of his truck and up the grand front steps of Alder House. The experience was nothing new; he'd visited on each of the seven previous Saturdays, but today was different. Over time he'd accepted that he would arrive, check in, and then be turned away, but now he had a different expectation, one that might not be met.

Sunlight grazed the back of his neck and a salty breeze toyed with the bottom hem of the henley he'd worn because Alek had a self-professed love of him in long-sleeved henleys.

Outside the lobby door, he took a fortifying breath and entered. The lobby was painted in varying shades of warm whites—Alek would say it looked like an evangelical's store-bought version of heaven. There wasn't a line to check in, so Ian gave his name and claimed his usual spot in an armchair beside an unlit fireplace with a mantle made of an enormous slab of driftwood.

With a spike of completely unwarranted adrenaline, he realized he'd forgotten his weekly box of offerings back at the truck. Calling them gifts wasn't exactly right, because in all honesty, he was practically prostrating himself at Alek's altar. Ian would circle back to the truck later; he couldn't risk delaying his visit.

A blonde-haired woman in high heels and an expensive-looking linen dress moved around the desk and headed for him. That didn't mean anything. A staff member always delivered the news directly to him. There was no calling of names across the lobby at Alder House. There was no guarantee that Alek had said yes.

"Mr. Stewart?" The woman bent down until they were at eye level.

Ian checked her name tag. *Helen.*

"Mr. Katin will see you now." She procured a sticker badge from her clipboard. On it was Ian's full name and the picture they took of him on his first visit. She passed it to him, and rose back to her full height. "Please keep your badge on at all times." Once he'd stuck it to the left side of his shirt, she said, "If you'll follow me, I'll take you through to the lounge."

Ian seemed to have lost the ability to talk, so he nodded and stood. Each step that followed was like fighting the strong pull of a riptide as the receding saltwater snatched the sand from beneath his feet.

Helen tapped a plastic card against a black badge reader beside a set of double doors that Ian had never been allowed to go through. The doors opened with a mechanical *ksh* into a small, windowless room with a wall of lockers on one side and a burly security guard waiting.

"You can put your belongings here," the guard said, pointing to the first available locker.

Ian emptied his pockets and placed his phone, wallet, and keys inside.

"Are you wearing a belt?" the guard asked.

Ian shook his head and the guard patted him down before pronouncing him free of potential weapons.

As if they were entering a prison, or an aviary, the guard double-checked that the doors remained closed behind them before buzzing them out of the room. The second set of doors led to a wide hallway with pale oak floors. On his right, a wall of windows framed a striking view of the sea.

They reached what must have been the lounge and nothing else mattered because there was only Alek—Alek backlit by a glow of sepia sunlight, sitting imperiously in a leather armchair.

Blood roared in Ian's ears. He raced across the room, dropped to his knees at Alek's feet, and laid his head on his lap because he was completely overcome with relief to see him again.

This was real. This was Alek. Tangible and warm and living.

Underneath him, Alek stiffened, and Ian started to pull away, but Alek laid a staying hand on his head and ran his fingers through his hair.

"I'm sorry," Ian sniffed, returning to his feet. "I should have asked if I could touch you."

With an amused smile, Alek waved a flippant hand. "You didn't do anything I didn't want you to do," he said in a faint Bulgarian accent. He gestured to the chair next to him. "Please sit."

With a nod, Ian did what he was told. He turned his chair until they were facing each other and let his starving eyes rake over him.

Alek was dashing in a casual black tee and the lounge pants Ian's mom had made for him. He filled out his clothes much better than Ian had expected, the muscles of his shoulders and chest outlined beneath the fabric and his lean biceps no longer drowning in his sleeves. His olive skin had tanned to a glowing, warm brown—it was actually the first time Ian had seen him look anything other than mildly anemic. His shiny raven hair had been trimmed and a closely buzzed beard shadowed the lower half of his face. The sharpness of his cheekbones had softened and the half moon hollows under his eyes disappeared.

"I take it you like what you see?" Alek said, a small smirk teasing the corner of his lips.

"You look so good, love." He stopped, distracted by how his voice shook. It was hard to talk, hard to even breathe with Alek sitting across from him, without knowing if he would come home.

"You look good, as well." Alek lifted a hand at him. "Have you taken up weightlifting in my absence? I was hoping you would look far more scrawny and heartsick."

Ian looked down. He hadn't noticed. "No. It's probably just from working. I had to keep busy…"

Alek nodded like he understood. "How is your mother?"

"She misses you. I miss you."

Alek looked at him, his pale green eyes sphinxlike. "I'll give you a tour," he finally said. "Perhaps we can find somewhere more private."

Ian scanned the room. Aside from an orderly posted by the doors and a few other pairings of patients and visitors, the room was otherwise empty, but a tour was a good idea. Maybe it would be easier to be in Alek's presence with a distraction to keep their conversation steered from heavier subjects.

"So that was the lounge," Alek said as he sauntered down the hallway with Ian at his side. He pointed at the wall of windows to their right. "That's the ocean. It's always there, glaring sunlight obnoxiously. And this is the cafeteria." Alek came to a stop.

The cafeteria was an open, airy room with a dozen or so small tables and one long communal one. Everything was clean, modern, and mostly white, save for the occasional wood accent. The western wall followed the theme with ceiling-to-floor windows, broken by a twenty-foot stretch of panoramic sliding glass doors folded back to bring the outside in.

Alek led Ian across the cafeteria, through the sliding doors, and down a path that weaved around manicured landscaping.

"Next on our tour is the rose garden," Alek said as they took a right at a fork in the path.

The rose garden was really a large lawn bordered by thornless peony bushes. A giant redwood tree stood on the bluff of the cliff, and behind it was a bench that offered a nice view of the Pacific, though the illusion of Alder House as anything other than a cage was broken by the towering chain link fence that lined the perimeter.

The bench was probably as secluded a spot as they'd find, if it had not been occupied by a very pretty young woman with blue eyes and black hair.

"We can find another spot," Ian said to Alek, but the girl had already jumped from the bench.

She shook her head slowly as she looked between the two of them, then said, "I promised I wouldn't imagine you having sex, but your description didn't do him justice. Alek, are you sure you wouldn't like to consider making your couple a throuple?"

Alek scowled. "I don't share, and you said you would behave."

Alek sat in the place she'd vacated while Ian looked on, unsure what to do. It would be rude to steal the woman's spot... Also, who was she anyway?

"Ian, this is my friend, Briar," Alek said. "I sent her here to reserve our seat."

Friend? Falling back on manners when uncomfortable, Ian thrust out his hand and shook hers.

"It's very nice to meet you," he said.

His eyes caught on the row of scars on her arms, most old and faded, but some fresh and raised and highlighted pink.

After a relatively strong handshake, the girl named Briar let go and turned back to Alek. "Just look at the wingspan on his hand." She clucked her tongue, then muttering something indiscernible, left them alone.

"If you're jealous," Alek said when she'd gone. "Don't be."

"I'm not. She's not your type."

"And what exactly is my type, Ian?" Alek's jade eyes were glossy, pupils dilated wide, challenging him.

Ian took the question as rhetorical.

"All the same," Alek said. "I haven't touched her and I have no desire to." Alek patted the space on the bench beside him. "Now come sit down."

Leaving a foot between them, Ian took a seat and looked out at the sea. When he turned, Alek was still watching him.

"I'm ready to tell you my story," Alek said.

Ian opened his mouth to argue, but Alek lifted his hand.

"You said you only wanted to know when I'd forgiven myself, and I'm afraid that might always be a work in progress. My first instinct is still to blame myself, but now I can fight it. I know that when it comes to my family, I did nothing wrong and I'll keep telling myself that until it sticks."

Ian's mouth went dry, his heart cantered in his chest. "You don't have to tell me... not unless you want to."

"If I didn't want to tell you, I wouldn't."

Taking Alek's hand in his, Ian said, "I'm listening."

Alek kept his eyes on the ocean and started with his name—Aleksandar Velishikov—and where he'd come from and who his father and his mother and his uncle were.

"The nightmares I have... there are things I can't forget, things that still remind me. The sound of water over river rocks, or worse yet, rocks clattering against each other, a piano bench dragged across the floor, the smell of smoke, ash underneath my fingertips." Alek met Ian's eyes. "My father drowned my uncle in the river behind our house. I was there and I was so scared. I tried to save my uncle, but it was too late. I know now that it wasn't my fault."

From there, Alek detailed the fire that followed and how he'd suffered to see his uncle and all of his things erased by the flames. "When my parents returned, my father acted as if nothing had happened, and my mother? She thought only of herself." He explained how he'd followed her to the burned-down house. "Again, I was there. She killed herself, and it wasn't my fault. I hate my mother. I'm still working on that too." Alek released a shaking breath. "But even if I hate her, she chose death at her own hands. She felt she had no other option. I know what that feels like."

Ian's stomach clenched with nausea at the thought of what Alek had suffered, at how close Alek had come to joining his mother.

By the time Alek finished, he'd confirmed everything that Ian had pieced together and explained the things he hadn't.

"How old were you?" Ian asked.

Alek looked down at his lap. "Eleven."

Violence exploded inside Ian. He wanted to destroy Alek's enemies and feast on his foes, but everyone was already dead and the only demons were Alek's own. Instead, Ian took Alek's trembling hand, and held it against his heart. Alek's face lifted to follow the movement.

It was too easy to imagine Alek as Aleksandar, a child with eyes too big for his face, scared and alone and with no one to love him. Ian fought to keep the rage from escaping through his clenched teeth. He lifted Alek's hand only long enough to kiss it, then held it tightly back over his heart again, wishing he could travel through time to save him sooner, to spare him from so many years of pain, to give back the love he'd lost.

"I still don't know if my uncle was my father," Alek said.

From his pocket, Alek pulled an envelope so worn and wrinkled it was shiny, as if it'd been worried over in his hands for years, which it probably had.

"This is the letter my uncle left me. I've never been able to read it. You make me brave, and I thought... perhaps you could be with me while I read it?"

"I'll do anything you ask."

45

ALEK

Telling Ian was one insurmountable hurdle off of Alek's list. At first it had been terrifying, but the more he said, the stronger he felt. Now for the next item on his list. He clumsily ripped open the envelope and unfolded his uncle's letter, but his hands shook and he couldn't read the words.

"It's okay, love," came Ian's low rumble. "I'll hold it for you."

Ian pulled Alek onto his lap, rested his chin on his shoulder, and held the letter out in front of them.

With a deep breath and Ian's steady pulse thumping against his back, and forests all around him, Alek read:

ALEKSANDAR,

Even the best-laid plans can go awry, and so if you're reading this, I'll write as if that is the case. Ideally, you'll soon be on your way to join me. If so, I'd rather you stop reading here and refer to the following page which will give you instructions on how to find me. But if that's not what happened, if I died and you must go the rest of the way on your own, there are some things I want you to know.

Firstly, you must know that I love you, that you are the best thing that has ever happened to me, that everything I have ever done since you existed has been with you in mind, because you are my son.

Your mother and I were friends first, long before my brother ever married her. She was fierce and vibrant and insatiably curious. I loved her before I even knew what love was.

But I wasn't the eldest son and my values didn't align with the family, and back then, and even now, sons and daughters are their parent's most valuable asset. It had been decided for as long as I can remember that your mother would marry my brother, but she was not an object to be taken.

I tried to convince her to leave with me, but we were both so young and she was scared to leave behind everything she'd ever known. The only choice we had was to love in secret.

After we found out about you, I finally convinced your mother to run away with me, and then, while we were still trying to sort out the details, our parents decided that it was time for your mother and my brother to marry.

I went to my father. Her father. I promised anything and everything to no avail. I told my brother the truth and begged him to let her go. He was furious. And your mother? She said she wouldn't risk your future, but she was scared too, and I understood. I still do. Your mother chose my brother and ended things with me.

I fought—I promise—I fought for you, for her, for us, but your mother was resolute.

After time passed and my brother's anger cooled, he agreed to let me remain in your life so long as he was your father, and I your uncle, and your mother was his wife, and nothing ever happened between me and your mother again.

I would sacrifice anything to maintain an active presence in your life, to spare you from the poison that runs through our family, so I agreed.

However cliche it may be, the day you were born was the best day of my life. You had a thick head of jet-black hair and bright eyes that soon turned a perfect mix of your mother and I, so vividly green but with the slightest hint of my underlying blue. When I finally held you, you looked at me like you knew and understood everything.

But I couldn't hold you forever. I had to give you back. It killed me to see you claimed as my brother's son. Every moment I spent apart from you was agony.

I know how your mother is, but believe me when I say that she loves you as much as she can. After you were born, she changed. She was sad and then angry and then apathetic. I was so worried about her, but she wouldn't listen and she wasn't mine. So I devised a plan.

Maybe I could save you both. Maybe I could fall in line and stash money away while making up for all the love they failed to give you.

I should have left with you years ago, but your mother wouldn't come and I couldn't leave her. I'm sorry for not taking you sooner, for any time you spent unhappy because I was greedy, because I wanted you both.

I hope that even if I am gone, I did succeed in saving your mother too. I hope that your mother leaves with you and the two of you are free and happy, but if I couldn't convince her, if she was scared, I want her to know that I understand and I love her and I always have.

But this letter isn't for her. This letter is for my son. My son, who has whole universes inside his head. My son, who can turn thoughts and feelings and senses into sound like alchemy, like me. My son, who is so much more than his talent. My son, who shows kindness in ways that are unexpected, who is passionate and slightly terrifying in all that he is capable of.

If I'm not here now, the fault lies only with me, and my brother. None of this was your fault. You cannot blame yourself. We all should have been better for you and I'm sorry that we weren't.

Even though I can't be there to watch you grow up, the fact of which pains me greatly, I already know how your story will end. You are a force that cannot be reckoned with. I know you'll find your way. You will always be my light in the darkness.

WITH UNENDING LOVE,
     Krasimir Velishikov, your father.

PS if you've decided to stay in Bulgaria and join in our family ventures, I'm not upset, so long as it was your choice and not made in fear.

THERE WAS a reason why Alek wanted to read his uncle's letter at Alder House; he wanted to have elephant-size doses of benzodiazepines on hand should he need to spend a few hours, or days, in a hazy give-no-fucks fugue.

Alek was completely overcome with the loss of his uncle all over again, but it was worse, so much worse than when he witnessed his uncle's death, because it wasn't his uncle who died, it was his father and the pain was like every single nightmare that replayed the moment of his father's death had all turned into arrows that pierced the center of his chest like a target.

He noticed the ringing first, a high-pitched keen that he

hadn't heard in weeks. His pulse was a violent, dizzyingly-fast staccato. He couldn't breathe; it was like he was pulling air through a mile-long straw. His vision tunneled.

Ian tensed around him.

No. "I'm okay," Alek insisted.

He inhaled deeply, forcing himself to think only of his lungs expanding, and then emptying. Once. Twice. By the third deep breath, the tempo of his pulse was noticeably slower. Another deep breath and the ringing had stopped. Using Ian like a metronome, Alek matched his breathing to Ian's calm and steady rate.

"I'm so proud of you," Ian said, resting his cheek against Alek's shoulder. "But I can't help but feel cheated."

Confused, Alek turned. Ian lifted his head. Their lips were inches apart.

"Your dad really knew how to write a letter and all I've gotten is pornographic Post-it Note animations from you."

Alek sniffed, smiling as he faced forward again. He appreciated Ian offering him levity if he wanted it, and he did. "I am positively shocked you were able to read any of that, given it's written in Cyrillic."

Ian nipped a light bite to Alek's neck, tickling him with his deep laughter. "Oh, I have no idea what that says—I'm just going off length alone."

"What about while we were passing notes in the hospital? Doesn't that count?"

"I'll allow it."

Alek filled Ian in on the contents of the letter. "I wish I'd read it sooner," Alek said when he was done.

"I know," Ian murmured, his mouth still on Alek's neck. "I'm so sorry, Alek," and it wasn't a token apology, an automatic response to a shitty situation, because Alek heard the sadness in Ian's words, the shared grief that was there.

Ian turned Alek to face him and the intensity in his dark brown eyes, the ardent love and awe, hit Alek like an anvil to the head. He saw stars.

"Thank you for telling me, for trusting me," Ian said.

"Thank you for loving me when I couldn't." Alek sat sideways on Ian's lap. "There's something else I need to tell you."

"Say what you have to say," Ian said, voice rough.

Alek's eyes narrowed. "You've gone very pale. There's no need to look so morose, Ian. I'm not about to break your heart."

Some of the color returned to Ian's face, but Alek would keep close watch so he could dive out of the way if Ian vomited.

"Before you saved me," Alek began. "Before you sent me here, I would have said I don't deserve you, that you deserve so much more than me, but I think you've always been exactly what I needed, and a lot of the time that wasn't fair to you, and though I may be able to forgive myself, I'll never stop apologizing for hurting you.

"I am so sorry, Ian. For the pain I've caused you directly, for the torment I can only imagine you've been through over the last six months, for the two months I left you alone while I've been here.

"I know I'm still getting better, that there's still work to do, and I might relapse now and again, but now that I know I want to live, I want to live with you, and if that's not what you want, or you'd rather wait until I prove that I can be well, I understand and I will respect that and—"

"Shut up and kiss me. Of course, I want you. I love you."

Ian yanked Alek by his shirt, his other hand in Alek's hair, and they collided in a kiss that was wet with tears and messy with emotion. Somewhere in the fray, Alek found himself straddling Ian's lap without knowing exactly how he'd gotten there.

The world was spinning so fast around them they might be swept off the edge of the cliff, but Alek wasn't scared because as far as he was concerned, not even the promise of death could stop this kiss—

There was a tap on his shoulder and a disembodied, "Ahem."

It took sheer force of will to pull away, but Alek did and when he saw Rick, a gentleman he'd spent a great deal of time with during his earlier bouts of twenty-four-hour suicide watch, Alek wiped his mouth and said, "Your timing, Richard, is as impeccable as ever."

Ian's ears were an adorable shade of crimson.

"Public displays of affection are not allowed," Rick said. "You may kiss like you'd kiss your great-aunt, but you cannot kiss like that."

"We were just leaving," said Alek, hopping off Ian's lap. "Come along, Ian. The last stop on our tour is my bedroom."

Breathless, Ian said, "You'll have to give me a minute."

A short while later, after Ian's erection had become far less likely to be seen by passersby, Alek led Ian to his room, stopping outside the open door.

"Are private displays of affection allowed?" Ian asked lowly, his face still flushed.

"Unfortunately, not. There are cameras everywhere but the bathroom. No audio, but still very Orwellian."

"Do you know when you'll get out?" Ian asked as he followed Alek into the room.

"About that..." Alek stepped aside.

His room was empty except for the packed duffle on the bed, considerably fuller now than when Ian had first brought it.

"I could stay," Alek said. He ducked his head and dragged his fingers through his hair. "As of last Thursday, I've elected to continue my treatment here on a voluntary basis, just until I decide where I'll go and how I'll receive follow-up care, but if I know where I'm going, and you're ready to have me, I can leave today." Alek's pulse thundered in his ears. "I'm not suicidal. Haven't been in weeks. My medications have reached therapeutic levels. I'm no longer seeing things that only I can see. There's nothing to keep me here, though I'll stay if you think I should."

"What does your doctor say?" Ian asked, his face impassive.

"Dr. Dhawan says, and I quote, 'I trust your judgment.' High praise, don't you think?" Alek grinned. "Dr. Dhawan's been treating me from afar. I've done the work, Ian. I'm ready, and until you sent that ad for the Victorian, and I finally read your letters, I was planning to go my own way to spare you from my drama and angst, to give you a chance at a happier life, but it wasn't just that. I was afraid. I *am* afraid. If I go back to you, I could hurt you again. You could leave me and that terrifies me. But what if I don't hurt you? What if you don't leave? What if we live happily ever after and I missed all of that because I was scared?

"*Fear is only proof you are alive*. My uncle—" Alek stopped. It would take some time to get used to. "My father always said that. I used to think he meant that I should accept fear as something meaningless, something as automatic as breathing, and something I could ignore just as easily. I spent years without fear and now I see I wasn't really living—until I met you—and loving you made me so scared I let fear rule me until it nearly ruined everything.

"I think I misunderstood my father's lesson. I think he meant that there's no reward without risk. That anything worth doing will be scary, but that I should do it anyway. That fear should be felt, faced, and conquered. That there is no life without something to fear. I want to be with you, Ian, even if it's scary. If you're ready, I'd like to leave with you today."

Ian chewed on his lip for an agonizing handful of seconds. "My answer is yes."

Relief made Alek's knees weak.

"But only if you marry me on Monday," Ian added with a wince, like the ultimatum was one he hadn't wanted to resort to. "I can't go through this again, Alek. I'm sorry, but if you're hospitalized again, I have to know how you're doing. It's not that I think you won't stay better—"

Alek lifted his hands. "I want that too. In fact, I'd marry you today if that's what you really want, but I don't think you do. When we marry, it will be for love and not fear." From the duffle, Alek retrieved the papers he'd left at the top and passed them to Ian. "I had Llewyn draft these. It's a so-called psychiatric advance directive—I've made my wishes known (and legally binding) that should I become mentally incapacitated again, you are to remain updated on my condition and make decisions in my stead. It's all the power you'd have as my husband. I want you to have it. I trust you."

"I didn't even know that was a thing." He held Alek's gaze. "Thank you. When the timing *is* right, the offer still stands. I want my ring back on your finger, and my last name at the end of yours." Ian hoisted the duffle over his shoulder and pulled Alek into a more G-rated kiss. "Let's get you back to the Victorian where you belong."

Alek pushed his lips into a pout. "Speaking of the Victorian, I worry our makeup sex will be interrupted by potential buyers. Are you sure there isn't an open house scheduled for today? Maybe we should stay somewhere else..."

Ian smiled wide. "Consider the Victorian off the market."

46

ALEK

I t was almost dusk when they arrived at the Victorian. The drive took longer than it should have because Ian had abruptly stopped on three different occasions for make out pit stops. They both would have gotten off if Ian wasn't so averse to the perils of road head and public indecency charges.

Ian flicked the blinker, the rhythmic clicking too loud in the silent truck. Alek opened his mouth to once again opine the uselessness of indicating a turn when they were the only ones on the road, but then he saw the for sale sign planted at the end of the driveway.

"Would you have really sold the Victorian?" Alek asked as the truck trundled down the gravel road.

"I would, but not until I'd exhausted all options and was sure there was no chance you'd come back." Ian's Adam's apple bobbed, his knuckles blanching on the steering wheel. "If you killed yourself, I wouldn't have sold it, but only so I could spend the rest of my life single-handedly reducing this place and any memory of the happiness we had there to rubble."

Alek flinched at the image of Ian so bereft he turned destructive. He imagined Ian, tears tracking down the dust that covered his face, chest heaving with a sledgehammer in his hand, surrounded by a house he'd ruined, waiting for it to collapse on him so he could forget that Alek had ever even existed.

While Alek's motivation for suicide had been to spare he and Ian from further pain, now that he wasn't drowning in depression, he realized how horribly misguided his intentions had been.

After Ian parked, Alek opened the door and stepped down onto the soft pine-needle laden ground. Home. He was home. There was a flash of memory from the last time he'd been there —rain lashing, thunder cracking, heart broken—but he didn't dwell on it, instead focusing his attention on the face of the Victorian. While he was away, the wisteria had climbed another ten feet or so to the second story. It likely wouldn't grow any taller than that until next spring; the winter frost would make it slumber.

Birds called, the truck door slammed. Ian climbed the front porch steps and opened the door with a familiar wooden scuff.

"You coming?" Ian asked.

"Yes," Alek called, moving to follow.

When Alek had first found the Victorian, abandoned and shrouded in mystery, he thought that was the beginning of their happily ever after, but he'd been wrong. Everything leading up until now had been a long slog, a struggle to drag his baggage everywhere he went, and now he was home and he was light, his hands were empty, and he was free.

Ian held the door open and Alek passed through and the Victorian smelled like it always did, like history and lumber and lemon wood polish. Ian dropped the duffle to the ground with a thud.

Alek looked at Ian. Ian looked at him, and there was no more poignant musing over the journey they'd traveled. Alek's need was a rubber band pulled tight—blessed be to Dr. Dhawan and her cocktail of medications for keeping his sex drive intact.

He gripped Ian by his henley and slammed him against the wall, biting kisses from his collar bone to his neck on his way to his ear where he promised, "I'll never leave you ever again."

Ian responded with a broken, crumpled sound as he pulled Alek into a possessive kiss that said so much more than *mine*—it was relief, and it was fear, and it was forgiveness, and above all else, it was the same promise back again. *I'll never leave. I'll never leave. I'll never leave. I promise.*

When they parted, Alek pulled Ian's shirt over his head and sucked bruising kisses into his skin, tracing his tongue along the muscles that had grown sharper and more defined over their separation. With a deep rumbling growl, Ian pushed back and then it was Alek up against the wall. They crossed the foyer, bumping into sharp edges of furniture, sendings things smashing and shattering when they hit the ground.

At the bottom of the stairs, Ian took off Alek's shirt. "Sit down," Ian commanded with a heavy hand to his shoulder.

Moving quickly to comply, Alek sat a few steps up. He expected Ian to stand over him, but instead Ian lowered to his knees and removed Alek's pants with a maddening lack of urgency.

Punctuated with kisses along the inside of Alek's thighs, Ian said, "I've spent two months regretting the last time we had sex." He lifted his eyes. "I'm so sorry for taking my anger out on you."

Alek scoffed. "It's not like I didn't enjoy myself."

Ian sat back on his heels, face turned serious. "You should be treated with love and reverence every day of your life."

The intensity of Ian's gaze made Alek's skin prickle. Flustered, Alek suggested, "Revere me by letting me suck your dick first, then."

Ian pressed his finger to Alek's lips. "Hush. I'm still apologizing."

Alek sucked the tip of Ian's finger into his mouth. Ian's mouth went slack. Alek smiled and reached to pop the top button of Ian's pants.

"No," Ian said.

Alek slumped back, crossing his arms with a pout.

"About framing you..." Ian went on as if there'd been no interruption. "I want to say sorry, but that isn't quite right, because while I *am* sorry, I don't regret it—it was the only card I had left and I played it, but I do wish I could have done it another way, one that didn't steal your freedom from you."

Ian had said as much over and over in his letters, but neither of them had addressed the topic until now.

"It's already forgiven. You did the right thing."

Ian's eyes narrowed, hopeful and suspicious. "Really?"

"Yes. Emphatically." Alek cupped Ian's cheek. "Thank you for saving me."

Alek wished he could say something more profound. Ian had suffered at Alek's hands for months, risked criminal charges by framing him, sacrificed the relationship he wanted so desperately, fronted his money to give Alek the best chance of recovery —all to save him. But for Ian, thank you must have been enough because his shoulders sagged, all the tension leaving his body.

"Now will you stand so I can thank you properly?" Alek said.

Ian grinned. "No."

"Are we really going to fight over who's dick to suck first?"

"We're not fighting because I'm sucking yours first," Ian said confidently, his jaw set into a determined line. "If you want to say thank you or sorry or whatever, you can be a good boy and make that noise I really like while I'm draining your come down my throat."

"When you put it that way..." Alek leaned back, grateful for the padded carpet runner that lined the stairs. "As you were."

The muscles in Ian's back flexed and stretched as he bowed over Alek's lap. With eyes wide and always on him, Ian took Alek deep, so deep that Alek felt like he was being sucked into a black hole. He grabbed ahold of Ian's hair just in case, because anything was possible when the impossible was, when Alek was back at the Victorian with Ian, and everything was forgiven.

Ian sucked him like a starved man feasting after famine, his filthy moans surrounding Alek's cock in hot vibration.

"I missed your mouth," Alek said on a gasp.

Ian made another ravenous moan that had hairs rising all along Alek's body like he was about to be struck by lightning. In what was likely only a few minutes—though Alek wasn't sure because all concept of time was warped like they were in a Salvador Dali painting—Alek made that noise Ian had asked for without even meaning to, that half sob, half moan laced with awe and disbelief as stars burst behind his eyes, nerves exploded like a blown transformer, and Alek came so hard he was worried every inch of glass in the house would explode from the intensity of it.

After swallowing, Ian rested his cheek on Alek's thigh, watching him with sated adoration, like he'd felt Alek's pleasure second-hand. When Ian tried to stand, Alek realized his fingers were still tangled tight in his hair.

"Sorry." Alek loosened his grip.

Ian stood, his hair ruffled, and hauled Alek, weak-kneed and very much still fuck-drunk along with him.

"Let me feed you before round two," Ian said.

Alek pulled to a stop. "I'm not hungry."

"Well, I'm thirsty." Ian took another step.

"How could you possibly be thirsty after swallowing two months worth of come?"

Ian stopped, brows raised. "You still can't come without me?"

Alek dropped his eyes and shook his head. "If you didn't take me back, I would have had no choice but to commission a sex doll made in your image."

Laughing, Ian tugged Alek down the hall.

At the swing door to the kitchen, Ian held out his arm like a *Maître d'* and said, "After you."

Alek shot Ian a shrewd look and leaned against the door, backing his way into the kitchen. There was a fresh reno smell— new paint, sawdust, varnish off-gassing—the scent always reminded Alek of when he and Ian first went into business together, how he would follow Ian from one worksite to the next, riveted by Ian even as he hung drywall, and especially when he used a power saw. Alek could almost taste the salt of Ian's sweat when he kissed him.

Alek turned around. The kitchen! Gone were the loathsome cantaloupe colored cabinets, the cheap linoleum, the hulking stainless steel fridge that matched nothing else in the house. The floor was a chessboard of black and white marble and the built-in shelves and cabinets layered thickly with decades of paint had been stripped down to the original satin birch, gleaming with a golden stain faithful to the period. Matching wainscoting reached up the walls to meet plaster painted Paris Green. Instead of an island, running down the center of the room was a 19th century servant's table that Alek had restored and kept in waiting.

Across the kitchen, Alek opened a tall cabinet added seamlessly alongside the original built-ins; as expected, concealed within was a luxury fridge any home chef would sell their soul for. The five-foot wide free-standing cast iron stove that Alek had lovingly rehabilitated was no longer collecting dust in their storage unit, but instead the focal point of a wall that Ian had tiled floor-to-ceiling with ceramic squares that at first looked a moody emerald green, but upon further inspection were alive with notes of absinthe and darkest forest pine as they shimmered in the last dying beams of cloud-filtered daylight.

"My, my, you've been busy," Alek said, turning to face him.

Ian had leaned against the door frame, watching with nervous anticipation.

"I love it to death, Ian."

"Yeah?" Ian asked, a shy smile growing.

"Yes!" Alek rushed back across the kitchen and barreled into him, throwing his arms around his neck, before kissing him.

"It's better than I dreamed of," Alek said when the kiss broke. He moved his palms to frame Ian's face. "You did this and the library in two months? You've outdone yourself. Opus, indeed."

Smiling wide now, twin spots of red on the apples of his cheeks, Ian dropped his hands to Alek's hips. "The crew helped. It worked out that we'd already emptied our schedule, kept them paid too."

"I know I'm supposed to be turning over a new leaf, but I don't know what I did to deserve you."

"Likewise, love." Ian pulled Alek closer. "I really thought I lost you for good this time."

"You will never lose me again." Alek sealed the promise with a kiss like the slash of a knife against a palm in a blood oath.

Alek turned to face the kitchen, quite intentionally grazing his ass against Ian's dick. "I can't wait to cook!"

"I thought you said you weren't hungry?"

"I'm not."

"Good," Ian said in a velvet bedroom voice that foretold what he said next. "Go get yourself ready for me and when you come back, I'm bending you over that table."

"Isn't there a door you can fuck me against? That table is over one hundred years old."

"I won't break it. Besides, you rehabbed it. It'll hold. And if not, you can fix it—"

"You'll be fixing it because it was your idea."

"Deal. Now hurry up. I waited two months for this."

When Alek returned, naked with a lube bottle in hand, Ian was seated at the table, his bare back to him. Alek's heart stalled and restarted without rhythm. He crept up behind Ian and draped his arms down his chest, kissing the back of his neck before taking a surreptitious sniff of his hair, and like before, Alek's synesthesia built the image of a forest in his head, stronger now, because he was smelling the real thing.

"Are you smelling my head?" Ian asked.

Perhaps not so surreptitious. "I have no idea what you're talking about."

Ian tapped the tabletop beside him. "Bend over."

Salivating, goosebumps rising in anticipation, Alek bent at the waist, rested his chest on the tabletop, and turned his cheek to the side. All at once he felt scared and vulnerable and safe— and hard, he was definitely hard again. Ian loomed behind him at the edge of his peripheral vision. With a gentle nudge to Alek's feet, Ian spread Alek's legs wider and kissed the base of Alek's spine. It was too much and not enough and Alek did something he never did—he begged.

"Ian, please. I need more. *Please.*"

Ian's mouth left him. "But what about the table?"

Alek growled. Tease.

"Patience," Ian said and reached a hand around to stroke Alek's dick. "It's been a while, and I don't want to break you."

"If you don't hurry the fuck up, I'm going to hop off this table and fuck you myself with every intent of breaking you."

Ian laughed. "That could be fun. Maybe later."

The bottle uncapped and Ian's lube-slicked hand returned to Alek's dick while the other worked a finger into his hole. They both moaned at the tight fit. Ian added more lube and coaxed another finger in, all while continuing languid strokes up and down Alek's dick.

Alek was reduced to wordlessness, instead making a series of primitive moans that bore more resemblance to speaking in tongues than human speech. Relentless, Ian dragged him to the edge of orgasm by the dick while massaging his prostate from within like he was trying to christen the new floors with a puddle of precome on purpose.

"That's it, love. You're almost ready for me, aren't you?"

More lube was added, and then finally, *finally*, Ian pronounced him ready.

Alek looked over his shoulder to find Ian holding a condom packet in his hand. "Have you slept with anyone since we broke up?"

Alek shook his head, summoning the words to answer, "There's only you. Only ever you."

Ian stilled, probably because Alek had very intentionally repeated the vow he'd first told him, the same vow that Ian had promised in return on that last dark night they'd been together.

"You're not speaking English," Ian said in Bulgarian. Terrible Bulgarian.

In English, Alek lied, "I thought you'd find it more romantic in my native tongue."

"Liar," Ian teased with a thrust against Alek's ass. Ian set the condom on the tabletop in Alek's line of sight. "I didn't have sex with anyone else either."

"Oh my god, Ian! I know that. Are you going to fuck me or not?"

"So demanding," Ian said with a laugh, so that Alek was caught completely off guard when the head of Ian's lubed up dick pressed against him... and then disappeared. "You know what?" Ian pinned Alek to the table with a hand between his shoulder blades. "I'm starting to worry about this table too, and I can't see your face and I want to see your eyes when I put my dick inside you." Ian's hand left him, and the cold caress of displaced air and footsteps heavy on the marble meant that he was already running. From a distance, Ian called, "First one to our room gets to top."

"Cheating prick," Alek grumbled to himself and pushed off the table before running after him. "You'll pay for that."

47

IAN

The floorboards creaked. Ian held his breath.

"Ian?" Alek called. "If you're going to jump scare me, it'll be the last thing you do."

"I wasn't going to scare you so much as tackle you." Lifting both hands, Ian emerged from behind the door. "I call a truce. Get on the bed, love, and let me make you come again."

Alek chewed on his tongue, likely debating the merits of revenge over surrender. With a curt nod, he climbed onto the bed, his long body stretched out, his dick standing straight up. Ian wanted to suck him again, but he wouldn't risk Alek's ire. Instead, he covered Alek's body with his own, helping Alek push his knees up, and with another generous helping of lube, slowly pushed his way inside.

Alek's head tilted back and his eyes slammed shut.

"Let me see those eyes I thought I'd never see again," Ian reminded, waiting to sink in deeper until Alek complied. He didn't have to wait long. Parting thick eyelashes, Alek gave Ian a look so unguarded and desperate that Ian felt like he was going to die if he didn't put Alek out of his misery. On a single, careful thrust, Ian buried deep.

"About time," Alek grunted and wrapped his hands around Ian's hips, joining them closer.

Ian nipped a bite to Alek's lower lip. "You feel so good wrapped around my cock, love. Back home where you belong."

Alek moaned his agreement.

Ian pressed his forehead to Alek's, cradled the back of his head in both hands, and began to move. Each thrust was pleasure, and a promise too.

"I'll never leave you," Ian said. "I'm yours forever and after that too. I won't let you get hurt. I'll keep you safe."

Maybe marriage really was nothing more than a legal document, because as far as Ian was concerned, he was saying his vows right now and what joined them was so much more than mere matrimony and the label of husband was woefully inadequate to describe the way their souls were chained together.

Anyone else would think that the hell Alek had put him through was unforgivable—his lies to conceal, to trick, to hurt—but Alek wasn't Lucifer cast out of heaven. He was Lucifer redeemed, an otherworldly beauty with a soul of secrets dark and twisted, the giver of a love so rare it was precious, and so Ian worshiped Alek with tithes of kisses, ardent accolades of praise, vows of unending loyalty, and love and love and love.

For each of Ian's breathless vows, Alek had one of his own. "I'll never leave you again. I promise. I'll never hurt you again." And when he ran out of vows, Alek chanted like he was casting a spell, "I love you. I love you. I love you."

Alek's back arched, tears tracked from the corners of his eyes, his fingernails dug hard into Ian's back, and then it was like the entire world was folding in on itself and an apocalypse was all around and Ian would die over and over again if it meant he could die like this.

Hot come exploded between them as Alek's body tightened, and then Ian was coming too, and when the dust settled, Ian was afraid to look around because they'd fucked like two gods warring, the love between them so magic he worried that maybe the world really had ended, and the paradise of them reunited again was the closest he would get to heaven, that he'd forsaken the entire world, forfeited eternity, so long as he could be with Alek and he would. He fucking would.

That night, Alek still had nightmares, but when Ian woke him with a kiss, Alek didn't flinch awake, shaking and afraid. Instead he pushed Ian into the mattress and forced two consecutive orgasms, and threatened a third unless Ian apologized for teasing, which Ian promptly did because the trouble with being multiorgasmic was that if Alek was in a vindictive sort of mood, there was definitely such a thing as too much of a good thing.

———

WHEN IAN WOKE NEXT, sunlight streamed through the windows, and Alek was watching him.

"I want to try the piano," Alek said, brushing the hair back from Ian's brow. "But I need you with me when I do."

"Let's go, then," Ian said, pushing the duvet off and pulling on his pants.

Downstairs, Alek sat at the piano bench on Ian's lap.

With hands hovering over the keys, Alek turned, a single eyebrow raised. "Aren't you going to time me?"

Alek explained the day before that the hand surgeon had cleared him to practice an hour each day, but with the caveat that Alek should listen to his body and stop when he felt pain.

Ian kissed the back of Alek's hand. "I'm sorry for being so controlling before. I was scared, but I shouldn't have stifled you. I trust you to know when to stop."

"Your trust... after everything." Alek's cheeks flushed. "That means so much to me. I'm sorry that I scared you."

"There's no need to apologize, but if you want to make it up to me, you could stop forcing me to watch horror movies with you."

Alek scoffed. "It's really not that scary, Ian. Any ghost or slasher that stumbled upon you would be very sorry, indeed."

"It's too stressful and there's no happy ending..."

"You're so cute." Alek moved closer until their lips were nearly touching.

If they were playing chicken, Ian wasn't going first. He moved closer still until a breath or breeze would be enough to join them. "So are you. Now stop procrastinating and play."

Alek licked his lower lip. "I was flirting, not procrastinating." He turned back towards the piano.

"If you don't want to play today, that's okay. You should do it when you feel one hundred percent ready."

"Oh, I'm ready." Alek dragged his palm lovingly across the top of the piano lid. He flipped through a spiral bound book of sheet music.

Ian held his breath. Both were so silent the only noise was the tick of the clock on the mantle, and then, Alek's hands moved, and music filled the room.

It wasn't Alek's music, but it was advanced, the notes coming fast, the intensity resonating deep inside Ian's chest. Alek's fingers glided over the keys with a movement so fluid and light it was like they were underwater, floating and buoyant, like there was no gravity and yet somehow Alek could still press the pedal and push on the keys.

By the time the song had finished, Ian's cheeks were sore from smiling. "That was beautiful."

"It's Scriabin. My own music is still lost, but it feels closer now, like the songs are under a veil instead of locked inside a safe."

Ian braced for Alek's disappointment, or fury. But it didn't come.

"Maybe it's like Dr. Dhawan said. With sleep, and time, it'll come back," Ian said.

Alek shrugged one shoulder, while his other hand absent-mindedly flitted up and down a melancholy-sounding arpeggio. "I'd like for my music to come back, but I'll survive if it doesn't. That's not to say I won't be disappointed. I still love music, but it's enough to be able to play anything as advanced as this. I don't need the piano anymore. I've learned other ways to cope."

Ian beamed. Alek was so different. He was still Alek, but healthy. At peace. Ian had tried to love Alek enough for the both of them, but it never worked because Alek had to love himself, and when he finally did, that's what changed everything.

Ian swiveled Alek on his lap and kissed him, because he didn't know how to say any of that, how to tell Alek that he wasn't just proud of him, that he was in awe of him, that he was his hero. Maybe Ian put Alek in that hospital, but Alek had been the one to save himself, and Ian respected that.

48

ALEK
SPRING THE FOLLOWING YEAR

Alek was waiting in his perch—the third story tower—the place where everything nearly ended and the truth began. Outside the window that he fell out of, the forest was shrouded in a blanket of gray drizzle typical of early May. What he could see of the sky had turned peach and purple, the sun already setting.

The renovated third story tower was his favorite haunt. Ian had kept his promise, adding a turret-top balcony overhead, but Alek hardly ever felt claustrophobic anymore. Ian had also added a small wood-burning stove in the back corner that whispered warmth into the room and allowed for tea to be brewed from the cast iron kettle.

Alek sat in a dark navy lounge chair the color of a starlit sky. His laptop lay open in front of him at a compact captain's desk made of burl wood and centuries of adventure.

Looking at his life now, it was hard to believe that he'd fallen from the window only a year before. He and Ian married five months ago, on the longest night of the year. Winter Solstice. Alek had originally wanted the wedding to take place in the greenhouse —as far as venues went, it was the obvious choice—but Ian vetoed, fearing it was bad luck, which was adorable because Ian was not superstitious, at all. Instead, they married in the library, beneath the glow of the full moon shining through the skylight. They were the only ones there, which was exactly how Alek wanted it.

An official wedding had been held at the courthouse earlier that day. Ian's mom, Dr. Modorovic, and Dr. Dhawan had attended—Oh, and Briar, freshly busted from Alder House. But that was boring bureaucratic nonsense as far as Alek was concerned. The real wedding was the private moment he and Ian shared, the secret vows that were passed between them with the Victorian their only witness.

Alek had wanted to marry Ian for so long he'd feared reality wouldn't meet his expectations, that because he no longer needed Ian's validation via matrimony their nuptials would be an anticlimax, but he'd been wrong. Becoming Alek Stewart, to claim Ian's surname instead of a fake one... It was the truest form of love Alek had ever experienced.

After two months of newly-wedded fucking, Ian returned to work part-time. Alek took on occasional pet projects, but wasn't willing to risk his wrists toiling away over someone else's antiques. He'd continued his study at the piano, but in careful moderation now. Nothing else had come back, and that was sad, but it was okay. Really.

His therapy with Dr. Dhawan continued, despite her frequent attempts to transfer him to an actual therapist. While Alek had made psychological strides, he still had a hard time opening up to those beyond his trusted circle, which was really a triangle made up of Dr. Dhawan, Ian, and himself. Ideally, Alek would graduate from therapy before Dr. Dhawan grew too busy for him.

Even then, he'd likely still see Dr. Dhawan for a while. She'd already adjusted his medication regimen twice; first discontinuing the antipsychotic as promised, and then increasing the antidepressant when Alek had started feeling tired all the time, which was one of the warning signs they'd identified for a return of his depression. If more adjustments were required, Alek wouldn't despair. He understood now that sometimes his medications would require tweaking, but it didn't mean he, or the medications had failed.

The droning hum of Ian's truck slowly rose over the sound of the forest settling in for the night—rain drops dripping on leaves, branches creaking as birds found their nests in the trees. Alek shut his laptop and went to the window. He liked to watch Ian like this, when he thought he was alone, when he was his most honest self, and that might sound a little stalkery, a little crazy, but Alek was a little crazy, or at least formerly crazy, and even if he hadn't had that bout of insanity, the feelings he had for Ian were so intoxicating, it would have made him crazy anyway.

When the truck parked and Ian stepped out, long-legged, broad-shouldered, as strong and reliable as the ocean tides, he lifted his eyes to the third story tower and met Alek's gaze without searching, like he knew he'd been watching. Alek's pulse stuttered at the contact, the connection between them like a slack cord pulled tight.

"I'll come down," Alek called.

"I'll come up," Ian answered.

"I'll meet you in the middle," was Alek's reply over his shoulder as he hurried down the stairs.

They embraced at the second-story landing and when Ian kissed him, entire forests grew inside his head. Time slowed in that way it did, in that safe place where only the two of them lived, and when they finally parted, they both were breathing fast.

Ian palmed Alek's cheek. "Are we celebrating?" His dark eyes were wide, searching for Alek's answer.

Alek leaned into Ian's hand. "Yes."

Ian stilled, but it was like the silence before an explosion. "Really, love?"

Alek nodded. "The Rose Foundation for Mental Health will break ground next summer."

Ian squeezed Alek up into a hug that lifted him off his feet. "Oh, Alek. I'm so proud of you."

Alek had never left flowers at his mother's grave. He never even knew if she was in the family plot that her headstone was placed atop, the one his own empty coffin had been buried next to. But that didn't matter, because though he'd never felt her love, he could love her now in this way.

Dr. Dhawan had planted the seed. Mental health treatment was lacking, especially for those who could not afford it. There wasn't enough funding or facilities. First Alek had considered turning his Big Sur property into a subsidized mental health treatment center for those who could not pay their way, but that was thinking too small. That's not to say he wasn't going to do that; he just wasn't going to do *only* that.

The widest reach, the longest impact, would be achieved by starting a nonprofit with a board of directors made up primarily of mental health professionals that worked in concert with other established advocacy groups. Alek sold off the olive leaf crown and cashed out a few long-term investments to kickstart the project. From there he'd courted benefactors with deep pockets and a vested interest in mental health reform.

The nonprofit would focus on political advocacy for founda-tional changes to the mental health treatment system on a nationwide level. It would be a long road and there was much work to do, and Alek wouldn't necessarily do most of it— securing donations and maintaining cash flow was more in his wheelhouse—but it would be an honor to his mother, a sign of respect.

With time, and months more of therapy, Alek had forgiven his mother. Her fate was what his would have been if he didn't have Ian. She wasn't a bad person. She wasn't cruel. She was depressed, and alone, and scared, and Alek wished he could have saved her, but he couldn't, so he would do what he could to help people like her.

———

THE NEXT MORNING Alek woke to the heady scent of wisteria drifting in through the window. He didn't need to look outside to know that the wisteria had bloomed for the first time since he fell, and he didn't need to go to the piano to confirm that the fresh scent was like a wave of a magic wand, a curse lifted.

He knew because the oppressive silence inside his mind was replaced with the familiar unending musical score that played the soundtrack to his every thought. The faint rain drops that bounced off the leaves were notes played, and Ian's steady breathing was wind blowing through evergreen treetops, and all of it—every sound he could hear—it all blended harmoniously with the beating of his heart.

Everything came back all at once but in order, too. It started with his first memory of the piano, his first memory ever—the scent of climbing wisteria, the scrape of the bench over the parquet floor, the weight of his *father's* arm against his own, his father's hands flying over black and white keys, and the music he made, each note that he played were like fireflies blinking in the dark.

Decades of Alek's own compositions reappeared like a cloak had been dropped, like the music that had once been knit into his fingertips and was severed by the fall, had been slowly stitching back together this entire time, and the final stitch had been sewn.

Alek crept out of bed and left the room without waking Ian. He didn't need Ian there with him.

Music made him brave.

He went to his piano and he sat on the bench and he lifted his hands over the keys and he played. The song that came said thank you. It said sorry and it said love and it said a thousand other things that really meant forgiveness.

The wisteria's first bloom after Alek's fall and the dark months that followed was like a rebirth, a phoenix rising from the ashes, a vow that whatever challenges Alek had faced, whatever sorrow he'd suffered, whatever might come next, life would go on, and Alek along with it.

THE END.

AFTERWORD

Thank you so much for reading *Never Leave, Never Lie*. Please know that I treasure each and every one of my readers and I'm so grateful you took a chance on my debut.

Your review can help others find Alek and Ian's story, so please consider leaving one on Amazon, Goodreads, social media, or wherever you normally recommend books.

You can connect with me @TheaVerdone on Instagram, Twitter, TikTok, and Facebook. Or visit www.theaverdone.com

If you'd like to be the first to learn of new releases and receive exclusive bonus content (including a spicy prequel scene featuring Alek and Ian), please subscribe to my mailing list.

With love and gratitude,
    Thea

ACKNOWLEDGMENTS

This book would never have happened without the support of my husband, who even now, is watching the kids so I can write this. Thank you for working so hard to make my dreams achievable, for listening to hours of anxiety-fueled rambling about plot and publishing, and for being my light in the darkness.

To my sister. You've always been my built-in best friend. A confidant. The only person who knows exactly what I'm going through. Thank you for always listening, for all your support.

My therapists and psychiatrists. There have been many of you over the years and I remember each and every one of you. I hope you never, ever read this because I will be incredibly embarrassed, but if you do, please know that you changed my life, but not just mine. My children will have such a better childhood now that they have a mother who is well. I'll never take for granted that I had access to care providers who never gave up even when I wanted to.

I've always felt like there was something very special about writing friends. Reading someone's stories is like an intimate glimpse inside their head. Which is why I cherish every single one of the friends I've made along this journey. However, there are some names that stand out.

(Written in order of appearance because I have anxiety about "ranking" people.)

To my original writing group—Alona, Jillian, Erin, and Lauren—thank you for being the first to believe in Alek and Ian, for all the feedback that helped shape this story into what it is now. But most of all, thank you for believing in me.

Lauren. Thank you for sharing your creativity and priceless PR help.

Alona. You will always be my reigning grammar queen. Thank you for copyediting and proofreading my book.

Masha. Sometimes it really does feel like fate brings people together. I am so grateful to be your friend, and not just because you make my writing better, or because you've been such a source of comfort to me. You inspire me with your humor and wit and your strength in situations unfathomable to most people.

Tara. Your feedback improved my manuscript immensely and your love for my guys and their story meant so much to me. You were one of the first people who really made me feel proud of my writing.

Iris. Thank you for reading dozens upon dozens of blurbs and for all the other guidance you've given me along the way.

Marc. Thank you for wading through pages of literary smut to offer feedback. And for your dad talks.

The Baguettes. My bread in arms. Thanking you is the yeast I can do. But for real, thanks for all the help and cama-raderie.

Daphne. I said I would write you a sonnet, but let's be honest, I had to google what constitutes a sonnet, so instead I'll tell you this: I could write an entire epic poem and barely put a dent in the list of ways you've helped me with this book from consulting the MW oracle to market research to emotional support. You are the kindest soul and I'll forever count myself lucky that out of all the people on that baguette list, you chose me. Thank you for everything, bestie!

N. T. Lovich. Your hilarious comments are my favorite. Thank you for your input on Slavic culture and for my newfound knowledge on the impact of a well-timed paragraph break. I'm so lucky to have you as a critique partner.

Lilian and Tracey. Your love for Alek and Ian has been a life raft keeping me afloat. Thank you for all your kind words and feedback, and for answering all of my self publishing questions. From body beats to spicy scenes to snappy end of chapter hooks, I've learned so much from you both.

Yoanna. I am so grateful for your help with my attempts at Bulgarian and all the other questions you answered.

And to every other beta and ARC reader who I've not mentioned, but helped turn this book into something beautiful and shared it with the world, thank you so much!

Thank you to all the fellow authors who have supported me on various discord groups, answering my questions and celebrating my milestones. You've helped me so much.

Bookstagrammers. Thank you for believing in Alek and Ian's story. Your passion for books and supporting authors is such a beautiful thing. All the hours you invest into reading and reviewing and making edits and spreading the word makes such a huge difference in helping these stories be told. Thank you!

———

To my parents: You shouldn't be here. I told you not to read this. Having said that, thank you for always believing in my writing and supporting my dreams.

To my daughters A&R (8 & 5 at the time of publication): This is the only part of the book I'll let you read. Thank you for always supporting me. Every time you said "I want to sell your book, Mom" and "We love your book!" meant so much to me. And to my son, M (2.5): technically you wrote this book with me because I often edited with you in my arms. Thanks for that!

ABOUT THE AUTHOR

Thea writes romantic stories about imperfect people haunted by inner demons and dark histories. Whether it's a crumbling gothic mansion, the ocean at night, or the isolated art studio of a suspected murderess, her settings are as alive as any other character. She writes her books from a desk that faces a forest in the Pacific Northwest, which is all she's ever wanted.

Made in United States
Troutdale, OR
02/27/2024